DIES IRAE

Other Books by BV Lawson

Scott Drayco Series

Dies Irae

A Scott Drayco Mystery

BV Lawson

Crimetime Press

Published in the United States of America.

For information, contact:

Crimetime Press
6312 Seven Corners Center, Box 257
Falls Church, VA 22044

Trade Paperback ISBN 978-0-9904582-7-2
Hardcover ISBN 978-0-9904582-8-9
eBook ISBN 978-0-9904582-6-5

Acknowledgments

Many thanks to the lovely folks on the Eastern Shore of Virginia who helped inspire some of the sights and scenes in this book. Both Cape Unity and Prince of Wales County are purely fictional and an amalgam of various towns and counties on the Delmarva Peninsula.

Likewise, Parkhurst College is fictional and is not based on any existing institution. Any resemblance to actual events, locales, or persons, living or dead, is entirely coincidental.

Special thanks to Alison Dasho for her insightful editorial assistance and encouragement with an early version of this novel and for steering me in the right direction. Also, I can't express my thanks enough to Charles, Lela, Sylvia, and Ben for their amazing editing expertise and assistance.

Most of all, I give my undying gratitude—to infinity plus ten—to my amazing family for their encouragement, especially my astoundingly patient husband Charles, who is, as always, my Supporter-in-Chief.

PART ONE

Seek not to know what must not be reveal'd,
Joys only flow when hate is most conceal'd.
Too busy man would find his sorrows more
If future fortunes he should know before.

—From the song "Seek Not to Know," poem by John Dryden
music by Henry Purcell

1

The chiming wall clock filled the room with swirled purple ovals that felt like grainy silk. Almost seven o'clock. How long had he been pacing? It only took five steps up, five back to cross the room. A sixty-step-per-minute rate that would wear a groove on the hardwood floors, if he kept it up.

He cast an eye over at his piano. Maybe pounding out a Prokofiev sonata would be more constructive. His arm would cramp up, but it would be worth it. Decision made, he headed toward the piano but was stopped by a rapping on the front door.

The man framed in the entryway must have come straight from work, wearing a traditional FBI suit and tie. Unless something had changed, those regulation-looking shoes were a pair of Justin cowboy boots disguised by the man's slacks. His jute hair still sported a military cut, grayer at the temples, but everything else was the same as Scott Drayco remembered.

Neither of them moved for a moment as a jump-cut-movie of memories played in Drayco's head. What would the soundtrack for that be? Something noirish with shrieking violins, to match the staccato beats of the pouring rain outside.

He waved Agent Mark "Sarg" Sargosian inside. "Better come in before you melt."

Sarg entered and stood just inside the door as he looked around. "Think I've come to the wrong place. A Spartan would feel comfy here.

And is that pine air freshener?" Sarg's tone was joking, but his right hand curled and danced at his side as if fingering a hat.

"Got tired of tripping over things. I have a piano, sofa, refrigerator and microwave. What more do you need?"

"According to Elaine, quite a bit. We traded in a perfectly good bed for one of those giant four-poster canopy things. With matching dresser and nightstand." Sarg tugged on his ear, a nervous habit that also hadn't changed.

"How did you get here? I didn't see your car."

"In the shop. Took the train to Union, then a cab. It's waiting down the block."

"Don't expect to be here long, I take it?"

"Depends on you. And your answer."

Sarg's call earlier in the day was cryptic, short on details and long on rambling non-sequiturs, unlike the blunt partner Drayco once knew. "You could have told me over the phone. Cheaper and faster. The train from Quantico to D.C. is what, an hour?"

"I owed you more than that." Sarg shifted his feet in place. "And this is too important. I need your help."

How many people had lived, fought and died over those four words? *I. Need. Your. Help.* Such simple words. Dangerous words. No-going-back words. Drayco's feet felt glued to the floor as Sarg continued to tug on his ear.

Drayco took a deep breath, then turned to walk in the direction of his living room, looking over his shoulder to see if Sarg followed. Should he make coffee? He hesitated a moment, then bypassed the kitchen and dropped onto his frayed red sofa.

Sarg lowered himself onto the chair opposite. Both legs bounced in rhythm as he looked everywhere but at Drayco. Ten seconds turned to thirty, then sixty.

Drayco leaned forward. "All right, let's hear it, Sarg. You said you needed my answer. What's the question?"

Sarg's legs stopped bouncing as he morphed into professional mode. "The BAU's assisting on a D.C. police case. I'm the lucky guy given the assignment. Two months ago, a Parkhurst College student,

Cailan Jaffray, was walking home after a late-night lab project. Never made it. Her half-nude body was found in Kenilworth Gardens, though the MPD thinks she was carted there after her murder. A knife through the heart, no weapon found. Signs of cauterizing around the wound, like the knife was heated."

Drayco sat up straight. Stabbing deaths were common, not so much heated murder weapons.

Sarg continued, "It was mid-August, so most of the campus was on summer break. A few people still around had motives. A former boyfriend. The victim's rival. A college groundskeeper accused of being a stalker. Shaky alibis, no concrete evidence."

"This type of case doesn't usually prompt the Park Police or MPD to draw in the Bureau."

Sarg nodded. "Most of 'em would rather swim in a pool of cottonmouths."

"Then I don't see why—" Drayco caught Sarg's glance over at him, the way he bit his lower lip. "Which important person's daughter was she?"

"Niece of a Parkhurst religion professor, her legal guardian. Not particularly important per se, but Parkhurst is an elite school. Progeny of senators, grandchildren of Supreme Court justices, other illustrious alumni."

The type of circles BAU Unit Chief Jerry Onweller liked to hang around in. If Drayco won the lottery, he'd bet his winnings Onweller was friends with someone in the Parkhurst administration. "All right. I see why they want Bureau help. Scandal-abatement. Why do you need me?"

Sarg pulled out a piece of crinkled paper from his pocket and handed it over. "The girl was a music student. Rather promising. She received three unsigned letters in nine-by-twelve white envelopes with no return address. She threw away the first two. This is a copy of the third."

Drayco unfolded the paper and studied it. It looked like an excerpt from ordinary sheet music with a treble line for soprano—or violin, since there were no words—and a piano accompaniment. Oddly, no dynamics or tempo or pedal markings. The key signature had no sharps or flats, yet the unfamiliar tune wasn't in either C major or A minor.

He played the piece in his mind, drawing out the notes slowly at first, hearing each chord, each arpeggio. The accompaniment was uninspired, and the dissonant melody wasn't musical in a traditional sense. More of an exercise or a joke, or possibly some sort of code.

"I'm surprised you didn't check with the music faculty at Parkhurst."

"The MPD did. Some had no idea, most didn't want to get involved."

"You said this was the third music puzzle. The MPD couldn't have known the victim threw away the first two unless someone told them."

Sarg cleared his throat. "That would be Tara." His eyes locked with Drayco's. "My Tara."

Dear God, Sarg's daughter would be college age now. Three years ago, she was a senior in high school. Now she was a student at Parkhurst? Where naturally, the bubbly teenager had made new friends, and among them, one murdered music student.

The ex-Army Ranger Sergeant would never beg, but the message in his eyes was clear. Whatever it took, whatever bitter pill he had to swallow. This was his little girl, and he was worried.

"You think I can help because I play the piano?"

"Partly. You were always the best at solving puzzles. And there's another connection you have with the case."

Drayco was still absorbing the news Tara might be involved in a murder, so Sarg's postscript took a moment to register. "And that is?"

"The lab project. The one the victim was killed walking home from. Some guy's dissertation. It's about that sensory thing of yours, seeing colors and shapes when you hear music."

"Synesthesia?"

"Yeah, the girl had synesthesia, like you. The MPD doesn't think there's a connection, but I thought you'd find it interesting. Maybe help you get inside her mind better."

Drayco studied the piece of paper before handing it back to Sarg. "This is similar to twelve-tone music. To most people, it sounds like cacophony. To me, it's like blue-orange branching twigs with a rough bark feel to it. But no two synesthetes are alike, so I can't tell you what the victim experienced."

Sarg took the paper but didn't fold it up. He was in danger of falling off the chair, perched on the edge. After another good half-minute of silence, he muttered, "Three years."

Drayco didn't have to ask what he meant. He knew full well how long it had been.

"Three years and I keep replaying the same day over and over." Sarg looked briefly at Drayco, then away.

Drayco knew this man well. To Sarg, guilt was an invading force to be vanquished, not allowed entry. "I was thinking of leaving anyway." Drayco lied. "You had a family to support."

"Wouldn't have lost my job. Probably."

"Yet, if I had to do it all over …" Sarg rubbed his boot tips together. "Hasn't been the same since." He cleared his throat. "I meant to call you."

"Me, too."

The silence descended on them again as Drayco considered his options. He could offer his services, only to find they weren't needed. Some would say refusing to help was justified payback. Or Sarg and the MPD might solve the case on their own, with or without the music puzzle.

But then, there was Tara. "Onweller won't want me consulting on this."

"I've thought of a way to smooth it over, make him see how much we need you. All nice and official, with pay."

The fusion of contrition and hope on Sarg's face sent a shiver through Drayco. He'd thought that bridge long burned, the ashes cooled and scattered. Yet here it was stretching out in front of him, inviting him to cross over. Should he take the chance?

The look on Sarg's face turned to disappointment when Drayco said, "You'd better not keep that cab waiting too long, or your fare will cost a year's salary." Then Drayco added, "And if I'm going to help, I'll need a copy of that puzzle."

Sarg passed the puzzle back and stood up, moving like a man ten years younger than the one who'd arrived. He paused, then thrust out his hand. Drayco shook it.

"I'll arrange everything with Onweller so we can get going first thing tomorrow."

"I'd like to start by talking to Tara. If that's okay with you."

"Done. And Drayco …" He opened his mouth to add something, then stopped himself in mid-speech. "I'll see you in the morning."

"You coming via Union Station again? If so, I'll pick you up."

The details settled, Sarg left to finish his expensive taxi ride. Drayco resumed pacing, but with a glance at the music puzzle, he headed to the piano instead.

Ordinarily, he'd use Chopin to relax. Right now he needed black-and-blue jagged rocks tinged with an iridescent burgundy, the coastal wavelines of Prokofiev. He massaged his right arm first to stave off the stiffness and pain, then launched into the color-tsunami of Prokofiev's fourth piano sonata. It soon carried him onto a distant shore where the only thing broken was the silence.

2

Drayco awoke to a cascade of light pouring through the window. Hadn't he closed the blinds before he went to bed? Then a soft, warm body slid into bed beside him, and he remembered. Darcie Squier stopped by last night. Well, he *had* invited her to visit him at his townhome, hadn't he? Just not to show up on his doorstep as a "surprise."

After finally succumbing to Darcie's relentless seductions on his trips to the Eastern Shore over the past few months, it was almost a relief to wake up and find her there after a night of lovemaking. A relief? He didn't have time to dwell on that thought as Darcie started nibbling on his ear before working her way farther south.

When it came to sex, she was like a reluctant nun trapped too long in a convent, doing her best to "Make up for lost time," as she'd told him. And perhaps she'd summoned up his inner caveman as she talked of years spent in her loveless marriage crying alone in her room—although her ex-husband's riches seemed to dull the pain.

Drayco still wasn't sure what his feelings for her were. He knew his Cape Unity friends didn't approve of her—their words "shrew" and "alley cat" came to mind. But after Sarg's visit last evening, having Darcie here was better than a Cacao Espresso Stout from the Fiddler's Green Tavern. He *needed* this.

But his mind just wouldn't shut off, and his meeting with Sarg kept coming back to him. Sarg's baffling music puzzle poked at his subconscious, demanding he pay attention. He'd even had dreams of it last night, the staves leaping off the page and forming a knife headed straight for his heart.

No more avoiding the inevitable. He headed to the shower to clear mind and body of distractions, but Darcie had other ideas. She followed him inside, helped him dry off, then made him breakfast before he dressed because "she liked watching him walk around nude." He was going to protest for equal time, but she looked rather fetching in the kitchen wearing only lacy red panties.

She was disappointed when he told her he couldn't take her sightseeing because he was meeting Sarg. Her pout lasted only as long as it took for a friend of hers on the phone to mention Saks Fifth Avenue and something about Saint Laurent croc-embossed leather booties. When she squealed to him they were on sale for "only" nine hundred dollars, he spit out some of his coffee and grabbed for a paper towel.

The last shoes he'd bought were black garden-variety loafers. If Darcie didn't have her ex's money to play with, Drayco had a feeling she wouldn't be hanging around him long on his crime-consultant salary. She needed a senator or lobbyist and a mansion in Georgetown or McLean. Humble Cape Unity and its coastal small-town life must feel like a death sentence to her.

As Darcie babbled on the phone with her friend, Drayco grabbed his copy of Sarg's music puzzle and played it in his mind again. What could it mean? But the tuneless line kept morphing into Prokofiev and then to Bach. Soon his thoughts were in Cape Unity on the Eastern Shore inside the Opera House he'd inherited. His life, as always, seemed to be surrounded by musical puzzles.

Darcie finished her conversation, grabbed one of the egg sandwiches she'd made and plopped onto the couch beside him. "What's that?" She peeked at the puzzle.

"Part of that case I mentioned. And why I'm meeting Sarg later."

"So that's the reason you can't take me to see the First Ladies' dresses." She peered over at the paper. "Doesn't look terribly interesting. Is it important?"

He held up the paper to the light. "Possibly. It was sent to a college student before she was murdered."

Darcie put her plate on the coffee table and slid closer to him. "What was she like?"

"What?" He turned to face her.

"The girl who got killed. Tell me about her."

She had a way of surprising him like that. Showing a deeper side of herself to him than she did to others.

Last night, Drayco searched the Web for traces of Cailan Jaffray's social media footprint. She'd appeared like a fairly normal college-age girl at first. Then he noticed a more pensive, darker turn to her online posts in the weeks leading up to her death. Premonitions? Or hidden secrets?

He replied, "Well, music was a passion of hers. So much so she didn't have a lot of time left over for her friends."

"Kind of like you were at her age?"

He nodded. "Being a classical soloist is like having a lover who demands all your time. And you gladly give it. Once it gets a grip on your soul, it won't let go."

"I'd love to have you think of me that way." She reached up to stroke his hair. "But you make it sound like I'd always be playing second fiddle. Or whatever the piano equivalent is."

"I can't perform anymore, remember?"

She winked at him. "Only the piano, Darling. But you can still play, can't you?"

"For short periods. Until my arm cramps."

Darcie moved her stroking to his right arm. "Was the murdered girl a pianist?"

"A singer. Opera."

"Oooh, now there's more my thing. All those lovely dresses and jewelry and gorgeous sets. Was she any good?"

"Quite good, by all accounts."

"Then why would anyone want to kill her? Unless it's a rival."

He blinked at her. "She did have a rival, for love more than music."

"Then where does that puzzle come in? A form of musical death threat?"

And there she was again—much sharper than she let on. "That's what we aim to find out."

"How was she killed?"

"Stabbed."

"Ah, now see, that screams a crime of passion."

Drayco didn't think Sarg or the MPD would want some of the details of the murder made public, like the wound cauterizing, so he didn't mention that. Yes, a crime of passion might involve a stabbing. But to take the time to heat the knife first? That screamed premeditation, not spur-of-the-moment passion.

It wasn't often his thoughts were so vivid they translated into sensory links, but he could swear he smelled something burning. Darcie sniffed the air and jumped up, running over to the kitchen. As he got up to join her, she met him at the archway holding a blackened blob speared with a fork.

He tilted his head. "That doesn't look like an egg sandwich. In fact, I'm not sure what the hell that looks like."

"It was supposed to be a cinnamon roll. If you like them well done, there are five more in the oven just like it."

He started laughing. She was a worse cook than he was, and that was saying a lot. He grabbed the fork and tossed the blob into the sink. Then he wrapped his arms around her and captured her lips in a deep, slow kiss. She tasted like egg and coffee and cream, and right now, it was like a little taste of heaven.

3

The morning drizzle tightened the District's notorious braided-knot commute into a noose of traffic. But true to his word, Drayco picked Sarg up from the train station in his faithful blue Starfire, and they headed toward Parkhurst College. Their only conversation in the car was Sarg reading snippets from the case file he'd made and answering Drayco's questions.

No talk of the upcoming Washington Capitals season opener. None of Sarg's tirades over his Fredericksburg neighbor, the one who staged Civil War re-enactments in his yard—with action figures as Confederates and garden gnomes as Union soldiers shot to smithereens with a BB gun.

When they pulled into a Parkhurst lot, it didn't take long to spy signs of the college's deep-pocketed endowments. The campus coffeehouse where Drayco and Sarg were meeting Tara at ten-thirty had gleaming new everything. Pop-art light fixtures that looked suspiciously like Chihuly, crisp red shirts on the baristas, and a spotless self-serve espresso machine next to a case of pastries a French chef would envy.

"No crumbs." Drayco examined the floor around the table he'd chosen, the most isolated one in the back.

"What?" Sarg slid into the booth opposite and placed his caramel macchiato and éclair on the table.

"I thought this was a college, not a five-star resort."

"From what these kids pay, might as well be. One of the lessons Elaine and I learned when the kids started applying to colleges. And why it costs so much these days. No more barracks dorms. Gotta have satellite TV hookups, WiFi, and sushi made to order in the dining hall."

Sarg wrinkled his nose as Drayco picked up the salt shaker and sprinkled grains into his plain black coffee. "I don't care what you say, Drayco, salt does not make bitter coffee taste sweet."

Those were the exact words Cape Unity's Sheriff Sailor had said to him a few months ago. Sailor and Sarg might get along like gangbusters. Or maybe like magnetic poles, they'd repel each other.

Drayco sniffed the coffee. Maybe not quite plain java, because he caught a whiff of hazelnut. "You must have picked the right stocks. Because I doubt most FBI agents can afford a college like this."

"Stocks? What are those? Nah, Tara's the market winner. Got a full scholarship due to her overall brilliance and superiority."

"So she's taking after Elaine, then?"

Sarg smiled briefly, and Drayco almost smiled back. At least they were talking.

He said, "That case file you read to me. It screams a love-affair-gone-wrong scenario. The victim's recent breakup with a boyfriend, Garrington 'Gary' Zabowski, plus the victim's rival, Shannon Krugh. And there's the fact Cailan had the date-rape drug Rohypnol in her system. Illegal in the U.S., but legal in Mexico, where Gary traveled over the summer."

"Yeah, but then you have those odd burns around the edges of the wound."

"And why was she moved to Kenilworth Gardens, of all places, after the murder?"

"Beats me. Didn't find anything like it in ViCAP records or checking with area PD sex-crime units."

Drayco thought about that for a moment. Where did Tara fit into this, if at all? Tara, a friend of Cailan and acquaintance of Gary and Shannon. Although Drayco didn't have kids, he felt protective of Tara. Last time he'd seen her, she still had braces, was smartly sarcastic and liked challenging him to word game duels. He hoped three years of college hadn't remade her into an über-sophisticate type dropping Ayn Rand and Sylvia Plath into every other sentence.

He reached for the salt shaker again but jumped up as something hot and wet spilled onto his leg. A hand with a pile of napkins frantically dabbed at the spot.

"Oh, dear Falkor, I am so sorry." Tara's face wrinkled up into a wreath of embarrassment, as she continued to blot his trousers.

He reached for her hand to stop her and smiled. "This must be an experiment for sociology." He wanted to put her at ease, despite a nagging thought—was the dousing intentional? He had no idea what her father had said about him in the three intervening years. He sat back down and motioned for her to take the seat next to Sarg.

Her long hair was still naturally blond and crowned with a plain headband, and she wore little makeup. Her sweater had swaths of red, orange, yellow, green, blue, indigo and violet. The colors of the rainbow.

And she'd called him Falkor. Her nickname for him when she'd first met him and learned Drayco's name was from the Latin word for dragon. She'd promptly dubbed him Falkor, the dragon from her favorite *Never Ending Story*.

Drayco looked to Sarg, who nodded, giving his tacit approval to start. "It's good to see you again, Tara. Although it's still hard for me to believe you're old enough to be a college student. How are your studies going?"

She rewarded his question with a small smile. "Oh, you know. Full of declensions, derivations, and learning how to dump coffee on people."

"Ah, so I *was* a project. I hope I helped you get an 'A'."

"The easiest one I'll ever get." She hesitated, biting her lip. "As much as I appreciate you helping me with my 'project,' Dad said you needed to ask me about Cailan's murder? I mean, I'm not sure how I can help."

Sitting there, watching the young woman in front of him looking confident and vulnerable at the same time, he had a sudden insight as to how Sarg must be feeling. Ready to pack her up and send her to a convent. Preferably one with a fortress and a moat.

He said, "I'm sorry to have to discuss such an unpleasant topic, Tara."

"The police have already grilled me, right Dad?" She glanced at Sarg.

Drayco said, "I'm mostly interested in those music letters Cailan received."

She stared down into what was left of her latte. "Cailan was a singer. Guess you know that. She was a finalist in the Met Opera Regionals, which is kinda big for someone her age. Anyway, she didn't think it was all that weird when she got the first letter. Creepy, maybe. She was angry when she showed it to me. And after she got the second one, she was furious."

"Did they look like this?" Drayco pulled out his copy of the third letter and handed it over.

Tara the A-student took a few minutes to study it. "I don't read music like a pro. But after calc and chem equations, you get a knack for memorizing stuff. It's close to the other two letters she showed me, though each was different. She sang the tunes for me. Well, mostly, 'cause part of it was out of her range."

That's one of the things Drayco had noticed right away. The top line of music jumped around too much to be intended as a singable melody, making it less likely the "gift" was from a composer sending Cailan recital fodder. "Why did she throw them away?"

"She thought they were from Gary. That he was ragging on her."

"Gary, the ex-boyfriend. Gary's also a music student, a composer, which is why Cailan suspected the letters were from him?"

Tara nodded.

"Why did she and Gary break up?"

Tara bit her lip. "Shannon."

"Gary's current girlfriend."

"Ex. They broke up last week, too, or so I heard. I haven't had much to do with them since ..." Tara looked away for a moment. "Gary is a spoiled rich brat and Shannon's mental."

Drayco asked, "You mean her bipolar disorder?" Sarg's case file was very thorough, complete with bullet points.

"That's not her fault, is it? Choosing not to take her lithium sure is."

Drayco exchanged looks with Sarg. Bipolar disorder left untreated could lead to some strange and erratic behavior. "Why not take her meds?"

Tara adjusted her headband. "Self-destruction is easy. Self-creation is hard. That's what Professor Gilbow says. I think it was more than that. Shannon likes being a bully. She gave poor Cailan no end of grief."

"Gilbow. That wouldn't be Andrew Gilbow, would it?"

"I've got him for psych."

Sarg interrupted, "Onweller arranged for us to consult with him on the case."

First Onweller, now Gilbow. Definitely not reconnect-with-your-favorite-people week. "We'll discuss him later. Tara, who besides you might be familiar enough with Cailan's schedule to know she walked to her apartment after her lab project?"

Drayco caught a slight movement from Sarg, whose voice dripped with blue icicles as he said, "Tara didn't have anything to do with this."

Tara looked from one man to the other, wrinkling her nose. "He meant do I know any other suspects, Dad."

Drayco nodded. "Other suspects and potential stalkers."

Tara continued to pass dark glances at her father as she answered Drayco, "I thought that, too. There was that weird hippy stalker guy. I mean, hello—the '60s were decades ago."

"The college groundskeeper?"

"Yeah, he followed Cailan around. I think he's this big opera fan." Tara giggled. "His name is Elvis, can you believe it?"

The sound of maple cloud-like tones seeped out of a small fanny pack case Tara wore. She pulled out her smartphone and stared at the calendar on the screen. "Ohmygod, I'm going to be late for Gilbow's class."

She drank the last half of her coffee in one gulp, grabbed her backpack, and started to slide out of the booth. She gave Drayco a quick look and said, "Cadet Tile."

Drayco scanned the room until he spied a young couple at a table, drinks in front of them. He replied, "Iced Latte," and Tara grinned.

Sarg stopped her before she left. "I want you to add Drayco's number to your phone. In case you can't get me for some reason."

Tara rolled her eyes. "Dad ..."

"Humor me, will ya? And put a screen lock on that phone like I asked you to."

Tara stuck her phone out at her father but dutifully typed the numbers into her phone contact list as Drayco recited them. Sarg added, "Don't be calling him unless it's an emergency."

Tara's pale face showed off her sudden red splotchy flush as she gave her father a quick kiss and waved at Drayco before hurrying off. He watched her go, then asked, "What was that all about?"

"You mean my overreaction or Tara's schoolgirl crush?"

Drayco's jaw dropped as he processed that last part. "What, me?"

"As my wife once pointed out, you have no idea the effect that dark hair and those purplish-blue eyes of yours have on women, do you? Especially the married ones for some reason."

"She's like a kid sister. Or surrogate daughter."

"There's only fifteen years between you. Hey, don't tell her I said anything, 'kay? I'll be crossed off her Christmas list. And her wedding list. And added to her shit list."

Drayco shook his head and took another sip of coffee. Should he be flattered or horrified? To him, Tara would always be the little girl who liked chocolate sprinkles on her gummy-bear ice cream. Sarg's pointed reference to married women, on the other hand ... No, he was not going to think about the charming deputy he hadn't seen in months. He didn't need another awkward personal relationship in his life right now.

Sarg lightened his tone of voice as he asked, "Cadet tile?"

"Anagrams, one of the word games Tara and I used to play." He drummed the fingers of his left hand on the table.

Sarg stared at Drayco's hand for a few seconds. "Whatcha got?"

"The usual counterpoint at the outset of a case. Different lines and voices entering, demanding attention, only to be turned backward and upside down."

"That music letter thing?"

"If you want to call it music. Unsingable melody, dissonant harmony, obviously created using a computer program. I doubt it was intended to be performed."

"So, a code."

Drayco switched to twirling his spoon. "A good guess."

"That should narrow it down, right?"

"Anyone anywhere can download music software from the Internet. And every student, every professor, every secretary or janitor has access to a computer."

Drayco gulped down the rest of his coffee. "Has Cailan's apartment been cleared out?"

"The lease was for a year. The uncle hasn't been able to bring himself to see it. Let alone remove her stuff. So he told the police to use the key he gave them whenever."

Sarg licked his fingers as he finished the éclair, then added, "The cops picked the place apart."

"Still …"

"I got Onweller to agree to bring you on board, provided you only work on that music angle. Don't think he'd be pleased for you to go beyond that."

"I don't have to worry what Onweller thinks anymore, do I? You're the one who wanted my help."

Sarg pursed his lips into a scowl, and Drayco braced himself. *Here we go.* But Sarg just slid out of the booth and turned toward the door. "You comin'?"

§ § §

Tara was angry. She raced to her next class as if there were rockets in her shoes, but those rockets weren't fueled by the clock as much as embarrassment. God, could she have been any more lame? She'd called him Falkor like she was in fifth grade. And dumped coffee all over him! Definitely a lame-oid.

Not that she was trying to impress him or anything. As if. Besides, it'd be a lot harder to impress a Scott Drayco than John or Gary. Tara stopped in her tracks and grabbed hold of a nearby bench as she took a deep breath. Gary, Shannon, Cailan. How had it gone so wrong?

When an image of Cailan singing "Climb Every Mountain" from *Sound of Music* popped into Tara's head, she blinked back tears. It was so unfair. Cailan losing her parents but still somehow managing to dream big. And then this happens.

Tara would never forget the first time she met Cailan. In orientation before their freshman year, when Tara promptly dumped coffee all over her, too. Maybe that had been an omen. Falkor—Mr. Drayco—had better look out.

She'd never understood why Mr. Drayco left the FBI. And whenever she asked her father, he always had some non-answer. "He wanted to start his own business" or "It was just time." She wasn't that dense. She saw the way Dad tensed up every time Mr. Drayco's name came up and caught that funny look in his eye.

It must have been big. Something so horrible that he and Dad hadn't spoken in three years. Maybe it was better for her not to know. At the same time, she was disappointed Dad didn't respect her enough to tell her the truth.

He'd probably withhold information about Cailan's murder, too. Worried how she might take it, maybe. But damn it, Cailan was a good friend, Tara had a right to know what happened.

Tara fingered the case with her cellphone. She'd saved the last text on her phone Cailan sent before she died. "Meet u @ gb @ 7."

They'd been looking forward to trying out the new Ethiopian restaurant ever since it opened. When Cailan didn't show up, Tara knew something was wrong. And when Tara couldn't get Cailan on the phone, she'd called everybody they knew, even Gary. But nobody had heard from her. That's when Tara called Campus Security.

Tara had never told Cailan about Dad's "threat assessment" rules. Maybe if she had, Cailan would still be alive. What if, what if, what if. She wasn't going to go down that road because it only led to insanity.

But why hadn't Gary or Shannon seemed all that upset by Cailan's death? Tara had started avoiding the "Deadly Duo," as she dubbed them, after the murder. Maybe that wasn't being fair, but Gary had dumped Cailan and started dating Shannon not long before Cailan was killed. Coincidence? Mr. Drayco used to say how much he hated coincidences.

Tara sighed and continued her way to class, walking this time. Why hurry? Another boring Gilbow lecture about some trivial abstract thing. She'd have to wait until after class to dwell on the important kind of psychology. The kind she'd been asking herself over and over since Cailan died. What leads a person to kill someone else like their life had no meaning? No textbook in the world held the answer for that.

4

Drayco was surprised to see Cailan's apartment located in a pricier neighborhood, on the third floor of a rowhouse. The line of renovated brick and stone rowhouses was left over from days when D.C. had more of a community feel, lost during the government box-building of the '60s. The blight of office cubes housing lawyers and lobbyists popped up like chokeweeds in the manicured lawn of the family homestead.

Old building, no elevator, thank God. Sarg took the stairs two at a time, whether to prove he was still fit or due to nervous energy, it was hard for Drayco to tell. Sarg opened the door with the key Cailan's uncle gave the MPD. Even after Sarg flipped the light switch, the end-unit apartment on the third floor was dim. The heavy burgundy blackout drapes over the window shades likely had something to do with that.

When Drayco pointed them out, Sarg put his hands on his hips and gave the drapes an accusing glare. "Thought I'd learned to know her from her file. But nothing that would explain this. A sleep disorder?"

"Or she wanted to practice and needed to dampen the sound."

Drayco's townhome didn't need sound muffling, thanks to being on the end and having a partially deaf neighbor. Otherwise, someone might have called the cops by now. Most people don't appreciate a live piano concert at five in the morning.

He said, "Did your case file include all the notes from the police investigation? Because they didn't find much in here. Or from her social-networking sites or cellphone records, for that matter."

"Didn't you notice the bullet points?" The note of disapproval in Sarg's voice was clear. Sarg was obsessive about his bullet points. He laid some empty evidence bags on a chair and handed over a pair of nitrile gloves. "It's been dusted, but just in case."

Drayco wasn't sure what he'd expected. The room seemed so ordinary, an interchangeable room that could belong to any other college girl. Except most college girls didn't have posters of tenors with matinee-idol looks like Jonas Kaufmann on the wall. He fingered the blackout drapes as he passed by. Soft velvet.

He picked up framed photos of Cailan posing with friends, including Tara. Another photo had a much-younger Cailan with two adults Drayco recognized from Sarg's case file. Cailan's deceased parents. They looked relaxed, happy, no hint of the tragedy to come.

The genes of Cailan's mother, a native of Guatemala, shone through in the girl's medium complexion and long black hair. Her pale gray eyes were from her father. Cailan oozed confidence, daring anyone to stand in the way of her dream to sing on the stage of the Met.

Sarg opened the closet door and pulled out a pair of well-used boxing gloves. "Bet you didn't expect these. Guess they're from that self-defense class a year ago. Or she took up boxing as a hobby."

He put them back on the same hanger as if expecting their owner to return. "I'm not feeling the love for this Gilbow fellow, Drayco. Don't care for self-important, media-whoring psychology gurus?"

"He was the prosecution's expert witness in a case Baskin and I worked after I left the Bureau."

"Ah, Benny Baskin, the world's most diminutive defense attorney. Been a while since I heard anything outta him."

"The same Benny Baskin who has a near-perfect record of getting his clients off. Save one."

"Let me guess. The Gilbow case. I'd heard Gilbow was pretty good in court."

"He can be charming, entertaining. And very convincing. Came up with a piece of psych theater using the Minnesota Multiphasic Personality Inventory—"

Sarg snorted. "Not that again."

Drayco wished those personality tests had never been invented. Lawyers used them as if they were indisputable mathematical proofs. Trait from Column A plus trauma from Column B equals evil. Any psychopath worth his salt could fake them.

He replied, "Gilbow had the jury in the palm of his hand. But Benny won on appeal. Gilbow appeared on a chat show afterward and hinted Benny and I were unethical. He referred to us—half-jokingly—as the shrimp and the pimp."

One of Sarg's eyelids twitched, and he covered up a sudden cough. "I think I might have heard about that."

Drayco stared at Sarg. "How? Onweller?"

Sarg looked up at the ceiling as he tugged on his ear. Of course, it was Onweller.

"I don't give a damn about the name calling. But after his 'unethical' comment, Benny and I had visits from ethics investigators."

"And Onweller wants us to consult with Gilbow. Goody."

Drayco continued to prowl around the room, hoping to find something to make meaning of the music puzzles. Not many books. Textbooks and a stack of commercial sheet music—Mozart, Fauré, Brahms, Puccini. He thumbed through each one. No puzzles, just a few notes in the margins. "Practice half-tempo," and "Work on *passaggio* here." He laid the books down and moved on.

Some of the compartment doors in a tall jewelry box on her dresser were open. More signs of the police search. He opened a heart-shaped locket hanging on a side hook.

The small photo inside was of a young man, the pouting mouth and two-toned bangs also familiar from Sarg's case file. So Cailan threw away the letters she thought were from Gary Zabowski, yet kept his picture in a locket? Talk about love-hate relationships. Or perhaps their breakup was a sham and Shannon found out?

Sarg stood in front of the bed. "What is it with women and pillows? Is it in their DNA? The pillow gene?"

Drayco moved next to him and counted no less than ten pillows of all sizes, shapes and colors. "We should ask Gilbow, the omniscient."

He sat down on the bed and examined the pillows one by one. He caught a whiff of a strawberry perfume. Hair gel? A sachet? When he picked up a red paisley pillow heavier than the others, he stopped and ran his fingers around the back. The fabric lined up in a way that hid a small, covered zipper.

He unzipped it, then reached in and pulled out two small dolls and a few photos. He held the dolls up to the overhead light. They were made of rough burlap cloth, with long black yarn for hair. In the front of each, over the heart area, someone had stuck tiny straight pins.

Sarg took the dolls from Drayco as he handed them over. "Voodoo? Really?"

Drayco reached into the depths of the pillow pocket for anything that might explain the dolls and eased out a piece of paper with block letters that said, "I'm watching you."

He next studied the photos, three in all. Possibly printed from a phone camera, though the phone Cailan carried with her was never found. It was hard to tell if the photos were taken at the same time. The first showed the dolls and the "watcher" note sitting on her bed. The image in the other two was identical—a mirror with letters written across it in a red substance that spelled BEWARE OF OCHOSI.

He surveyed the room for the mirror in the photos, but not spying one, got up and headed into the bathroom. When he held the pictures to the side of Cailan's mirror, they were a match. He rejoined Sarg. "Looks like she got some effigy dolls and someone threatened her. I don't recall this from the bullet points."

"Can't believe the MPD didn't think to look inside those." Sarg frowned at the pillows.

Drayco handed the photos and dolls to Sarg to put into the evidence bags. "Do you have her uncle's office schedule? Think we could button him down for a few questions?"

"He's high on my list. And who better to discuss voodoo with than a religion professor?"

Drayco cast one last survey around the murdered girl's room. He thought of the boxing gloves on the hangar, waiting. The room had stayed the same since her death and held the air of a life frozen in time. Or an empty vase waiting for a budded flower that would never open.

He'd agreed to help Sarg out of curiosity over the puzzle and concern for Tara. Seeing Cailan's room, learning more about her, feeling the tendrils of the music connection wrapping around his inner core—he was angry. Angry at whoever did this, angry at Cailan for not being more careful, angry that violence had so much power to silence lives and music.

Gilbow would spout something regarding displaced anger, no doubt. Injustice plus sacrifice equals tragedy. Drayco avoided looking at Sarg as they headed out the door.

5

Walking through the corridor in the Rudolph Arts & Humanities Building, it was obvious the Parkhurst rainmaker riches also watered the classrooms. Drayco peeked into one room and saw large video screens, computers everywhere, comfy padded chairs. The whole place smelled like freshly printed money.

He imagined Cailan here, walking to class, laughing with friends, worried about nothing more than being late, or maybe an exam. Had she had hints of what lay ahead? Was that why her social media postings had taken a darker turn? When he passed a couple of co-eds, he had the urge to shake them. To give them a lecture on situational awareness. *Don't let this happen to you.*

Troy Jaffray's office was at the very end of the hall. Drayco was already forming a picture of the office belonging to the respectable man from Sarg's file with the tanned face, ruddy cheeks, and thick lionesque mane.

The Troy Jaffray who opened the door resembled a washed-out sepia version of his photo. And the chaotic clutter in the room wasn't at all what Drayco envisioned. The professor took one look at Sarg's suit and narrowed his eyes. "Not another detective."

Sarg pulled out his badge, and Jaffray examined it. "BAU, that's Behavioral Analysis Unit, right?" Then he turned to Drayco. "And you are?"

Sarg answered instead. "This is Dr. Scott Drayco. A consultant helping us with your niece's case, Professor Jaffray. You can speak freely in front of him."

The expression on Jaffray's face made it clear he didn't want to speak to either of them, freely or no. "Doctor Drayco? Psychology, I assume?"

"Criminology. And we just need a few moments of your time."

Jaffray opened the door wider and motioned toward a couple of chairs in front of his desk. Drayco and Sarg made it to the chairs without tripping, no thanks to the piles of books on every available patch of real estate. Overflowing bookshelves lined the room, with more books filling up the sill, blocking the one window. Peeks of mid-afternoon light vainly tried to peer in. Did all the Jaffray family have something against windows?

The professor sank into his desk chair. "I'd heard the police were calling in the FBI. Guess that means they're getting nowhere or have given up. Let me save you some time and summarize, shall I? Yes, I have an alibi. No, I haven't a clue who would want to kill my niece. And I have no faith whatsoever the police will find out who did."

Sarg cleared his throat. "About that alibi—the police haven't been able to pin down the taxi you said you used from BWI airport."

Jaffray grunted. "Maybe they don't want to."

Sarg added, "I'd think a religious man would have more faith in justice than that, sir."

"The Buddha said 'those who are free of resentful thoughts surely find peace.' The way I'm feeling right now, it means a lifetime without any peace."

Jaffray tilted his head and studied Sarg. "Sargosian, that's Armenian, isn't it. You must attend the Armenian Apostolic Church."

"My wife does."

"Ah, a lapsed sheep. Or one who substitutes civil justice for the religious. But you," he studied Drayco, "Don't look Armenian. I detect a little Greek in you. Orthodox?"

Drayco smiled briefly. "Unorthodox, perhaps. I hate labels as a rule, but if a label it must be, try truthseeker."

"The Talmud says the wisest among men is he who learns from all." Jaffray stared at Drayco's eyes. "The Buddha was said to have eyes like yours. One reason the blue lotus has come to symbolize wisdom."

"I'd feel a lot wiser if I got to the bottom of those music puzzles sent to your niece prior to her death. You told the police you didn't know anything about them. Have you recalled any details since?"

"They were a mystery then and now."

Sarg pulled out a pen and notebook from his pocket. "Mr. Jaffray, was your niece involved in any cults? Like voodoo?"

The professor's eyes widened, and he answered slowly. "None of which I was aware. Why do you mention voodoo in particular?"

Drayco opened the briefcase where he'd placed the items from Cailan's room for safekeeping and turned it to where Jaffray would see. "Give these a look, if you will."

Jaffray peered at the figurines through their plastic evidence bags. "These dolls are crude, amateur. More someone's idea of what a voodoo doll should look like, not something from a true practitioner."

He studied the pictures. "Beware Ochosi. Ochosi is a figure in religions including Santeria and voodoo. The hunter-magician spirit who represents justice. His symbol is a crossbow."

Drayco closed the briefcase. "Those items were found hidden in a pillow in your niece's room. The mirror in those photos is from Cailan's bathroom. We don't know if she wrote the message or someone else did. As a warning."

Jaffray perched his chin on top of his tented fingers. It was a gesture that might easily be taken as a prayer posture. But if prayer, it was the supplication of a wretched man. For the rest of him was slumped and rounded, like a mishandled book, warped and bent.

He sighed. "My niece and I were close, but we had the usual disagreements. Typical teenage rebellion. Cailan was most adamant about getting her own place. So I was increasingly out of the loop about her personal life. That's why I have no knowledge of her dabbling in voodoo or anything else."

Jaffray got up to reach for a book and handed it over to Drayco. "Here's a book on religious practices of the Caribbean. Consider it a loaner. Maybe it can answer your questions."

Sarg looked up from his notebook. "Gary Zabowski. Cailan ever talk about him?"

Jaffray shook his head. "I found out about Zabowski from the police. More of that personal life she kept from me."

He rubbed his eyes. "She did tell me she was already making plans for her forty-seventh birthday. To mark the date she outlived her mother."

Sarg stopped writing and cleared his throat. "Any thoughts on other motivations for her death, sir?"

"I've thought about this hundreds of times, Agent Sargosian. Drugs, revenge, cults, insanity."

"Any unusual motives? Had Cailan been ill, for instance?"

"Ill? Unless you're talking mental illness and suicide, I'm not sure why that would matter. She knew I'm not a fan of any form of suicide, assisted or not. The Buddha said mercy and killing can never go together."

"So no mental illness, then?" Sarg's pen hovered over his notebook.

"As far as I know, Agent Sargosian, she was perfectly healthy, mentally and physically. Sargosian ... Sargosian ... that sounds familiar. Do you have a daughter at Parkhurst?"

"Tara's her name."

"I remember her. A very good student, attentive. And I don't use idle flattery. She looked familiar. Is your family from the Eastern Shore, by any chance?"

"No sir, Glendale, California, originally."

"I could have sworn she was an Eastern Shore girl. That's where I'm from. I do some teaching at Eastern Shore Community College from time to time."

Drayco knew that tidbit from Sarg's bullet points. His subconscious had put it out of his mind, no doubt because his own experiences on the shore were less than idyllic thanks to two murder cases. He spoke up. "I'm familiar with the area."

"Nice place, if you can get past the poverty and smells from the chicken-rendering plants. My mother lives on the shore. I'm the one who broke the news of her granddaughter. And how I broke the deathbed promise to Cailan's mother I'd take care of her little girl. Keep her safe." Jaffray passed a hand over his face and closed his eyes.

As Drayco listened to Jaffray, he noticed something missing from this room. He looked again, making sure he hadn't missed it in all the clutter. Most religious traditions were inexorably linked to music—Gregorian Chant and illuminated manuscripts, Chinese Dongjing scrolls, Indian Vedic works. Yet despite the mountains of religious paraphernalia lying around, he didn't see a single music-related icon.

"Professor Jaffray, how did Cailan get interested in music?"

"Not from me." The glare Jaffray directed at the books on his desk was so intense, Drayco half-expected them to catch fire. "If you'll excuse me, I have a class to get ready for. And I wish you better luck finding her killer than the police did with my brother's hit-and-run."

Drayco and Sarg retraced their steps down the same long hallway as before, minus students this time. The only sound was the echo of their footsteps on the parquet floor. In its emptiness, the building's institutional beigeness was suffocating.

Drayco again took note of the classrooms, how small and intimate they were. No TAs used here. A big selling point, like college Crackerjacks—a prize PhD in every class.

Drayco said, "So Tara had Jaffray as a teacher. What did she think of him?"

"A bit dry, but she learned a lot."

"Wish I could say the same for us. More dead ends, few leads. No closer to who sent those letters or why."

Sarg held open the door. "Oh ye of microscopic faith." He used his cellphone as they walked to Drayco's Starfire, and from the fragments Drayco heard of Sarg's end, he had a good idea of where they were headed next.

So Troy Jaffray had a bad encounter with musicians? Or did he just hate music? And why was that notion so distressing? Music had meant so much to Cailan. A girl who heard rainbows in music, like Drayco did.

He squinted at the sliver of sun turning water crystals amid bone-colored clouds into the halo of a sundog, like the glass prism he once gave Tara. The brief glimpse of sun disappeared, taking the sundog with it and leaving behind the crisp autumn air and smell of decaying leaf mold.

Sarg ended the call. "You know how to get to Kenilworth Gardens, right? Gotta couple of park police meeting us there."

Drayco didn't ask how Sarg explained to Onweller the necessity of visiting Kenilworth to solve the music puzzle. The broader case was their game, not his. His game was the music puzzle and nothing more. Funny thing about games—they often said more about the creator than the creation itself. Something he and Troy Jaffray could probably agree on.

6

Kenilworth Aquatic Gardens was an odd choice to dump a body. Anyone planning such a thing would have few access options, a fact verified by the two park police from the Major Crimes Unit. "Bordered by marsh on three sides. Only way to get in would be the main road leading into the visitor's center." Detective Jackson Smith motioned toward the road behind Drayco. "Anacostia Street."

"What about a canoe?" Drayco surveyed the wetlands, trying to gauge how someone would manage it.

Smith frowned. "It was night, so it was dark. And it was low tide when the marsh often loses up to ninety percent of its water."

Drayco inhaled the fishy, earthy smell that reminded him of the Eastern Shore. He'd grown to like it. "So how did they get through the locked gate? The fence is too high to climb for most people. Worse if you're carrying a body."

"The NPS says no keys have recently gone missing. Someone could have made an impression for a key. Or used burglar's tools."

The grass was half-green, half dormant-straw, typical of October. Back in August, the Mid-Atlantic was in the middle of a drought which meant dry, crunchy grass. Sarg's file noted there'd been no footprint evidence thanks to that and the dozens of tracks from a Girl Scout group the day before Cailan's body was found.

The second detective, Tawna Grayson, motioned for Drayco and Sarg to join her in an area ten feet from the boardwalk. She kept looking at her watch, a message so unsubtle, she might as well have shouted at them to "hurry up." She'd made it clear she was upset she and her colleagues might not get credit for the collar. But she hated cold cases even more.

"Thought you'd want to see where the body was found. Park opens every morning at seven. Mostly bird watchers at that hour. One of the poor unsuspecting Audubons came across the corpse." She frowned. "Don't see the appeal in looking for every red-crested, black-beaked thingamabird."

A large white bird made a splash, followed by a greenish-gold croaking sound, catching Drayco's attention. "That egret over there is impressive."

"I prefer my birds smothered in gravy." Detective Grayson walked in a circle around where the body had lain. "Not a lot of blood, no weapon, just a body with a stabbing wound in front. No one saw anyone. People in Anacostia tend not to see things—if they want to stay healthy."

Sarg didn't appear impressed with the egret, either. He'd never been a water fan, one reason he told Drayco he'd gunned for the Rangers and not the Seals. He said, "Lots of homes in this area. And no one saw any unusual cars, vans, trucks at that hour?"

"Nothing unusual, or so they said."

They paused as a white-top helicopter flew five-hundred feet overhead and the noise drowned out their conversation. Like most people in the metro area, Drayco resigned himself to the constant parade of helicopters day and night—black hawks, Bells, Dolphins, Sikorskys. With the highest concentration of VIPs, military and intelligence per square meter on the planet, it was to be expected.

After the helicopter noise faded to a low roar, he said, "Any NPS vehicles come here late at night? After closing?"

Detective Smith answered. "Occasionally. If you're asking whether someone saw one that night, no."

Grayson edged toward their car. "If you need anything else, you know the number."

Smith hung back for a moment, lowering his voice. "This is her first big case with the division. She's none too keen on leaving it unsolved. And having the Feds come in rankles. But we all know how much connections matter."

Drayco asked, "Connections?"

"Unit Chief Onweller being golfing buddies with Parkhurst President Thackeray. Guess we should have known the FBI would be called in sooner or later. Apparently Thackeray and the college trustees hate the notoriety. Makes Parkhurst look bad."

"Right." Drayco waved him off, so the officer could rejoin Grayson, already buckled in the driver's seat with the engine running.

Drayco waited until they pulled away, which took all of five seconds with Grayson's lead foot. "Golfing buddies?" His suspicions about Onweller and the Parkhurst administration had come home to roost.

"It's not relevant to the case."

"The hell it isn't. It means once again I'm in political quicksand where I could get sucked down along with the truth. And so could you. Did you know about this and conveniently forget to tell me?"

Sarg tugged on his ear and then gave an unconvincing shrug. "You wanna be the body or should I?" Sarg looked up at Drayco. "On second thought, guess I'm closer to Cailan's height."

They walked in silence back to the visitor's center and counted out the steps it would take to reach the dumping site. Sarg placed his jacket over the area where Cailan was found and then lay down.

Drayco started at the parking lot and retraced the most likely path the murderer took. "Depending upon the size and strength of our killer, I'd say three minutes might do it unless there were accomplices. Since the police couldn't isolate any tracks ..."

Sarg raised his head. "How well did you see me from the lot?"

"In the dusk like now, you could be mistaken for an animal or a group of birds on the ground. In the dark, you'd be impossible to see."

Sarg hauled himself up. "So this guy drives in after dark, drops off a body tra-la, trots away and nobody sees him."

"Maybe somebody did."

"What do you mean?"

"Something they see all the time. So they didn't think anything of it."

"That why you were asking about the NPS vehicle?"

"I'm not suggesting an employee per se. Have any NPS cars or trucks been stolen recently?"

"Dunno. I can check." Sarg squinted into the gathering gloom. "A real peaceful place. Hard to believe it's in the heart of the city."

The nation's capital had so many of these areas. Drive along the GW Parkway and you'd swear you were on a road in the forests of Shenandoah. Until you reached the clearing where you can see the National Cathedral and monuments rising up across the Potomac River, like the Emerald City in Oz.

And here in the middle of town lay the aquatic gardens of Kenilworth, the water lilies, cattails, and wildlife mute witnesses to a desecration of their grounds. Someone's joking idea of a "final resting place?"

Drayco asked, "Can you arrange a meeting with Shannon Krugh, Cailan's rival?"

Sarg brushed the grass off his jacket and put it back on. "If you pick me up at Union Station tomorrow, I will make it so. A chat with Gary Zabowski, too?"

"And that hippy stalker, Elvis Loomis."

"Anything else I can arrange for you, my liege?" Sarg made a mocking bow.

Drayco bit back a retort. Their old rhythms and patterns were off, making him uncomfortable around Sarg. And he didn't like being uncomfortable around Sarg. But few wounds healed in such a short time.

Meanwhile, an unsolved puzzle and a murder case were getting as cold as a January wind off an ice-packed Chesapeake Bay. That was one helpful fact in their favor—at least the killer hadn't dumped Cailan's body there.

7

Drayco was early to his morning appointment with FBI Unit Chief Jerry Onweller, a meeting the man's secretary had arranged late yesterday. She hadn't given a reason, but Drayco had a good idea what it was about—to lay down the law. Keep him in his place.

As he walked into the BAU offices at Quantico, he was surprised when several former colleagues greeted him with slaps on the back and good-natured ribbing. Maybe there really was a part of him that missed being part of a team, the surrogate family he never really had. He fingered the unfamiliar "Visitor" ID tag, which hung crooked no matter how much he tried to straighten it.

The secretary ushered Drayco into Onweller's office, with the signed photo of J. Edgar hanging in the center of the room. Onweller shared Hoover's bulldog jowls, only Onweller sported a lot more hair, with a thick salt-and-pepper brush top above half-rimless glass frames. The man still had the same gun-shaped air freshener on his desk, shooting out cherry-scented puffs. Drayco pulled up a chair without waiting to be asked.

The Unit Chief, who'd had the back of his chair to Drayco, twirled around and stared at him, barely blinking. So that was the way he was going to handle this, with the silent treatment? Finally Onweller said, "I never pegged you to screw up the way you did when you left."

It was telling that Onweller said "when" you left, not "before" you left. Drayco didn't have time to react before Onweller continued, "You were being looked at for a promotion by the Section Chief down the line. Something that didn't surprise me. So I gotta ask myself, why would a man throw all of that away and lose everything he'd worked for?"

Onweller picked up a card and tapped it rhythmically on his desk. "Especially someone with such attention to detail."

Drayco ran his hand along the armrest. "Mistakes happen."

"Not with you. You were plenty sharp to shoot that kidnapper three times to incapacitate and not kill. Yet you overlooked where he was hiding, missed seeing his gun, and allowed him to shoot Agent Sargosian and kill that young officer? Your write-up on the incident was barely more than a page and unusually vague."

"It all happened very fast."

"Yes. I can imagine." Onweller continued tapping the card. "There were some who questioned my decision to promote you in the first place, due to your youth. This confirmed their suspicions."

"Perhaps they were right."

"Bullshit."

Shocked, Drayco sat up straighter. Was that why Onweller had always been harder on Drayco than Sarg? And that part about going to bat for Drayco despite his youth—that was a curveball. A curveball wrapped in a skin of guilt. For in protecting Sarg, Drayco realized he'd essentially stabbed Onweller in the back. Unintended collateral damage.

Onweller stared at him a few seconds longer, then asked, "Sargosian tells me you haven't solved the music puzzle sent to Cailan Jaffray. Is that correct?"

"That's correct." He stopped himself from adding, "Sir."

"Are you anywhere closer to solving it?"

"Possibly. I hope so."

Drayco waited for the inevitable "you're off the case" edict. But Onweller surprised him again when he said, "I guess even boy geniuses need extra time now and then."

An insult or a joke? Onweller's face was blanker than a fresh piece of printer paper. Drayco didn't have long to ponder that, as Onweller added, "Stick close to Sargosian and don't be striking out on your own. This is a sensitive matter."

"I understand your ... position." Drayco deserved a medal of honor for not adding, "Seeing as how you're golfing buddies with Parkhurst President Thackeray." Instead, he said, "No one wants to solve that puzzle more than I do. I owe it to Cailan."

"Yes. Well." The Chief stared at the gun air freshener, then pushed a button on top, forcing out more puffs of cherry. Literally clearing the air?

Drayco left Onweller, not knowing what to think about their meeting. It felt a little like being sent to the Principal's office, only to be patted on the head and shuttled back to class. Maybe he should have brought along an apple.

§ § §

Drayco made the short trip to Fredericksburg to pick up Sarg at his house, and they headed back up I-95 toward the District. Sarg prattled on about everything from his wife's new macramé kick to a new hardware store where they sold the perfect avocado slicer. It wasn't until they cleared the D.C. border that he said, "I didn't see any of Onweller's blood on you. What did you do, take him a fruit basket?"

The way they were already thinking alike again was a little scary. "If I had, it would have been all lemons and limes."

"That good?"

"It wasn't horrible. About what I expected."

Sarg grunted sympathetically, then said, "I do have one piece of news. I'd like to say it's good news. But I'm inclined to think it isn't."

Drayco turned onto the Parkhurst campus and headed for the visitor parking lot. "At this point, I'll welcome any news."

"Your hunch was right. Park service says they had an SUV stolen. One of those white numbers you see all the time. And get this—the oh-so-intelligent employee left his Park Service uniform in a dry-cleaning bag inside. Size medium, could fit an average man or woman."

"And they didn't think to tell investigators sooner because ... ?"

"It was stolen a year ago. They didn't think there was a connection."

Drayco maneuvered into one of the few spots left and parked. "Why do you feel this is bad news?"

Sarg exhaled loudly. "Tara."

It would blast a hole in the love-triangle theory. Drayco had a vision of all the times he'd seen Sarg laying down the law with Tara and her older brother, Michael. Through all that bluster and discipline, Sarg was a good father. Working with violence at your day job but having your kids several degrees of separation away, not so bad. It becomes torture when there's only one degree of separation.

"And you thought having her attend a local school meant you could keep an eye on her."

"Should've encouraged her to go to one of those small Corn Belt schools."

"This could still be a love triangle gone wrong." Drayco hauled himself out of the car. "Let's go meet one-third of that triangle, shall we?"

The music school building was grandiose, even by Parkhurst standards. Architecture designed by Michael Graves had contemporary steel cross beams flying from the roof and soaring tall glass windows in front.

Sarg examined the gleaming façade. "Parkhurst sure ain't Ivy League—they wouldn't dare let any ivy grow here."

The chairman's secretary greeted them and ushered them into the recital hall. And what a hall—a black-painted cloud with dotted lights like stars, an enormous pipe organ and seating for a thousand. She herded them up onto the stage and had them wait, saying Shannon Krugh was supposed to meet with them in one of the greenrooms.

As the secretary scurried off, Sarg whispered, "You could fit a circus on this stage."

Drayco barely heard him. The piano was calling, as always. A gleaming Bösendorfer Imperial Grand, with sensual curves he couldn't help reaching out to touch. The smooth finish would feel cold and lifeless to most, but to him it was electric. As he listened closely, he almost heard the instrument "breathing" with kaleidoscopic room sounds vibrating off the strings on the soundboard. Maybe no one would notice if he sat down in front of the keyboard for a minute?

Sarg came over to take a look. "Looks bigger than usual."

Drayco walked all the way around the instrument, then rubbed his fingers over the bass end, with its black matte finish. "It has an added subcontra octave, instead of the standard eighty-eight keys. Mostly for Busoni transcriptions of Bach's organ works. Most schools can't afford these beauties."

"How much?"

"This type starts around a hundred-eighty grand."

Sarg whistled. "You ever play one of these?"

Drayco moved his hand to finger the contours of the smooth rim, recalling one concert in Chicago where the audience had him back for three encores. "Long ago in a galaxy far away."

Sarg opened his mouth to reply, but then the secretary returned. Drayco studied her more closely. She looked to be in her 40s, chestnut hair cropped short, dressed in the same conservative Parkhurst attire on staff everywhere. Except this woman's pinstripe suit had a red pocket handkerchief, and she was wearing red earrings in the shape of the letter C with flames on the edge.

"Are you a hockey fan?" Drayco asked.

She tilted her head up at him and smiled. "Name one person from Calgary who isn't."

She motioned them into one of the greenrooms behind the stage. "We figured it would be best to have you talk with Shannon in private. She's been through a lot since Cailan's death." The woman's smiled dipped, and she thrust her hands into her jacket pockets. "I guess we all have. One of our brightest talents."

They entered the greenroom where Shannon Krugh sat in a chair looking in a mirror braiding her dyed-pink hair. "These are the two gentlemen from the FBI here to see you, Shannon."

The girl paid scant attention to the secretary, who nodded at the two men and left. Shannon's right leg and foot bounced rhythmically on the floor. Combined with the frenetic braiding, she was like a plane ready for takeoff.

"I've talked and talked and talked to so many policemen, I think I'm all talked out. Like, I'm kinda busy, you know? Midterms are coming up, and I have to study if I want to keep my scholarship, and of course I do, so can we get this over with real fast?"

Sarg sat down in another chair opposite her. "We just have a few questions for you, Miss Krugh."

"Great! So lay it on me and I'll answer whatever. It's not like I've got anything to hide. Gimme what you got. I can take it."

Sarg squinted at Shannon through narrowed eyes. "Since you don't have anything to hide, why don't you tell us about bullying Cailan."

Both of Shannon's legs were bouncing now, in rhythm. "I don't know where you heard that. I mean, we weren't the best of friends, and she was jealous when her boyfriend dumped her for me, but I wouldn't call that bullying, would you?"

"No, but that's not all we—"

"And it's not like I don't have to be on best behavior, with this scholarship and all. I mean, I'm not swimming in dough like all the other kids. So why would I jeopardize that?"

Sarg tried again. "You were music rivals, too. Both singers, right?"

"Sure. She was a music student, I'm not, but we both sing. Sang. Well, I still sing. You know what I mean. And yeah, she got most of the attention. And the awards, but then look who she is."

"What do you mean, who she is?"

"Professor's niece, for one. And all that money she had coming to her. And being His Royal Highness Gilbow's goddaughter and all. I mean who am I to compete with that?"

"Is that why you sent those music puzzles, because you felt threatened by her success? Wanted to scare her?"

"The police asked me that, and I don't know anything about music puzzles. And I mean why should I, because I got a 'D' in the one music theory class I took."

Drayco had chosen to stand, his arms crossed. Watching her, listening to her, it was clear what was going on. He smiled gently at her. "How long have you been off your lithium, Shannon?"

She stopped bouncing and twirling. "I hate it. You can't drink too many liquids, you can't drink too little. It makes me cold all the time. And I itch. And food doesn't taste right."

"Does your doctor know all this?"

"I always take it right before I see him. He doesn't have to know." She lifted her chin with a defiant pout of her lips. Then she jumped up off her chair, sat on the edge of a dressing table and let her legs swing over the side.

Drayco kept a steady gaze trained on her. "Is that why you got into voodoo, because you were off your meds?"

She met his gaze for a brief moment, then avoided looking at him. "You're the one who's on something. My parents would kill me if they found out I was involved in some cult or whatever. You should ask Gary, Mr. I'm-better-than-anyone-else. He's into all kinds of weird things, so he's the one you should ask about drugs."

Drayco walked over and sat beside her on the dressing table. "Are you a soprano or mezzo?"

"Soprano." She pulled out some wintergreen-scented gum and started chewing.

"You're familiar with the opera *La Gioconda*?"

"Of course." Her eyes widened. "I see what you're getting at. Gioconda wanted to stab her rival, okay, but I never touched Cailan. Nor drugged her."

She slid off the table and headed for the door. "The police told me all that, so it's like you're tripping me up or anything." She paused before slipping out the door. "It would be a real operatic thing of me to do, wouldn't it? Killing Cailan? My best role yet."

Shannon blew a big bubble at them and then ducked into the corridor, where another young woman joined her. Her companion was a few years older, with thick makeup like a Hollywood starlet. The woman frowned at the men and guided Shannon down the hall and through an exit.

Sarg said, "Geo condo?"

"A Ponchielli opera."

"Didn't know you liked opera."

"I don't."

Sarg got up out of his chair and stretched. "Yup, day keeps getting better and better. I've got a whole new appreciation for lithium."

Drayco folded his arms across his chest. "Gilbow's goddaughter? You holding that tidbit in escrow, like Gilbow and Onweller being best buds? It wasn't one of your bullet points."

"That goddaughter thing is news to me, too. Onweller never said a word."

Sarg walked to the doorway and planted himself in the middle, his hands pushing on both sides of the frame. "Look, I admit I made a mistake three years ago. A mistake and a decision I've regretted every day since. And will for the rest of my life. But I've never withheld any intel from you. I didn't tell you about Onweller being chummy with the college president because I was afraid you'd turn me down if you knew."

Drayco didn't reply. What could he say? Sarg was right about the intel. The real elephant trampling through that room was something neither of them had discussed. Why hadn't Drayco contacted Sarg during those three years? It wasn't just up to his former colleague to try and glue their friendship back together. Sarg had to live with his guilt. And Drayco? Excuses about being too busy felt like a cop-out.

Sargosian unblocked the doorway and headed into the hall. "Guess this means we get to consult your favorite windbag after all. I'll go rescue Cailan's boxing gloves. You take those, I'll get him another pair, and let you two duke it out."

The image of Gilbow flat on his back in the middle of the boxing ring cheered Drayco up. "Were you able to get in touch with our Prince Charming, Gary Zabowski?"

"We see him in an hour. First, I have a treat for you."

"Oh?"

"We're going to see the King."

8

The "king" turned out to be more of a jester. Baggy black-and-white checked pants, white T-shirt, long dark hair and a beard that reached to his chest. Drayco looked at the man's feet, half-expecting to see oversized floppy shoes, but he sported only ordinary sneakers. He knew from Sarg's case file that Elvis Loomis, alleged Cailan stalker, had a rap sheet including drugs, DUI and domestic violence on an ex-girlfriend.

They'd arranged to meet him at the Campus Security office, where he sat in an interview room. Not far from the room, Drayco spied a row of Segway patrollers emblazoned with Parkhurst Campus Security on the sides. Those things went for several grand each.

Sarg, getting more foul-tempered by the minute, strode right on in and slapped his hands palm-side down on the table. "All right, Mr. Loomis, let's cut the crap. Why were you stalking Cailan Jaffray?"

Elvis Loomis mimicked Sarg by slapping his hands on the table and leaning in. Both men were reverse images of each other, the scowling nobleman in his dark suit and the grinning jester in his costume. "She was pretty, she had a pretty voice. Knew she'd be a big star some day. I wanted her autograph. End of story."

"You were seen following her on more than one occasion. Did you need that T-shirt and a hat autographed, too?"

"Already told all of this to the po-leece. You suits are all the same. Jump on the fucky-duck who don't conform. Cause anyone who's done time is always up to no good."

"You hit a woman once. Is that a hobby of yours?"

"She said I hit her. I didn't. But who's gonna believe me?" Elvis peered over at Drayco. "That your good cop?"

Drayco hid a smile and waved.

"Does he talk?"

Drayco walked to the end of the table to get a better look at Elvis' face. "How'd you get this job with your background, Elvis?"

"Hey, the good cop does speak. This job, my friend, came via a recommendo. Used to be groundskeeper for a congress-critter. I do good work, ask the Dean."

"Oh, we will all right." Sarg pulled out a chair, but didn't sit down. "A campus is filled with lots of young women. That why you wanted the job, Mr. Loomis?"

Elvis leaned back and laughed. "I needed the bread, but yeah, that's a perk. Place is full of hot young chicks. I dare you not to look at any of them parading around in skimpy clothes and tight jeans. I'm not a eunuch, for chrissakes."

Sarg growled. "I have a daughter that age."

"Don't get your thong in a wad, man. I'm the guy who trims trees and mows lawns. Never hurt nobody."

Elvis squinted at Drayco while motioning toward Sarg. "Call off the bad cop, 'kay? Or arrest me or whatever. His negative energy is harshing my buzz."

Drayco slid into the chair Sarg had pulled out. "Where did you hear Cailan sing in the first place?"

"College concerts. The only kind I can afford—free. Besides, opera's my thing now. Callas, Sutherland, Fleming. Does the soul good."

Drayco smiled. "Music does, yes. How did you become an opera fan?"

"In jail." When he saw Sarg open his mouth, Elvis hastily added, "We had this warden who was like that Arizona dude—the one who makes inmates wear pink uniforms. Our warden's idea of torture was to play opera through the intercom. Had some of the guys ready to gnaw their arms off, but me, I began to dig it. When I got out, I haunted Clayton's CD Cellar, looking for bargain discs. Got hundreds of 'em."

Sarg butted in. "You collect voodoo dolls, too?"

Elvis' words echoed Shannon's. "Didn't know G-men were allowed to do blow on the job, man. Voodoo dolls?" He spread his arms out wide. "My religion is the entire universe. Everything else is myth, man."

Drayco pushed the paper with Cailan's music puzzle in front of him. "You enjoy puzzles, Elvis?"

Elvis looked at the paper and his lips curled into a smile. "They're okay, but I don't read music. Ironic, huh?"

Drayco got up and handed Elvis one of his cards. "In case you think of something that might help."

Elvis took the card in one hand and waved with the other. "Bye-bye, good cop."

Drayco and Sarg allowed Elvis to return to his gardening and headed to the car, where Sarg thumped the hood. "An innocent autograph stalker? Don't buy it." Sarg shook out his hand, flexing the fingers. "And you were easy on him. Seeing as how he's a potential murderer."

Drayco glanced at Sarg's hand. No damage. "He doesn't strike me as a master liar. And if he honestly can't read music, it would be hard for him to create those puzzles. Computer software or no."

"Still think he's hiding something. And it's possible the guy who sent the puzzles isn't the same one who killed her."

"I didn't say Elvis wasn't hiding something. Necessarily. And you're right, we could be dealing with two separate culprits. If Elvis killed Cailan, I want to nail his sorry ass as much as you do."

Sarg started to thump the hood again, but stopped and rubbed the paint with his sleeve. "You kept Leonora, eh?" He patted Drayco's Starfire again and sighed. Well, I'm rustier than this old-girl-of-a-car. Haven't been out in the field for far too long. Hell, you've done more with your solo consulting. I've become a goddamn police research librarian. Not what I bargained for."

"It's like *Klangfarbenmelodie*."

Sarg stared at Drayco like he'd lost his mind.

"It means altering the color of a note or melody by switching instruments in the middle of it. But it's the same music. Maybe you're not out in the field on a regular basis anymore, but you help law enforcement agencies do their jobs better. It all serves the same purpose."

Sarg perched on the hood of Drayco's car for several moments, not saying anything, his hands stuffed in his pockets. He squinted skyward as a flock of geese honked loudly overhead, V-ing their way south. "I haven't cooked a goose in a looooong time. Truth be told, I've never been fond of cooked goose."

"Maybe if you smothered it in gravy."

Sarg valiantly fought to hide a grin, grabbed the car keys from Drayco and whirled around to the driver's side. "I lined up a visit with Mr. Gary Zabowski. But we may not be there long."

"What do you mean?"

"His father isn't just an attorney, he's a partner in a Philadelphia firm that's argued cases in front of the Supremes. Pulls down several mil a year."

"Yet Gary told you to meet him at his apartment?"

"I figure Dad Esquire or some other legal beagle will be there. Hate to disappoint you."

"Oh, I'm a disappointment sponge. I soak it up."

Yet Gary was the one person who intrigued Drayco the most. Composer Gary, in the center of the stormy love triangle, most likely candidate behind the music puzzle. Was the *La Gioconda* reference more of an apt one than he'd thought? If Gary was like the male romantic interest in the opera, he'd sail away to safety while the woman who loved him was sacrificed. No wonder Drayco didn't like opera. Too much like his day job.

Drayco said, "Been a while since you drove the Starfire."

Sarg hopped into the driver's seat, and Drayco buckled himself into the passenger side as he said, "You still drive like an old woman?"

In reply, Sarg accelerated backward and did a full 360 in reverse before pointing the car in the direction of Gary Zabowski, composer, lothario, and—if they were lucky—puzzlemeister.

9

It was a sleepy, tousled Gary Zabowski who answered their knock a few minutes shy of one o'clock. He had on briefs barely covered by a T-shirt that said "Composer by Day, Cage Fighter By Night." Without a word, he motioned them toward a leather sofa behind a low table cluttered with empty cans of beer, Red Bull and takeout boxes with grease stains. Then he vanished into the kitchen. The sounds of running water and grains pouring out of a bag hinted he was making coffee.

He was alone. No father, no lawyers.

Sarg pointed at the table. "Resembles your place, or the way it used to be. And your cuisine."

Drayco didn't think the aroma of stale beer and cigarette smoke mingling with decaying kung pao chicken was like his place at all. But he had to admit, he wasn't a neat freak. A reaction against his father's OCD cleanliness, perhaps, or it was the comfort he found in clutter. Sarg had often spent part of his visits playing maid.

Gary's computer setup on the other side of the room drew Drayco's attention. A desktop unit and large monitor, two laptops, an electronic piano keyboard, a small mixer and two large speakers.

The monitor had a project open, and Drayco took a closer look. Gary was working on a string quartet. As Drayco scanned the screen, he thought the music had some Bartók touches, which surprised him. It was a lot more tonal than what many young composition students were writing these days.

"You're here about Cailan and those music puzzle thingies, right?" Gary opened a new can of Red Bull and dumped some into his coffee, then set it down to light up something that looked like a clove cigarette, banned for sale in the states. He blew out a puff of sweet-smelling smoke and grinned at them. He was a kid used to getting what he wanted.

Gary said, "Could have saved you the time and bus fare. Didn't make those puzzles, didn't kill her and don't know who did. We done now?" He pushed past Drayco, grabbed the chair in front of the computer and spun it around to sit down, coming within inches of knocking into Drayco's knee. He didn't apologize.

"You're a composition student, right?" Sarg called from the sofa, where he moved to avoid sitting on a gooey, green patch.

Gary waved his arm at the equipment. "What do you think all this is? State of the art, cost thousands. I charge it up and Dad pays the bills. Dad's rich, in case you didn't know. Thinking of ponying up a big chunk of change for the new Parkhurst law school so it'll be named after him."

Gary didn't need an attorney, he had his ego to protect him.

"You dated Cailan, dumped her for Shannon Krugh. Were you aware of their rivalry and Shannon's bullying?" Sarg apparently thought better of sitting on the stained sofa and joined them so that he and Drayco were bookending Gary.

"That's a big ten-bore, Mr. Cop Man. Shannon runs hot and cold. It's why she didn't have a lot of friends at the music school." He blew a big cloud of smoke first in Sarg's direction, then in Drayco's. "It was fun dating a bipolar chick. Kinda like having two girlfriends at the same time."

"Did you know about voodoo dolls or threats directed at Cailan?"

"Yeah, Cailan told me."

Sarg's eyebrows shot up. "She did?"

"She didn't tell anyone else, only moi. Happened while we were still dating. I wouldn't put it past Shannon to have done it. But she never fessed up to it."

"Was Shannon involved with any cults?"

"Shannon? Would have guessed Cailan of the two. I mean it's always the quiet ones, right? Wouldn't touch those culty weirdos with a ten-foot light saber."

Sarg put his hand down on the computer table, hitting a stack of CD cases that clattered to the floor. He bent down to pick them up but grabbed something under the table instead. He straightened up to take a look, flipping the cover of a book around so Drayco could see it.

The pictures on the cover were of nude men and women engaged in various sex poses. Sarg opened to the middle and turned it sideways. He said, "I'll never look at caramel the same way again." Then he flipped to the title page. "Local publishing company. Friends of yours?"

Gary snatched the book out of Sarg's hands and threw it under the table. "If you want to look into Cailan's death instead of my reading material, talk to Liam Futino. I saw them arguing at the Café Renée the day she was murdered. I could tell he had it bad for her." For a split second, Drayco noted a hint of wistfulness on Gary's face.

Drayco asked, "Who's Liam Futino?"

"Just a guy she knew. Nobody important."

Sarg pulled out his notebook to jot down the name. "Important enough to argue with, apparently. Know why they were arguing?"

Gary shrugged. "None of my beeswax."

Spurred by Sarg's book discovery, Drayco prowled around the room for other surprises. He made a circuit, noting a pile of video games stacked on a table. The game on the top was one of the popular role-playing titles, the usual good vs. evil, lots of nasty weapons, lots of CGI blood.

Drayco picked it up and scanned the description. This one included casting spells. He put it back and continued his prowl, stopping by the sofa for a minute to stare at the floor, before returning to where Gary sat. "Why did you dump Cailan for Shannon?"

Gary shrugged again. "Too trusting, too needy, too desperate for love and attention. I prefer things free and easy, no baggage."

He must use a different dictionary from Drayco's—Shannon's bipolar disorder didn't count as baggage? "You had an alibi for the night Cailan was killed?"

"Reed and I were hanging out at Tuchman's. It's a bar in Georgetown. Reed Upperman's a doctoral psych student. I met him through Cailan, who was in this project of his on freaks."

Sarg's cellphone emitted a series of beeps, and he pulled it out of his pocket. Gary snickered. "You use the default ringtone that came with that phone? Oh man, geezers and technology."

Sarg ignored him and headed toward the back of the room for some privacy.

Gary pressed a save button on his computer keyboard and closed the project Drayco was looking at. "You carry guns, right? I prefer Glocks. Go on the range and practice when I get a chance."

"That so?" Drayco hadn't carried a concealed weapon for the first couple of years after leaving the Bureau. It was like being cold, stark naked at first. But it meant no chance to use it, to potentially kill someone. It wasn't until he had a nasty run-in with a client's ex-con brother that he started hiding a gun in his car.

Gary spun in his chair to face Drayco. "Bet packing a gun makes you feel big and tough. You ever shot a guy?"

"Yes." From across the room, he sensed Sarg tense up.

"You kill him?"

"Aiming to kill is a last resort. Keeping the bad guy alive for questioning is the better way to go."

Gary turned to his computer, tapped a few keys, and strains of Blue Öyster Cult's "Don't Fear The Reaper" blared out of the speakers. "Too bad. That would be the only fun part of a gig like yours. At least with my money and degree," he held up a hand and rubbed his thumb against his fingertips. "I'll end up doing something a lot more lucrative than low-paid cop."

"A typical composer makes mid-five figures and teaches at a college. Hardly lucrative."

Gary tipped back in his chair and looked up at Drayco. "You enjoy making people squirm? I'll bet you were the kid who aimed a magnifying glass on insects and watched them burn for the hell of it. I mean, why else do your kind of job?"

Drayco took a step forward, towering over the younger man. "Because my job is a hell of a lot better than making light of people's suffering. You should try that sometime."

Sarg finished his call and rejoined Drayco and Gary. "Onweller. An update. We through here?"

Drayco replied, "We're through."

The two men let themselves out, where Sarg immediately breathed in a deep lungful of smoke-free air. "That boy is not getting anywhere near Tara."

"She has better taste than that. Although he's right about having plenty of money to burn. Did you get a good look at his watch? A Breitling. Costs five grand."

"So you're a watch connoisseur now, good for you."

Some things about Sarg hadn't changed, although his "mockservations" were usually aimed at people low on Sarg's esteem-ladder, not his former partner. Drayco said, "It has a chronograph and E6B flight computer, two features he probably never uses."

"But he could have used all that computer gear to create the music codes. The MPD is putting their money on him."

"Yet they didn't mention the stain."

Sarg stopped in his tracks. "What stain?"

"That couch you were sitting on. It's been moved recently, judging by rug indentations. But it doesn't quite cover a rust-colored stain on the side nearest the wall."

"Blood?"

"Psychic detective I'm not. Got a test kit and search warrant on you?"

"When the MPD questioned Gary, it was at the second district station. Not enough cause for a search warrant, what with Gary's alibi and attorney-daddy."

Sarg paced along the sidewalk. "This might be probable cause. We should call the MPD."

"What would that accomplish? There could be a dozen reasons for that stain. A Bloody Mary, red wine, ketchup, all required homework for Party 101."

Drayco had spent many a night in the UMD library when he was a student, looking for some peace and quiet to get away from the Garys and their parties that lasted until God a.m. "The MPD isn't going to touch Gary unless they have a stellar reason. Besides, I'm supposed to focus on the music puzzles, remember?"

Sarg sighed. "Okay, so what next?"

"A talk with Reed Upperman about that lab project. There's hardly anything in the MPD reports."

Sarg headed toward the car. "Upperman and Gilbow are both on my 'next' list. But it'll have to wait until tomorrow morning. There's some big department confab this afternoon."

Drayco slid into the driver's seat. "Ninety minutes until your train. My townhome isn't far away. Beats sitting on one of those hard chairs at Union."

Sarg hesitated, then climbed in. "They are pretty hard. My ass stays numb for hours afterward."

Drayco turned on the engine as Sarg tugged on his ear hard enough to rip it off. Maybe this wasn't a MENSA-grade bright idea, but Drayco pointed the car in the direction of his home, anyway. Crawling, baby steps, walking. That was the usual order of things.

10

Sarg had barely set one foot inside Drayco's townhome, when he picked up the mail pushed through the slot in the door. His "maid" instincts must be kicking in, even in Drayco's newly Spartanized digs. At one time, Drayco would be amused. Right now, it was as welcome as an invitation to a tuba recital.

"Bill, bill, bill. Second notice?" Sarg lifted one envelope up to the light. "Here's a legal looking something addressed to Scott Ian Hoover Drayco." Sarg waved it in the air. "Ian I knew. But Hoover?"

Drayco snatched the letter from him. "Blame Brock. If it were up to me, I'd change it. I may still."

"He would name you that, wouldn't he? How's your dear ole former G-man Dad doing these days? Still consulting?"

"We did a case together not long ago."

"Bet that was as much fun as an impacted wisdom tooth. Or my shitty crown. You tell him you were back with the Bureau, at least temporarily?"

"Not unless absolutely necessary."

Sarg tugged on his earlobe, making Drayco ask, "Okay, out with it. What's on your mind?"

"Guess I was just wondering if your father blamed me for you leaving the FBI."

"I never told him why I left."

Sarg stopped in mid-tug. "You didn't? Nothing about me and—"

"I didn't think he needed to know."

The flashing red light on the answering machine Drayco kept for business purposes got his attention. When he pressed PLAY, a high-pitched male voice came out of the speaker, "Mr. Drayco, this is Rick

Paddington with Topol Global Security. We were wondering if you'd had time to consider our offer—" Drayco pushed the stop button.

"Topol Global Security? What offer?"

"For a full-time job. I was recommended."

Sarg put the bills down on a table by the door. "I thought you liked the consulting thing?" Then Sarg glanced at the stack of bills. "I read about that case over on the Eastern Shore, where a client bequeathed you that Opera House. Why don't you sell it and live off the proceeds?"

So Sarg had kept tabs on him? Drayco shook off the surprise and moved toward the refrigerator, with Sarg trailing along behind. "I enjoy helping people. But the townhome, the office rent—D.C. isn't cheap. Insurance, taxes, it all adds up."

"So again, I say, why not sell that Opera House? It's not like the dead client who gave it to you would raise a stink, pun intended."

"It's tied up in legalities, for one. And ..." How could he forget the faces of the people who'd come up to him, bursting with gratitude he was going to restore the historic building and bring more jobs to the depressed area? One woman cried as she gave him a hug, others volunteered for one committee or another. "And it may be a while before it can be sold."

He reached into the fridge and pulled out a Manhattan Special. Drayco chugged down some of the espresso soda, enjoying the bittersweet tang.

Sarg looked over his shoulder and exclaimed, "Ha!" and pulled out a bottle of his favorite beer. "You hate this brand. Don't tell me you've kept these since the last time I was here?" Sarg shot him a suspicious stare.

Drayco took another swig of his soda and grabbed Cailan's music puzzle. After staring at it for a few moments, he strode to a bookshelf to snag one of the volumes and bring it to the chair. He flipped through the pages until he found the section he was looking for, then compared the book and puzzle side by side.

Sarg pushed a newspaper aside on the sofa, sank down on the leather cushions and put his feet up on the coffee table. "I know that look. You've got something."

Drayco studied the paper. "Schumann."

"One of those German composers, right? Sending puzzles beyond the grave?"

"Schumann read a book on cryptography and allegedly tried his hand at creating a musical cipher-wheel. Three rows of the alphabet, with the letters in one row all natural, the next row all flat, and those in the last row, sharp. Turning the wheel yields forty-two settings—the number of all possible arrangements of accidentals in the seven white-note scales."

"So you'd need a copy of the wheel to decode it."

"Or this book." Drayco compared the wheel in the book to the music notes in the melody on the letter-puzzle. He grabbed a pen and envelope from the coffee table and wrote something down, then handed it over to Sarg. "If our letter-sender used Schumann's scheme, this is what it says."

Sarg read the two words aloud. "CAILAN AVENGE," and put the paper down. "Someone taking revenge on Cailan or Cailan needs to avenge something else?"

Drayco got up to get another soda, and Sarg yelled out to him, "Bring me a refill will you? I'm not driving." Sarg picked up the newspaper and scanned the headlines. "Huh. There's been another one."

Drayco handed him the beer. "Another what?"

"Warehouse arson. Wouldn't make big news, except—"

"Except these warehouses are owned by a U.S. senator. It was on the TV news, too."

Sarg tipped the bottle. "This is the third fire, same MO, gasoline accelerant. An ATF agent I know says Senator Bankton calls them every day, putting on the big squeeze. Big surprise."

"Thankfully, you're not working that case." Drayco stared up at the ceiling. "Getting back to ours, are we sure all the music faculty at Parkhurst were cleared in Cailan's death?"

"All faculty, spousal units and kidlings were at a retreat in August when Cailan was murdered. No students around, either. Last big hurrah before fall classes."

"Except Gary, the composer."

"And Shannon, the singer."

A knock on the door startled both of them. The mail had already come and he rarely got visitors, unless it was Mrs. Wiseman, his neighbor. Drayco hopped up to respond. He opened the door and stood there in shock before a slow smile spread across his face. "Tyler. What a surprise. Do come in." Two extraordinary visitors in two days, but this one was an unexpected pleasure.

"Thanks. I'm in town for a conference and had a little free time before it starts." Her voice still had the same unusual coppery shimmer, like tinkling wind chimes. She stepped into the living area, and it was Sarg's turn to jump up. The woman paused when she saw him. "Is this a bad time?"

Drayco pointed at Sarg. "This is FBI Agent Mark Sargosian."

"Your former colleague?" She held out her hand to Sarg, who shook it. "Drayco's told me a lot about you."

"Really?" Sarg looked askance at Drayco, and then his gaze dropped to the ring on Nelia's left hand.

"And this is Deputy Nelia Tyler, with the Prince of Wales County Sheriff's Department."

"Right. That Opera House case in Cape Unity. Is your husband in law enforcement, too, Deputy Tyler?"

Nelia shook her head. "An attorney. Up in Salisbury, Maryland."

"You don't sound Virginian. Transplant?"

"The Eastern Shore accent is a little different."

"It's enchanting. To go with a very lovely lady." Sarg smiled. "You'll have to tell me all the dirt you have on this guy. I need blackmail material."

Nelia laughed. "It's a deal."

Sarg looked from Nelia to Drayco. "I can take a cab to Union …"

Drayco said, "Nonsense. I'll drive you to the station. Tyler, ever been to Union Station?" When she shook her head, he added, "Host to several presidents, kings and World War I troops."

"I'd love to go, if you don't mind me deadheading."

Drayco certainly didn't and was glad to see Sarg and Nelia getting along, making small talk along the way. The snatches of conversation were about the sheriffs' conference and one of the scheduled speakers Sarg knew from the Bureau.

After a promise to meet tomorrow and tackle Andrew Gilbow, Drayco dropped Sarg off at the station and asked Nelia, "Had supper yet?"

"No, but I'm not sure I feel like a fancy restaurant."

"Then I've got just the place for you." Drayco pushed the music puzzle to the back of his mind for now, and refused to dwell on Sarg's disapproving look as he'd headed into the station. He'd gotten that from Sheriff Sailor, too. And he was getting more than a little irritated by it.

§ § §

Drayco stopped by Thai Tanic and ordered carryout, then drove Nelia to the Jefferson Memorial. It was past peak tourist season on a late afternoon, so they were by themselves.

He guided Nelia to the top of the stairs, with the Jefferson statue behind them bathed in a haloed spotlight as dusk approached. The Tidal Basin lay in front where the first hints of fiery red and orange dappled the leaves on cherry trees across the water. Could be a painting hanging in the National Gallery of Art.

Enough daylight remained for him to make out Nelia's warm, intelligent brown eyes and the sprinkling of tiny freckles across her nose like facets on her diamond-shaped face. A light wind blew strands of her blond hair into her eyes, and she pushed them away so she could see to eat her Pad Thai.

"Not used to being sans hat?" He'd only seen her without it on a few occasions.

"Honestly, I hate hats. Especially brown ones." She slurped up a few noodles.

"It looks nice. Your hair, I mean."

"And here I figured you were going to say brown deputy hats are a real turn-on."

He laughed, and dug around in his curry, trawling for the last shrimp. They ate in companionable silence for a few minutes and watched the black squirrels scampering around. Drayco pointed at them. "Believe it or not, those are descendants of eighteen Canadian squirrels released at the National Zoo while Theodore Roosevelt was president. They've taken over the capital area."

"They look like they're wearing tiny uniforms. I'll try to remember to take a picture while I'm here for my conference." She finished her meal and set the container down. "The National Sheriffs Association Conference. They're combining the summer and winter events into one this year. It's a big deal."

"Where's Sheriff Sailor?"

"Important court case where he has to testify. I'm his designated replacement. Frankly, I think he'd break his own leg to get out of the conference. Except the golf tournament part." She pantomimed holding a golf club and making a putt. "Tim suggested I play hooky if the weather was nice."

"How's Tim doing?"

She stared at a pair of squirrels chasing each other. "He's stable. MS is unpredictable, so he has good days and bad days."

When Drayco worked with Nelia before, he'd been able to tell when it was one of the "bad" days. They must be frequent on those weekends the commuter-marriage-couple got to see each other, because Nelia seemed most withdrawn on Mondays.

He filled her in on the details of Cailan's murder, prompting her to say, "You are a magnet for bizarre cases, aren't you? I got the impression you never wanted anything more to do with the FBI. Does this mean you're thinking of going back?"

"I'm not sure they'd take me, even if I wanted to." With Onweller near retirement, it might be possible. As he'd laid it out for Sarg, going solo cost money. Having autonomy and not having to deal with bureaucracy was worth it, at first.

Maybe the happiest people weren't the ones who wanted to make a difference. Cailan Jaffray wanted to make a difference through her music, a difference with her life. Making plans for what she wanted to do on her forty-seventh birthday, the day she would have lived longer than her mother.

The wind picked up and blew ripples across the Tidal Basin. Nelia said, "It's lovely. Much better without all the tourists around."

"The day tourists, you mean. The night tours are just getting started. You can see all the monuments lighted up at night from boat, trolley, car, Segway, bike, or the old-fashioned way, on foot."

"Guess the locals are jaded, but I get thrills every time I come to the Mall."

"I used to. This is the Disneyland part of D.C. Then you have the underbelly, the part that most tourists never see. Drugs, gangs, shootings. And the part I deal with more often than not, the middle belly."

She smiled. "Middle belly?"

"Where most people live. Where the most crime and illegal activity occurs but is rarely reported. There's a hell of a lot of stress, jealousy and anger in this town. The veneer of civility is there. Parties and teas, charities and back-slapping. I'll wager there's as much drug use, sex crimes, and fraud. And a whole lot of back-stabbing."

Nelia said, "I read a study recently. Middle-belly fat is the most dangerous kind, the type that causes heart disease. And kills more people."

"There, you see?"

"So this case of yours is a middle-belly murder?"

He grinned at her. "A good title for a bad novel. Or a self-help book on how to lose weight."

Nelia grabbed their empty cartons and got up to throw them in a garbage can. Then she held out her hand to help him up from the steps. "Let's go play tourist. I could use a nice long walk by those lighted monuments."

He took her hand and bounded up. Okay, so he might be a tad jaded about the monuments. His thoughts wouldn't be on them, anyway, with part of his attention on the music code and the other on the woman next to him. He hadn't realized until she showed up on his doorstep how much he'd missed her.

11

The Chesapeake Bay Bridge was the technological equivalent of a sea serpent. The weekend car hordes streaming across were like fish getting eaten one by one until they backed up inside the sated bridge's gut. He'd wanted to fly himself over, but the FBO where he rented a plane was booked solid. So here he was, driving into the beast, getting swallowed.

When he was finally disgorged on the other side, he drove down U.S. 13 into Cape Unity. There was something about the Eastern Shore that helped him de-stress. The tang of salt air, the heron sightings, the much slower pace of life. Besides, Sarg practically commanded him to take the weekend off.

He wasn't entirely sure why he'd come. Guilt? Loneliness? Anger? The triad of useless emotions. If Drayco were honest with himself, he'd admit working with Sarg was harder than he'd thought it would be. That triad of emotions was happily munching away at the walls of his mental lockbox where he kept his darkest memories, and those memories were trying to break out. He didn't like it one bit.

He pulled up in front of Cypress Manor and was a little surprised nothing had changed since Darcie's divorce from Town Councilman Randolph Squier. Darcie had defended the name of the place when Drayco poked fun at it. Yet even she had to admit it didn't make any sense after the last cypress tree died off years ago.

Darcie, to her credit, didn't let him wallow in angsty mud. She'd barely let him put his overnight bag inside the door before she dragged him upstairs to the bedroom for a refresher course on why she was such a good tonic for his mood.

Once they'd dressed and made their way to the kitchen table where she'd wisely purchased bakery cinnamon rolls this time, she showed him once more how she was full of surprises. "I couldn't stop thinking about that murdered girl, Cailan."

At his raised eyebrows, she added, "Oh, don't look so surprised. We do have the Internet here. I looked it up. The murder, I mean, and her name and all. *The Post* said it was likely someone she knew. Not one of those random things. But I don't think it was a love triangle, after all."

He took a bite of the roll. Not bad. Lots of cinnamon and toasted pecans. And definitely not charbroiled. "All right, so tell me how you arrived at that conclusion."

"The news hinted a boy was involved but didn't mention his name. I'll bet it's because his Daddy is somebody important. Anyway, girls are afraid of snakes, right? Well, all the girls I know. So why would Cailan agree to meet a boy at night in a place full of snakes?"

He grinned at her. "Snakes aren't so bad."

She shuddered. "I think she was dumped there. I mean, if it was a crime of passion, he'd have stabbed her some place they went all the time. After an argument or whatever."

Well, she definitely had the dumping part correct. Score one for Darcie. "Fair enough. What else?"

"The newspaper said nothing was removed from the body. I've read about these things in books. The murderous lover would have taken some token, like a ring or necklace or a photo. Kinda like a scalp in the old days."

"Her shirt and bra were missing." Probably to make it easier to drive in the heated knife, but that was mere speculation on the M.E.'s part.

Darcie frowned. "That's hardly the kind of token a lover would take. No man develops attachments over clothing they give to a woman. Now jewelry, on the other hand …"

"So, they got frightened off by a noise before they could remove it."

"They certainly weren't frightened enough not to dump her there, right?"

"True." He reached out and held her now-ringless left hand. "Have you heard from Randolph lately?"

"My ex bonded out on bail. He's got a good attorney. Probably won't spend much time in jail for the embezzlement. We only speak through our attorneys, so I haven't seen him in months."

"Do you miss him?"

She squeezed his hand. "I should have gotten out long ago. I admit I married him as much for his money as I did love. Does that make me shallow?"

"Darcie, there are dozens of reasons people get married. Or stay married. Love, politics, money, convenience." An image of Nelia and Tim popped into his head. "Surely a part of you loved him?"

She twirled strands of her hair around her finger. "He treated me like a queen. I'd rather be treated like a goddess. Venus, maybe. She's the goddess of love and passion, right?"

When he said yes, she got up and came around behind him and nibbled along his neck. Being in the presence of a love goddess wasn't such a bad way to spend part of a weekend.

§ § §

On Sunday, Drayco stopped by the Lazy Crab B&B to visit with one of his favorite people in the world, Maida Jepson. If there was one person who grounded him squarely in the center of a peaceful universe, it was Maida. The Crab still looked the same, with the inn's garden sporting late-blooming pink phlox, purple asters, and goldenrod.

As usual, she welcomed him with sweet tea so thick it needed a knife. It wasn't as good as one of her famous toddies, but since he was driving to D.C. later, he had to pass on the alcohol.

It didn't take long for her to suss out his mood, and she asked him point blank about his latest case. He couldn't tell if she was more surprised at the music puzzle angle or the fact he was working with his former FBI partner.

She'd never pressed him on why he left the Bureau. Nor did she press him on it now, hovering around him with as much tea as his pancreas could handle. In her own way, Maida was like one of Troy Jaffray's Buddha-like figures, which made it unsurprising when she came out with an astute insight into the music puzzle.

"I don't know much about Schumann's ciphers. But surely the murderer could have come up with something better than that. 'Cailan Avenge'? Sounds like he's playing a game with you law enforcement types."

He'd briefly entertained the same thought, but discounted it. "Our murderous puzzlemeister didn't send the notes to the police or FBI. So if that was his plan, he's not very bright."

"Hmm. I'm not a composer—"

"Or a murderer."

"Or a murderer, but it seems like an awful lot of trouble to go to just to annoy someone. It has to have a deeper meaning. Why else use music when a simple word cipher would do?" She smiled at him. "Whatever it is, you'll figure it out."

Drayco smiled back, then looked around for signs of Maida's husband. "Don't tell me I missed Major again."

"He ran up to Salisbury for some new doorknobs. We had a family with kids who thought it'd be fun to put superglue in the locks. I don't suppose you can stay overnight? I know Major would love to see you."

"Wish I could. But I have to get back this evening."

"You'll return soon, I reckon. That Opera House of yours will bring you back to us, sooner or later. How are the grants coming?"

"Good. It's looking good." It was the truth—the preliminaries to restore the building were shaping up nicely, if slowly, but it wasn't a topic he wanted to dwell on right now. Instead, he cast his eye on a plate of muffins on the counter. Orange and green muffins? For Halloween, perhaps?

Her gaze followed his, and she got up to bring the plate over. "A new creation of Lucy Harston's via Lost-In-Tea Party shop. Sweet potato and jalapeño." She handed him one. "Don't be wrinkling up your nose, young man. They're actually pretty tasty."

He took a small nibble. Not bad. And then the jalapeño kicked in. He grabbed his glass of tea and gulped half of it down.

She sat in the chair across from him. "You don't look very happy these days. Working with your former partner that hard?"

"It's not easy, I'll grant you. But better than working with Gilbow."

"Gilbow?"

"A psych professor, the murdered girl's godfather. He and I have butted heads on a case or two before. You might have seen him on TV, hawking his books and pearls of wisdom like a televangelist. Perhaps a part of him thinks he created the universe in a few days. Or at least he's in the center of it."

Maida shook her head. "He must have had a horrible childhood. How else can you explain his over-compensation by trying to make the world revolve around him?"

After filling him in on the latest Cape Unitarian gossip, Maida made him promise to return soon. He'd already been planning on it, especially when he lined up an architect to draw up restoration plans for the Opera House.

That Grande Dame of a building was where he found himself now, standing in the middle of the stage in front of the Steinway. It wasn't that long ago he was Cailan's age, his piano career bright with promise, getting accepted into the Tchaikovsky competition in Moscow. That was only a few months before the carjacking and his injury.

He'd survived the attack on his life, but Cailan hadn't. If she'd lived, perhaps she would have stood here one day herself, in recital or in a staged production. What was there about Fortune that was so willing to paint bulls-eyes on musicians? So many seemed to die young or simply fade away.

He inhaled the familiar aromas of the century-plus building, with its musty original-fabric seats, layers of dust, and the earthy smell of old oil and grease. He was relieved to note there were no aromatic traces from the two men who'd died on stage. The crime scene crew had been very thorough. When blood seeps down through hardwood floors, it can sometimes mean a lingering stench for years.

Drayco walked around to the piano keyboard and caressed the white and black keys with his fingers. The historic piano was quickly becoming an old but cherished friend. Each and every piano had as much character as most people, one reason pianists had their favorites. This one was the aging diva who could still sing circles around young upstarts, all while wearing a sonic cloak of shimmering rubies and garnet stones.

He started to sit down but stopped. He couldn't. Not right now. The tightness in his chest must be from all that caffeine. He'd grab some decaf and Skipjacks nuts at the Novel Café on the return trip to D.C.

Before turning out the lights, he paused for a moment to listen. Even silence had color since nothing was truly silent. Right now, the jagged rust-colored shards of sound piercing him from the building's creaks and air handler were more searing than soothing. He'd hoped coming to the Eastern Shore would clear his head. But even now, all he could think of was CAILAN AVENGE.

12

Drayco awoke with the vague impression he was drenched in sweat, though he wasn't wearing a stitch of clothing. Was he floating? Floating out the window, floating into a warehouse, hearing colors and shapes bouncing off walls.

A corrugated sulfur spike pierced his senses: a gun firing. Then his shock and horror as he saw the red stain spreading over Officer Decker's chest and a matching stain on Sarg's leg. The room in the corner Sarg had skipped wasn't unoccupied …

A blue-tipped fork of a bird call shot through his bedroom window, and he focused on it, willing himself out of the sleep paralysis. Then he was free.

He swung his legs over the side of the bed and ran his hand through his hair. The alarm clock showed it was only four, but he got up and headed for his piano. Good thing he wasn't supposed to meet Sarg until noon because he was in no shape to drive.

He needed something challenging to take his mind off the dream, something like the devilishly difficult "Ondine" by Ravel. It was just the ticket, with shimmering, modal ripples of sound and finger-knotting chord tremolos.

Six hours later—one-sixth of which was spent soaking his right arm in warm water—Drayco left the house to Sarg up from Union. Autumn skies were usually one of the perks of living in the Mid-Atlantic. Maybe that was why the leaden overcast sky greeting Drayco this morning was disappointing. The look on Sarg's face as Drayco picked him up at the station didn't do much to help.

Sarg hopped in and slammed the door. "This day keeps getting better and better. Train was late, some rail maintenance thing. So it was sardine city. Then the guy at the shop tells me my car's going to cost three thousand to fix, so I asked him if he was putting on gold-plated mufflers. And a round, doughy fella who's never seen the inside of a gym got the last *pain au chocolat* at Union Station."

He pulled out a plain cheese danish and ate it over the bag. "What'd you have? The usual burnt toast? Or one of those godawful peanut butter marshmallow fluff concoctions of yours?"

"Just coffee."

Sarg winced, moved his jaw from side to side and then rubbed his cheek.

"Didn't you ever do anything about that crown of yours?"

Sarg took some more tentative bites before wolfing down the rest of the pastry. "Comes and goes."

They made it to the Parkhurst psych building ten minutes early, which gave Drayco time to study the place. The windows were so shiny and new, they probably received their share of bird strikes. Was that why groups of birds had such violent names? *A wreck of seabirds, a murder of crows.*

Sarg stared up at the gleaming contemporary three-story structure with criss-crossing windows like a Picasso painting. "An entire building for psychology? I can understand music since you gotta save room for that canyon-sized performance hall."

"I checked out the psychology department's website this morning. A goodly part of the building was built by an ego fed on chat-show appearances."

Sarg grinned. "Really don't care for this guy, do you?" He studied Drayco's face. "You look a little pale. Bet you popped a couple of NoDoz. More of those dream paralysis things?"

"Hadn't had one in a long time." Until Sarg showed up needing his help. Drayco held open the door. "Shall we get this over with?"

They found their prey in his office lair, the pristine neatness a stark contrast to Jaffray's clutter. Not a stray paperclip anywhere. Neatly hung, organized frames of various university degrees and certificates lined the wall and shelves. A few occasional oddities, like a painting of mistletoe or the jar containing liquid surrounding what looked like a human brain.

The Great One himself turned around, holding a book in his hands he shut with a loud thump and slid back on a shelf. The overhead light gleamed off his shiny, egg-shaped skull, as he peered at them through his rimless round wire glasses. "You," he looked at Sarg, "Must be Agent Sargosian."

Then he turned to Drayco, "And you I didn't expect. Slumming with the FBI, are we?" Gilbow's green-pebbled voice rattled Drayco and made him wonder if that was part of his distaste for the man.

Drayco walked over to look at one of the degrees on the wall, from Patuxent Academy High School. "You grew up around here?" He'd never bothered to learn Gilbow's background, other than his professional biography and court tactics. And the man's bio never mentioned his younger years.

"My family moved here when I was in middle school so my father could open an offset printing business. When it failed, he became a cop."

"Did you meet Troy Jaffray at Patuxent or here at the college? We understand you were Cailan's godfather."

"She was another of my advisees. Troy wasn't keen on her being a music student. Wanted her to have something more practical to fall back on."

"Like psychology."

"Better than being a starving singer waitressing in a sleazy club. I can't fault him for that."

"Did you talk with your goddaughter much?" Drayco fingered the slick glass of the jar with the brain. From the size and shape, the organ was most definitely human.

"I wasn't as close to her as my wife was. I'm afraid my knowledge of Cailan was more of her career, as her advisor. So if you're asking about boyfriends, enemies, the typical suspect line of questioning, I can't help you."

Drayco spied photos on the walls of Gilbow arm-in-arm with celebrity hosts from national TV programs. And the spines of several books showed they were all authored by Gilbow. Psychology was lucrative for a few people, anyway. "Did you have Shannon Krugh in any of your classes?"

"Krugh. Krugh." He tapped his chin. "Yes, I remember her. A delicate face that didn't match her personality. I found out from Cailan the young woman had bipolar disorder."

"Were you aware she was bullying Cailan, sir?" Sarg asked.

"Wouldn't surprise me one whit. Poor judgment, risk-taking, all hallmarks of bipolar. It's not the same as schizophrenia. I've been called to testify in a lot of insanity-defense cases on that subject. Sociopaths sometimes displace their anger on other victims. Something you should look into."

Gilbow frowned. "Then, you people allegedly do profiling, right? I must say I haven't been impressed with what I've seen in the courtroom from FBI testimony."

Drayco moved closer to Gilbow by the side of the desk, towering over the other man by a good seven inches. "Gary Zabowski. Was he also in one of your classes?"

"I can ask the secretary to go through my roll books. I take it he's a suspect, too. Provided you with a half-dozen lies, did he?"

Sarg was gritting his teeth. "Then you do know him, sir?"

Gilbow turned his left ear toward Sarg. "You'll have to say that again, agent. I'm deaf in my right ear."

Sarg raised his voice. "I said, it sounds like you know Gary Zabowski."

Gilbow winced. "I'm not deaf in both ears, Agent, just the one. It doesn't matter if I know Mr. Zabowski or not because I can already tell a lot about him. It was Nietzsche's belief that the lie is a condition of life. A colleague of mine at UM found most people tell a falsehood once every ten minutes."

"Do you count yourself among that group, sir?"

Gilbow smiled. "I think I like you, Agent Sargosian."

Drayco made a note of that to use against Sarg later. "Professor Gilbow, Cailan was involved in a lab project with one of your doctoral students, Reed Upperman. A project involving synesthesia?"

"It's his dissertation. Promising lad. I'll let you ask him for details. He only meets with me every now and then. Pretty much runs it himself. His office is on the second floor, in the labs."

Sarg nodded. "Yes, sir, we're going there next. By the way, my unit chief, Jerry Onweller, said he'd contacted you."

"Good man, Jerry. I gave him my opinion, naturally, since Cailan was my goddaughter. And since we're dealing with college students, I fear it will boil down to a relationship gone awry. An act of profound wretchedness—the murderer willing to destroy another even if it entails destroying the self."

"Did the police or Onweller tell you the manner of death?"

"You're referring to the use of the knife and unusual burn marks? Young people often go through a period of religious experimentation. I wouldn't be surprised if there were a ritualistic aspect to this case. Human sacrifice is a feature of some occult belief systems. That's more Troy's bailiwick than mine."

"However ..." Gilbow bent over to slide out a book from a lower shelf, and flipped through the pages and held it out so they could see violent icons from the past. War illustrations from cave paintings, a battle between barbarians and Romans carved on the Ludovisi Sarcophagus, the mummy of an Incan child sacrifice.

"It's unfortunate humans can't channel their energies for good. Take my wife, Adele. She finds the academic life boring, so she gets her thrills from skydiving and bungee jumping. Does a lot of fundraising, often combining the two, like a bungee jump to raise money for a new cancer center at the college, a favorite cause of ours. Adele's sister died from colon cancer."

The door opened, and a tall brunette older than a college student breezed in along with a cloud of sandalwood perfume. "Sorry, dear, I don't want to interrupt."

"Your timing is excellent. We were just discussing the cancer center."

"Really? I don't recall seeing these gentlemen at the planning meetings, but new blood is always welcome."

"This is Agent Mark Sargosian with the FBI, and this is consultant Scott Drayco. They're here about Cailan."

"Oh, I see." Adele Gilbow pulled out a chair and sat down. "Murder seems so much worse when it hits young people. And Cailan …" She paused and swallowed. "Cailan was such a lovely, vibrant girl. We miss her."

Drayco said, "Were you and Cailan close, Mrs. Gilbow?"

"Please, call me Adele. Mrs. Gilbow makes me sound like a dowager." She smiled briefly. "I guess I was a surrogate mother figure. No one could replace her own Mom."

"So you don't know anyone who'd want revenge on her? An anonymous letter she was sent prior to her death, a music code, spelled out 'Cailan Avenge.'"

Her eyes widened. "She didn't mention it at all. Avenge? Whatever can that mean? Cailan was well liked with plenty of friends." She thought about it for a moment. "I suppose it may have been that rival of hers, Shannon. Music is a cut-throat business, as bad as beauty pageants."

Judging by Adele's sprayed hair, artful makeup, and the way she walked as she came in, she had first-hand knowledge of pageants. And from the adoring look Gilbow was giving her, it worked for him.

"Are you ready to go to lunch, dear?" Gilbow grabbed his jacket from the back of his chair and put it on. His dismissal of the other two men was clear.

"It was lovely meeting you both," Adele said, with a parting wave.

Before they disappeared from view, Gilbow called out over his shoulder. "The Bureau is paying me for my services. Do call if you need help. I charge by the hour."

It was a lot more than Drayco would be compensated, a point Gilbow probably knew. If grad student Reed Upperman were like his mentor, Drayco would be earning every penny.

"I'm still wondering why Onweller neglected to tell us Cailan was Gilbow's goddaughter." Sarg tugged on his earlobe.

"A test, perhaps."

"Of who, you or me?"

Drayco stopped in front of a small wall fountain with dancing lights. It shimmered like the Ravel piece he'd played this morning. "You don't have to worry, as far as Onweller is concerned. I made sure of that when I left the Bureau, didn't I?"

Sarg sucked in a deep breath through his teeth. "You took the fall for me, yes. As if I'm ever going to forget that. Or learn how to live with it."

Drayco sighed and ran his hand under the water, enjoying the coldness on his skin. Unlike so much else at Parkhurst, this felt real, almost alive. "Let's go find out about this mystery project Cailan was involved with. It's quite possibly the last thing she did before her death."

13

Sarg and Drayco took the stairs—they'd shared a loathing for technology-trap elevators ever since being stuck in one for hours—and headed up toward Reed Upperman's domain. A security camera near the corridor ceiling pointed toward a door that said "Rodent Room."

Mini-skyscraper racks filled with their doomed dwellers lined the walls, tended by two students in white lab coats. The cages were claustrophobically small. Maybe Drayco could sneak back in later and liberate a few white Wistar rats? Probably wouldn't go over well. Despite the ventilation system, whiffs of musky ammonia from rat urine followed Drayco past the room.

He poked Sarg in the arm. "So what did you think of Gilbow?"

"People pay him big bucks? I'm in the wrong business." Sarg stopped as they came to a lab with 313 above it, and looked through the glass window. "Think that's our guy?" Sarg opened the door, and they walked in.

The man who sat hunched over a computer monitor looked to be more Drayco's age than a typical grad student, with short, curly hair harboring a few strands of gray. His days-old stubble and wrinkled shirt, combined with a wastebasket full of food wrappers, made it look like he lived there.

He had on loose-fitting leather pants that didn't match the rest of the image until Drayco spied a bicycle partially hidden in a corner of the room. On the desk next to the computer lay a bowl of slippery white things that looked like eyeballs alongside some shriveled brown bundles. Lychee nuts and dates. An odd combination.

Reed Upperman jumped out of his chair when Sarg called his name. "I didn't expect anybody today. Hoped I could get caught up."

He adjusted the headlight-thick glasses on his nose. "Look, if you're here to sell lab equipment, talk to the chairman, Dr. Gilbow. He's the one who makes those decisions. But if you're offering a new infrared eye-tracker, I'll put in a good word for you."

Sarg made the introductions while Drayco walked over to examine a chart on the board. It had rows and columns with shapes, colors, numbers, words and letters of the alphabet. Of the ten rows, one was half blank. Drayco pointed to the chart. "Is this what you're working on?"

"Part of my dissertation. It's on synesthesia." He pronounced it sin-uhs-zee-zhuh, instead of thee-zhuh.

"Only ten subjects?"

"We're a small college, Dr. Drayco. Since most synesthetes are female, I had a devil of a time finding subjects, let alone a couple of males. More subjects makes it easier to get time on the new fMRI scanner. Even post-docs come to blows over scheduling."

"Any particular type of synesthesia? Grapheme-color? Odor-color?"

"Any type I can get. With sixty known forms and thirty different combinations of senses, I won't be able to cover them all. How did you know? Are you a synesthete?"

Drayco drew his finger under one of the header rows on the chart. Reed stood and took a few limping steps to get a closer look. "Sound-color synesthesia. You a musician by any chance?"

"Of a sort."

"We find sound-color synesthetes are drawn to music. Perhaps why several of my subjects are musicians. Like Cailan Jaffray."

Drayco studied the chart. The subjects were identified by a number and not by name. "Which one is Cailan's?"

"Third one down."

Drayco moved closer to the chart. The data collecting started during the spring term, and Cailan's was the partially blank row. The last set of data was taken the night she was killed. It was like a half-formed ghost reaching out to him, and he fought the urge to touch the chart. "She had grapheme-number synesthesia."

Sarg held out both hands. "Can you summarize all this in a sentence or two? Without too much psychobabble?"

Reed peered over his glasses at Sarg. "Psychobabble is a derogatory term, Agent Sargosian. The equivalent of me calling you an agent of the Fumbling Bunch of Idiots. To answer your question, synesthesia is the crossing of two or more senses. People experience numbers, letters or sounds with colors, shapes or smells. In your partner's case, he hears sounds and sees colors and shapes. Cailan had one of the more common types, seeing numbers and letters in color."

Drayco remembered when he'd first discovered not everyone saw paintings in their minds when they heard sounds. He was sixteen, on tour in London, and it came as a complete shock to him. "Reed, how did you recruit students like Cailan to be in your project?"

"I posted a note on the bulletin boards around campus, on the psych website and had a notice in the school paper."

"How was it worded?"

"As vaguely as possible. And not that they'd be paid. Didn't want to bring in the riffraff who'd pretend, for the money. More than one research project's been scrapped because of that. Cailan was my best subject." He sighed. "Now I'll have to try to recruit someone else."

Reed looked up at Drayco, with a hopeful expression. "I don't suppose—"

"Not really," Drayco smiled. "Were the labs always held on Tuesday and Thursday night from eight to nine?"

"Not counting snow, ice, and the occasional power outage. After Cailan's murder, I realized it happened not long after she'd left one of our sessions."

"Do you remember her being anxious or afraid? Or meeting someone?"

"I've tried to recall that night many times. Cailan seemed happy, as I think she was up for some sort of award. She always left by herself, and I'm pretty sure she was going straight home."

"That was two months ago. Are you sure your memory of that night is correct?"

"That same night I got a call from my own little girl after she sprained her ankle. She lives in Pennsylvania. I don't get to see her much."

Reed took off his glasses to rub them with a cloth from his pocket. "I do recall Cailan once mentioning this strange guy who followed her around. Said he was on the maintenance staff."

Sarg said, "Medium height, on the skinny side, long beard?"

"Sounds like the man she described. She was more grossed out than frightened."

"Do you have a list of the other students in the project?"

Reed pursed his lips and studied the computer screen. "I have to okay it with Dr. Gilbow and the college. Our subjects are covered under the HIPAA agreement through Health and Human Services."

"We'll take care of that."

"Is there anything else?" Reed turned away from them as he scrolled through several screens and scribbled something on a pad beside him.

Dismissed again.

Outside the building, Sarg prodded Drayco about his synesthesia. "Yeah, yeah, you don't like to discuss it. Must be neat, though, huh?"

"It is what it is. It doesn't make me into some Super Detective."

"So my voice has colors too?"

"Gold and green, shaped like a sine wave. The same colors as Reed's jade dragon stone necklace."

A female student walked by in jeans so tight they looked painted on, topped by a knitted sweater that allowed her bra to show through. Sarg grunted. "Elvis Loomis is right. All the girls dress like what we antiques used to call sluts."

"You do know that's—"

"Sexist. Natch."

"You might appreciate it more, if you didn't have a daughter that age."

Sarg growled. "Better not catch Tara dressing like that."

Drayco glanced back at the psych building. "Tara wasn't in Reed's project, was she?"

"Not that she told me. You bet I'm going to double-check." Sarg sat down on a bench, surveying the campus scenery. "I'm inclined to agree with the MPD detectives. Avenge Cailan due to synesthesia? I'm putting my money on jealousy."

The college carillon chimed in the distance, the chalky magenta setting Drayco's teeth on edge. But at least it added some interest to the buttoned-up campus without a stray leaf in sight. Even a mud puddle or two would make it look more like a real college setting than an artist's conception.

Sarg frowned at another girl walking past in knee-high black boots and a flaming purple miniskirt. "Onweller's golfing buddy, the college president, called him this morning to ask how it was going. Like we'd swoop in and have it all figured out in two days."

Drayco joined him on the bench. "Could happen."

"If you were that Super Detective."

Sarg's gaze followed a young man walking by with his low-hanging pants exposing half his underwear. "At least we don't have a U.S. senator breathing down our necks like my ATF buddy. Nasty arson case, that."

"Senator Bankton, right? Why does that name sound so familiar? Other than politically." Drayco wracked his brain. "There was a TV evangelist named Bankton. Any relation?"

"Same guy. Made millions charming sweet little old ladies out of their bank accounts. Now he's charming lobbyists out of theirs. Hell, I had an aunt who was a big fan. Loved the theater of it all. Bankton's wife is a former pianist."

Drayco scrolled through a mental list of all the pianists he could think of, coming up blank on a Bankton. "What's her maiden or stage name?"

"Melanie Marsee."

"Still not ringing a bell."

"She played for Bankton's services before they got married. She was real good, better than the crappy music on those other shows. She sure hit the jackpot. Bankton's worth millions."

To gold be the glory, amen. "Speaking of money, I double-checked Troy Jaffray's finances. He and his deceased brother were both shrewd investors. They got in with one of those dot-coms early, then cashed out at its peak."

"Well now. Maybe that Liam Futino guy Gary saw arguing with Cailan the day of her death was smitten with Cailan for her money. Not her music."

Drayco watched a little enviously as a Campus Security officer glided past on a Segway. "I suspected Futino might be a musician, so I called around. He plays at a club called The Basement in Georgetown, off Wisconsin above the C&O. Starts around five for happy hour."

Sarg looked at his watch. "Guess I'll call Elaine and tell her I'll be late."

"Can you check with MPD to see if they viewed feeds from that security camera in the psych hall? It's aimed at the Rodent Room—if the scan is wide enough, it should have captured Cailan coming and going the night of her murder."

"Something else that wasn't in the official report."

"Might not matter, if the college doesn't keep archived video feeds."

The Metropolitan Police Department was one of the ten largest in the country, and not without its share of controversies through the years. Abuse of overtime, inadequate training, ethics probes. And it had lost a vast majority of arbitration cases.

Drayco knew some of the homicide detectives. They were honest, thorough, and frequently overworked. Most didn't make enough salary to afford to live inside the District where they served. But the lapses on this particular homicide case were a little disturbing.

He got up and stretched his arms behind his head and then stretched out his legs. Being tall was a disadvantage, at times. Nothing fit right, including benches. "My caffeine quota is low. Why don't we get a quad espresso at Café Renée?"

"Where Liam Futino and Cailan argued? Good idea."

Two young men wearing backpacks sailed past them on skateboards. Drayco needed to try that some day. "Aren't you going to tell me what you undoubtedly dug up on Futino after we talked to Gary yesterday?"

Sarg grinned. "It's fun keeping you in suspense. Like all of our other players, nothing in ViCAP, nothing in local crime databases. On the surface, he appears clean."

"So did Ted Bundy." Drayco yawned. Maybe he'd make it a quintuple espresso.

"You think a place named Café Renée will have good *pain au chocolate*? Ever since I missed out yesterday, it's all I can think about. What did you call it once? An ee-day fix-ay."

Drayco tried to relax and enjoy a moment of companionship with Sarg, like the old days. It was hard, with the dream that started off his morning dogging him all day. After three years, the details of that day at the abandoned warehouse were as vivid and clear as one of the video recordings they hoped to get from the psych building. Sarg wounded, two men dead. And one career ended, thanks to Drayco's fabricated report. Gilbow was right. People do lie every day.

14

The waitress sported the nametag "IQ," which she told them stood for Irene Quillen. IQ blew out a huge bubble of gum, as she studied the picture of Cailan that Sarg was holding. The bubble collapsed into a concave membrane of purple goo, which matched the color of her hair. Or at least half. The other half was a natural-looking red.

"That's her. She came here a lot with this guy during my shifts. He was kinda cute, if you like older men and geeks." She was answering Drayco, but kept looking at Sarg and smiling. "I like older men."

"Describe the guy." Sarg slipped the photo into his wallet.

"Like I said, kinda cute." She scanned Drayco's body. "Not near as tall as you."

Sarg tried again. "Can you give us a few more details about Cute Guy?"

"Curly hair. Soulful face. Had a little mole on his cheek." She blew another bubble. "Don't think I've seen him on campus."

They weren't here to order anything except a drink, and Drayco handed back the menu she'd given him. "Are you a student at Parkhurst?"

"Sure am. Bowling Industry Management."

Drayco tried to disguise his glance at Sarg, who mouthed the words silently, "Bowling Industry Management?"

"Do you remember the last time you saw them here, together?"

"Um, yeah. They were usually quiet, but that day, they argued. And he looked so sad, like someone kicked his puppy."

"You didn't happen to overhear what they were arguing over, did you?"

"It's as loud as a rock concert in here after five. Can't even hear myself think."

It was a minor victory to verify Gary's account of Liam Futino and Cailan. But what did it tell them? Only that Cailan had a blow-up the day she was murdered. There were millions of different reasons for arguments. Few led to murder. Still, why keep this man a secret, the "soulful" and much older Liam?

At the moment, IQ was staring soulfully at Sarg, and Drayco couldn't help asking, "How did you get into Bowling Industry Management?"

IQ stopped chewing her gum. "My Dad's idea. I'd changed my major four times. He told me I had to pick something and stick with it or he'd cut off my allowance."

"Are there a lot of job opportunities in that field?"

"Beats me. I opened the catalog, closed my eyes and dropped my finger on the page. And there it was." She chewed slowly. "I always thought astronomy would be kind of neat, ya know? My father said there was no money in it."

Sarg raised his arm to wave at someone coming through the door. Tara came bounding over and kissed her father on the cheek before sliding in next to him. IQ frowned, took Tara's drink order, and flounced toward the kitchen.

"Glad you took my call, sweetie."

"Oh, Dad, like I'd block your calls." She smiled at Drayco. "I promise not to spill anything on you this time."

"Deal."

Sarg reached for the salt shaker, which he passed over to Drayco in anticipation of the arrival of coffee.

Tara looked around the room. "Never been here before. I love the ceiling, it's so retro chic. Faux pressed-tin tiles from the nineteenth century. Did you know they were only used in North America? Well, mostly."

Sarg said to Drayco, "Nice to know those tuition dollars are paying off. My daughter, the next Martha Stewart."

Tara punched him in the arm. "It's from my art history class. We did a unit on architecture."

"Okay, then you're the next—what's that guy's name? The one who designed Disney Hall?"

"Frank Gehry, Dad. He did the Guggenheim Museum in Bilbao, among others. A real star-chitect."

Drayco said, "Are you majoring in art? Your father's been keeping your major a secret. Please tell me it's not Bowling Industry Management."

"Any business degree is a good career move. Parkhurst doesn't have you declare a major, except for music, until you're a junior. So I had to pick one this fall. I considered physics but went with biology. Should help me get into grad school."

"Already picking out grad schools?"

"Not the place, just the degree. I can't decide between pharmaceutical research and criminal forensics. My heart says forensics, but the other pays way better."

There was a certain irony in that—one path would create drugs, the other would nail people for abusing them. He wouldn't try to influence her decision, but forensics could sure use more Taras.

Drayco waited while IQ dropped off two coffees and an Italian Tarocco soda, then apologized to Tara for interrupting her schedule. In reply, she took a loud slurp of soda. "Buy me lots of these, and I'll make time."

"Gary told us Cailan was in a relationship with a man named Liam Futino. And they argued the day she died."

The blood-orange soda was turning Tara's lips red. "Was this recently? 'Cause after Gary dumped her, she said she didn't want another boyfriend. Never said a word about dating anyone."

"What about cults? Voodoo, witchcraft?"

"She would have laughed herself silly instead. Now, Shannon, on the other hand. She dabbled in everything."

It was the exact opposite of what Gary had said. Drayco had no problem taking Tara's word over his.

Tara had matured so much, and he compared her to the man sitting next to her. Same oval face, high forehead, hazel eyes, and a hawk nose. Researchers who claim they can tell personalities from nose shapes say owners of hawk noses prefer to carve their own path. And don't care what other people think.

"Tara, Troy Jaffray hinted he and Cailan were having problems. Did she discuss it?"

"They'd had a falling out. Cailan wanted to be a singer, her uncle didn't approve. Mr. Jaffray's dead wife was a musician. Don't think he wanted to be reminded of that."

She looked stricken. "I just realized he's lost his wife, brother, sister-in-law and now his niece. Oh, that poor man."

Her face grew pensive as she took sips from her Italian soda. "He wanted Cailan to have a double major. In case the music thing didn't work out. He got steamed. Threatened to cut off money for her degree when she wanted to concentrate on her music career."

She bumped her glass, spilling some soda.

Drayco pushed a napkin over. "Was she afraid of him?"

"Maybe some. Guess he was a little overprotective. He really cared about her." She flashed a quick glance at her father.

Drayco smiled at her. "Fathers, and father-figures, worry about their daughters. Good ones do, that is."

"But I'm careful."

Sarg shifted in his seat. "You'd better be careful. A friend of yours got herself murdered. Let that be your wake-up call."

"Threat assessment, Dad. You and Mr. Drayco taught me that."

Drayco winced at the "Mister" part. "Then you remember that in an emergency, you should take deep breaths, don't panic and stay focused."

Tara huffed and wagged her head from side to side. "Now I've got stereo fathering."

"Listen to what he said, Tara. Good advice."

"Yes, Dads."

She slurped up the last of her soda and slid out of the booth. And when I get a hangnail, I'll give you both a call to let you know how I'm doing."

Sarg watched her as she left. "I've faced down enemy soldiers and all flavors of criminals and not thought anything of it. But a twenty-year-old daughter ... that terrifies me."

As Tara strode confidently out the door, she reminded Drayco of the self-assured Cailan in her photos. Evil so often preyed on the weak, but not so much in this case. And that was what terrified *him*.

15

After a call to The Basement Club in Georgetown to see if Liam Futino was there, Drayco learned he'd called in sick. "Change of plans, then," Sarg noted. "You got his home address, too?"

In reply, Drayco pointed the car in that direction. He hadn't gotten far when he pulled over to a curb and rolled down the window.

Sarg said, "What are you—" Then he saw the woman on the sidewalk, wearing a brown uniform.

Drayco called through the open window. "Tyler, aren't you supposed to be at a conference?"

"I am. There was a three-hour gap with nothing to do. So I hopped on Metro to Foggy Bottom and picked up the shuttle bus for a walking tour of Georgetown." She held up a bag. "And a souvenir, naturally."

"Are you headed back?"

"There's a workshop on cybercrime I'm signed up for. Starts in an hour."

"Hop in. We're headed to Petworth. The Conference Center's on the way."

She looked at Sarg and hesitated. "Maybe that's not such a good idea. I mean, if you're on the clock …"

Drayco waved her inside. "Nonsense. And it's an easy route via K Street."

She relented and slid into the back seat. "Nice to be with law enforcement types who aren't in brown suits. Well, mostly brown. A few black and blues. Lots of hats." She must have opted not to wear hers today, her blond hair twisted into a French braid.

Sarg turned around from the front seat. "How long have you been a deputy?"

"Six years. First in Gloucester County, then Prince of Wales."

"How'dja get into deputying?"

In the rear view mirror, Drayco saw she was clenching her jaw, probably not aware of it. "I was in law school for a semester. I met my husband there, we got married. I think the average law school tuition is twenty to thirty thousand dollars. Per year. Per person. Police Academy was a lot cheaper. One of us had to work to pay the bills."

"Drayco here tells me you're a damned fine deputy. Helped him out on a couple of cases over in your neck of the woods."

She laughed at that. "We do have woods, I agree with you there. And Drayco is also very good at what he does. Sheriff Sailor is not easily impressed."

"Drayco also told me of your husband's illness. I was sorry to hear it. I thought I read about a promising new treatment for MS?"

Tyler looked out the window, as if sightseeing. "He has the worst kind. Primary progressive. Most treatments are aimed at the intermittent, relapsing form. He had to walk on crutches first. Now it's a wheelchair." She added quickly, "But some patients live for a long time, we're told."

They pulled onto Mount Vernon Place and in front of the Washington Convention Center, and Nelia hopped out. It wasn't until they'd pulled away that Sarg pointed out Nelia left her shopping bag behind. "Looks like you have an excuse to see her again while she's in town."

"I'll see she gets the bag, if I have to mail it to her."

Sarg's face was skeptical. "What is it with you and married women?"

"Sarg, you know very well I don't—"

"Yeah, a regular Boy Scout." As they headed up New Hampshire Avenue, he added, "A lovely woman. And an unhappy one, if I can still read women right."

"What is happiness, but a lone mourning dove singing after the rain."

"More of that philosopher guy you quote all the time? Bertrand Russell, right?"

"Pure Drayco, by way of Confucius or Buddha. You'll have to ask Troy Jaffray."

Sarg pulled out the case folder. "So, Cailan kept her relationship with Futino enough of a secret nobody knew except Gary. Who found out by accident. Wonder why Gary would tell us and not the police?"

"If he feels threatened, more of a suspect, he may be trying to focus our attention elsewhere."

"Even with attorney-daddy ready to pounce?"

Drayco hadn't imagined that brief, wistful look on Gary's face. "Perhaps on some level he still cared for Cailan and was jealous of Liam."

Their route took them past Rock Creek Cemetery. Drayco was drawn to cemeteries and had visited this one before. It was the *crème de la crème* of the dearly departed, the final resting place to justices, congressmen, actors, Civil War veterans and author Upton Sinclair.

Historically interesting, but he preferred small, isolated cemeteries, where the un-famous spent their eternity in the same anonymity in which they lived. Each unadorned tombstone held a story, a lesson, a reminder—don't take anything for granted.

Futino's house was one of the sand-and-brick rowhouses built in the 1920s and '30s, with a front porch above street level. Two small children with blond hair rolled by on silver scooters, trailed by a purebred Pomeranian. Signs of the changing D.C. demographics. Petworth was eighty percent African-American in the '60s.

Looming across the street, a larger building took up three lots including extra parking. Drayco immediately dubbed it the "Psycho House," looking like it had jumped out of the classic Hitchcock film. A thirtyish woman in a pumpkin-colored dress and matching hat got out of her car in front of Psycho House. She stared at them for a few moments, then walked over. "You here to see Liam?"

Drayco smiled at her. "Are you a neighbor of his?"

"No, I work for Monument Catering. As our slogan says, 'Big or Small, We Do it All.'" She pointed across the street. "That house is a rental. For parties, weddings, whatever. I've got a retirement dinner there tonight."

"Are you a friend of Mr. Futino?"

"He's often sitting out on his porch when I'm here for an event. We've chatted." She smiled as she said the words and moistened her lips. "I was hoping he'd be here today, but I don't see his car."

Drayco took a stab in the dark. "Did you happen to have a catering event on the night of August thirteenth?"

She thought for a moment. "I have parties here once a week, sometimes more." Her face brightened. "The thirteenth. Yes, I remember thinking how unlucky it was to have a baby's christening party on Friday the thirteenth."

"Did you talk to Liam that evening?"

She gasped. "Oh my God, he's not in any trouble, is he?"

Sarg always kept his ID in his pocket. His hand was there, too, as if ready to flash his badge any minute, but he didn't haul it out. "He's not been charged with anything, ma'am. Routine info gathering."

"He wasn't home on the thirteenth. I remember because … not to be superstitious, mind you. I was hoping nothing bad had happened to him. On account of the day."

"What time was this, ma'am?"

"Around supper. Maybe he had a hot date." Her face made it clear she wasn't thrilled with the idea. She brightened when she saw a car headed in their direction. "There he is now. We're all in luck."

Liam got out of his car like a man decades older than his years, stiff, shuffling. He didn't pay any attention to them until their female companion called out to him. That made him look up, and he smiled. "Hello there, Janet. Wouldn't get too close if I were you. Cold, flu, some microscopic intruder is munching away on my innards."

She tutted sympathetically. "If I'd known that, I would have brought you chicken soup."

He replied, without much enthusiasm, "Wouldn't want you to go to any trouble."

"Oh, it's no trouble at all. Let me set up for tonight and I'll be back to take care of you." She waved at Drayco and Sarg and entered the house across the street.

Liam looked at the two men with foggy eyes. "Do I know you?"

Sarg held out his badge. "Can we talk with you for a few minutes, sir?"

Liam scrunched his face into an expression of pure misery. He didn't shoo them away, motioning for them to follow him inside, where the air smelled unusually sterile, with hints of ozone. Drayco spied a large air filter in one corner.

The living room's buttermilk-colored walls and parquet floors were accented with framed prints of famous jazz musicians. The only color came from mini-explosions of red in one lone throw pillow, a red and beige checkerboard area rug, and a potted plant with a flower called bleeding heart, if Drayco remembered it correctly. A violin lay on a table in a corner.

Sarg sat on the edge of the sofa and pulled out his notepad and pen. "Mr. Futino, we're told you were friends with Cailan Jaffray."

Liam leaned against a table but didn't sit down. "Friends? Sounds so ordinary. Like a mere house window instead of stained glass."

Sarg said, "Yes, you were friends or no, you weren't?"

"Yes, yes, yes, we were friends. We shared a love—no, make that a passion—for music."

"According to our source, you shared a lot more than that. And you argued with her on the day she died."

"We had sex, if that's what you're asking. But that's not all it was. I loved her." Liam rubbed his hands over his face. "Totally unrequited. She was getting over a breakup, and I was the rebound remedy."

"Is that why you argued, Mr. Futino? You wanted something more from your relationship than she did?"

"We never argued over that." Liam slumped even further. "We were arguing about—I don't recall. It hardly matters now. Her uncle or something."

"When you learned of her death, why didn't you go to the police?"

Liam took off his glasses to rub his eyes. "A guy I jam with had a run-in with the law once. Mistaken identity thing. Attorney fees bankrupted him."

"So you felt sure you'd be a suspect?"

"You're here, aren't you?" Liam put his glasses back on.

"What did you do after that argument with Cailan the day she died? Did you go to work?"

"I came home. I was home all night. Safe, sound, sleeping, all the while Cailan was going through what must have been sheer terror."

"So you were home at what time?"

"We usually met at the Café Renée around five. So, I guess I was here from seven or so onward."

Sarg exchanged a quick look with Drayco and made some notes in the pad. Was Janet the caterer mistaken?

Drayco took the time to make mental notes, studying the open violin case on the floor that held spare strings, a box of rosin, a mute, a tuner. The lid held a few photos under the bow holder, and Drayco recognized Cailan in one. "How did you and Cailan meet, Liam?"

"She came to a club with a few friends one of the nights I was playing. We got to talking and we really connected. Or so I thought at the time."

Drayco noticed a cellphone lying on a table and pointed to it. "How did you and Cailan arrange meetings? Your phone number didn't show up in any of her records."

"I loathe phones. I only use that thing for emergencies and gigs. If Cailan and I wanted to talk, I showed up at her place. Or she showed up here. Old-fashioned, I guess. But kinda nice."

"You said Cailan was upset with her uncle. Did she say why?"

"The usual things. Money. And he was none too pleased with her being a musician. I can imagine how he'd feel knowing she was dating one."

"He didn't know?"

"She wanted to keep our relationship secret. Maybe that was the reason. Or maybe she hoped her ex would come crawling back."

"Her ex being Gary Zabowski?"

"Yeah." Liam's eyes held the first spark Drayco had seen in him. "A pampered prince. From the kind of family who thinks an honest day's work is to call their inside trader."

The spark turned to fire as he added, "Cailan showed me a couple of Gary's compositions. Sad thing is, the kid has real talent. He might have a big career if he wasn't such a slacker. He didn't love Cailan. Or appreciate her."

Liam got up and headed to a media cabinet. He bent over and fiddled with a few settings, then straightened up as a piano transcription of the intro to Puccini's aria "O mio babbino caro" sounded through the room. Moments later, a soprano voice began to sing.

"That Cailan?" Sarg asked, and Liam roused himself from listening with an annoyed expression. But he nodded.

Drayco had heard plenty of singers, and though he wasn't an opera fan, he could tell Cailan possessed a rare gift. A lyrical tone and radiant warmth not unlike a young Renée Fleming, with interlocking violet triangles

Liam started coughing, a slight cough at first that soon turned into a violent spell, as he gasped for breath, tears streaming down his face. Drayco made a beeline for the table with the violin and picked up something he'd spied earlier, an inhaler, which he handed over. The other man shook the canister, forced it into his mouth and pressed the pump.

When he settled down and was breathing normally, Drayco asked, "Asthma?"

The other man fiddled with the inhaler. "I can control it most of the time."

Drayco had seen his cousin in the throes of an attack, often during D.C.'s notoriously pollen-heavy spring. Stress was another common trigger. The cold or flu Liam was coming down with would make it worse.

Sarg put his notepad away. "Can we get you something else?"

"I'll drink a glass of water, take some pills, go straight to bed." He seemed to have forgotten Janet and her chicken soup.

Drayco said, "Just a couple of other items, Liam. Did Cailan mention a stalker, a guy named Elvis Loomis?"

"Once. Wondered whether she needed to get a restraining order."

"Did Cailan mention some unusual notes she'd received in the mail, ones that contained sheet music?"

Liam shook his head. "Sounds like something Zabowski would do."

Back inside the car, Sarg said, "Gary didn't lie about one thing. Liam Futino did have it bad for Cailan. Still does."

Drayco glanced back at the house. "I'm a little sorry we'll have to sic the MPD on him."

"Yeah, but they can do all the leg work, talk with neighbors, try and verify his shaky alibi. Why is it suspects are always home alone?"

It was too early in October for the time to have flipped from daylight savings to standard. The dance of light late in the day was definitely changing, with the longer shadows of autumn tripping over newly obscured sidewalks and yards. It was dark enough to need the headlights before five. By the time Sarg's train pulled in to Fredericksburg, it would be pitch black.

Sarg turned on Drayco's satellite radio and flipped around until he found a channel he liked and sat back with a happy sigh.

Drayco said, "What is it with you and polka?"

"My grandfather listened to polka when I was a kid. Every time I hear it, I picture Papik and Tati dancing around the living room." Sarg added, "Besides, it annoys you."

Drayco leaned forward to switch the station, but Sarg batted his hand away.

Drayco said, "I'll get back at you by playing Stockhausen sometime."

"Shtok houses"?

Drayco gritted his teeth, though not at Sarg's comment. Listening to any music on the radio while driving was dangerous for him. The colors and shapes were more distracting than a construction zone with flashing lights at night in the pouring rain. Polka wasn't so bad. He

almost laughed when he realized polka music made him see green
blobs.

§ § §

Tara knew her Dad and Mr. Drayco wouldn't like what she was up
to, but she didn't care. She'd never tailed anybody before. Maybe she
wasn't doing it right, but it seemed like this was how they did it in the
movies. She was convinced Gary Zabowski was involved with Cailan's
death somehow, and he was acting weird. Even for him.

She watched as he ducked into Jedd's Emporium on the strip two
blocks from the psych lab. Should she go in? Gary knew her by sight,
so waltzing right in there probably wasn't a bright idea. How else could
she find out what he was doing?

Maybe it wouldn't be so bad—Jedd's was half imported goods and
half party supplies. The place was so packed with bins, baskets, and
racks of costumes, she could dodge almost anybody in there.

Upon opening the door, she immediately spied Gary in the back,
so she moved behind a display of hats. When she peeked around the
bowlers and pith helmets, he was still there and arguing with someone
she couldn't quite see.

Well, she'd come this far. She looked to her right and saw a
possible solution to her dilemma. Moving as nonchalantly as she could
manage, she sidled over to shelves filled with masks and pulled out a
rubber witch's face. She checked a mirror on the counter. Yep, it
covered her entire face.

She picked up a shopping basket and threw a pair of gloves and
tubes of body paint in it. Just another customer shopping. She added
another item or two as she worked her way to the back of the shop.
Then she slid into a row next to Gary, separated by jars of pickled
ghost peppers and boxes of chocolate-covered insects.

She still couldn't see the person Gary was arguing with, so she
moved one of the jars aside a few inches. It was that hippy custodian,
Elvis, the one who'd stalked Cailan. His face was red as he waved his

arms around. Gary, Mister I'm-Better-Than-Everyone, just smirked at the other guy.

What were they arguing about? She bumped into the shelves, and a box of the chocolates tumbled down toward the floor. With athletic grace she didn't know she had, she reached out and caught the box in her basket.

She held her breath for a moment, but the two men kept talking. Then, she heard Elvis say "It's worth more than that. You short-changing me?"

Gary uttered a muted laugh. "It's a fair price. Besides, what are you going to do, turn me in? You're in this as deep as I am. They'd arrest both of us."

Elvis grumbled, "Your Daddy'd get you off. Not me. I'd be the one going down for this."

If only she could see them better. She did hear what sounded like Gary opening up a wallet and pulling out some money. Then came a crinkling sound, like a bag. Gary said, "See, this works for both of us. Win-win," and before Tara could react, he came around behind her shelf and started toward her.

She reached out for a jar of the peppers while Gary grabbed some of the chocolates. He glanced at her jar and then her mask and laughed. "So that's what witches eat. Who knew?"

After he'd paid for the chocolates at the front register, he left, and Elvis followed soon after. Tara waited ten minutes, then put back all of the items including the mask. She explained to the cashier, "Forgot my wallet," and headed outside. She breathed a sigh of relief when she saw no signs of either Gary or Elvis.

So what did she do now? If she told her Dad, she'd get the lecture and a docked allowance. Maybe this whole exchange had nothing to do with Cailan's murder? And maybe she should have bought those peppers. They'd make her so sick, Dad would feel sorry for her. But at least she had a new appreciation for detective work—enough to know it wasn't genetic, because she didn't like it all that much.

16

Sarg's car was out of the shop, but the next morning he took the train, anyway. "In my next life, I wanna be a train engineer. Riding the rails, seeing the sights."

"Blowing the horn to avoid hitting drunks walking on the trestles. Or cars jumping the gates." Drayco felt like blowing the horn himself, narrowly avoiding a red-light runner as Leonora's brakes squealed in protest.

"You can be a downer, you know that?" As they pulled up in front of the warehouse where Elvis Loomis had a loft apartment, Sarg added, "Talk about downers."

No worries of D.C. gentrification here. The billions of dollars being spent on the Capital Riverfront along the Anacostia and Potomac Rivers a few miles south hadn't reached this place. Amazingly, the building wasn't condemned, and Elvis proved he did indeed live here when he opened the door.

He was in a mellower mood than in their last meeting. Probably had to do with the tangy aroma of marijuana Drayco smelled on his clothing. Was he in mellow-mood when he'd followed Cailan around, worrying her so much she considered taking out a restraining order?

"I must be important to have such esteemed dudes hovering around my hovel. Come on in. But I'm not paying out any lawsuits if you fall through the floor."

He led them upstairs to a room that if anything, made the exterior look fashionable. A new-looking laptop perched on a small table in one corner. Otherwise, the decor consisted of peeling paint, cement block tables, and rickety tie-dyed furniture like '60s escapees through a time machine. One of the few places to sit was a lounge with one of its front legs missing, propped up on stacked wooden blocks. Drayco eyed it skeptically.

"I think we'll stand," Sarg said.

"Suit yourself." Elvis flung himself down on the lounge. It jiggled, but held.

A clicking of heels behind them made Drayco and Sarg whip around as a woman in a form-fitting dress and ebony hair joined them. It was the same young woman who'd left with Shannon at the music school.

Elvis blew kisses at her. "Happy Ilsley, the Feds. Feds, Happy Ilsley."

She walked right up to them and looked them both up and down. "You are," she pointed at the ring on Sarg's hand, "married. And you," she looked at Drayco's ringless hand, "aren't."

"Miss Ilsley, I'm Agent Mark Sargosian with the FBI and this is Scott Drayco, who is consulting for us."

"Umm. What other consulting do you do?" She pinched Drayco's butt, which made him jump.

Elvis just laughed. "Oooh, dude, you're pinch-worthy."

Drayco regretted his decision to leave his jacket in the car. He was absolutely not going to look over at Sarg.

Happy smoothed her dress with her hands. "I doubt you're here for a threesome." She looked at Sarg. "I can tell you're the disgustingly happily married type, so you wouldn't be invited. This is about that murdered singer, am I right?"

"Yes, it is, Miss Ilsley." Sarg flipped out his notebook. Drayco knew he used it as much to prod his subjects to concentrate and get down to business as he did to get details.

"I was at work."

"And I was here in a drunken stupor." Elvis grinned up at them and stroked the beads in his beard. "That's what I told the cops. And I'm sticking to it."

"Where exactly do you work, Miss Ilsley?" Sarg's pen poised above the paper.

"I work at a club. Do waitressing and stuff."

"What's the name of the club?"

She walked over to a table to pick up a pack of cigarettes, pulling one out that she lit up. "You haven't heard of it. Just this little dive." She blew smoke in perfect rings that circled to the ceiling. Sarg held his pen above the paper and stared at her.

"Okay, if you must know, the Potomac Pleasure Palace." Sarg jotted it down. Drayco guessed Sarg knew as well as he did the "Palace" was a strip joint, one of a handful within the District. The owner, interviewed recently by *The Post*, preferred to call it a "Gentleman's Club."

Drayco moved out of the smoky line of fire. Onweller would be thrilled if word got back Drayco and Sarg smelled of cigarettes and marijuana. "Happy, how did you meet Shannon Krugh?"

She smiled at him. "Been to a rave party?"

"I'm allergic to loud noises."

She laughed. "We could have a lot of fun together, I'll bet. That's where I met Shannon, at a rave. She's a good kid. Not uppity like those other Parkhurst divas. The kind that look at you and see white trash. But then, she doesn't have money. She's regular folk."

"Unlike Cailan Jaffray?"

"Ask Elvis. I didn't know her."

"Did Shannon talk about her?"

"Some. They both wanted the same boy. Shannon won out."

Elvis was humming to himself. On the surface it sounded tuneless, but Drayco detected hints of Bellini. Elvis stopped and said, "'Mira, O Norma.' A rivalry between this Druid priestess babe Norma and this other chick over the same guy. Don't know what either Shannon or Cailan saw in that kid, Gary. Money, I guess. Always comes down to money, don't it?"

Drayco said, "Speaking of Druids. Since you're on campus a lot, you pick up on any cults, any voodoo, animal sacrifices?"

"Whoa, that's heavy. Me? Don't believe in anything that doesn't come out of a can, bottle, or bong." He was grinning as he said it, though his hands gripped the edges of a tie-dyed throw hanging over the lounge. "Religion is the true evil, man."

Elvis relaxed, stretched out on his side and propped his head in one hand. "Didja know my padre was a Pentecostal preacher? Hellfire, holy water and a whip he used to keep his brats on the straight and narrow. Beat me right on over to the other side, didn't he?"

Elvis seemed to notice Sarg's ring for the first time. "You got kids, Agent Gozian?" Sarg wisely didn't answer. "I got a kid. Ill-ee-jit-a-mit son. In Californ-eye-ay. Haven't seen him in five years. And he's seven, now."

Happy stubbed out her cigarette and grabbed her purse. "If you're going to get all maudlin on me, I'm outee. Besides, I've got to practice." She winked at Drayco on her way out, walking in the odd way models do on a catwalk, heel-toe, heel-toe.

Elvis watched her go and sighed. "She doesn't love me. Says she does. She'll flirt with any guy who's got his equipment intact." Elvis sat up and managed to fold his legs into a lotus position on the lounge, with his knees protruding over the side. "Her money plus my money equals no cardboard tent under a bridge."

Drayco said, "What did she mean, practice?"

"She's a singer too. Not opera. Got an audition coming up for a plum role at Signature. Has ambitions of New York, don't they all? Too bad she wasn't friends with Cailan. That godmother of hers is all pally wally with one or two of the Board of Trustees. Raises money for 'em."

"Adele Gilbow?"

"Yep, yep, yep. That's the one. Her husband's a dick-amundo. She's okay."

"You've met them?"

"I run into everybody on campus, in passing. You can tell a lot about a person by how they treat peons, don't ya think?"

Drayco eyed Sarg, who'd once said the exact same thing. He looked over at the laptop in the corner. "Does Happy read music or does she learn her songs by ear?"

"Dunno. Ask the Tony-winner wannabe herself. I think I seen some music here somewhere," Elvis squinted around the room.

Sarg stowed his notebook. "Mr. Loomis, in your stalking of Cailan, did you see anyone else, well, stalking her, too?"

"Stalking sounds so cloak and dagger. What you dudes do, right? If you mean following, there was this one guy. Curly hair, glasses. Hadn't seen him before. Or since."

"You don't know his name?"

"Can't say I do. Had a kinda John Doe-ish look to him." Elvis grinned.

They let themselves out, afraid Elvis would break his neck trying to navigate the steep stairs in his condition. Drayco had a moment of *déjà vu* that he couldn't quite place and shook it off.

He stopped to study a yawning mini-chasm in the asphalt, one of thousands that made D.C. a Pothole Paradise. "If Happy can read music and is proficient with that laptop, she, Shannon and Elvis could have conspired together on those puzzles, if not the murder."

"I told you he was hiding something." Sarg pointed to an original VW bug parked in front. "Guess who that belongs to?"

"The world's last remaining hippie."

"Uh huh." Sarg looked at the bug, then up to the loft, then back to the bug. He hadn't made a move toward Drayco's car but kept shifting his feet in place. "It's nine-thirty."

"And we should go so we can keep our appointment at ten."

"Uh huh."

"You going to be okay?" Sarg had agreed to set up the appointment, but Drayco knew he wasn't happy about it. It was one of his least favorite places though he'd kept his fears hidden from everyone at the Bureau except Drayco.

"Just drive. And turn on the air conditioning."

The only time chronic-popsicle Sargosian liked air conditioning was when he was afraid he was going to throw up. They climbed into the car, and despite the 50-degree day, Drayco cranked up the AC to max.

17

When the District's one and only public hospital, DC General, closed after two hundred years of community service, it became the temporary headquarters of the Chief Medical Examiner and labs. Deputy Medical Examiner Harriet Zachman greeted them, her hands full of reports she plonked on her desk. The one on the top was a Report of Investigation concerning a thirteen-year-old boy.

Zachman scrunched her nose while glancing at the report as if it were a personal offense. "I'll be glad when we move into the Consolidated Forensic Lab. Right now, it's more work we don't need."

She led them to the refrigerated body storage rooms. "Guess every step is one in the right direction. Especially after the problems in the '90s."

Some of that went all the way back to when Drayco was a grad student. The old facility was plagued by unsanitary conditions someone likened to a third-world country—roaches, rodents, no air conditioning, and unrefrigerated bodies, some piled on top of each other. Add in low morale, rapid staff turnover, uncertified pathologists, and it all led to a backlog of over a thousand cases, including homicides.

New leadership and help from the military had made a difference. As Drayco and Sarg walked through the lab area, the improvements were noticeable, to both the eyes and the nose. Zachman even made them wear shoe covers.

"Most of the time we need the sixty to ninety days we're allowed to close out a case. What with thirteen hundred autopsies a year. That's one reason we still have Miss Jaffray's body. Unusual, but not unprecedented. Plus, her guardian authorized us to keep it as long as we needed."

She put on plastic gloves and a paper cap over her Halle Berry-pixie hair. Was her golden skull necklace her choice or a gift? Drayco had never seen one like it before.

"I'd let you speak with our Supervisory Medicolegal Investigator, but there was a shooting this morning. Sixth time this month some dumb kid got in the way of a drug deal gone bad. The Narc Division loves it when our guy shows up. We got more law enforcement officers in the twenty-some-odd agencies covering the District than we do citizens. Talk about pissing contests."

Their paper shoe covers made a soft swishing on the concrete floor. The only other sound was a slight turquoise humming from the fluorescent overhead lights. The relative quiet made it feel like Drayco was in a church crypt.

Zackman stopped in front of a row of shelves stacked with body bags. "Don't get Bureau types much. Not for shooting victims, most connected to drugs or gangs."

She handed Drayco the case file with exam pictures and then stopped in front of one shelf and zipped open the bag. "And yet, here you are for a Parkhurst College student. Money doth have its privileges."

Even in death, it was easy to tell Cailan Jaffray had been a lovely young woman. The victim-corpses he encountered in his line of work always drew him in. Fragile and broken shells of what once held life. The M.E. dissected the pieces to tell a story, while Drayco tried to bring them back from the dead, jagged piece by jagged piece.

Cailan was more petite than in her photos, making the sutured lines across her body seem that much larger. He was so intent on studying her, it took him a moment to see Zachman's concerned face and her hand reach out behind him.

"Are you all right? Need a filter face mask?"

Sarg was as pale as the body on the slab. He straightened his shoulders. "I'm good. Wish I'd skipped breakfast."

Sarg had never been comfortable in the morgue. But as he said, it wasn't the same as a battle when you had an adrenaline chaser to keep you focused. Drayco raised a few fingers on his hand at Sarg, their secret code indicating he'd do most of the talking.

Drayco pointed to the stabbing wound in one of the photographs taken of the body prior to dissection. "It's not shaped like a 'Y' or 'L.' So the knife wasn't twisted out?"

She shook her head. "Very clean, straight in, straight out. Double-edge knife. See the diamond shape in that photo?"

It was a well-defined diamond, at that. "I guess you can't determine the length of the blade."

"I can tell you the wound depth was six inches, straight through the heart. No abrasion from a hand guard. So the blade is longer."

"And very little blood when the body was found in Kenilworth."

"She should have had six liters for a woman her size. Although she bled internally, about two liters are unaccounted for. So she bled out somewhere else. And the blood left had separated into clot and serum. Several hours passed since the stabbing took place."

"Defensive wounds?"

"No, but with the amount of Rohypnol in her system, and the fact it looks like the bleeding stream was projected, my guess—she was lying on her back."

Drayco handed the folder over to Sarg. Maybe if he had something to read, it would help. "Sounds like a large blade." Drayco studied the suturing on Cailan's chest. "And possible a woman could have thrust it in."

Zachman nodded. "If the blade tip was sharp. Judging from the entrance wound, I'd say it was."

"Those odd singe marks. The police report noted you believe the knife was heated somehow?"

She walked over to the folder in Sarg's hands and flipped to one particular photo. It was a close-up of the wound. "The knife was plunged in and out rapidly leaving tiny burn marks on the skin. Not long enough to cauterize blood vessels or organs."

"No way to tell how it was heated?"

"Those details are more your thing than mine. Stove, charcoal grill, matches. Take your pick."

Drayco had brief images of Gary and his clove cigarettes. Happy Ilsley and her Marlboro Lights. Elvis and his joints. All lit with matches.

Sarg had regained some of his normal coloring, but kept his eyes glued to the file as he spoke. "She was naked from the waist up. No sexual molestation?"

"Nope. After you called, I had one of our toxicologists do a retest. He found out something that may interest you. In addition to the Rohypnol, there were slight traces of methotrexate and misoprostol."

Sarg looked at Drayco, who said, "An abortion."

"Our tox screens don't routinely look for that. These days something like Rohypnol is high on the list, the reason her blood was tested for that right away. The latest lab results indicate the M&Ms were in her system a few weeks. That can happen after a successful abortion."

Drayco said, "Could you tell how far along she was?"

"Such drugs are prescribed at clinics if the patient is less than seven weeks in her pregnancy." Zachman added, "No signs she'd been pregnant before, if that helps."

"There aren't many clinics in the area. Agent Sargosian can put the paperwork through."

Drayco saw Sarg still looked a bit green, so he tried to wrap it up. "Dr. Zachman, what about those fibers you found?"

"Oh yes, the fibers. I didn't have high hopes of finding any. But these were in her mouth. Two small, red cotton fibers."

"A gag, possibly. Maybe the crime scene was in an area where the murderer was afraid sounds would carry."

"That would mean our *unsub*," Sarg accented the word, "drugged and then gagged her. Unless the fibers had traces of Rohypnol, too?" Sarg liked to give Drayco a hard time for his dislike of using FBI jargon.

Zachman smiled and shrugged. "Did I mention thirteen hundred autopsies a year, Agent? Hire us some more staff, and we'll see what we can do. That's another layer of technology we can't afford to use right now."

"You've been very helpful," Drayco rescued the file from Sarg, to flip through one last time. "If you do find anything else …"

"Of course. Anything to keep you and your HBO happy," she said as she ushered them toward the front, which made Drayco grin. So Harriet Zachman knew some Bureau-ease, with her High Bureau Official jab. A very observant woman, of both the dead and the living.

Sarg took several lungfuls of air as they left the building. "October air smells different, don't you think?"

Drayco took the hint and didn't mention Sarg's morgue-a-phobia. Bad enough he was kidded during FBI training and given the motto "Easy come, queasy go Sargosian." Maybe it was because they knew he was an ex-Ranger, supposed to be one big bad dude.

But something else was at play now, a suspicion verified when Sarg leaned against the sign outside the entrance. "I may be a lapsed churchgoer. But I gotta pray I never have to see Tara laid out like that. I mean, what if this thing isn't a tragic love story, like an Elvis Loomis opera."

"We're not talking serial killer. Yet."

"That's what I keep telling myself." Sarg had dust on his pants from the sign, which he patted off, leaving clouds trailing behind him. "So you get the afternoon off, while I get the joy of appearing in court to wrap up that Atkins case the BAU consulted on."

"I'll need it to gather my strength for the party."

Sarg grimaced. "Don't know which part of that pisses me off more. That Gilbow thought it would be amusing to invite us or that Onweller practically ordered us to go."

When Sarg passed along that news item earlier today—what Drayco called a "command performance" at Andrew Gilbow's party tomorrow evening—he guessed the man was joking. Parties were unpleasant medicine you sometimes had to take to treat the ailment. Or in this instance, the case. *Hors d'oevres* sleuthing.

Sarg found a silver lining. "Ya think they'll have good wine and grub? I wouldn't mind some Rumaki or calamari tapas." He'd obviously recovered, to be thinking of food.

Drayco grumbled, "Definitely no humble pie on the menu."

Cailan's music puzzle poked at him, nudging his subconscious. CAILAN AVENGE. Avenge who, what? And what if his reading of the music code wasn't correct? He'd be the one choking down several slices of humble pie.

As if sensing Drayco's mood, Sarg said, "Not gonna stand me up are you?"

"What about Elaine? Onweller said to bring her."

"She's got some church gig not even guilt could get her out of. As you may recall, she loves parties."

"I guess it's an X-chromosome thing, like pillows."

"Don't tell Elaine that. I'll be sleeping on the couch for weeks."

"Your court appearance isn't until one, right?"

"Why?"

"Want to go bowling?"

Sarg eyeballed the building they'd left. "Bowling over body bags any time. But isn't it early for bowling?"

"Not if you're Shannon Krugh. I found out she works at a local bowling alley part time."

Their earlier interview with Shannon was on safe territory and a little like the old "Name That Tune" game, trying to guess a song after a couple of notes. She hadn't impressed him as someone who was passionate about music, more like something she fell into.

And though he tried not to let the colors and shapes of people's voices prejudice him, for some reason, the cayenne-colored thumbtacks in Shannon's tones was unsettling. Maybe it was the bipolar coming through. Or perhaps it was something altogether different.

18

The Patriot Bowling Alley was a symbolic landmark of the old-new, ramshackle-glitz schizophrenia in the District. Like other buildings in this block, it dated back to the mid-twentieth century. Its Modernist blandness hadn't been renovated since.

The rainbow spray-painted graffiti on one side looked more like bored-youth scribblings than territorial gang markers. A sign loomed over the door with an outsized bowling bowl tilted down toward entering guests, threatening more of a head-strike than a pin-strike.

Over in one corner of the parking lot, a pile of fresh lumber, gleaming steel, and paint cans hinted at the tired building's visions of rehabilitation. Far more interesting was the sight of Shannon Krugh and Gary Zabowski in the middle of a heated argument. It was so heated, neither of them noticed Drayco and Sarg as they approached.

Gary's outstretched arms gestured close to Shannon's face. "You can't keep it. I don't care about the other junk. Burn, sell, give away everything else. But I need that laptop."

"You told me it was a gift." Shannon crossed her arms over her chest

"I said it was a loaner. And I think I'd had three bottles of Rolling Rock at the time."

"You're filthy, stinking rich so why do you care so much about one little laptop computer?"

"Because it's not mine. I got it from Cailan."

"You gave me something that belonged to her? You're pathetic."

"Technically it wasn't hers. It belongs to Dr. Jaffray."

"Oh for God's sake, Gary. You're not good enough to be pathetic, you're not good enough to be pond scum. You're the crap pond scum eats."

Shannon whirled around and strode over to a backpack lying a few feet away, pulled out a laptop computer and brought it over to Gary, thrusting it under his face. "Take it. I can use the computers at the library instead."

Drayco and Sarg were so close now, Drayco chimed in, "Tell you what. Why don't Agent Sargosian and I make sure that laptop makes its way back to Dr. Jaffray." Drayco held out his hand.

Shannon and Gary froze in place. Gary recovered faster and only hesitated a moment before letting Drayco take the laptop. "Fine, but it's your responsibility now. I want that on record."

Gary climbed into a blue sports car he squealed up to around fifty miles per hour before he even got out of the parking lot. Shannon ignored the car and the two men and bent over to yank at her backpack, only to miss on the first try. "Goddamn it," she yelled, giving it a swift kick before finally rescuing it.

Drayco asked, "Mind if we ask you a few more questions?"

She walked toward the entrance. "My shift starts in five minutes. You want to talk, you'll have to follow me in," and she disappeared through the front door.

Sarg turned to Drayco. "The Bureau forensics geeks will want to look at that laptop."

"Let me get first crack at it. You can hand it over tomorrow."

Sarg tugged on his earlobe. "That's not standard protocol."

"Gary and Shannon both used it after Cailan's death. So there may not be anything left connected to her. And you know the Bureau and MPD will fight over it. Then it will vanish forever into some evidence locker."

"But Onweller—"

"Doesn't have to know." Drayco held out his hand toward the bowling alley. "Shall we go in?"

The interior of the bowling alley was as dispirited at the outside. Garish painted signs above the lanes tried their best to draw attention away from worn carpeting and burned-out lights. The walls hemmed in the smell of stale beer and greasy french fries.

It was a far cry from elite bowling alleys—more like exclusive high-tech Hollywood clubs—with projection screens and furniture designed by architectural school rejects. He made a mental note to ask Tara about that.

They spied Shannon in front of the rental desk, the sole staff member in sight. Sarg asked, "Are you one of those server girls or do you rent the shoes?"

Shannon knocked her booted foot on a tool case in front of her. "I'm a lane mechanic."

Sarg looked at the tool case then back at Shannon. She picked up an ohm meter, smiling at Sarg's obvious confusion. "I get called in whenever the main mechanic needs a hand or time off. My dad was a lane mechanic. Taught me everything I know."

Drayco recalled the waitress at Café Renée and her Bowling Industry Management major. "You know Irene Quillen?"

Shannon dropped the ohm meter into the case. "IQ? I'd say her IQ is as high as a five-year-old would bowl."

"And yet she said she wanted to study astronomy. Until her father said it wasn't lucrative."

"He told her that?" She put her hands on her hips. "Why is it everyone is always trying to tell you how to run your own goddamn life." She scowled over at the lanes, then straightened up and turned back to Drayco and Sarg. "I'll bet you two never bowled before."

Sarg said, "Sure." Then he turned to Drayco. "You have, right?"

"Nope."

"Brock didn't take you bowling?"

"Too busy. He pitched a baseball to me once."

Shannon picked up a bowling ball from a rack and handed it to Drayco. "We don't have much of a crowd in here as you can see."

Only one other man was bowling at that moment. Drayco watched the man take his stance, position the ball in his hands, then roll the bowl down the lane, knocking over all the pins.

Drayco handed the laptop to Sarg and said, "Seems easy enough." He rolled the ball down the long wooden path. It curved over toward the gutter, arced into the middle of the lane, and proceeded to nail a strike.

Sarg groaned. "You're a bowling shark, aren't you?"

"I did what he did," Drayco indicated the other bowler.

"You do know it's not that easy."

"Why not?"

Shannon reached up into some cubbies behind the service desk and pulled out a ribbon that said "Bowling Star," and handed it to Drayco. As she'd reached up, the sleeves on her shirt fell toward her elbows, exposing her wrists and forearms and the angry, snaking lines of self-cutting marks.

Drayco knew a thing or two about scars. He envisioned Shannon taking a knife to her skin during a depressive phase, alone at the time. Alone and bleeding. It was a wonder she was still alive.

Shannon showed neither depressive nor manic signs today, making Drayco suspect she was definitely back on her meds. "Was that the first time you've seen Gary since the two of you broke up?"

"I've been avoiding him. Well, trying to avoid him. As you can see it doesn't always work."

"Was he violent toward you while you were dating?"

"Gary's all bark, no bite. And he's a lousy drunk, weepy and useless."

"So he never threatened you?"

"Threatened, no, taunted, yes. That's what I get for dating above my station. And like always, the rich guy screws the poor girl in more ways than one."

Sarg said, "Did you do any drugs together?"

"Do I look like a nun? Show me a college student who doesn't do drugs or alcohol, and I'll show you someone whose name is on an altar candle."

"What drugs are we talking here, Miss Krugh? Marijuana or worse?"

Shannon pursed her lips together. Sensing she was about to clam up, Drayco asked, "Do you like Parkhurst, Shannon? Have you made a lot of friends there? Your parents must be proud of your success."

She leaned with her back along the counter and then hoisted herself up onto the top. "Parkhurst is Parkhurst and I don't do friends. I mean when you're different, you grow up fighting off bullies. Not that Parkhurst has bullies, just snot-nosed stuck-ups. As for my parents— they expect a lot."

"You have one friend. Happy Ilsley."

"We hang out together. Sing, dance, drink, smoke, fuck, ogle guys' butts." She smirked at Drayco. Happy must have talked to Shannon after leaving them with Elvis at the loft this morning.

"Did you sing together?"

"Duets?" She laughed. "Duh. For fun, natch. She's way better than me. She'll be rich and famous, and I'll be her groupie."

"She must read music fairly well."

"She's okay, a little shaky. So I guess I got her beat there."

"Did you enjoy your trip to Cozumel?"

Shannon's eyes widened. "How in hell did you know that?"

"The MPD learned Gary was seen in the company of a young blond for a few days while he was in Mexico over the summer. I'm guessing your pink dye came after. And with your hair pulled up, I can see that tattoo on your neck. The one with the warrior god and his tongue sticking out. A popular Mexican souvenir."

"Gary flew me down to stay with him for a week. I didn't tell my parents. He says come on down, he pays the airfare, so I said, hell yes. "

Sarg frowned. "You have a passport?"

"The college helped me get one last year. They were planning on taking a music school production to Europe. Fell through, natch."

A man entered the front door, saw the three of them and immediately started in on Shannon. "Krugh, I'm not paying you to socialize. You're supposed to be working on that solenoid."

Shannon glared in the man's direction, then whispered, "Yes, massah," and hopped off the counter. She added in a low voice to

Drayco and Sarg, "Sex on the beach for real is a hell of a lot better than the drink."

Drayco hid a smile and asked, "By the way, is there a password to access the laptop?"

"Primadonna. Real original, huh?"

Drayco and Sarg left Shannon to her solenoid. But as they exited the building, Drayco held out a hand to stop Sarg, then pointed to someone else in the lot. Someone with a familiar long beard, inspecting a weed trimmer lying in a small patch of grass.

Sarg always had to walk faster than Drayco to keep up, but this time he beat him by two seconds. "You work here, Elvis?"

Elvis Loomis straightened up so fast, he dropped the trimmer in mid-buzz. Cursing, he bent over and picked it up. "My other gig laid me off. Said it was budget cuts. You and me know the truth. They think I'm a killer. Who knows? Maybe I am. Don't know what I'm doing or where I am half the time."

Sarg pressed him, "Do you know Shannon Krugh? She's a friend of Happy's and works in this bowling alley."

"I know her through Happy, sure. She put in a good word for me. S'how I got this here job. Don't pay a lot."

"When did you get laid off?"

"Two days ago. Right after you showed up at Campus Security. Coinkydink? Don't think so. Thanks for that, by the way."

"Why didn't you mention it when we saw you this morning, Mr. Loomis?"

"None of your damn business. Want to know if my navel's pierced, too? All the same importance, ain't it? Meaning shit."

Drayco suspected it had more to do with how high Elvis was. Sarg seemed to agree, asking, "Why don't you tell us about those recreational pharmaceuticals that keep you from knowing where you are half the time. Bought any Rohypnol lately, sir?"

"Ro hip what?"

Drayco said, "Roofies."

Elvis dropped the weed trimmer again and cursed some more. "Why didn't you say so? That stuff ain't worth it. Hell, if I want to feel drunk, I'll buy beer. Much cheaper. And if I want the runs, I'll get me some prune juice."

"What about giving roofies to someone else, say Happy, Shannon or Cailan?"

"I may not be a college boy, but I got brains to keep my yap shut. You wouldn't believe me if I said yay or nay. So why bother?"

Elvis tugged on the weed trimmer's starter cord and winked at them over the deafening buzz of the motor, as he attacked a clump of sad-looking turf. Elvis wasn't using any ear protection. If he kept that up, it wouldn't be long before he'd go deaf from that noise, close to 100 dB. So long to his beloved opera. Drayco was sorry he no longer kept disposable earplugs in his car to give to him.

They hurried into the car to close the doors and shut out the buzzing. Now that they could hear each other, Sarg said, "Shannon's a lane mechanic? There are days I feel like a fossil."

"A cash-starved lane mechanic."

"Meaning?"

"Might make her more vulnerable to bribes or selling drugs. We need to get the name of her doctor. She may have more than one, getting extra prescription meds she sells to students. Seroquel, or Suzie-Q, is a bipolar drug popular with cocaine and meth addicts. Fights the comedown."

"I can search Virginia's PDMP for controlled substance abuse."

"Last time I checked, Seroquel wasn't on the list."

"And why, pray tell, did you check that? Something I should know?"

"A case I consulted on."

"Is NoDoz on there?"

Drayco laughed, as he watched several sparrows circling around one of the few large trees on the street. He said, "If NoDoz and caffeine show up on that list, I'll be one of the first arrests."

19

Drayco was a workaholic to the core, a trait that had chased off a few lady friends. But for once, he was grateful to have the afternoon off, thanks to Sarg's court case. He wasn't as grateful for Sarg's news that Onweller wanted to meet with both of them at Quantico tomorrow morning.

Why was it so hard to work with Sarg again? Those early days seemed a long time ago, when they paired up after Drayco's former partner died in an accident and Sarg's retired. Then later applying for and being accepted into the BAU together.

Getting in had been Sarg's career-long goal. When Drayco made it in after only four years as an agent, Sarg defended his qualifications to those who'd grumbled about the influence of Drayco's father. Not that it mattered. He'd worked hard, paid his dues. And words weren't sticks or stones. Make that redwoods or boulders.

He got up to make a peanut butter and mayonnaise sandwich, thought better of it, and grabbed the Manhattan Special he'd set beside the pile of mail he hadn't bothered opening. Especially the one on top, the rent overdue for the office he kept downtown. The few high-profile clients, the law enforcement agencies he'd consulted for, paid reasonably well. But those recent Cape Unity cases were *pro bono*, and work was unpredictable.

He could just see giving up the office and meeting potential clients at the local coffee shop. Yes, Mr. Drayco, my son was murdered, the police haven't found a motive, I need your help, and no, I don't want any whip on my caramel macchiato.

He grabbed the remote to turn on the TV and flipped through channels, stopping on a local newscast that made him sit up straight.

Andrew Gilbow was being interviewed about the "cold case" of the poor murdered Parkhurst student, who the reporter had learned was Gilbow's goddaughter. Drayco turned up the volume.

"It's not often I'm asked to offer my forensic psychology services on something so personal. When the FBI asked me to help, I was happy to do whatever I can."

Yeah, right. Not the FBI as a whole had asked, just Gilbow's pal, Onweller.

The reporter asked if they had new leads and were close to solving the case.

"I'm sure the detectives are … trying their best. The success rate with such cases is low. Cailan was a special girl. She deserves justice." Either Gilbow was a good actor or genuinely upset because Drayco hadn't heard his voice break before. On the other hand, he implied Sarg, Drayco, and the MPD were no better than Keystone Cops. Typical.

The story cut to the reporter interviewing Parkhurst President George Thackeray, who said, "We feel this was an isolated incident. The other members of our student body have nothing to worry about," then tilted his head at an empathetic angle to add, "Our hearts go out to this unfortunate student and her loved ones."

Drayco turned the TV off when the news moved on to another story and stretched out on the sofa, his legs propped on the table. Despite the NoDoz, he felt the fog of sleep roll in and surrendered to it.

It didn't take long this time for the nightmares to kick in. The colors and shapes of the various sounds in the room served as a backdrop for the action in front of him he was too paralyzed to stop. Sarg and Drayco and the young MPD officer were back in the abandoned building. The officer's informant thought he'd seen the kidnapped woman here, but not recently. It was a lead, possible clues, nothing more, so they split up.

But the warehouse wasn't empty. The late afternoon light through the broken windows was dim, but Sarg had ignored a room as he rushed past. A mistake that proved to be deadly. A dark shape emerged from that room and then everything happened at lightning speed.

In the wake of the firestorm, the officer—the son of a city councilman—lay dead, Sarg shot, and the suspect severely wounded by Drayco. He could have shot to kill. One bullet right through the forehead, something he'd nailed many times on the range. Some grumbled he should have. But then the suspect couldn't tell them where the kidnapped woman was being held before he died.

In the background, a noise grew more insistent by each second. He focused on one color in his mind and used that to pull himself out of the paralysis. Someone was knocking on the door. He slapped his face several times, and feeling mostly awake, he headed to the front. There on the step stood Nelia Tyler.

"A woman I met at the conference offered to drop me off." She hastened to add, "So I could pick up that bag with the souvenirs."

"Is she waiting for you outside?"

"I told her to pick me up on her way back."

Drayco pointed to a table near the door. "There's your bag."

"So it is. Guess I should have told Martha to wait."

Nelia stood in place for a moment, then walked over to take a peek inside the bag. "Looks like everything is still there."

"Cat burglars don't find any challenge in pilfering goods already in our possession."

"Lucky for me you don't have a snow-globe fetish."

They looked at each other, Drayco not recovered from his nightmare enough to pretend away his discomfort, Nelia looking equally uncertain. Her eyes widened when she looked at the coat rack which sported a red negligee hanging on a peg. Drayco grabbed it and folded it up in his pocket. Darcie had left it behind, and he'd hung it up there last night as a reminder to return it next time.

Nelia's cheeks were the same color as the negligee. Drayco apologized, "Sorry about that."

She smiled slightly. "Looks like your house is Grand Central Station when it comes to items left behind by women."

Drayco rubbed his neck. "My life is a lot more boring than you think."

"I ran into Darcie Squier in Cape Unity last week. She was quick to mention you and she were seeing each other."

"Seeing? That sounds like a couple of blind people who just got corneal transplants."

She laughed. "I figured she might be embellishing things a bit."

Drayco waved her inside. "Come on in. I can give you the ten-cent tour."

She smiled. "As long as it takes less than an hour."

He decided not to take her upstairs where the bedrooms were, which meant the ten-cent tour only took five minutes. She put her hands on her hips and nodded with approval. "Low maintenance, no clutter. My kind of decorating. The couch could use a few pillows."

He stifled a grin as Sarg's words echoed back to him, *What is it with women and pillows?*, then led Nelia to the front corner of his home, saving the best for last. "And this is my pride and joy." He put a hand on the piano, centered in a room intended for a den, with rough stone walls and bookshelves on either side of a small fireplace.

"It's a beauty, all right." She scanned his face. "But since you seem tired, I'll take a rain check on a private recital."

He got a beer and handed it to her as she slid onto the sofa. To make room for her drink, he picked up the mail from the table and carried it to the kitchen counter. One letter that wasn't a bill stood out, and he brought it with him. A white nine-by-twelve envelope.

"Your winning lottery notice?" Nelia tipped back the beer as he admired how she was one of those rare women who could chug a beer and still look like she'd walked out of charm school.

"Official documents don't usually come without a return address." He slit it open and angled it so the standard-sized sheet of printer paper inside slid out on its own. Then he picked up the edges of the paper between his fingernails to avoid obscuring the sender's prints. If this were like the other notes, there wouldn't be any.

Holding it up to the light, he looked for watermarks. As with Cailan's note, it was the type of mass-produced printer paper found over the country. If they had a suspect, they could match the paper to his printer. Color printers left secret embedded serial number and manufacturing codes. And black-and-white printers left unique patterns caused by the rotating drum in the toner cartridge, like a fingerprint. The only printer he'd seen at the homes of any of their suspects was Gary's.

His expression must have alarmed her, for she hopped up to get a good look at the letter. "A music score? Isn't that the type of letter your murder victim received?"

Drayco retrieved his copy of Cailan's letter and compared the two. They were indeed similar, with the same software-generated music staves containing a simple harmonized melody. As with Cailan's music puzzle, no key or time signature. He placed the letter on the table, got the Schumann book he'd used for Cailan's letter and studied the music wheel.

"Is there an embedded code with this one, too?"

"I can make a phrase using the cipher-wheel. I'm just not sure it's what the sender intended. It spells out CODA OR DA CAPO."

"Coda means the end of something, doesn't it?"

"It signals the end of a movement or an entire piece. *Da capo* literally means 'from the head,' but in music it's an instruction to repeat the previous section. It's usually abbreviated D.C."

"Cailan was sent letters before she was murdered. Do you think … would someone be targeting you? I'd hate to see you get shot like on your first trip to Cape Unity." Her voice was light, teasing. She placed a hand on his arm, and he wasn't sure she was aware she was doing it.

He passed the paper over so she could get a better look. "I'm more concerned it means someone else is in danger. Sarg's daughter, for instance, or another of Cailan's friends. 'Da capo' sounds like someone's planning a repeat performance."

"You think they sent this to you instead of the Park Police or MPD because of your background?"

"I don't know. Regardless of who sent it, I'd say the message is 'catch me if you can.'"

Nelia pointed to a curious drawing at the bottom of the paper. "What does that mean?"

The small figure depicted a man sitting cross-legged wearing antlers on his head and holding something circle-shaped in one hand. "I don't know. It wasn't on Cailan's note."

"Your life may be boring, but your cases aren't." Nelia grinned, adding, "When I leave the big city tomorrow, guess I'll have to content myself with the Eastern Shore's exciting world of convenience store thefts and public drunkenness."

"You're leaving so soon?" He'd hoped they might have more time. To catch up.

"The Sheriff's budget could only afford part of the conference." She didn't explain, but Drayco knew the county board kept cutting the Sheriff Department's funds. They might never get back the deputy position that got axed two years ago.

Nelia's cellphone chirped, and she pulled it out of her pocket to read the text. "My ride is outside." Once more she stood by the front door, the picture of indecision until she stuck out her hand.

He shook it, like one professional to another and tried not to hold on too long. Being around Nelia was like sitting on a piano bench with his three-year-old legs swinging over the edge, as he picked out "Traffic Cop" on the keyboard.

She was smiling as she made for the door. Then she stopped dead, whirled around and grabbed her souvenir bag. "Almost forgot what I came for," and waved as she let herself out.

Drayco closed his eyes for a moment. His timing had never been good when it came to long-term relationships with women. Why should this be any different? She was off limits with a very sick husband and a loyalty streak a mile wide.

He really should call Sarg and let him know about the note. But he'd promised to give Cailan's laptop computer to Sarg in the morning, and this might be his last chance.

After spending an hour on the laptop, he guessed Cailan must have received the computer shortly before her death. At first, he didn't find signs of her presence. Then he found a folder Shannon must have overlooked. It was labeled "CJ." It included websites bookmarked for pepper spray, self-defense tips, how to handle stalkers, the occult, and a fortune-telling site.

Drayco clicked on the occult site. It was a page on voodoo, a topic she likely would have researched, thanks to those dolls. He also looked at the fortune-telling site, which led to saved results from a quiz. He got a lump in his throat when he read Cailan's results, "Something wonderful waits for you right around the corner."

The Great God of the Internet coupled with pseudoscience crap had struck again. With so many people lulled into believing everything they found on the Web, he expected computer shrines to pop up in homes soon. Worship the new Oracle of Dell-phi.

Then he came across a bookmarked page on abortion clinics. Ah, Cailan. Was Gary the father? Liam? Or some other man whose identity she'd tried to hide like she had with Liam?

Maybe young people had similar problems decades ago. But instant access to all this info—recipes for drug cocktails, sites selling pepper spray, rape statistics, conspiracy theories—was making them less happy and more paranoid. It was hard to tell if increasing rates of teenage depression were cause or effect.

There were no signs Gary used the computer, and the only trace of Shannon was a research paper for a philosophy class. He made a copy of the paper on a memory card.

Drayco's finger hovered over the power switch, briefly harboring the idea of researching excuses to get out of Gilbow's party tomorrow night. He wasn't sure which he least looked forward to—the party or the meeting with Onweller. Perhaps Sarg could find a reason to enjoy himself at Gilbow's bash if they served Rumaki or calamari tapas. Even that didn't appeal to Drayco.

Too bad Nelia couldn't have stayed longer. Or gone to the party. Did she still have that taxiway-blue dress and high heels that set off those shapely legs usually hidden under deputy-brown slacks? Disgusted with himself, he flipped the power switch to "off."

20

Drayco was early to his morning appointment with Onweller, but there were no signs of Sarg. Knowing how Onweller valued punctuality, Drayco headed on in. He'd just taken his seat when Sarg opened the door and explained his delay with one word, "Traffic," then laid a report on Onweller's desk and sank in the chair next to Drayco.

"All right then," Onweller was suddenly all business. "What's this new music puzzle that came to you, Drayco?" Upon being handed the letter, he adjusted his glasses on his nose and took a hard look. "You compared it to the other one?"

"Very similar, down to the paper, printer, evenness and darkness of the toner." Drayco explained what he thought it meant, both translated and musically.

"Adds a new wrinkle to the proceedings. I'd decided we wouldn't need your services any longer since you figured out the first code."

Sarg moved around in his seat. "That would be premature. We're continuing to get new leads."

Onweller picked up the report Sarg had placed on the desk and flipped through it, reading Sarg's latest bulleted list. "Almost all of the suspects here, Shannon Krugh, Gary Zabowski, Liam Futino, Elvis Loomis, fit the love-gone-wrong scenario. You have an outlier motive, Elvis Loomis and religion?"

Sarg cleared his throat. "Loomis was the son of an abusive preacher. It's obvious he doesn't think highly of religion. And Cailan Jaffray was the niece of a religion professor. A possibility."

"Hmm. And this lab project? Reed Upperman? Doesn't seem connected."

"We haven't found anything concrete yet." Sarg seemed to be choosing his words carefully. He hadn't agreed with Drayco's own belief that the timing of the attack, heading home after a lab session, wasn't coincidental.

But Sarg appeared to be playing diplomat. "That brings me to something troubling us, sir. Why hasn't the college put out notices to the students and their parents about Cailan—as a warning and to ask for tips?"

"The students have gotten the word from the bloodthirsty media, Agent. President Thackeray asked us to be discreet. Since it's likely to be a crime of limited associations, it makes no sense to stir things up with negative publicity. Not with several important funding projects in sensitive stages with wealthy donors."

Sarg pinched the bridge of his nose. "Phrase it in a general way, then. A reminder for students to go out at night with a buddy, things like that."

"Washington is a violent city, Agent Sargosian. Crime is big business here whether it's white collar or no collar. Which is why all incoming Parkhurst students have to sign a code of responsibility that includes an awareness of the campus' location. And to act accordingly."

Code or no code, if the victim were anyone other than the niece of one of the college's professors, a lawsuit might be in the cards. And still could be if any one of those wealthy parents decided to pull their little darling from school and demanded a tuition refund. A romance-murder made things so much easier for Onweller's golfing buddy. The sour taste in Drayco's mouth was worse than a vinegar cocktail with a lemon chaser.

He said, "Dr. Gilbow was on the local news last night, speaking about the case. Was he authorized to do that?"

Onweller frowned. "I asked for his input, so technically he's helping us. Anyone can give their opinion on TV in a free country."

He riffled through Sarg's file. "I'm certain you'll pinpoint the unsub soon. And I must emphasize the soon part. With only eight agents in our unit and new requests for investigation support, we can't afford to have you tied up on this case, Sargosian."

Onweller handed the file back to Sarg. "Because of this new music note, and only because of this new music note, I'll spot you a couple more days. Make sure you use the time wisely."

After they'd been dismissed, Drayco and Sarg regrouped in Sarg's office. "I am seriously beginning to regret sending Tara to that college."

Sarg had a dartboard he pulled out and hung on the wall when he needed to let off steam. He tossed three at the board in rapid succession, missing the center by a wider margin than usual. "And I'm tired of Onweller's pissy attitude lately."

Sarg tried three more darts, which were farther off-center. He scowled at the copy of the note sent to Drayco. "Not many people know you're helping with this case. Just the people we've talked to."

"Unless they've told others."

"Yeah, okay, but how would they know to send it to you? We didn't tell a soul *you* were the one to figure that code out."

"Why don't we ask one of that small circle, Troy Jaffray?"

Sarg thumped a stack of materials in his inbox. "Sounds better than working on my regular docket."

Despite the tension and the awkwardness at times, Drayco could tell Sarg was enjoying the chance to get out of the office and pound the pavement. Maybe it was just a case of greener-grass-envy, but Sarg must be getting as frustrated as Drayco had with the shifting of the Bureau's focus. More counter-terrorism, less of the "ordinary" day-to-day crime often buried in the back pages of newspapers.

Sarg threw one last dart, a bulls-eye, and pushed his inbox aside. "You're driving, hotdog."

21

One of the last people Drayco expected to run into on the way to Troy Jaffray's office building was Shannon Krugh. She walked right past Drayco and Sarg, then stopped and whipped around.

"You," she pointed first at Sarg and then Drayco, "almost got me fired."

First Elvis, now Shannon. At this rate, they were going to have to open an unemployment bureau for their suspects. Not that they owed said suspects any particular favors. Drayco pulled out the memory card with the copy of her research paper and handed it to her.

She stared at it with suspicion.

"It contains the paper for your philosophy class, from that laptop computer. Thought you might want a copy."

She grabbed the card. "Did you read it? The paper?"

"Only the title page."

"Didn't you want to dig into my psyche or whatever and see why I killed Cailan? I mean, everyone thinks I did it. Wasn't like I was Miss Popular before, but now …"

Her fading Pepto-pink hair, tattoo, and hole-pocked jeans desperately tried their best to mark her as stylish. But they were more timeworn than trendy, from what he'd seen Parkhurst co-eds wearing. At any other school, Shannon's new-found notoriety might be fashionable.

He replied, "We like to keep our minds open."

She chewed on her lip. "You're the only one. You and Happy."

Shannon rolled the memory card around in her hand and stuffed it into her pocket. A slow smile spread across her face. "Maybe I should take this as a sign. Happy says I need to take this whole mess and re-evaluate stuff. Make a few changes."

Drayco smiled back. "Change can be good."

"So they say." She turned to leave, adding in parting, "Tuesdays are law enforcement bowling nights. You should come."

As she continued on her way, Sarg said, "Call me cynical, but I doubt she's really changed."

"People do, you know. Change."

Sarg shrugged. "More often than not, they turn into more of what they were before." He looked sideways at Drayco. "It wasn't wise—and maybe not legal—to give her that copy of her paper."

"I'm surprised you didn't ask the title."

Sarg let out an exasperated sigh. "Okay, what was the title?"

"'Should Reason Be the Sole Basis for Determining What Actions are Morally Right or Wrong?'"

If Sarg didn't have both of his hands folded across his chest and stuffed under his armpits, one of those hands would likely be tugging on his ear. As it was, he just shook his head.

They walked the rest of the way to Jaffray's office in silence, leaving Drayco to examine more of the campus. Was the pristine landscaping some of Elvis' leftovers?

The air smelled cleaner here, like someone sprayed giant cans of odor neutralizer around. More signs of the carefully controlled Parkhurst image. Send your pampered darlings to Fantasyland College, and we'll send them back with a riffraff-free degree.

Not so much in Troy Jaffray's jumbled office, where the professor was smoking a pipe, perfuming the air with an aroma reminiscent of burned chocolate. They'd no sooner walked through the door when he said, "I doubt this meeting will do any good. Unless you have news of the monster who killed Cailan."

Sarg said, "We received a new music puzzle. Well, Drayco did, it was addressed to him."

"And this helps us how?"

"Well, sir, it means we've hit a nerve with that monster. Makes it more likely he'll slip up."

"Likely? Isn't that the same as saying you're a little bit pregnant?"

The sight of Cailan's pale wax-doll body in the morgue popped into Drayco's mind. How young she'd seemed. No obvious way to tell she'd been a singer or—briefly—a mother. He asked, "Were you aware your niece had been pregnant?"

Jaffray froze and stood there unblinking for several moments. Then he sank into his desk chair. "Had been? Then did she—"

"An abortion. We're in the process of contacting area clinics. They won't be able to tell us who the father was unless he came in with her."

"How far along?"

"Considering the chemicals found in her system, maybe seven weeks."

Jaffray gripped the edge of the desk. "What else have you found out about her that I didn't know?"

Sarg answered. "She had a recent relationship with a thirty-two-year-old by the name of Liam Futino, a violinist. They argued the day she died. He says it was over you."

"Me?" Jaffray lifted his head.

"You were pressuring your niece to drop the music career and go into psychology, sir. And one of her friends said Cailan was afraid of you."

"I never threatened, nor hit, nor so much as yelled at that girl. Why in the world would she be afraid of me? If anything, I thought I was too indulgent in trying to compensate for the death of her parents. And from what you just told me, I was right."

"Cailan had some money coming to her. Was that from her parents, sir?"

"Their estate. The Will outlined that if anything happened to them, their money would be placed in a trust fund for Cailan until she turned twenty-one."

"How much money are we talking here?"

"My brother was good with finances, Agent Sargosian. Better than I. He encouraged me to invest in an Internet startup years ago. He cashed out at the peak, but I was more timid and got out before the stocks went through the roof. He had over a million saved up. All of that was to go to Cailan."

"And now that she's deceased?"

"Is that an accusation, Agent? Are you implying that since the money reverts to me, it's the reason I murdered my own niece?"

"Just considering all the angles, Professor. And we didn't know until right now that the money goes to you."

Red splotches popped out on Jaffray's neck. "And you wondered why I didn't have much faith in law enforcement. Accusing me while the real murderer goes free."

"We're not accusing anyone right now." Sarg pulled out his notebook. "Simply trying to get more information. For instance, the knife used to kill Cailan. And how it was heated before it was used."

Jaffray didn't appear to hear Sarg at first, then turned to him, distracted. "What? Oh, yes, Andrew alerted me to that. Your Chief—Onweller is it?—wanted his expert opinion."

"That's odd, sir. When we asked Professor Gilbow ourselves, he said, and I quote, 'That's more Troy's bailiwick than mine.'"

"If he means religion, yes, there are certain religions that have used heated daggers or knives. Remind me of the type of weapon it was?"

"Double-sided, six inches, possibly longer. We don't know about a hand guard or any markings or patterns."

Jaffray reached to the bookshelves on his left and retrieved a book. Just as Gilbow had done, Jaffray opened it and pointed at a page as he pushed the book toward them on the desk. "Examples of ceremonial double-edged knives. One of the most common is the Athame, used in Wiccan and other Neopagan practices. And as for being heated, certain witchcraft traditions associate the Athame with the element of fire."

"What about Satanism, Troy?"

Jaffray acknowledged Drayco with a flick of his head. "Human sacrifice and knives have been associated with devil worship, but that's all in the past. Human sacrifice in the Western world is rare these days. The Santerians sacrifice animals, but that's it. If anything, I'd say this was staged to look as if it had a religious angle. Like that voodoo doll you showed me."

"Do you have any enemies who'd want revenge? You told the police you weren't aware of any threats to you or Cailan."

"That's what I said, and that's what I meant. Have I failed some students? Yes, but so has every other professor on the planet. They don't go around killing family members of professors to get back at them. They'd kill the professor first."

Drayco pulled out the DA CAPO music note he'd received and indicated the drawing at the bottom. "Does that look familiar?"

Jaffray studied it. "Maybe Cernunnos. A horned deity worshipped by Iron Age Celts across Europe. Until the turn of the first century."

"What does this Cernunnos represent?"

"Depends upon the context and the culture. It's sometimes associated with the Druids."

"Aren't the Druids mostly myth?"

"Our knowledge of them is. The main source of information is from Caesar, and the Romans weren't known for being charitable toward other cultures. The Druids are a lost civilization. Modern interpretations of their religion and culture are whatever people want them to be. This Cernunnos fellow here? He's sometimes regarded as the God of Death or Guardian of the Otherworld. The modern concept of Satan came from him and his horns."

"So this comes back to Satanism and human sacrifice."

"If you have someone running around sacrificing people in imitation of Druids, we have no record they used such practices. Although," Jaffray hesitated. "It's interesting the early Irish Celts believed the gods are fond of music."

Sarg said, "There aren't many people who would know that, are there, sir?" The implication hung in the air, a circling hawk spying its prey in an open field.

The red splotches on Jaffray's neck had spread to his face, now a single crimson mask. "Your killer is out there, gentlemen. I've had pressure from the college, pressure from MPD, and pressure from Campus Security. Now the FBI joins in when all I want is a little peace to grieve."

Drayco studied a shelf filled with religious icons—Shiva, a small replica of the Pietà with Mary and Jesus, the Buddha. After their last encounter with Jaffray, Drayco researched Buddhism. Gautama Siddhārtha, the Supreme Buddha, was reported to say that you will not be punished *for* your anger, you will be punished *by* your anger. Jaffray seemed to have forgotten that.

Jaffray passed a shaking hand over his face. "You didn't tell me what your new music note said, Mr. Drayco."

"It said CODA OR DA CAPO, meaning—"

"The end or a repeat. If it's the latter, that crime will be on your heads, not mine. The only thing I've done wrong is to have loved too many people too much. And now, I would like you to leave. Unless it's to tell me you've arrested someone for the murder of my niece, I don't wish to hear from you further."

Sarg snapped his notebook shut, hopped up, and didn't look at Jaffray as he left through the office doorway. Drayco took more time to follow, pausing to peer through the partially open door in time to see Jaffray pull a bottle out a desk drawer and guzzle down a third of it. Framed within his cluttered office, Jaffray blended in with the piles of yellowing print books behind him.

22

He hadn't come up with a good excuse to get out of Gilbow's party. Flu? Nope. Sprained ankle? He *could* make that happen, but probably shouldn't. Food poisoning? Tempting, but no. It wasn't as bad as being trapped like the rats in the Parkhurst psych lab cages, but close.

Money and power swarmed into the District each workday morning, then swarmed back at night. Many of those commuters lived in neighborhoods like the one Drayco was currently navigating in North Arlington. Areas within D.C.'s borders—the Harbour, Kalorama, Georgetown—could match the price tags of these mini-castles. But on this side of the river, you got a lot more real estate. And the privacy that went with it.

He continued north on Chain Bridge Road toward the Gilbow residence, through a set of gates, up a snaking driveway, to find—another castle, this one crafted from a light gray stone. Large urns ringed the entrance, with buried evergreens shaped into twisting topiaries circling to nowhere.

Topiaries. Drayco hated topiaries. He shared a moment of sympathy with the evergreens until he remembered *they* didn't have to spend a few hours at an ego-fest.

He pulled into a space in the circular drive where a bored attendant motioned him to park. Not much room left, the drive crammed with enough BMWs to start a dealership, and a few smug hybrids in-between.

A familiar voice called his name, and he turned to greet his former partner. Sarg studied Drayco's attire, or lack thereof, specifically one article of clothing. "Still allergic to ties, I see. You think they're going to rise up and strangle you? Attack of the killer ties?"

"They serve no valid purpose. Unless you're trying to impress people with your Italian-silk designer neckwear."

Sarg flipped up his own paisley tie. "Nope. Sears."

"Well, shall we go in and get this over with?"

"God, yes. The only saving grace is Gilbow wants everybody to clear out by ten. Apparently, he's OCD about watching the local news. Probably hopes he'll see himself on TV. He's a regular TV whore."

They had barely set foot in the foyer when Sarg muttered, "Get a load of this place. Self-help books and TV appearances really do pay well."

From the marble floor and columns in the entry to the cascading crystal chandelier above, the home was a better status symbol than a mere Italian-silk tie. Drayco pointed out an innocent-looking cherub statue at the top of the stairs. "The work of Panax Security Systems. Smile, you're on hidden camera."

"Been doing research for your new job?"

"Potential new job. Panax Security is popular with the wealthy in the Metro area. It's a competitor to Topol. And I haven't said yes."

"Security Cameras, locks, bodyguards. So exciting."

"You left out the part about rubbing elbows with celebrities."

"Looks like you can get a head start on that. I've spied an ABC anchorman, a D.C. councilwoman, and a man I swear is one of the Washington Capital's coaches."

Drayco took a measure of the crowd. How many millions in salary dollars did it represent? Washington, D.C., land of extremes. Where the most privileged and powerful in the world shared geography with the most downtrodden and powerless, all within a few miles.

Sarg turned toward him but instead collided with none other than Reed Upperman, munching on a scallop wrapped in bacon. Drayco and Sarg had agreed they'd divide and conquer, so Sarg grabbed Reed by the elbow. "Show me where you got those scallops. I don't suppose you saw any Rumaki?" and he guided Reed away.

The first guest Drayco ran into on his own was a surprise. "Evert Bauer?" The man took a few steps back, which allowed Drayco to get a better look. Someone Brock helped during his FBI tenure, a man who resembled a Scottish deerhound, with a floppy gray mane and a long nose. One of the few who didn't aspire to be alpha, as long as he was in on the hunt.

Bauer stared at him and then his face broke out into a broad grin. "Scott Drayco. You haven't aged much. But ten years ago you were what, twenty-six? Me on the other hand," he ran his hand through his hair, which was fifty percent white. "See what working with students can do?"

"You teach at Parkhurst now?"

"Three years. Political science. Assigning homework is easy. I send the kids out to watch Congress in session." He laughed. "We lose more poly-sci majors that way."

"I can imagine."

Bauer bounced on the balls of his feet. "I'd heard you were riding solo these days, a consultant like your padre. You here on business or pleasure?"

"When I'm lucky, they're one and the same."

"I doubt you'll find much pleasure here. Gilbow's parties have good grub, but they're hardly entertaining. Unless you engage in the sport of gossip."

Drayco studied the crowd, trying to imagine himself at a Washington Capitals game instead. "Who are the home and away teams tonight?"

"The home team would be Gilbow himself. He's a fine teacher and does a lot of good in the community. Book, charities, so forth. It's oil and vinegar with the other faculty. He's the vinegar, by the way. The rest of us skid along behind him."

Bauer gestured to a young man passing by with a tray and exchanged his empty glass for a full glass of grapefruit and vodka. From the slight slur in the man's words, this was Bauer's third or fourth glass rather than his second. The professor smacked his lips. "Where were we?"

"I think you were going to fill me in on the away team."

"Oh, ha ha, yes indeed. Have you got a year or two? Extra-marital affairs, DUIs, who cheated who out of a chairmanship. Even some cocaine. And people think college faculty are dull."

"Any of those affairs involve students?"

"It would make for a juicier tale, eh? But I'm not aware of any. Not that they don't happen."

Drayco eyed a tray of food as it passed by. Was that what Rumaki looked like? "There must have been a lot of chatter over Dr. Jaffray's murdered niece."

"Chattering like magpies. Or maybe starlings, huddled together en masse in their protected little tree."

"How do the faculty members feel toward Dr. Jaffray?"

"Well liked. A lot of that may be the sympathy factor. It's fatal to be related to the man."

Drayco lunged to the left to avoid being sideswiped by another tray-carrying waiter. "Any of those affairs, DUIs or stolen chairmanships connected to him?"

"You'd expect a religion professor to be a paragon of virtue. Clichéd, but he fits the role."

"And his murdered niece?"

"Almost went to one of her recitals once. Wish I had. Didn't have her as a student. The faculty who did said she was an average scholar, polite, quiet. The type who never raised her hand to ask questions."

"Too quiet and polite to have affairs with any faculty?"

Bauer wagged his finger at Drayco. "That's a minefield there, son of Brock. I like my legs and feet intact." He belched, in tune. "Don't look now, the object of your questions approacheth. I think I need a food chaser for this cocktrail, er, cocktail. If you'll excuse me."

Jaffray reached Drayco moments after Bauer left, and Drayco steeled himself for another argument. But after glancing in the other man's direction, Jaffray said, "Bauer must still be sober. Did he start singing yet?"

"Not unless belching counts."

"Another glass or two and he will. He seems fond of Black Sabbath."

Drayco smiled. "The lampshades around here look too big for him."

"Everything associated with Andrew Gilbow is larger than life. I bet you hate having to work with him."

Jaffray was drinking a plain soda, exactly what you'd expect from a paragon of virtue. He raised his glass to look at the effervescent bubbles. "Sometimes I wish I could get drunk like Evert. Would make it easier for me to apologize."

"I'm sorry?"

"No, that's what I'm supposed to say to you. For my attitude when you were in my office earlier today. You meant well."

"Truce, then." He held out a hand, which Jaffray shook. "Evert Bauer was saying he wished he'd made it to one of Cailan's recitals."

"Her recitals always did pack the auditorium."

Jaffray clutched his soda glass in both hands and didn't seem to notice the condensation rivulets flowing down his wrists. "Her death was most inconvenient for Parkhurst. The college took a financial hit from bad investments. They need to nab more rich kids to boost the coffers. Cailan ungratefully put a crimp in their plans with her murder."

"Professor, is it possible the deaths of Cailan's parents weren't accidental? Someone hated your brother or his wife—enough to want to hurt their daughter?"

A booming voice over Drayco's shoulder heralded the arrival of their host, as Gilbow butted in. "I asked him that, didn't I, Troy? Something similar came up in a court case where I was an expert witness. You and I should sit down and compare notes, Drayco. Wouldn't want you wasting your time on ground I've covered."

Drayco looked at Jaffray, not Gilbow. "What was your response to that question, professor?"

"That we don't always know our family as well as we should. But I think it unlikely. My family was perfectly ordinary." Jaffray's pale face looked yellow in the glare of the chandelier. "And now I think I'll try some of your always-delicious buffet, Andrew."

Gilbow waited until Jaffray was out of earshot. "It's amazing he turned out as he did. His brother and sister-in-law may have been ordinary, but his parents were drug addicts. His father died a couple of decades ago. His mother was placed in an institution."

"Is he clean?"

"Troy? I've never seen him drunk or high. I have no idea what he does in the privacy of his own bathroom. Nor is it any of my business as long as it doesn't affect his teaching."

Gilbow pointed at Drayco's empty hands. "Is none of our food or drink offerings to your liking?"

Before Drayco could reply, Gilbow added, "Perhaps the piano in our study over there is more your taste. You'll have to play something later. Anything except those goddamn waltzes Adele loves. Onweller told me your music background. Impressive. Sorry some young punk ended it all. A carjacking, wasn't it? That would make a good lecture sometime—failed dreams intersecting with crime and the psychology of revenge. I should have you in as a guest lecturer."

A woman called Gilbow's name and off he went, ready to perform in front of a new audience. But it was another woman who'd caught Drayco's eye. Tall and willowy, she had on lacy gloves, a throwback to another era. She also wore a maroon dress—stylish enough to show she'd kept her youthful figure, but conservative enough to suit a senator's wife.

After Sarg had informed him of Melanie Bankton and her televangelist performing background, he'd looked her up. He was positive this was the same woman. He took advantage of the departure of a group of people she'd been chatting with to approach her.

"Mrs. Bankton?"

She turned to him with the polite smile of one who'd mastered the art of robotic rituals that are part of a political wife's circuit board. But then she got a big smile on her face. "Don't I know you?"

"My name is Scott Drayco, and I—."

"THE Scott Drayco?"

Drayco was so startled, it took him a moment to recover. "I'm *a* Scott Drayco."

"The pianist?"

"Not professionally these days. But once, yes."

"Should have recognized you sooner. I have all four of your recordings. I remember thinking we'd be hearing a lot from you. Then you vanished."

Drayco had his own programmed reactions, too, when it came to questions about his piano past. For a moment, he almost broke that programming, sensing she'd be someone who'd understand. But he remembered where he was and why he was there. "It's a long story. I understand you played the piano, too?"

She half-smiled, shifting her glass of wine from one gloved hand to the other. "You were an artist, I was a dabbler. The difference between Picasso and a kindergartner's finger painting. But I really did enjoy it. When you're playing, it's so easy to forget anything else exists, isn't it?"

"Another pianist I knew called it 'soul teleportation.'"

She nodded. "I like that. So, what brings you to this … delightful occasion, Scott Drayco?"

"A murder, to be frank."

Mrs. Bankton's eyes widened, but she quickly recovered. "I hope you don't mean you're going to commit murder before the evening's over. Sometimes I feel like that myself at one of these things."

"Trying to solve a murder."

The dawn of realization spread across her face. "You must mean Andy's goddaughter. Kate? No, Kay Lynn? I'm not very good with names. I do recall her recital I attended."

"Cailan. And I don't recall anyone else calling Dr. Gilbow Andy."

She laughed. "I suppose not. He hates it. We've known each other for years. I was a wild child, he was the straight-laced type. I did my best to corrupt him."

She glanced around as if looking for the man in question, and almost lost the grip on her wine glass. When she noticed Drayco looking at her hand, she raised her glass to take a sip of wine. "Despite my current social status, I think parties are as much fun as a colonoscopy."

"You know more people here than I do."

"I saw you talking to Troy earlier. He's such an interesting man, isn't he? Hasn't looked the same since the death of Cailan." She pronounced the name slowly, this time. "I would love to have you over to play the piano for us sometime."

A trio of women in satin, sequins and sapphires swooped in and herded Mrs. Bankton toward the marble fireplace and a group of more satin, sequins and sapphires. She looked over her shoulder and mouthed the words "I'm sorry," as she was led like a lamb to the slaughter.

The string quartet started playing. The round russet circles of the Beatles' "Eleanor Rigby" mingled with dozens of purple, brown and red voices in branching patterns and the pewter spirals of glasses clinking. This was another reason he hated parties, the overwhelming dissonance of competing sounds and their colors.

Making a beeline for the open door leading to the pool and garden, he drank in the cool night air with relief. When he felt a presence behind him, he turned to see Adele Gilbow looking up at the sky. "The light pollution is hideous, but you can still see a few stars."

Drayco followed her gaze and noted Cassiopeia rising over the treetops. One of his favorite constellations, with its W-shaped line of blue-diamond pinpoint stars.

At the sound of a string quartet in the house switching to a waltz, Adele tapped his shoulder and curtsied. "May I have this dance?"

She placed one hand on his shoulder and used the other to clasp his hand, and off they went. "So you do know how to waltz, Mr. Drayco. I was half-afraid I might end up with sore feet from being stepped on."

"Blame my cousin. Used me as a guinea pig when she was learning to dance for her prom."

"They still waltz at proms? Thought it was all jiggling around these days."

"They waltzed at hers. I think the theme had something to do with the Dark Ages."

Adele laughed. "Andrew loves waltzes. The music, I mean. He can't dance to save his life. Don't tell him I said so. He hates to admit weakness as I suspect you've discovered."

Drayco steered Adele away from the pool to stave off a sudden bath for them both. She saw him looking toward the pool, with fountain sprays jetting in from both sides. "I know this looks a bit much, Mr. Drayco. Quite different from my childhood and Bohemian parents, living in a wigwam with my six siblings. One extreme to another."

"Like fire and water?" Drayco indicated the lights and electric tiki torches switching on around the pool.

"In a way. I did keep the vegan part of my upbringing. Couldn't kill a fly, let alone eat one."

"You're not serving insects on that buffet of yours, are you?"

"Insects are a sustainable and readily accessible form of protein. Make good brain food."

Drayco glanced over at the house, thinking he should have looked closer at that buffet. His expression must have given him away because she laughed. "No, we don't have any insects tonight. At least in the food."

The waltz music ended, and she released his hand. "Andrew says I'm easily bored, flitting from one experience to another. But I wouldn't mind if they struck up another waltz right now."

"Ah, but I'm sure your dance card is full."

"Even so, I'd save a slot for you."

Sarg strode out into the pool area with two glasses in hand. Adele hesitated, then waved and blew them a kiss before heading toward some other guests.

Sarg looked askance at Drayco. "Am I breaking up something between you and Mrs. Gilbow?"

"Thankfully, yes."

"Thought we'd compare notes, though pickings are slim. Gary is considered a problem student. Due to his powerful lawyer-father, the college overlooks his behavior. Gilbow doesn't like Reed Upperman all that much. Maybe because Gilbow can't use Reed to further his career."

Sarg paused to take a sip of wine. "Reed doesn't have a lot of friends but hangs out with Gary. Which is odd on its own when you think about it. No one has anything bad to say about Cailan. Maybe no one wants to speak ill of the dead, but I find that hard to believe. This is a catty group of people. And everyone contradicts everyone else."

Sarg handed the second glass over to Drayco, "Guessed you might need one by now."

Neither man had to say anything else. They watched the guests around the pool and commiserated silently between sips of wine while watching Cassiopeia slowly rise.

§ § §

The three of them sat in the car in front of the fence, looking over at the closed gate that appeared to be floating on pillows of fog. Tara was surprised at the lack of lights, but the park was supposed to be closed, right? The darkness hid their car but also made it hard to see what lay on the other side of the fence. Tara shivered from the lack of heat, now that the car engine was turned off. This was a lousy, miserable, horrible idea.

The young man next to her unbuckled his seat belt and opened the door. His words were slurred, and Tara didn't catch the first part. She did hear him say "Because we'll always regret it if we don't. Besides, it's just an old garden with very dangerous ... birds." He laughed.

Tara gripped the wheel of the car. They shouldn't be here. She shouldn't be here. Her father would be furious. Hopefully he wouldn't find out since he had that party at Professor Gilbow's. She looked at her watch. He'd probably be driving back home right now. Part of her wished she was with him there, not here.

As first dates went, this wasn't turning out like she'd hoped. Tara had flirted with John for weeks hoping he'd notice, and he'd finally asked her out. Even if it was to a party where they hooked up with Jessica, who'd also had too much to drink.

When they found out who her father was, John and Jessica had ganged up on Tara to go see where they'd found Cailan's body. Tara offered to drive them tomorrow when Kenilworth was open, but they'd insisted on coming *now* and refused to leave the car until she relented.

John slipped out of the car with Jessica close behind and headed over to the gate. Tara groaned, but followed. They examined the chain-link fence, six feet high, seven if you counted the three lines of barbed wire at the top.

Tara felt more hopeful. "Looks like we can't get in guys, so why don't we come back tomorrow, 'kay?"

John rattled the fence in frustration. "I can climb it. I've done it before on other fences."

The more Tara got to know drunken—and uninhibited—John, the more she thought her interest in him might be fading. Just as she hoped she'd be able to coax him and Jessica back to the car, John yelped with glee.

He'd been walking along the fence, looking it up and down, and now pointed to a small opening underneath one section. Before she had a chance to say "Wait," he'd dropped on his back and shimmied half-way under the fence. When his blue-jeaned legs disappeared, Jessica promptly copied his actions and within seconds, she'd joined him on the other side.

Tara was furious. At them, at herself. At anyone and anything around her which included a fence pole that she kicked. And regretted, when waves of pain traveled up her foot.

She folded her arms and paced with only a slight limp in front of the fence opening. Should she join them or wait until they'd had their fun? When they discovered nothing over there except grass and trees? In the darkness, with the one security light twenty feet away casting shadows, even the grass and trees were hard to see.

Then Jessica screamed. Screamed and screamed nonstop until she started sobbing hysterically.

"Jessica! What's going on? What's the matter?" Tara peered through the spaces between the links in the fence, but still couldn't see anything. She was pretty sure she heard John throwing up.

Tara took a deep breath and ran to the car, where she'd forgotten her cellphone. As she ran, her instincts kicked in. So did her father's constant reminders of taking a "threat assessment."

She looked around the area, realizing how vulnerable she was at that moment. She reached the car and grabbed her phone to call for help. As she did, she noticed a car without its lights driving away slowly. Hadn't the driver heard Jessica's screams?

PART TWO

For by that knowledge of his destiny
He would not live at all but always die.
Enquire not then who shall from bonds be freed,
Who 'tis shall wear a crown and who shall bleed.

—From the song "Seek Not to Know," poem by John Dryden
music by Henry Purcell

23

Late-morning fogs were rare in the capital this time of year. Drayco watched the misty layer of clouds thin, allowing the ghostly shapes to morph into trees and buildings. It was eerily beautiful. He and Sarg stood in front of the apartment complex as they waited for the two MPD officers to exit ahead of them.

Drayco and Sarg trudged up the one dimly lit flight of stairs and onto a landing, where the door to one room was propped open. As in Cailan's apartment seven days ago, Sarg handed Drayco a pair of nitrile gloves. "They've been through most of it. Promised to let us in, if we used these."

This time, it was Shannon's apartment, where an officer in uniform was bent over a stack of papers he flipped through. He looked up with an annoyed expression on his face which quickly relaxed. "Drayco. You slumming with the suits?"

Sarg said in a voice so low only Drayco could hear. "Why is it everyone says *you* are the one doing the slumming?"

Drayco said, "Gonzo, good to see you. Still racking up the bowling trophies?"

"Our league placed first in our division this year. I bowled a 215."

"Detective Bill Gonzalez, meet Agent Mark Sargosian. His daughter is one of the young people who found Shannon Krugh's body."

Gonzalez nodded sympathetically at Sarg. "We've been here all morning. Found these," he handed Drayco some pictures. "Maybe a motive, maybe not."

Drayco and Sarg looked at the photos. They were of professional quality, some in color, some in black-and-white. And all were of Shannon stark naked.

Drayco handed them back, and Gonzalez placed them inside a plastic sleeve, saying, "It's not a big place. Hallway, one bathroom, a small kitchen and this living area. If you can find something we didn't, I owe you a steak dinner."

Sarg studied at the brightly painted walls. "It's very … pink."

Drayco headed to the bedroom as Sarg followed. "You said on the phone Tara was taking this well."

"She's a tough kid. Foolish at times. If she were a few years younger, she'd be grounded for a month. No, make that a year."

"And her schoolwork?"

"Wanted her to take a few days off. She put her foot down so hard, I thought it'd go through the floor all the way to China."

Drayco stepped around a basket of dirty clothes waiting to be washed. "How does Elaine feel?"

"She agrees with Tara. So, after spending most of last night at the police station, Tara still made her eight o'clock psych class. I'm going to meet her in an hour , see how she's doing. She protested, I insisted. You're welcome to come along."

They stepped inside Shannon's former bedroom. More pink walls. The bedspread was red with pink and gray pillows, all recently moved, and the sheets pulled up, exposing the mattresses. Sarg grabbed one of the pillows and checked for zippers as in Cailan's room, then shook his head.

Underneath the pillow lay a small teddy bear, its fur missing in some places. Sarg picked it up and held it in his hand for a moment. Taking a deep breath, he replaced the bear.

Drayco understood. Here they were, pawing through a victim's belongings, caught between clinical detachment and empathetic bonds with inanimate objects. It was hard not to shed pieces of your soul.

He noticed a tool chest that was a smaller version of the one they'd seen Shannon use at the bowling alley and opened it. After spying something at the bottom, he pulled it out and showed it to Sarg. "A lock-picking kit."

"Guess that answers the question of how she got into Cailan's apartment to leave the voodoo messages."

Drayco nodded, then tossed the kit back into the chest with a sigh. "At least we got to see the body in situ this time." Sarg had called Drayco on the way to Kenilworth after first contacting the MPD, and he'd met them there last night. Shannon was found in the same location as Cailan, give or take a few inches. As with Cailan, Shannon was topless.

This time, they could be certain about the weapon, because the knife was still in the body. It was an Athame knife, like the one in Troy Jaffray's book. A box of long-handled matches lay near the victim, with one spent match on the ground. Her shirt, bra and jacket were found in a park trash can.

Drayco picked up a bottle of prescription pills from the nightstand. The label read LITHIUM CARBONATE, 300 mg capsules. It was filled four months ago but was half full. Impossible to tell whether she'd taken any recently. Hopefully, the tox report would provide that detail.

He sat on the edge of the bed, trying to match Shannon's belongings with the girl he'd conversed with for a grand total of thirty minutes. Perhaps the pink was from the manic side, the black from the depressive. The clarinet lying in one corner, manic?

The two cross-stitched pillows, one of a black rose, the other of a dog with red eyes and white horns—depressive? What of the framed pictures of Jefferson Airplane and Janis Joplin in all their psychedelic-colored glory? They hung at skewed angles, indicating the detectives took them off and put them back.

A coffin-shaped incense holder next to the bed held ashes that still smelled of sage. If Cailan's room symbolized the modern template of a co-ed's habitat, Shannon's was that habitat on acid.

Sarg pointed to the posters. "Must be what it looks like inside your head when you listen to an orchestra." Sarg had been pestering him nonstop about the synesthesia.

Drayco ignored him and got up to retrieve a matchbook from a table. He flipped it over, then showed it to Sarg. It was from the Potomac Pleasure Palace. "Guess Happy gave it to her," Sarg said.

"Hmm." Drayco walked to a bookshelf, a misnomer since it didn't hold a single book. He fingered a familiar-looking tiny doll lying there, sans pins. If they'd needed evidence Shannon was behind Cailan's voodoo dolls, they didn't have to look any further. It was identical to the one they'd found hidden in Cailan's pillow.

He picked up the sewing basket next to the doll. It had one spool of thread and a measuring tape inside, with a few pins pushed into the cushioned top. She must have used most of them on Cailan's doll effigies.

Despite being almost empty, the basket was heavy. With his gloved fingers, he pried open the bottom of the basket and pulled out several pieces of paper, all the same size.

Sarg came over to take a look. "Paycheck stubs. From the Potomac Pleasure Palace. And they're made out to Shannon Krugh."

"So, Happy Ilsley did some recruiting on the side. Maybe those icons from the hippie era over there are no coincidence—gifts from Happy or Elvis."

After going through the room some more and not finding anything else of interest, they rejoined Gonzalez in the living room and handed over the check stubs.

"I like my steaks medium rare," Drayco said.

Gonzalez placed the evidence in a new bag. "Naked photos and a strip club. They didn't have college majors like that in my day."

Drayco glanced over at the pile of papers Gonzalez had thumbed through earlier. He slid out a plain white nine-by-twelve envelope peeking out the middle of the stack. A familiar-looking envelope, with computer-printed lettering and no return address. It was already open, so he lifted out the contents. Another sheet of music with an unsingable melody.

Drayco handed it over to Sarg. "Our *Da Capo.*"

A second detective Drayco didn't recognize popped into the hallway to let them know they'd found something in the trunk of Shannon's rusting eighteen-year-old Honda. Drayco and Sarg joined him downstairs and saw what he'd collected—a can of red paint, a brush and another small voodoo doll. "This some kind of cult thing or a joke?" The detective asked.

Drayco couldn't answer that. Perhaps just proof of Shannon's bullying. Or that Shannon was indeed involved in a cult. Or used by someone else who was a member. The one person who could say for certain had just taken Cailan's place at the morgue.

§ § §

Drayco handed Tara the latte he'd ordered for her, as he joined her and Sarg at a corner table at Café Renée. Tara's face had a healthy color, and the hand that accepted the latte was steady. She smiled at him and said "Thank you, Mister Drayco." She appeared to be half-joking, but Falkor was back on the shelf, maybe permanently.

Drayco could tell Sarg was doing his best not to hover, but he was doing a lousy job. Tara patted her father on the arm. "I'm okay, stop worrying. It's Shannon who's not okay. Well, and John and Jessica. That John wouldn't last an hour in the Rangers, Dad."

Tara herself would do fine in the Rangers. She'd asked to be allowed to see Shannon's body when the police arrived, though Sarg had objected at first. The police were thrilled, hoping she could ID the body since the other two students weren't coherent at the time.

To her credit, Tara hadn't flinched or looked the least bit green, something she hadn't gotten from her father. She even had the presence of mind to make the observation, "That's a weird blood pattern, isn't it?"

One of the MPD detectives later told Drayco, "Hope her father's encouraging her to go into law enforcement."

Drayco was secretly hoping she'd pick forensics over pharmaceutical research. But this wasn't the time or place to discuss that. He was just happy she was alive and enjoying a latte like a normal college kid.

Sarg, the model of tact, blurted out, "Don't see what you like about that John guy. You can do better."

"Other than the fact he's gorgeous?"

She smirked as Sarg muttered, "He won't be when I get through with him."

"He's got a sensitive side, Dad. He doesn't show it to most people because they'll make fun of him. He writes poetry. And he brought me a purple rose to our first date because he knows I like them."

Her father just pursed his lips into a scowl.

Tara seemed to have something else on her mind, looking up, then down at her latte every few seconds. She removed the lid and stirred the foam into coffee whirlpools. "I didn't like Shannon. I knew she had a mental illness. Sometimes I think that's an excuse to justify bad behavior, when the bad behavior was there all along. But I am sorry she's dead. Did you know she and Cailan sang a duet once?"

Tara stirred some more. "They had different voice teachers who thought pairing mezzo Cailan and soprano Shannon would be a great idea. They got through it without killing each other." She lifted her head and looked stricken. "I mean—"

Sarg patted her hand. "We know."

Drayco gave her a few moments to take sips from her latte, then guided the focus back on last night's drama. "Tara, do you recall any more details about that vehicle you saw drive away?"

"I've tried. All I remember is what I told everyone. A white SUV without its lights and maybe a stripe on the side. I couldn't tell if there were, like, police lights on top or a logo or anything."

"And you didn't get a glimpse of the driver or any passengers?"

"Wish I had."

The look on Sarg's face told Drayco Tara's father had mixed emotions about that. Her eyewitness description could help track down the driver. But that eyewitness status could also make Tara a target.

Sarg stretched his arm along the backrest of the blue vinyl seat. "The NPS is fit to be tied, thinking it's either the stolen SUV. Or an NPS employee."

Tara watched Drayco sprinkle salt in his coffee and wrinkled her nose. "Guess this means Shannon is off the hook as killer?"

Sarg played with the straw in his iced macchiato. "Actually, the MPD is leaning toward murder-suicide."

Tara looked at Drayco. "Dad said you found more of those music puzzles. And one came to you. Did Shannon do all those? I didn't think she was that good a student. I mean, why would she bother sending one to you if she was just going to kill herself?"

"I'm not convinced she did. One was sent to her, too."

"Well then, who—"

"That's what I aim to find out."

Tara picked at her scalp, a mannerism he thought she'd outgrown. She didn't say anything for a minute, and he was worried he might have misjudged her toughness. Until she blurted out, "Math coins."

Sarg put a hand on her shoulder, a concerned look on his face, but relaxed when Drayco said, "Macintosh. Are you sure it's not a Gala or Red Delicious?" He looked at the lone apple sitting in a basket on the counter near the cash register.

"You can tell by the green and red," she replied. "And it's a fresh Macintosh, too, not a moldy one left over from the dinosaur era."

Sarg groaned, while Tara and Drayco exchanged a conspiratorial smile. They were both well aware Sarg still had a 1990s Mac Classic II in his home office.

Tara asked, "So if it wasn't a murder-suicide, who did it?"

Sarg clenched his teeth. "We don't know yet, but stay as far away from Gary Zabowski as you can."

Tara patted her father's hand. "Threat assessment, right Dad?"

Drayco took a sip of his too-hot coffee and hoped the white SUV had seen as little of Tara as she had seen of it.

24

The same blue sports car Gary Zabowski drove at the bowling alley looked out of place in front of his apartment. Sarg shot it a wistful look. Drayco briefly considered warning Sarg's wife Elaine her husband would be angling to get a sports car now their baby birds had flown the coop. Did Sarg not recall how they used to poke fun at Middle-aged Miata Men?

Gary didn't look surprised to see them, waving them in with a shrug. He took off his shirt, threw it in a pile in the corner and grabbed a different one. But not before Drayco caught a whiff of sweet smoke. Not cloves this time. Marijuana.

"Look, I heard about Shannon, okay? A friend of a friend called. It's all around campus by now. I'm surprised the po-leece haven't dropped by yet."

Sarg pulled out his notebook. "The friend's name, Mr. Zabowski?"

Gary crossed his arms. "All I have to do is sic my father on you and he'll turn you into minced-cop-burgers."

Drayco nodded toward the window. "That your car in front?"

"A Lotus Exige. Cost seventy-five grand. A high school graduation present from my Dad. He gives me anything I want."

Sarg put pen to paper. "Since you have nothing to fear, where were you last night?"

"Reed and I were at a club, knocking back some brewskis."

Sarg flipped back several pages. "At the same Tuchman's bar in Georgetown where the two of you were during Cailan's murder? If I were you, I'd avoid going to that bar with Reed Upperman. Seeing as how people tend to get killed when you do."

Gary went over to his desk and sat in his swivel chair, twirling it around. "We go there a lot. Ask the staff."

The layout of Gary's apartment looked the same as their last visit, maybe dustier and more cluttered. But the pornography book was gone from under the desk. Girls seemed drawn to Gary, so why masturbate to a book when a warm live body was one phone call away? Unless he got off on photos …

Drayco asked, "Did Shannon give you any pictures of her in the nude? Ones she had done professionally?"

"Sure, why not?"

"Who took them?"

Gary cleared his throat. "Uh, she didn't say."

"Did you do anything with them? Sell them, pass them around, send copies on your cellphone?"

Gary looked up at the ceiling for a few moments. "I might have texted some to a friend."

"Did your friend share them?"

"I told him not to. But yeah, he did."

"With how many people?"

"Several. Shannon found out and was furious. She was afraid she'd lose her scholarship."

"Did you do the same with Cailan?"

"Cailan? She wasn't that type. Very into her career. Always thinking ahead about how this thing or that thing would look when she became a big star."

Drayco picked up a matchbook lying on one of the tables and flipped it open. It was from the Potomac Pleasure Palace, with a phone number scrawled on the inside. A number he recognized from Sarg's notes. "How long did you and Happy Ilsley date?"

Gary stopped moving in his chair. "How did you—" and he noticed the matchbook. "Shannon worked there. Could have been hers."

"But it's Happy's phone number written inside, not Shannon's."

"No bigs, we went out a few times." He looked from Drayco to Sarg and back. "You can't tell Elvis. He doesn't know."

Drayco walked over and took a whiff of the shirt Gary had taken off. "Is Elvis your source for marijuana?"

"Elvis and I have this arrangement. He needs money, I need weed."

Drayco frowned, and Gary added, "Reed gave me that look, too. Said to be careful or I'd get in too deep."

"You and Reed seem to be close, despite your age difference."

"What of it? Is there some age-gap rule?"

Drayco perched on the edge of Gary's desk. "Just wondering if he talked about his dissertation project much."

Gary relaxed. "Mixed brain signals or something. Sounds woo woo or whatever."

"Cailan was in that project. Was Shannon?"

Gary laughed. "Shannon was so obsessed with Cailan, she'd do anything to get inside her head. So yeah, she signed up for the project. Needed the money. Told me later she was faking it. She didn't have that syness-whatever but looked it up at the library and learned the lingo so she'd get in."

Drayco didn't have to look at Sarg to guess his pen was poised in mid-air as he digested that bit of news. It wasn't a smoking gun since both victims shared music classes and acquaintances in addition to Reed's project. Still.

The college said they were close to getting HIPAA clearance to release all the names in Reed's project, but hadn't yet. Drayco suspected they were dragging out the process, hoping it wouldn't be necessary. If they'd handed it over sooner, could it have prevented Shannon's death?

That thought made Drayco see red for a moment and not from any sounds he was hearing. "Does Reed know Shannon was faking?"

"I told him last night. Don't owe her anything now."

"But you owe Reed."

"As I said, we're drinking buddies. A good drinking buddy is rarer than a girlfriend. I can get a date," Gary snapped his fingers, "Like that. Women hit on me all the time. Even professor's wives. One of the biology teachers and old man Gilbow's wife."

"Adele Gilbow?" Drayco exchanged a glance with Sarg. Drayco refused to admit it was *schadenfreude.*

"Don't think she really meant it. Some women play that game to keep their husband's interest. Get the male protection-property thing going."

Drayco gave him a small smile. "You'd better watch out. Someone will think you've been paying attention in psych class." He handed the younger man a copy he'd made of the latest music puzzle, the one sent to Drayco. "This look familiar?"

Gary held it up to the light, then reached over to his electronic piano keyboard and tapped out the melody. "This is junk."

"Can you tell which software created it?"

"A dozen or more could've made this."

"What do you use?"

"Sibelius. Top of the line. Steve Reich, Michael Torke, the best composers use it."

"This music puzzle is quite basic. A melodic line with piano accompaniment. No key signature, meter signature, no tempo markings. Cheaper software could have created this, right?"

"Sure. You can download a free trial of some programs." Gary tilted his head as he handed the paper to Drayco. "You into music?"

"You might say that."

"An instrument?"

Drayco nodded at Gary's keyboard. "Piano."

"So why aren't you playing piano instead of cops and robbers? Music not noble enough for you? If it's power trips you're after, you should've become a conductor. They have egos the size of a galaxy."

Sarg didn't move his gaze from his notebook. "So I take it you're aiming to be a conductor."

Gary opened his mouth to retort when Sarg's cellphone rang. Gary smirked as he heard the same basic ringtone as the last time. Sarg indicated to Drayco he was heading outside, leaving Drayco alone with the young man.

Gary stared at Drayco with defiance. "If you tell anybody about the weed or clove cigarettes, I'll say you planted it. Elvis won't rat me out."

"I don't care. About the weed or cigarettes. I do care that a lot of young people with a lot of potential are being wasted. Some dead and others well on their way."

Drayco reached over Gary to the electronic keyboard and played the first few measures of Chopin's "Funeral March."

"You think that's supposed to be funny?" Gary said.

"I think you'd better listen to Reed Upperman. Before you get in too deep."

Gary pulled out a joint hidden behind the computer, lit it and blew smoke in Drayco's direction. "You my priest now?"

"Confession is good for the soul. Let me know when you're ready for a little redemption."

As Drayco left, he heard music streaming through Gary's speakers inside the apartment. Music Drayco couldn't identify that he guessed might be a Gary Zabowski original. Liam Futino was right, Gary did have talent, even if his music set off an explosion of chili-red barbed wire in Drayco's head.

25

Elvis Loomis was one hundred percent sober this time. And a sober Elvis was not a friendly Elvis. He greeted their knock by opening an upstairs window and pouring out a can of beer. They jumped back to avoid getting doused.

Sarg called up to him, "Looks like you drank something that didn't agree with you. Good thing you weren't trying to assault a federal officer. 'Cause that'd get you a couple years at FCI in Petersburg."

A few moments later, Elvis opened the door and headed up the stairs without a word.

Sarg said, "Yay. We're invited to the party," and they followed Elvis up, tiptoeing around cans and papers on the floor of the loft.

Sarg parked himself on the edge of a table across from the wobbly lounger where Elvis took refuge. Drayco went on the prowl as he liked to do, looking for the unexpected. Like the little nugget of gold Sarg had dug up and mentioned on the drive over, "Guess who owns the warehouse loft Elvis and Happy live in? Just guess."

Drayco had earned a perfect score for putting two and two together on the first try. "That wouldn't be Senator Bankton, would it?"

"One of the many owned by him and his wife. Now isn't that special?"

Special wasn't the word for it. Nor did Drayco want to use the word "coincidence," because it was the same as an expletive to him. But it did add greater weight to his room-prowling. Even if he did find something to tie Bankton to the murders, having a senator involved would be several levels of headaches above Drayco's role in this case.

Sarg asked, "Know why we're here, Mr. Loomis?" Sarg didn't pull out the notebook, maintaining eye contact with Elvis.

"Got a call from Gary, so I can guess. I offed Cailan and now Shannon, right? You're going to ask where I was. And I'm going to tell you here, drunk, where else?"

"Ah, yes. Your good friend Gary. The same Gary who's underage and who you're plying with alcohol and drugs. Maybe you're headed to the lockup, after all."

Elvis snorted. "Good luck with that. It's like that river-in-Egypt thing. De-nial. Gary, me, we know nothing'."

"Someone else might rat you out. Your gal pal Happy, for instance."

"You mean Beatrice Meredith Stedner, don't you? That's her real name. Thinks she's going places. Little Beatrice Meredith, from Winchester, Virginia, home of apple butter and Patsy Cline. Used to sing in the church choir and now thinks she's the next big Broadway star. Reckon that's the only thing she and Cailan had in common, a desire for their name up there in lights."

Drayco asked, "Is she here?"

"You just missed her. Beatrice-Happy, that is. She's over at Signature, rehearsing. Got the part she auditioned for. Goodie for her."

Sarg frowned. "I'm more interested in the roles you and Shannon played. She give you some of her prescription meds to sell?"

Elvis huffed. "Now why didn't I think of that? Might could've bought me a new muffler for my elderly bug out there," he nodded toward the parking lot.

"What about your landlord? Are there any unusual roles for him in your little drama?"

"Landlord? Don't know about any of that. Happy's the one who found this place, on some website. She writes the checks."

Drayco bent down in front of a crumbling wooden case filled with compact discs, many still sporting Clayton's CD Cellar stickers. Elvis hadn't lied when he said he had hundreds of them. He scanned the titles and pulled out one recording that was totally unexpected and waved it at Elvis. "Reverend Forest Bankton and his Crusade Cavalcade?"

Elvis cackled. "Found it here when we moved in. Almost squashed it with the ole bug. But it had music, so I gave it a listen. That Bankton joker's wife has some decent stuff on there. You know, those Ave Maria thingies, with Bach and Schubert. Couldn't bring myself to squash Bach."

That was something Drayco and Elvis had in common. Bach was eternal, universal. Playing through his counterpoint fired every neuron in Drayco's brain. "You have any recordings of Cailan or Shannon singing?"

"I wish, oh man, how I wish I did. Don't think Cailan made many. Shannon never shared any of hers."

Sarg growled. "You, Happy, Gary, Shannon. Quite the little play group, weren't you?"

As Sarg waited for Elvis' non-reply, Drayco spied a tall cabinet along a wall, with the door ajar. He opened it farther, and it squeaked, catching the attention of both Elvis and Sarg. Drayco pulled out a folded-up tripod and an expensive camera and held them up before stowing them again. "Perhaps the quartet shares nude pictures?"

"So I do a little photog on the side. It's art, man. All aboveboard. Some of the girls at the strip club want to earn extra moolah. I take their pictures, they use 'em to get gigs."

Sarg said, "I can imagine the type of gigs nude pictures get."

"I don't ask. And I never made out with any of my clients. 'Specially not the young ones. I got a kid of my own, for chrissakes."

Elvis pulled his legs into a pretzel and leaned on them, resting his chin on the backs of his hands. "You gotta wonder where the fathers of those girls are. Dudes must be AWOL. Like me."

He looked at Sarg. "You on good terms with your kid?" and answered his own question. "'Course you are. Me, I figure it's better to be out of sight. Won't turn into my father that way. In case it's genetic."

"You're afraid you'd hit your boy?" Drayco said.

"Hit?" Elvis let out a loud laugh. "Beat to a bloody pulp you mean. That's religion for you. Institutional hatred and pre-joo-diss. My God says I can beat you. Or kill you. And I'll be rewarded in the sweet bye and bye."

He hopped up, retrieved a hand-rolled joint from a drawer, and lit it. "Hypocrites, all of 'em. Like Cailan's uncle, the religion prof. You know he's been to Happy's club? Yeah, Mr. Godman is right there with the others, ogling the bouncing boobs and booty."

So the paragon of virtue had a little demon standing on his shoulder. Drayco didn't have to look at Sarg to know they were thinking along the same lines. This bombshell dredged up a lot of new possibilities—sex, blackmail, vengeance.

The thought of Troy Jaffray as murderer was never appealing to Drayco. Still wasn't. Maybe it was because Troy reminded him of a wise conductor who'd once taken Drayco under his wing. A man who'd said the reason Beethoven was able to continue to write music even as he went deaf was because his soul could still hear.

Elvis took a few puffs on the joint, then several more. He already acted more relaxed. Drayco felt Sarg stiffen next to him and knew by-the-book Sarg would love to see the police nab Elvis on narcotics charges. But friendly Elvis was helpful Elvis.

Drayco asked, "Did Troy Jaffray know Shannon?"

"Saw him talking to her at the club. Guess that means he knows her. Happy didn't like him. Slashed his tires."

Sarg leaned forward. "What kind of knife did she use?"

"Huh?" Elvis was nice and relaxed now and smiling. "I don't know. Yay long," he held his hands six inches apart. "A knifey-knife. The kind that cuts things."

As they let themselves out, Elvis was humming to himself and murmuring the words "prodigal son." And he didn't pour beer on them as they left.

26

The last coral slivers of twilight had faded into a bluish-gray sea of washed-out stars when they caught up with Happy Ilsley at her rehearsal. It was Drayco's first visit to Signature since the move to its new digs—where fine art met dramatic art in an industrial way. Exposed ceiling ducts, curvilinear orange chairs, and giant wall-sized posters greeted them in the lobby. Metal stairway steps glowed with rainbow-colored accent lights.

Once in the main performance space, they watched Happy and her fellow cast-mates in action. Happy, the extrovert, had snagged the lead in the musical. Casting against type, it was a role that called for her to be vulnerable and afraid. She was convincing. Her rich voice was well-controlled, darker than Cailan's, with a touch of Patti Lupone. It had amber rectangles with crinkly crimson edges.

They'd timed their visit to coincide with the rehearsal wrapping up. Sarg and Drayco corralled Happy into one of the seats at the back of the hall with her face still flushed from the physical exertion of blocking out steps and stage movements.

Sarg positioned himself so that he stood in the row to her right, and Drayco sat beside her to her left. It was an old trick of theirs, assuming counter-angles so they could examine an individual's body movement for signs of lying or stress. They naturally slipped into that pattern.

Drayco asked, "I understand you've been here all day, rehearsing?"

"Isn't this place amazing? I'm having so much fun, it should be a crime."

He blinked at her choice of wording. "Have you chatted with Elvis lately?"

"Lord no, I need to focus. I even turned off my cellphone."

He nodded. "I didn't think you'd heard the news."

"News?"

"Late last night, Shannon's body was found in Kenilworth Gardens. She'd been murdered, like Cailan."

Her reaction took Drayco by surprise. The glow on her face vanished, and she sat very still. Then she turned to him and started shaking him, sobbing so hard she couldn't catch her breath. Slowly, she gathered her composure and wiped the tear streaks off her face with the sleeve of her navy leotard.

"I'm sorry, Happy. But we need to know if you have any idea of who might have done this or why."

She answered through her sniffles. "It's gotta be random. Shannon was a nobody, like me. One of the invisibles. That's why we got along so well." She managed a small smile. "I had four older brothers growing up, and I always wanted a little sister. Shannon was like that sister."

Sarg asked, "A little sister you lured into strip club life, Miss Ilsley?"

Happy glared at him. "Look, she needed the money. Badly. Working two jobs, doing the school thing full time. I made sure no one touched her. It's not that kind of club. No full frontals, pasties required, no groping and no giving out phone numbers. Just a bunch of lonely men getting away from their nagging wives for an hour. Maybe remember when life was full of promise and dreams."

Drayco tried to stretch out his legs in the cramped seat, remembering why he didn't go to a lot of plays. "Yet the Potomac Pleasure Palace does encourage that innocent-young-girl vibe. No staff over thirty and waitresses in schoolgirl uniforms."

Sarg looked askance at Drayco, but it was Happy who asked, "You been there?"

Drayco gave up sitting in the chair and stood, balancing himself on the back of a seat in front of her. "I called them up yesterday and asked."

Happy nodded. "I would have remembered a customer like you."

She gave a quick, wild glance around the hall and lowered her voice. "Don't tell them about the stripper part, please? Bad enough my mother's disappointed in me. It broke her heart when she found out. If I end up on Broadway, I'm going to get her a front-row ticket."

Drayco said, "What does Elvis think?"

"He's not thrilled about this," she waved her hand around. "But it's time he grew up and stopped leeching off me and everyone else. He's long outgrown that hippie act. Makes it way too easy for him to avoid responsibility."

"Like being a father."

"Like being a father who's not like *his* father."

"The same father who turned him against religion and made him think it's bunk. Do you agree with him?"

She'd stopped sniffling, but her nose was running, so Drayco pulled out a handkerchief and handed it to her. He'd picked up the habit of carrying them around from his piano days, to wipe his hands. Or in one case, to wipe blood off the keys after a glissando mishap.

"Thank you," she smiled up at him. "I don't hate religion. I hate hypocrites."

"Troy Jaffray, for example?"

She clutched the handkerchief. "I admit it—I slashed his tires, all four of them. Mr. God Professor waltzing in paying his money to ogle the naked girls." She started singing, "Tits and ass" from *A Chorus Line*, "Where the cupboard once was bare. Now you knock, and someone's there."

Sarg didn't look impressed. "Pretty good reason for bumping off Cailan Jaffray, Miss Ilsley. You admitted you were jealous of her. Maybe jealous of Elvis' obsession with her, too? And you hated her uncle enough to slash his tires. A triple revenge whammy."

She looked at him frostily. "I don't kill. Tires, maybe. Not animals or people."

"Okay, then, maybe you can show us the knife you used to kill those tires."

She shook her head. "I threw it away. And yes, I destroyed evidence. But only evidence I slashed Jaffray's tires. Nothing more."

Drayco asked, "Elvis said he was drunk at home when both Shannon and Cailan were murdered. Can you verify that?"

She hesitated. "I was here last night until eleven. Went out with a couple of other girls from the cast afterward. Don't know where Elvis was."

"And when Cailan was killed?"

When she didn't reply, he prompted, "Did Elvis tell you to say you were with him at home?"

"I don't remember. Maybe. I wasn't working at the club that night."

They were both lying about alibis, but that didn't mean it was to cover up murder. And what about Troy Jaffray, what was his excuse? Could Drayco have been so wrong about the man? "Happy, was Shannon having an affair with Professor Jaffray?"

"Oh dear Lord, I hope not. She never said anything."

"Elvis said he saw Shannon and Troy chatting at the club."

"We all chat with customers, it's part of the deal. Look, I was protective toward Shannon. Watched how guys treated her. Made sure she didn't get harassed."

Happy took a deep breath, then popped out of her chair. "Look, I have a lot of things I need to do."

She turned to head out the door, still clutching the handkerchief. Then she whirled around and patted Drayco's shirt, pasting a smile on her face. "Sorry about the meltdown. If you ever want to return the favor and pound me, you've got my number." And she left, with the same heel-toe catwalk gait he'd noticed before.

Back in the theater lobby, Sarg scanned his notes before putting them away. "Let's say we're talking two killers. If Jaffray offed Shannon, he copied the other guy's MO. Unless he stabbed Cailan, too. I mean, he is an expert on ritualistic killing and those Athame knives."

Drayco was about to reply when a different woman's voice sounded behind them, "Fancy running into you here." They both turned to see Adele Gilbow, who must be taking a break from bungee jumping and skydiving. "Agent Sargosian and Dr. Drayco on the case of Shannon Krugh's murder, I assume?"

The look Sarg shot Drayco spoke volumes. Just as Gary had said, the crime scene was barely cleared and yet most of the campus knew. The texting and Twitter hotline strikes again.

As if reading their minds, she added, "Jerry Onweller called Andrew this morning and informed him of the tragedy. My first thought was serial killer, but Jer said something about a murder-suicide? I think he wanted Andrew's analysis on Shannon's state of mind. Since he had her in class."

She sighed. "In fact, there's been a flurry of calls. Caleb Thackeray phoned Andrew and Jerry. He was furious."

Sarg said, "I'll bet."

"Poor Shannon. I didn't know her, but Cailan talked about her some."

Sarg asked, "What specifically?"

"As I mentioned earlier, their music rivalry. And they had a falling out over some boy. Gary, I believe? Cailan was afraid of Shannon." Adele swung her purse around in front of her. "I have to confess, I didn't take her fears seriously. And now, it's too late. For both of them."

She opened her purse and pulled out a photo. It was identical to ones they'd found hidden in Cailan's pillow, with the warning painted in red on Cailan's mirror. "Cailan gave me this. I know you're going to judge me for it, but I thought she'd done it herself to get attention. When I showed it to Andrew this morning, he said I should give it to you."

Sarg took the photo. "You must be stalking us."

"Jerry Onweller said you'd be here. I thought I could kill two birds with one stone. I'm friends with one of the theater's board members, and we're headed out for cocktails and some fundraising battle plans."

The friend in question waved at Adele. The woman was clad in gray pants, gray shoes, gray sweater and gray hat. Didn't get much more neutral than that, the Switzerland of outfits. Adele and her friend headed outside.

Sarg had mini-thunderclouds gathering across his face. "Since when does Onweller have the authority to deputize a psych buddy of his into the FBI? 'Cause it sure looks like he's going behind our backs."

Drayco was less surprised at Onweller's behavior than Sarg was, having the benefit of time and distance. He was instead obsessing over what Adele Gilbow said about not taking Cailan's fears seriously. It made him think of the "Da Capo" puzzle folded in his wallet.

Had it warned them of Shannon's death? Here he'd been, angry at Parkhurst for not turning over the list of students in Reed's project, wondering if doing so earlier would have prevented the second tragedy. Was he just as guilty? Then again, sometimes taking a threat seriously may prevent the surprise of the tragedy, but not its execution.

27

The small makeshift shrine inside a display case at the Parkhurst Music School held a smiling photo of Cailan with a copy of the press release announcing her Met regional award. Tall glass candles decorated with musical notes, crosses, and the Parkhurst logo stood like spires among red carnation bouquets and stuffed animals.

The case had a new addition since the last time Drayco was here, a photo of Shannon. Maybe she hadn't been popular at the music school in life. But in death, they hadn't forgotten her.

Sarg was meeting Drayco on campus in a couple of hours, before noon. This gave Drayco a chance to talk one-on-one with Cailan and Shannon's fellow music students. Some were reluctant to open up at first. But when he approached it by "talking shop," one musician to another, the walls fell, and all of a sudden they were full of opinions and theories.

Gary's name popped up, as did mentions of "that creepy guy," whose description matched Elvis. No one knew of any cults. Most were ready to believe it was murder-suicide.

The one boy who'd been the most helpful seemed to be indifferent to the whole issue at first, making *Phantom of the Opera* jokes. But he turned serious when he recounted a brief conversation with Cailan two days before she was killed. "Said she was worried. Maybe a little scared. After getting these weird notes in the mail."

"With music on them?"

"She didn't give details. Just said she'd figured out who was sending them, and it wasn't who she'd thought."

Wasn't who she thought? This was the first time anyone said Cailan knew the sender's identity. He asked the young man, "Did she give a name?"

The young man shook his head, so Drayco asked, "When was this?"

He replied, "That's what freaked me out. It was the day she died. I kept quiet about it because … My family doesn't like publicity, you know?"

Doesn't like publicity? After learning the young man's name from other students, Drayco did a little cellphone research on the boy's father. Wall Street investment banker. Right. He'd have to let Sarg handle that one.

The other tales—of rampant cheating, who was addicted to prescription drugs, which students were most likely to show up in class drunk—made Drayco depressed. These kids had everything those a few miles east of the Anacostia River lacked, wealth, privilege, opportunity. And the main difference seemed to be they could afford lawyers to keep them out of jail.

On an impulse, he ducked into the recital hall, which was empty and dark, except for a small spotlight on stage. The Bösendorfer called to him, and who was he to ignore such a command? He slid onto the bench, pushed up his sleeves, and launched into a Bach prelude and fugue. His hand didn't cramp this time, another frustration of his—it was unpredictable.

Since his arm was in unusually good shape and not wanting to waste the deep timbres of the instrument's rich bass end, he switched to Debussy's *La cathédrale engloutie*. He still loved the warm, complex sound of his Steinway, but the dark, bell-like timbre to this Bösendorfer lighted up his brain like a field of black and yellow tulips in the middle of a thunderstorm.

He heard footsteps on the stage and stopped playing as a woman joined him and leaned on the edge of the piano. She smiled. "It's lovely to see you again so soon. Here I was thinking it was going to be an ordinary day."

"Is there such a thing for you, Adele? Your husband says you're the thrill-seeking type."

"What else is an English major good for? Mostly I meet people for brunch or tea. Whenever or wherever there's money to be shaken from wallets and purses. Today, I'm trying to help set up a music scholarship in memory of Cailan. Is that why you're here?"

"When Agent Sargosian joins me, we're going to visit Reed Upperman."

"Reed's such a dear young man. Andrew and I are both fond of him."

Maybe *she* was, but Sarg's intel at the party indicated Gilbow himself was not. "Has Reed talked about his dissertation project?"

"In passing. Andrew doesn't like to discuss work at home, but Reed's project sounds fascinating. Being able to experience so many senses all at once."

She walked around the crook of the piano and sat beside him on the bench. "Andrew told me about the brutal end to your piano playing. You're still exquisitely good. Thinking of starting a second career?"

Second? He'd moved on to a third and might soon be switching to a fourth. "I can't practice the long hours it takes to be a concert pianist."

Adele looked at his left arm, exposed by the sweater pushed above his elbows, and then reached over to trace the uneven pink scars trailing down his right forearm into his wrist and hand. Scars not all that different from the ones he'd seen on Shannon, except his had the chance to heal.

Adele said, "What a pity. We need more musicians in this world, not fewer."

Drayco moved his arm to his lap and turned the conversation back to Reed and his project. "Cailan was one of Reed's synesthesia students. Surely she must have mentioned him?"

Adele continued to stare at his scars. "It's amazing such sensitive hands could kill. I notice you don't carry a gun. I'm glad. I hate guns."

She switched her attention to his face. "Cailan didn't discuss school as much as you'd think. I suspect she was worried it would get back to Andrew. Or her uncle. We mostly talked girl stuff."

"Did she mention her disagreement with Troy?"

"He was a doting uncle, if a stodgy one. I never can get him to come bungee jumping with me. If there were a contest for stodgiest professor, it would be a tie between Andrew and Troy. Cailan just wanted to sing. It wasn't as if she wanted to be a prostitute. Or join the army and be sent to one of those unpronounceable countries."

"Was she afraid of him? Of her uncle?"

"He had a temper, but who doesn't? Me, Andrew, we all do." She fingered his scars again. "You're not very fond of my husband, are you? Every time I mention his name, you look cross."

"He's well respected in his field."

She laughed. "Oh dear, you really do dislike him. He thinks highly of you."

Drayco stared at her, stunned. "He hides it well."

"Oh, he can bluster and babble with the best of them. Jerry Onweller's told him a lot about you."

Drayco shook his head. "Not sure Onweller knows what to make of me."

"Ah, to see ourselves as others see us. The poet Robert Burns was right."

Bobby Burns meant well. But if people really could see themselves from the viewpoint of others, it would mean more money for psychoanalysts. And sales of Gilbow's self-help books.

Right now, Drayco tried to see Adele through the eyes of a twenty-year-old boy. "I chatted with Gary Zabowski, Cailan's ex. To be honest, he said you came on to him."

"It's possible. I meet a lot of Andrew's students. And I am an incorrigible flirt."

As if to prove the point, she reached over and held his hand, but seemed more intent on studying his fingers. "Seems like a big jump from pianist to FBI. Or crime consultant."

"Not as much as you think. A lot of analysis in both."

She smiled at him, released his hand and slid off the bench. "You're an unusual man, Scott Drayco. And now, I'd best head to my appointment before I forget what I came for."

Once she'd left, he ran his index finger silently along the black keys, then launched into the Debussy, picking up where he'd left off. His music career, the FBI days—his past kept stalking him like a bounty hunter.

He reluctantly ended the Debussy and bid farewell to the Bösendorfer to go meet Sarg. The college had gotten a release from HIPAA regulations, and Sarg and Drayco were to get the names of participants in Reed Onweller's project. Two days too late to help Shannon. Maybe not too late to prevent another murder.

28

Reed wasn't alone. He and Andrew Gilbow were in the middle of an intense discussion but stopped talking when Drayco and Sarg walked into the lab. Gilbow greeted them with a full-blown scowl. "I knew you'd turn up here sooner or later. Another tragic death. And the death of a dissertation."

Reed turned his back on Gilbow and limped over to take a seat, balling his fists in his lap. "I'm sorry about Shannon's death. Genuinely sorry."

He took a deep breath and looked at Drayco. "But I also found out Shannon Krugh was faking synesthesia the other day. Guess you know all about that."

When Drayco nodded, Reed confronted Gilbow. "This doesn't have to mean my project is through. I still have eight participants."

Gilbow thrust his hands in his pants pockets. "It won't be that easy. Graduating at the end of the year looks doubtful."

Sarg had no sooner opened his mouth to speak, when Gilbow handed him a piece of paper, adding, "Here's the list of the students in Reed's project, Agent Sargosian. Not that it matters."

Sarg looked at the list. "And why is that, sir?"

"It's highly unlikely it had anything to do with the deaths of the two girls. Especially since Shannon wasn't a true synesthete."

"But no one knew she was faking. The link could still be there."

The caution-flag wrinkles on Gilbow's brow unfurled slowly. "According to Reed here, Gary Zabowski knew. But even though beer-stewed college kids aren't the model of discretion, Agent, you have a point."

Drayco read the list after Sarg handed it over, not recognizing any of the other names. "So you believe Gary is our murderer?"

"I don't know the young man in question personally. He fits some of the serial killer profile. In his early twenties, higher-than-average intelligence."

Drayco folded the list and put it in his pocket. "I'm not as enamored of blueprint profiles as you are."

"Well then, Dr. Drayco, what is your expert opinion on our killer? Or killers, if a copycat is involved."

Drayco would take inordinate satisfaction if he were able to prove Gilbow wrong, but his own bag of theories was half-empty. "I think I'd like Reed to tell us more about Shannon's behavior during recent lab sessions."

Reed hesitated until Gilbow nodded at him. "You understand I'm not speaking on behalf of the college or Professor Gilbow. Just my own observations. I was already worried about her participation in the project before I knew she was a fraud. The bipolar probably should have disqualified her."

"Her unpredictability?"

"Among other things."

Drayco perked up. "Other things?"

Reed nodded. "I caught her trying to erase Cailan's data in the computer."

Sarg asked, "You believe her capable of murdering Cailan, then?"

"Capable of suicide, yes. Murder, no."

Reed reached to turn off his computer monitor, and his hand bumped into a switch, sending a sudden loud noise through the speakers hanging on the wall. Drayco winced, but the others were unaffected. When Reed quickly turned the switch off, Drayco said, "That is an amazingly ugly sound."

Reed's face lit up. "Really? How so?"

"Brownish-green spikes that feel like hot tar on bare feet." Reed grabbed a pencil and jotted something down.

Gilbow peered at a wall clock. "I'd be happy to talk more with you gentlemen whenever my schedule allows. Right now, I have a class on the first floor. If you'll excuse me …"

Reed barely looked up from his notation as Gilbow left. "You feel textures with sounds, too, Drayco? That's three senses involved at the same time. Amazing. I do wish I had you in my project." He put his pencil down and sighed. "Gilbow's right. It may not matter."

Sarg moved a stool next to the table to sit. "Your dissertation really under the gun?"

"I got a leave of absence from U Penn to finish my degree. Taking an additional semester is a non-starter."

The painful noise from Reed's machine still rang in Drayco's ears. He tried to ignore it. "Surely something can be worked out."

Reed rubbed his forehead. "Did you know I only get to see my kids a couple times a month? Makes me wonder if it's all worth it."

Sarg pulled out his notebook and laid it on the table but didn't open it. "Mr. Upperman, would I be right in saying this dissertation is your last chance at U Penn? If you don't get it, you won't be given tenure?"

Reed pulled out a cloth and removed his glasses to clean them. "It's hard to get tenure without a PhD, sure."

Sarg tapped the notebook. "We contacted your school. There were complaints you were getting too graphic in your Abnormal Psych class, using personal sexual references. And you also wanted to add midnight classes?"

"Political theater and sour grapes, that's all. The Dean and I don't see eye to eye on a lot of things. You can't teach Abnormal Psych without the 'abnormal' part. As for the midnight classes, that's not a new idea. Even community colleges have added them."

Reed smiled mockingly at Sarg. "Unless you suspect I'm a vampire?"

"No sir, I can see your reflection in that mirror over there," Sarg nodded his head at the wall.

Reed got up and limped over to a coffee machine in the corner. The coffee, the color of burned wood, smelled just as appetizing. "If you want to know my sad story, Agent Sargosian, you could just ask. My marriage is on the rocks. So is my career. And the funny thing is, I'm not sure I care."

He gulped down several sips of hot coffee, without so much as a cringe. "You know any police psychologist openings?"

Sarg said, "If you're referring to a profiler, there's no such position at the FBI."

"I mean forensic psychologist. Psychometrics, PTSD. Criminal case consultations. Fascinating stuff."

Drayco immediately remembered Dr. Simms, the FBI psychologist he'd been asked to see prior to leaving the Bureau. It hadn't struck Drayco until now, but Simms resembled an older version of Reed, minus the glasses. Reed could squeak by under the maximum age limit to qualify as an FBI agent.

Reed limped to his chair, and for a moment, his leg buckled under him, making him spill some coffee on the floor. Drayco reached him in two long steps to steady him, rescuing the coffee before it could cause burns.

Reed slipped into his seat and massaged his leg. "Legg-Calve-Perthes disease. Doesn't bother me most of the time."

The chart of synesthesia subjects made a window frame behind Reed's head. A thick red line now covered up a row Drayco assumed was Shannon's, X'ing her out of the project. Another trace of her existence fading away.

Soon, her Facebook page would be deleted, her belongings packed up and returned to her family. One seven-billionth of the planet's voices silenced forever. Few would notice or care about the lane mechanic who wanted to be a singer.

Reed's voice had dark blue edges it hadn't before. "Well, gentlemen. If I have any hope of avoiding my PhD meltdown, guess I need to get back to work."

As Drayco and Sarg headed down the hall, Sarg asked, "You're in a mood. Gilbow cooties?"

Drayco stopped in front of the stairs. "Psychology, religion, music. Supposedly, three of the four pillars that enlighten the human condition. We're up to our necks in all three, but they're hardly enlightening. If we run across a poet, we'll have a complete set."

"Would it help if I quoted one of my famous limericks?" Sarg held open the stairwell door.

"Over a beer later. Beer and limericks, the real solution to all of life's problems. Can religion come close to that?"

"You may be right, but don't let Elaine hear you."

Sarg's joking made Drayco less gloomy, but it didn't explain his mood in the first place. He hurried to beat Sarg down the stairs rather than pull a Gilbow and psychoanalyze himself.

29

They walked from the psych lab to the humanities building, as Drayco cataloged every college landmark to add to his mental map. Mostly, he watched the students. The Parkhurst vibe wasn't like UMD or other schools in the Metro region—Georgetown, GWU, Catholic U.

It felt more like Stepford U, with students who were stand-ins for the real thing, tolerating their four-year sentence as a mere formality. The stamp of legitimacy to access the parental bank, now and in the future.

Sarg's pocket buzzed, and Drayco watched with fascination as Sarg pulled out the cellphone and typed furiously with both thumbs. When he finished, he pocketed the phone. "Tara. Can't keep in touch with either of my kids, otherwise. They don't know what a letter is, they don't e-mail and making a phone call is so twentieth century. It's all about texting."

"You're good, for a geezer."

"Careful, junior. You'll be there soon."

On those mornings Drayco hadn't gotten much sleep, he felt he was already in full-fledged geezerdom. "Tara doing okay?"

"Seems to be. Says she is. Doesn't mean I still don't wanna send her to her grandparents in North Dakota until this thing is settled."

Troy Jaffray's office was familiar to Drayco now, but the man sitting in his chair was barely recognizable. Jaffray's jacket was as rumpled as if he'd slept in it. His hair had a greasy shine, and the circles under his eyes were dark craters on a barren moonscape.

He seemed to sense who they were without looking up. "I'm surprised you want to talk to me. None of the others does."

"The others, sir?" Sarg took a seat, while Drayco remained standing.

"After Cailan's death, the police kept me informed on everything. They were sympathetic, helpful. Now I'm persona non grata."

Sarg placed his hands on the edge of the desk. "Sir, you want to tell us why you didn't mention your visits to the Potomac Pleasure Palace? Where Shannon worked?"

Jaffray lifted his head. "Shannon?"

"The same girl who bullied, and possibly killed, your niece. Shannon Krugh, the girl who was found dead night before last at Kenilworth, like Cailan."

Jaffray shook his head. "The police asked me about the Krugh girl. I didn't know about the bullying until after Cailan's death. And I don't remember seeing Shannon before."

"Isn't that a bit coincidental, sir? You hid the fact you went to a strip club where this girl worked, but don't remember her. Even though you were seen talking to her, and her best friend slashed your tires?"

The professor opened his mouth, then snapped it shut. They waited for the better part of a minute until he replied. "That dancer— Happy, I think was her name. She accused me of being a hypocrite. She attacked my tires in a fit of pique. But I had no idea the other girl worked there. Perhaps I would recognize her if I saw a picture."

Sarg pulled one out of his pocket and held it up. Jaffray squinted at it and sank into his chair. "She looks familiar. I didn't know her name at the club."

"Did you date any of the dancers, sir?"

Jaffray's lips tightened into a straight line. "Is this why the police won't talk to me except to ask my whereabouts? I'm a suspect in this girl's death?"

"We're not ruling out possibilities right now, sir."

"Why in the name of all that's good and true would I do such a thing?"

"Revenge for her behavior toward Cailan. Or when she spurned your advances."

"I didn't date any of those women, Agent Sargosian. Nor was I interested in so doing. It's been a long time since my wife died and I … I wanted a little fantasy of being with a woman again."

Drayco uncrossed his feet where he'd been leaning against a wall which caught Jaffray's attention. He stared at Drayco for a moment. "The man with the Buddha eyes. Do you still feel wise, Mr. Drayco? Because I'm finding that I don't."

"I believe the Buddha said, 'Chaos is inherent in all compounded things. Strive on with diligence.'"

Jaffray smiled briefly. "The Buddha also said, 'Just as a candle can't burn without fire, men can't live without a spiritual life.' And I'm finding it hard to strive or to burn."

Drayco stepped over a pile of books and reached up to one of the rare empty slots on the office bookshelves. "The book with examples of ceremonial double-edged knives. It's missing."

Jaffray pursed his lips. "That's the least of my worries at the moment."

"Troy, did the police tell you how Shannon Krugh's body was found and their theory?"

Recognition dawned on the man's face. "There was a knife again, wasn't there?"

"The police haven't traced its origins yet, but it was an Athame knife."

"Ceremonial. Yes, that would make sense. I recall the police saying something about suicide." He raised an eyebrow. "But if it's suicide, why am I a suspect?"

Drayco replied, "I can't speak on behalf of the MPD or FBI. But I don't buy the suicide angle."

Sarg piped up, a note of irritation in his voice. "It's a solid theory."

Drayco glanced sideways at the dark shadows that came out of nowhere to dance across Sarg's face. Shadows that connected with the drum-tight upward pull of Sarg's shoulders. Drayco had a good idea why Sarg was upset, but the impending blow-up would have to wait.

Jaffray propped his elbows on the desk. "In the interest of full disclosure, I spoke with that young man. Liam Futino. He called, wanting to talk about Cailan. He loved her deeply, and for that I am grateful. Even if she didn't appreciate it."

Drayco said, "Did he mention Shannon at all?"

"My memory isn't the best right now. Stress does that to the mind."

Jaffray's bloodshot sclera and the slight tremor in his hands made him look a decade older since Drayco last saw him. Jaffray was correct, stress can induce those symptoms.

But a yellowish tinge to his skin hinted at something else. It was the same sickly pallor he'd seen on Jaffray at Gilbow's party, but the significance hadn't registered then. Drayco asked, "Are you referring to stress from your niece's death or something else?"

Jaffray traced his finger up and down the spine of a book in front of him on the desk. "Statistics are funny things. For instance, even when surgery is possible, only fifteen percent of people with pancreatic cancer live five years. That's what my doctors tell me."

Troy Jaffray, professor of religion, had out-Job'd the biblical Job. "How long have you known, Professor?"

"Two weeks. The doctors want to shoot both barrels at me, surgery and chemo. For what, I ask? Pancreatic cancer is the same as a death sentence. You delay it for a few years, but you still die."

Drayco didn't know what to say to that. He had the sudden urge to go tackle some Beethoven sonatas.

30

The Basement jazz club in Georgetown lived up to its name. Hidden away on Cady's Alley, far from the trendy restaurants and boutiques of M Street, it lay beneath a building left over from the industrial water-district days.

Drayco stopped short at the top of the stairs that led to the entrance. Taking separate cars only postponed the inevitable confrontation. "Okay, out with it. What's rattled your cage?"

Sarg thrust his hands in his pockets and paced back and forth. "You. And this insane quest. It's like one of those infinity strips, folding back into itself. We haven't found anything that proves this wasn't a murder-suicide. In fact, all arrows point in that direction. As much as I hate to admit it, and I really, really do hate to admit it, the Metropolitan Police and the college are probably right."

"Even the dead are innocent until proven guilty. Those puzzles—"

"Shannon could have done those puzzles. Maybe Gary helped her, thinking it was all one big joke."

Drayco half-expected him to add, "And I didn't need to bring you in on this." He looked up at the sky, but the vast expanse of infinite universe was no match for light glare from the District. "Why did you ask my help, Sarg? The music background angle was an excuse, wasn't it?"

Sarg stopped pacing. "When I said it hadn't been the same since you left, I meant it in more ways than one. I second-guess myself all the time. Worse, then I ask myself what you would have done."

"You're second-guessing your decision to bring me on board?"

"Yes. Maybe. I don't know." Sarg headed toward the entrance. "Ah hell, let's get this over with."

With the tension hanging in the air like an unresolved tritone, Drayco led the way as they descended into the bowels of the club. It was deep enough to lie below the level of the C&O Canal that lay just beyond. The walls were quarried rock, the same blue granite and fieldstone on the District's oldest structure, the Old Stone House up the road.

Except for two men at the bar putting away shots of Jim Beam, Liam Futino was the only person in sight, warming up his violin on the micro-stage. As they approached, he stopped playing. He twirled the bow in his hand at his side, then planted both bow and violin on the piano.

Sarg motioned to a table in the corner, complete with blue tablecloth and oil lamp. Liam trailed them to the corner and tripped as he stumbled into one of the seats. He looked as bad as Troy Jaffray, minus the yellow pallor.

Sarg had told Drayco he wanted to beat the afternoon gridlock on I-95 down to Fredericksburg and didn't waste any time. "Troy Jaffray said you called him to talk about Cailan. Is that true, sir?"

Liam nodded, picking at his one gold stud earring. "I thought he of all people would know what I was going through."

The barking tone Sarg used earlier in the day with Gilbow and Reed was becoming more of a growl. "And what are you going through, Mr. Futino? Guilt? Remorse? Fear of getting caught?"

Liam shrugged off Sarg's accusations. "I don't date a lot. Too much like war. Little battles and strategies. Winners and losers. When I met Cailan, none of that mattered because I knew—" His voice trailed off, and he swallowed twice. "I knew she was the one."

The pianist in Drayco was interested in hands, which gave away a lot more than people realized. Liam rubbed his hands together, the fingers on his callused left hand interlaced with the fingers on his other. He wasn't fidgeting or covering, the hand versions of lying.

When he looked into Drayco's eyes, he was on the verge of tears. "You could tell how talented she was, Mr. Drayco. I saw it when you listened to that recording. I was connected to her in a way I never felt with anyone else."

Drayco motioned for a waitress and had her bring over a glass of water which Liam sipped while draining his emotions. "She got pregnant. She didn't tell me right away, but did eventually. Said she was about two months along."

Sarg said, "So you told her to get an abortion, is that right?"

"She asked for some money to buy a nice dress for an upcoming recital. I handed it over, gladly. Only afterward did she tell me she'd used the money for an abortion." Liam rubbed his hand over his eyes. "Maybe she guessed I'd have wanted her to keep the child. Hell, I would have even raised it on my own, if I had to."

A man with a large instrument case slung over his shoulder walked into the club, looked at Liam, and frowned. The man opened the case, pulled out a sax and started tuning. The amorphous teal paramecia it emitted contrasted with the smudged, brass exterior of the instrument itself.

Drayco said, "Was that why you argued with Cailan the night she was murdered?"

Liam grimaced. "She said we were through. For good. That I was too old for her. Made me feel like some dirty pervert."

Sarg uttered a "Huh," and added, "Guess you took that hard. Hard enough to kill her?"

"I could never hurt Cailan." Liam leaned back. "And I have an alibi."

Sarg leaned in. "You told us you were alone at the time, sleeping."

"That was a lie. Couldn't face my disgust, I suppose. For where I really was."

"Yeah? And where was that?"

"I was angry with Cailan, hurt and confused. I wanted to ease the pain. Forget her."

Liam pushed the glass away as if looking at his reflection in the water offended him. "There's this woman I've seen hanging around the club. I was pretty sure she'd be available. So we went to a hotel. Had a marijuana appetizer followed by a vodka chaser and then sex. I don't remember a lot, but that's what I wanted. To be numb."

Drayco asked, "Available because she's for hire?"

"I'd never done that before. First time for everything, right? I don't know her name or where she lives."

"Can you describe her?" Sarg pulled out his notebook.

"Tall, thin, long red hair. With a pierced nose. One of those silver rings that goes through the nostrils."

"Were you also with her two nights ago?"

Liam rested his head in his hand. "Two nights ago? I was at a jazz concert at the Kennedy Center."

"Anyone see you there?"

"Two thousand people, or however many that place seats."

"I'm talking about someone who could ID you personally, sir."

"Didn't see anyone I know. Got there right before it started. And we had a late-night weekend gig here, so I left the concert early. Not sure why my social calendar is of such interest to you, Agent."

"Were you aware Cailan was harassed and bullied by one of her colleagues?"

"She talked about it a bit, sure."

"Well, two nights ago that colleague, Shannon Krugh, was found dead in the same location where Cailan's body was recovered."

Drayco waited for the moment when Liam would realize what Sarg was potentially implying, but Liam just shook his head. Finally, he replied, "I guess what goes around, comes around."

A drummer and a pianist joined the saxophone player in warming up, all three casting curious looks at Liam and his companions. As patrons started filing in, Drayco nodded to Sarg. He left Liam to his sorrow and his music as he and Sarg headed up into the light-polluted skies over Georgetown.

Sarg grumbled about wasted efforts and how it was going to take him an hour and a half to get home. Drayco didn't feel like arguing and let him go. But he wanted to hang around a little longer.

People-watching was one of his favorite hobbies. Not on the same level as the piano, but it was probably a better psych experiment than any touted in Gilbow's classroom. He collected good watching spots like others collected places to watch the Fourth of July fireworks on the Mall.

He had spots everywhere, from Capitol Hill to Adams Morgan to Anacostia. Each session created its own socio-symphony, each person a different instrument, each snatch of conversation a separate melodic line. The only way to truly understand a symphony of people is to learn all of the various parts.

At this moment, though, he wasn't people-watching per se, more like person-hunting. And when he spied his target, he moved in.

§ § §

Except for her five-eleven stature and pierced nose, the auburn-haired woman wearing a white ruffled top tucked into black jeans could blend in with shoppers at Mazza Gallerie. Or in this case, people walking the streets of Georgetown. As he approached, her vacant expression morphed from blank canvas into secretive Mona Lisa, exhibiting an eternal, knowing hint of a smile just for him.

"Looking for someone?" She leaned in closer and twisted the plain silver chain around her neck.

"That depends. You fill the bill, but I'll need to ask you a few questions first."

"You'll love my answers."

"Let's find out." Drayco guided her off the main street onto Cady Alley, away from curious stares by pedestrians. He spied a half-hidden bench nestled between black chokeberry bushes.

She gave a quick look around as if nonchalantly checking out the scenery. He recognized a tactical survey. Women on the streets who survived knew they were one careless mistake away from being a crime statistic and newspaper headline.

She turned her full attention back to him. "My rates are competitive and I'm very flexible, in more ways than one. My one rule is no glove, no love."

"I'd like to ask you about one of your clients."

She scooted away from him and folded her arms across her chest, with a scowl. "A cop. Just great. You're losing your touch, Alice."

"Is that your name—Alice?"

"Look, when I was talking rates, I meant my manicure and pedicure business, okay? That's not against the law."

"Even if it were, I wouldn't arrest you because I'm not a cop."

She loosened her self-hug, but one foot was still poised in front of her, ready to run. "Far as my bank account's concerned, same difference."

"Two young women are dead and there may be more. I'm not asking you to get involved or give me your real name." Drayco was glad Sarg wasn't around to hear that part. "Just a few questions, I promise."

She chewed on the inside of her cheek. "Promises are same as lies in my business."

A fading bruise lingered on her chin that makeup hadn't managed to cover. The souvenir of one of those promises. "You may not be able to help, since this is going back a couple of months, to August."

"These girls you mentioned. Were they ... were they in the biz, too?"

"Both were college students. One moonlighted as a stripper."

Alice gave a tight-lipped smile. "I have an A.A. in Business Admin, can you believe it?"

She dropped her hands to her sides although her feet were still positioned in sprint mode. "Guess that girl who moonlighted, she needed the money, huh?"

"She was on a scholarship and her family wasn't wealthy. She's originally from the Virginia end of the Eastern Shore."

Alice's eyes widened. "You shitting me? That's where I'm from, well, the Maryland part. A postage-stamp town you've never heard of."

"You'd be surprised. I've got a place on the Eastern Shore myself. In Cape Unity." A rundown empty Opera House could count as a place, of sorts.

"My mother still lives over there with my daughter. I'm hoping to save up so my little girl can go to college one day."

"What about that business degree?"

"This ... manicure business ... pays better. Not many jobs over there, which is why I'm here. Got more blue crabs than people on the shore. People eat the crabs, but the crabs don't bother them. People 'round here," she pointed toward the street. "Bother whoever, whenever. They'll eat you whole."

A slight smile played around her lips, and she looked him up and down. "I don't put out for free."

He pulled out his wallet and peeled off some bills he handed to her. She snatched them and tucked them into the envelope-style purse slung over her shoulder. Then she fished out a small business-style ledger. "What's the date in August?"

"He wouldn't have given you his name."

"They never do. That's not the kind of notes I keep." She flipped to one page. "Take this one, for example. September fifth, five p.m. Mr. Cheap Blond Toupee." She glanced up. "I give 'em the only names I need. Mr. CBT, 50ish, wears a girdle. He's in sports marketing, wife thinks he's in a meeting, smells like peppermint Tums and garlic. Enjoys toe massages and dressing in a loin cloth."

"Is this a form of accounting or a form of insurance?"

"Take your pick." She flipped a few more pages. "August which day?"

"The thirteenth."

"Lucky thirteen?" Her smiled faded as she read the entry. "Mr. Sad Musician. Curly hair, glasses. Calluses on left hand. Most of my clients I forget the next day, but this one … he near broke my heart. Didn't want to talk, so we had a few drinks and joints instead. Who's Kay Lynn? Is she one of those dead girls?"

Drayco nodded. "Did you put a time down?"

"Nine p.m. Usually, I boot 'em out after their time's up, but he was as good as passed out. I wasn't much better. When I woke the next morning, he was still there."

"Have you seen him since, say two nights ago?"

"I've seen him around, but he doesn't acknowledge me. And he hasn't asked for my services again."

Drayco leaned forward with his arms propped on his knees and considered her information. It cleared Futino for Cailan's murder. But not for a revenge killing against Shannon, with or without the help of

Troy Jaffray. Loose ends of cases like this dangled and twisted around as kites tossed in shifting winds. Good thing he liked kites.

Alice reached over and ran her hand through his hair. "You paid for more than an hour, and you've only used ten minutes. I know a place nearby where I can make those other fifty minutes really count."

Alice's parted Valentine-red lips were doing their best to seal the deal. Nelia Tyler had found it funny when a prostitute in the Prince of Wales County lockup came on to him. Until the woman realized he wasn't a lawyer or cop and couldn't help her out. Tyler never wore lipstick on the job. Too unprofessional. With her natural beauty, she didn't need it.

Drayco said, "Some other time."

"You promise? I don't get your type, only the losers. It'd be nice to have some real fun for a change."

He smiled at her. "Promises are lies."

31

Looming shapes, muted colors, distant sounds, and whispered voices hovered around him. Silhouetted blobs focused into familiar faces so detailed, Drayco felt he could reach over and touch them, if he weren't paralyzed.

He held up used food wrappers and said, "Someone's been here recently." In the rear corner of the main warehouse room, Officer Decker straightened up after retrieving an object on the floor and yelled "I've got something." Then the flash of a dark figure hurtled out of the room Sarg had hurried past without searching.

The corrugated sulfur tones of gunshot echoes reached Drayco's ears as he turned to see Officer Decker falling to the floor with a bloom of red growing on his chest. Another shot, more sulfur tones, Sarg down. Drayco fired his own gun, one-two-three, hitting the shooter's arm, leg, chest.

Sarg was breathing, he must still be breathing …

Drayco's clothes were drenched with sweat. He'd fallen asleep on the couch watching the Washington Capitals game, after temporarily abandoning attempts to solve the music puzzle from Shannon's room.

In his first crack at the puzzle, no phrase combinations of the Schumann wheel made any sense. That was not acceptable. This was not going to be the first puzzle of any kind he couldn't solve.

He grabbed a Manhattan Special from the refrigerator and headed to the piano. Caffeine and Bach usually did the trick. Setting the drink aside, he concentrated on his fingers as they dug into the keyboard and let his mind flow with the notes.

So many things about this case felt off. The puzzles, Kenilworth Gardens, the murder-suicide theory. A Troy Jaffray-Liam Futino collaboration, cloudy motives from Elvis and Happy.

Gary Zabowski certainly had all the right criteria-music knowledge, computer skills, a strong tie to both victims. Sarg and Gilbow both would say Gary had some elements of the sociopath. Drayco didn't trust easy solutions.

Solutions. That damned puzzle of Shannon's. What did it mean? He launched into Bach's Italian Concerto, but after a few measures, his hand cramped. He stopped and tried again, but it took even fewer notes for the pain to shoot up his arm. He banged his hands down on the keyboard, then patted it by way of an apology.

Maybe it was the pain, maybe the anger sharpening his brain. Because he suddenly remembered Schumann wasn't the only composer who loved music codes. Olivier Messiaen created something he called a communicable language, using a musical alphabet to encode sentences. It was much more complicated than Schumann's—a combination of word painting, numerology, fixed note durations, Latin declensions and matching vowels to various notes.

Drayco hopped off the bench and grabbed a Messiaen biography from the shelf. He'd been fascinated by the composer since he heard "Quartet for the End of Time" and later discovered they had something in common—Messiaen was a synesthete.

After re-reading the section on codes, Drayco headed to the sofa, grabbed Shannon's puzzle and stared at it, focusing on one repeated pattern. Grabbing a pad of paper, he made a chart of notes and letters, arranging them in different ways until he found one that spelled out a phrase: DEATH STING IS SIN. One of Messiaen's coding rules was that only verbs, nouns and adjectives were allowed. No pronouns.

"Death sting is sin?" Drayco read it aloud. A biblical reference, if he interpreted this correctly.

Death and sin, a possible ritualistic MO with a possible ritualistic dagger. Why did the puzzle sender switch methods, if this was indeed the same sender? More importantly, did Shannon's death really mean the end, the coda, or would there be more repeats, more victims?

"The sting of death is sin." One of Drayco's grandmother's favorite Bible verses, from First Corinthians. What had Shannon done that her murderer deemed to be a sin, had blamed on her?

He must have fallen asleep again on the sofa. It took several seconds of the Prokofiev ringtone on his cellphone to wake him. He glanced at the time, 2 am, and at the caller ID—Nelia Tyler.

It wasn't Nelia on the other end. A man's slurred voice yelled, "Goddamn bloody bastard. You're fucking my wife. Don't lie to me because I'm an attorney and I know all about lying." Then came a series of loud burps and more slurring. "You'll pay for your sins. You'll pay all right because I'll see that you pay."

A "thunk" signaled the phone being dropped, followed by murmured voices. The murmuring continued, and then he heard faint snoring in the background.

Nelia picked up the phone and immediately apologized. "I'm so sorry. Tim had a bad day, and when he gets that way, he starts drinking. Then he starts in on the crazy talk."

Drayco had never seen Nelia cry, but he detected an unusual huskiness. It was hard to tell, since voices lost their color over cellphones, the limited bandwidth squeezing formants and harmonics into a gauzy gray mess.

"Are you okay, Tyler?"

"We'll be fine. He just needs to sleep it off. I'll call you tomorrow or in a few days. I feel I owe you a big crab cake dinner from the Seafood Hut, but—"

"Yeah. But." He hung up with her and tried to get back to sleep. Before the phone call woke him, he'd switched from nightmares about Sarg and the shooting at the warehouse to dreams of giant stinging bees attacking him. With the added adrenaline from Nelia's husband's drunken rant, Drayco would end up watching the clock rather than sleeping.

He got up and grabbed a book of conversations between Messiaen and critic Claude Samuel and began reading. Messiaen, the composer, was also Messiaen the theologian and ornithologist.

Drayco read one passage, "My faith is the grand drama of my life. I'm a believer, so I sing words of God to those who have no faith. I give bird songs to those who dwell in cities and have never heard them. Make rhythms for those who know only military marches or jazz. And paint colors for those who see none."

Colors for those who see none. Drayco got up again, this time to find a recording online to download to his stereo system. Messiaen's haunting "Vocalise" for voice and piano filled the room with silver and blue, ethereal soap-bubble shapes. The mezzo on the recording sounded a little like Cailan. But this soprano was still alive, still performing and recording.

He conducted a Web search and found a bio of the singer, who'd be forty-seven now. The same age Cailan once said she'd envisioned a big birthday gala to celebrate living to an older age than her mother.

He switched off the recording and the lights and sat on the couch in the dark.

32

Another weekend, another visit from Darcie, ostensibly to pick up a dress she ordered last time. After receiving the "DEATH STING IS SIN" note and that disturbing late-night call from Tyler's husband, Darcie was a welcome distraction.

She brought him a cup of tea at the table where he sat checking his computer for more social traces of Cailan, Shannon, and their friends. He looked at the cup. Tea? He had tea? Must have been in the cabinets for years. He sniffed the brew. Earl Gray. Well, at least he'd been neglecting the best.

She looked around the room. "Kinda lonely here by yourself, I imagine."

He blinked at her. Was she suggesting she move in with him? He started to bring out the usual string of excuses for why that wouldn't be a good idea, when she added, "You need a dog. Or a cat. You do like animals, don't you?"

Drayco thought about Shoggoth, the black Savannah cat who'd almost adopted him in Cape Unity. Sort of half-dog, half-cat. "Yes, but I doubt they'd love my schedule. But thanks for the reminder."

"Reminder?"

He got up and went into the kitchen long enough to grab a bowl and pour in some kibble. Opening the back door to his postage-stamp yard, he placed the bowl beside the door. "Stray cat," he explained. "I hate to see an animal starve. It's too skittish to make friends with—I think it was abandoned and has trust issues."

"I didn't know you were a pet psychiatrist, too." Darcie sat beside him when he reclaimed his seat at the table and peered over his shoulder. "How's the case coming? Anything new?"

"I spent last night with a prostitute."

She almost dropped her cup. "That's not funny."

When he saw the way her lip trembled, he apologized. "I was merely asking her some questions about the case."

She glared at him. "I'm surprised you don't think of *me* that way."

He pushed the computer away and reached for her hand. "Of course I don't. Besides, if anything, I'm the gigolo. Your bank account is a lot bigger than mine."

That prompted a smile. "I like that. My own private gigolo." She took a sip of her tea, then asked, "I repeat, so how's the case coming?"

"Not well. There was another murder. Another Parkhurst co-ed."

"More music puzzles, too?"

"Unfortunately. As mocking as the others and equally unsolved."

"See, I told you it wasn't a crime of passion."

He couldn't argue with that. Just *what* it was a crime of, however, was still up in the air.

Darcie massaged his right arm. He looked at her with a raised eyebrow. "I appreciate the attention, but what prompted that?"

She continued massaging without missing a beat. "Because I want you to play the piano for me."

"I could soak that arm in warm water like usual."

"This is a lot more fun, don't you think?"

He smiled and let her work on the arm for a few minutes, then headed to the piano. His baby, his Steinway, always looked like it was chiding him when he stayed away for too long. He sat in front of the keyboard. "What do you want to hear?"

"Something romantic."

He flipped through a mental list for a moment, then dug into Chopin's Nocturne Opus 27, number 2 in D-flat major. It was one of the first Chopin pieces he learned to play, and it remained one of his favorites. The opening cantilena was quick to transport him into that alternate reality where nothing else existed except him and the piano.

So much so, that when the last notes died out, he was surprised to find he wasn't alone. And then he saw Darcie standing there.

The same Darcie who watched him through watery eyes as she sniffled.

"Didn't you like it? Or not romantic enough?" he asked.

She wiped her eyes. "It's absolutely horrible."

His eyes widened, then she added, "Horrible you don't get to play for other people. You are so good and so sensitive. It's a crime against the universe you aren't doing this for a living. Isn't there some surgery they can do on your arm?"

He shook his head. "They already did. Besides, the window of opportunity for a piano career is long gone. I'm too old now to start over."

"Thirty-six is too old?"

"In piano years, yes."

"Oh." She chewed on her lip. "You should give a recital at the Opera House. As a fundraiser, maybe."

"Think anyone would come?"

That made her laugh. "You'd pack the house." She joined him on the bench. "You are one of a kind, you know that? A detective pianist with synes ... synesh ... oh, you know what I mean."

"Synesthesia."

"That's it. Did those murdered girls have it, too?"

He blinked hard. Where had that come from? He hadn't mentioned it, and those details weren't in any of the news accounts. He looked over at Darcie, whose eyes were full of innocent curiosity.

When he didn't answer, she said, "I'll take that as a yes."

"I shouldn't discuss details of the case."

"Aren't you worried the killer will come after you, too?"

"Unlikely, since the victims were co-eds."

She put her head on his shoulder. "What's it like living with that synes-thingie?"

He pointed at a painting hanging on his wall, a Jackson Pollock knock-off with blue and gray swirls and a thick texture from embedded burlap. "When I hear sounds, they're like that."

"Even voices?"

"Yours is like red piano felt. It's quite pleasant."

"It had better be!" She lifted her head to kiss him on the cheek. "Have there always been people who had that gift?"

"I'm not sure you'd call it a gift. But synesthesia has likely been around a long time."

"I can imagine how well that went over in the Dark Ages. They probably thought it was from the devil and burned them as witches."

She was probably right about that, too. It was hard to imagine one of those Dark Age-holdovers going around killing girls with synesthesia at Parkhurst College. Still, the world was filled with people killing others in the name of some God due to some perceived "wrong" belief.

He didn't buy into the love-triangle theory, but the motive had to be something more mundane than witchcraft or a mini-religious war. Whatever it was, he had that feeling he got when the answer was bubbling under the surface of his brain.

Since Sarg had the weekend off to take Elaine to a harvest festival in Fredericksburg, maybe Darcie's visit would help Drayco see the problem in a new light. Or maybe he'd go ask Abraham Lincoln for some advice. Because he was finally going to take Darcie on that sightseeing tour, starting with the Lincoln Memorial.

33

Onweller called a sudden ten o'clock meeting without saying why, making Drayco scramble to get there on time. He couldn't blame Sarg for shifting around in the low-slung chair in the Unit Chief's office waiting for Onweller's latest pronouncement. Fighting the desire to do the same, Drayco sat up straight. Maybe not the picture of calm, but as good an impression as he could manage. This must be about the new musical puzzle. Had to be.

Onweller didn't look at Drayco directly, but over the top of his head. "President Thackeray wants to express his gratitude for your hard work. We both agree with the MPD this case boils down to a troubled girl with mental problems who killed her romantic rival. And then herself after the boy broke off the relationship. A murder-suicide."

Drayco had suspected and dreaded this was coming. It didn't make swallowing the poison pill any easier. "But why send one of those music puzzles to herself?"

"All part of her mental illness. The girl had bipolar with classic behavioral symptoms from being off her meds. In one of her manic phases, she killed Cailan Jaffray. In a subsequent depressive state, she took her own life. The police found a suicide note tucked away in one of her textbooks."

"Dated recently?"

Onweller flipped over a page and frowned. "Well, no, it was dated a year ago. But it shows she was suicide-prone."

"Her car wasn't found in the lot. That's a long way to walk from the college or her apartment."

"I think Agent Sargosian's hypothesis is correct here. The Krugh girl had an accomplice. He dropped her off then helped her carry Cailan Jaffray's body into the gardens."

Maybe it was a lost cause to argue, but Drayco didn't care. "Shannon wasn't a good student. In fact, she was in danger of losing her scholarship. I can't see her coming up with those music puzzles."

"If Agent Sargosian is correct, the accomplice created those puzzles. That boyfriend of hers, Gary Zabowski, is a perfect candidate. No doubt, he sent you that new 'sting of death' thing."

Drayco tried hard not to grit his teeth. "Are you willing to bet other lives on that theory? Because that's what's at stake if you're wrong. We finally got a list of names of the other people in Reed Upperman's project. We should at least warn them."

Onweller's staccato tones were as pleasant as the sound of a piano string breaking. "We won't require your services anymore, Drayco."

He eyed Sarg, "And Agent Sargosian is being reassigned to the Bankton warehouse arson cases. The senator's lost faith in the ATF to solve the situation and has requested the Bureau's help. Since Sargosian has worked arson cases in the past, he's the perfect choice."

Sarg remained silent. Like Onweller, he avoided looking at Drayco directly.

As Drayco stared unflinchingly at Onweller, he caught a brief hint of uncertainty on the man's face. It was swallowed up in steely resolve as he finally met Drayco's stare. "Agent Sargosian, I think we're finished here, and you can return to your office. I've sent the arson files there."

Onweller jumped up after Sarg left, planting his palms on his desk. "I know how you think, Drayco. Always driven to find some reason for the insane things people do. But no matter how hard you try, sometimes it just is what it is. Like that young punk who ended your piano career. Life is unfair. For every Shannon Krugh or every young thug, there are a dozen more. We have to accept it and move on."

Drayco rose from his chair. "Shannon Krugh wrote a paper on reason and determining what's morally right or wrong. I don't want that to be her epitaph. Those music puzzles weren't created by that girl. And I don't believe they were created by Gary Zabowski. There's a deeper layer to this. The whole thing's off-key."

Onweller eased back down, but his eyes never left Drayco's. "You have a keen mind. But forgive me for not wanting to trust a man who'd take the fall for someone else's mistake."

Drayco swallowed hard, biting back a hundred different retorts. He knew Onweller wouldn't understand his reasons for protecting Sarg, one of the few people he'd been close to for any amount of time. Nor did the Chief understand Drayco as well as he thought he did.

"I can't let this go. Those puzzles do mean something more."

Onweller tented his fingers together. "Nevertheless, you are not to pursue this further. As far as President Thackeray and Parkhurst College are concerned, the case is in the hands of the MPD, who can tie up any loose ends. I must insist you stay away from Parkhurst students and faculty. Or I can and will have you arrested for obstruction of justice and witness tampering."

Drayco headed for the door, but before he left, he pointed to the seal on the wall. "Fidelity - Bravery - Integrity. I hope you haven't forgotten what those words mean. Because I haven't." And then he walked away.

34

Drayco picked at his burger without much enthusiasm. He'd spent most of the day at home following the drama in Onweller's office, catching up on paperwork and bills—lots of bills—before coming here. The waitress refilled his cup of coffee, and right after she left, a man slid into the other seat across from Drayco, reached for the salt shaker, and handed it to him.

Drayco grabbed it. "You must have taken a wrong turn on I-95, because this is a long way from Fredericksburg."

"I promised Elaine truffled risotto for dinner this week. One of her faves. You tried buying truffles in Freddyburg? Fugeddabout it."

"How'd you know I'd be here?"

"Figured you'd want to drown your sorrows." Sarg looked around the table, "Yet I note a decided lack of libations. And I figured of all the places you'd head for, it'd be Tuchmans."

"Might have been another bar someplace."

"Yeah, but this bar was where Gary and Reed allegedly met the night Cailan was killed. Aren't giving up on this thing, are you?"

"No. But I hadn't expected you to."

Sarg stared at the salt shaker. "I know it looks like I got you kicked off the case. By agreeing with Onweller on the suicide-accomplice thing."

"Et two, Brute?"

Sarg rubbed his eyes. "When I married Elaine, I decided the 'richer or poorer' thing didn't matter, because I'd make sure we were always richer. Then the kids came along and I said, okay, so maybe not richer. But it didn't matter because having a family was worth it. What I hadn't counted on was what I'd be willing to do for that family. Like ask a friend to take a bullet for me. Not once, but twice."

Drayco didn't say anything right away, the silent seconds ticking by. Sarg lifted his head and seemed surprised to see Drayco smiling at him. "You want to—even need to—believe the suicide angle, because it means Tara is safe. Can't blame you for that."

Sarg ran his finger along the table. "Didn't think it through clearly until after I left Onweller's office. But yeah, this solution wraps everything up in a neat and safe little package."

Drayco signaled for the waitress to join them. "Whatever the man wants, Heather, add it to my tab. And do you mind repeating to him what you told me?" Drayco pulled out a photo from his wallet. "About this guy?"

"Other than he's a real babe and I hope you'll bring him by sometime?" She winked at Drayco. "Of course, you can bring yourself here anytime you want, and I'll die happy."

She wrote down Sarg's order as he dictated it. "As I told hottie here, I work most nights. Have been for months. I'd have remembered the guy in that photo. And I've never seen him." She shimmied off to the kitchen.

Sarg grinned. "She's kinda young for you, don't ya think?"

"Perhaps you didn't notice when IQ was giving *you* the eye. Heather's flirted with all the men in here, because it makes for bigger tips."

The trade inside the bar had picked up, so Heather only had time for a smile as she dropped off Sarg's grilled asiago sandwich. He took a bite. "Not bad," and then eyed Drayco's burger wistfully. "Elaine and Tara are on a vegetarian kick, so I said, okay, as long as I get to keep dairy. Vichyssoise ain't the same with soy milk."

Drayco winced as Sarg pronounced it "vishy swah," with his farm-boy accent, prompting Sarg to grin. "You can say it, I can make it."

"Why didn't you become a chef, Agent Sargosian? Those TV chefs earn a lot more than a humble federal agent."

"Doing something for a living can suck all the fun out of it."

Drayco had a fleeting image of himself up on a stage at a piano, the audience indistinguishable from every other audience, night after night. Traveling from one city to another, handed off from one stranger to another, not having the time to see the sights before it was onto the next concert hall.

Sarg picked up his knife and used it to peer under the bun on Drayco's burger. "Good God, man. There's pineapple and mayo and french fries on that thing. Where in hell did you learn to eat such weird combinations?"

Drayco knocked the knife away and took another bite of burger. "When you're left to your own devices as a kid, you make do."

Sarg grunted in sympathy, but seemed to be enjoying his own meal a lot more, until he winced again and rubbed his cheek.

Drayco fingered the picture of Gary he'd shown the waitress. Either she was mistaken, or both Gary and Reed lied. "I've never turned my back on a case."

"And you're not about to start now, yeah, I got that. You know you won't be paid. And you won't have any official backup. And if Onweller gets wind of it, he's liable to do something drastic."

Drayco chewed some more of the burger, but it wasn't firing any of his taste buds. Might as well be eating the small wooden board the burger was served on. "If I were still at the Bureau, maybe I could help more."

Sarg stopped taking tiny bites of the sandwich and put it down. He pushed the plate around, then said with a nervous laugh, "What, you mean like me, newly assigned to that high mucky-muck arson case?"

"Maybe I should seriously consider that corporate security job."

"A terrible waste of brain."

Drayco sat for several moments, not eating, not talking, observing the other patrons. Anything to avoid eye contact. Sarg appeared happy to do the same.

"Those paralysis dreams I've been having. They started after you showed up at my townhome. The dreams are all the same. The warehouse, the shooting."

Sarg nodded.

"I agreed to take the fall for you, but not just because of your family. I also didn't want to lose another partner."

Sarg gaped at him. "Yet you did, didn't you? I'm not dead, but still gone. Now *you're* the one who doesn't have anyone to watch your back."

"Better than watching someone shoot yours. Again."

"We don't go out in the field much at the BAU, you know that. Besides you made it into the quarter-inch club. Reynolds didn't call you 'dead-eye Drayco' for nothing. Must be those magic piano hands make you shoot like that. The Rangers would have loved you."

Drayco smiled. "Too independent for them."

"You were never comfortable with the idea of having to shoot someone. But I knew you'd come through when the chips were down. Always trusted you to do the right thing."

Sarg picked at a fingernail, then tapped it on the table as if shaking out invisible dirt. "I've obsessed about that day. Forgot my training, let my guard down and a good man got killed. And yeah, I was worried about my family. I was selfish."

"Selfish?"

"I'm pretty good at what I do, but you … you're a natural at figuring out connections, looking at problems from unique angles. I knew you'd land on your feet. Thrive, even."

Drayco forced a slight smile. "I've done okay."

"Maybe you'd do better if you stopped going to such great lengths so people won't suffer from their own mistakes." Sarg motioned for Heather to bring the check.

Drayco pushed his plate away. The hamburger had sounded good when he ordered it. Sarg clucked his tongue, pointing at the uneaten hamburger. "You're never going to be big and strong that way. It'll stunt your growth." He reached over and cut off a portion and popped it in his mouth, a blissful expression on his face.

Sarg wiped off the grease. "So where do we go from here?"

"We?" Drayco grinned. "You've got an arson case."

Sarg tugged on his ear. "That's another suck-up case. I hate suck-up cases. I don't like you going it alone. And if you're right and this isn't a murder-suicide, my daughter may still be in danger. Whatever you need, I'm good for it."

Drayco grabbed the check the waitress brought. "Your official access to databases could come in handy."

"Done."

"Although those databases won't help with the music codes, my new-found obsession. They just don't fit the vibe of the murders. More an afterthought."

"I'm a simple polka boy. You evil classical musicians are a different animal altogether."

In reply, Drayco reached over and dropped the remainder of his burger in Sarg's coffee.

35

"Do not fear to be eccentric in opinion. For every opinion now accepted was once eccentric." One of Drayco's favorite Bertrand Russell quotations. Quite apt, in the here and now. He was restless and drove around after parting ways with Sarg. No particular destination in mind, weaving through a steady rain past the monuments as the floodlights set them off, one by one.

They were modern stone temples with their statues of demigods posing for eternity. Statues of marble and bronze that hid feet of clay. Drayco shoved his own foot down on the accelerator to avoid side-swiping a car whose driver was glued to a cellphone.

The frenzied Power City was light years away from the laid-back lifestyle fifty miles across the Chesapeake, where the Eastern Shore only recently got broadband. He had a sudden craving to hear the voice of Nelia Tyler. Nelia was one of the few people other than Sarg who'd understand his reasons for not dropping this case.

Drayco hadn't planned on it but realized he'd turned onto the road that led to Cailan's apartment. He parked the Starfire in front. A beacon of light shining through her window beckoned him upstairs as rain bombed his windshield with loud "thwacks."

The door to Cailan's apartment was ajar, so he pushed on past into the living area. He startled two men, one sitting on the sofa, the other bent over several cardboard boxes piled in the room. It was an unlikely pairing.

The man dipping his hands into a box straightened up and faced Drayco. "What are you doing here?"

"Saw the light on. Wanted to make sure no one was in here who shouldn't be. It appears I caught you packing Cailan's things."

Troy Jaffray picked up more books and papers and tossed them into the box. "I heard from Andrew Gilbow the FBI was off the case. Shannon Krugh killed Cailan and herself. End of story. Guess I should be relieved."

"You're not?"

From the couch, the other man piped up, "We can't believe it's over, that's all. And I thought when they nailed the monster, I'd feel better."

Drayco confronted Liam Futino. "I'm surprised to find the two of you together."

Jaffray grabbed a tape gun and ripped off a long piece of tape to cover the box top, then sank onto the arm of the sofa. "I wanted to hate Liam. I really tried. After talking to him on the phone, it was clear he's every bit as devastated as I am."

Drayco examined the photo Liam held in his hand. "A memento?"

Liam stared down at the photo of himself and Cailan, both of them smiling, his arm around her shoulders. "I expected her to throw out all the photos of me. Of us. A friend took this one. I had him print out a copy for us. And she kept it."

Drayco hadn't spied any photos of Troy Jaffray when they first searched the apartment, and he didn't see any around now to be packed up. Had she thrown those out?

Liam still had his coat on, a very dry coat. And the only indentations in the plush throw rug in front of the sofa were a set of shoe prints as if he'd been sitting there for sometime. Drayco asked Jaffray, "Did you arrange to meet Liam here or did you find him here?"

Jaffray cast a quick glance over at his companion. "I would have arranged it. If he'd asked."

Liam reached into his pocket and took out a key he held out to Jaffray. "Cailan gave it to me when we started dating. After she broke up with me, she wanted it back. I just never got around to it. Wasn't going to steal anything. I hoped …" He slumped into the sofa.

Drayco asked, "You came here looking for something in particular?"

Liam cradled the photo in his hand. "When Cailan first told me she was pregnant, I could tell she wasn't happy. I urged her to get a sonogram, hoping it would help her bond with the baby. Don't know if she did, but I thought … maybe she kept a copy of the sonogram. Of our baby."

None of the three men spoke for a few moments. Any notions Drayco entertained over Liam Futino pursuing Cailan as a potential money tree had long flown off his mental radar. Now, he was convinced. Both men were pictures of the kind of grief that cauterizes open wounds in memory and turns them into black scars.

Jaffray broke the silence. "You're wondering if we collaborated. Wreaking vengeance by killing Shannon and framing it as a suicide."

"It crossed my mind. The police might think so, too."

"I got the impression the police were following the FBI's lead which begs the question—what are you doing here, Drayco?"

Drayco walked to a table holding a portable digital device, the same model other students carried at the music school. How many times had he listened to his own practice sessions, to catch the weak spots in his playing, head off slips in technique?

The device had a built-in external speaker, and he pressed the PLAY button. Cailan's clear, rich voice even sounded good singing scales in compressed mono. He let it continue playing for a few moments, then switched it off.

As both Jaffray and Liam sat still with tears in their eyes, Drayco said, "Scales are mathematical marvels built on ratios and semitones. When the ear hears an interval as consonant, the brain relaxes. When the ear hears dissonance, the brain instinctively wants to resolve it. Everything about the murders of Cailan and Shannon is dissonant."

Jaffray blinked away his tears and stared long and hard at Drayco, finally giving him a curt nod. "I hope you find more resolution than I have."

Drayco picked his way through the boxes toward the door and looked back before heading out. Jaffray placed a hand on Futino's shoulder, and they concentrated on Liam's photo of Cailan, as if doing so would magically bring her back to life.

Drayco stood very still in the dark, grateful the rain had stopped. After leaving Jaffray and Liam, he'd walked the entire length of the path Cailan took from the psych lab to her apartment and was almost back at his starting point.

Two minutes ago, someone began following him.

Thorn-covered bushes that lined a sharp right turn in the path hid Drayco as he waited for his follower to come into view. Whoever it was didn't seem to know anything of the art of tailing. Too much foot scuffling and a near-stumble or two. When the culprit lurched around the turn, Drayco saw why.

Gary Zabowski appeared, spinning around in all directions to spot his suddenly missing prey. The smell of beer surrounded him in a cloud as if he'd been doused in *Eau de Frat Boy* cologne.

Drayco maneuvered behind Gary, waited a moment, and loudly cleared his throat.

Gary stopped spinning and would have fallen to the ground if Drayco hadn't caught him by the elbow and hoisted him up. "Think I just had my first heart attack," Gary slurred.

Drayco said, "Skulking around will do that to you. Why are you following me instead of staying at the bar you left?"

"I was at that bar, 'cause I can't come here, without going to that bar first."

"You do this … whatever this is, often?"

Gary pulled his arm out of Drayco's grasp. "Whoever took Cailan did it while she was walking home. I used to walk her home." He deflated like a balloon. "My breaking up with her got her killed."

His words were slurred, but Drayco could translate easily enough. Swaying in the winds of his guilt, Gary was in no condition to walk, let alone drive. Drayco anchored a firm grasp on Gary's shoulder. "I'm taking you home."

Gary didn't argue and allowed himself to be shepherded to Drayco's car, staying mute all the way to his apartment. Drayco walked him to the door to be sure he made it inside. But their path was blocked by a man wearing a confidence-cut suit and a frown of annoyance.

Gary squinted at the man in concentration. Then he put a hand to the side of his mouth and attempted a whisper so loud, it scared a cat on the stoop next door, who hissed at them. "That is Mister Lawrence G. H. Putnam, Esquire, Attorney-at-Law, and mouthpiece. That's what they call 'em in those black-and-white movies, right? Mouthpiece?"

Gary fumbled for his key and managed to open the door, then made a sloppy salute with one hand as the other arm waved them inside. Putnam didn't bother looking around, like one who'd been there before.

"I've been trying to get you on your cellphone all day, Gary. Your father is very upset. He says you called President Thackeray at his office and threatened him with a lawsuit if you were thrown out of school. Something about being a murder suspect. That's preposterous, Gary. Thackeray himself told your father one of the two dead girls was behind it all."

"She didn't do it." Gary flopped down onto a chair and belched.

"I daresay the police know what they're doing, Gary. And your father doesn't have time to deal with these games of yours. He's a very busy man." Putnam pulled out his wallet. "It is money you're after? Your father told me to give you whatever you need."

Gary folded his arms over his chest and didn't answer.

Putnam pulled out several hundred-dollar bills, so crisply new they lay as flat as if they were fresh off the Mint assembly line. "If you need more, let me know. And don't be calling Thackeray or anyone else in his office." The attorney turned to leave, pausing a moment. "You don't want to disappoint your father, do you?"

Gary waited until the attorney was gone, then mimicked him in a sing-song voice, "You don't want to disappoint your father, do you? Too late for that. I was born, wasn't I?"

Drayco left Gary long enough to duck into the kitchen. He spied what he was looking for, a jar of instant coffee he combined with water heated in the grease-encrusted microwave.

He handed the cup to Gary, who peered up at him with scrim-covered eyes. "I gotta be the only bum on campus with a lawyer stand-in for a daddy-o." Gary took the coffee and gulped down a sip. Drayco doubted he was the only one. Not at Parkhurst.

"I didn't know if you take milk or sugar," Drayco said.

"Depends. This tastes different from when I make it. S'okay."

Drayco didn't tell him he'd also found the salt shaker on the counter. "You argue with your father much?"

"Hell, that would mean we talk. You heard mouthpiece. Daddy-o is a very, very busy man who can't be bothered with little, what do you call 'em? Annoyances. And I'm one of those annoyances."

Gary gulped down some more coffee and sounded fractionally more coherent. "They're divorced. My parents. Mom spends all her time shopping, partying, high society stuff. Guess she didn't like all those young women throwing themselves at my father because of his moolah."

Drayco got up to make himself a cup of coffee, trying to ignore the filthy microwave. What were those red blobs in there? A new life form? Smelled a little like rotting pizza. "I'm familiar with difficult father-son relationships. But he must care about you on some level."

"He cares about himself. I'm a reflection of him and his genes. Therefore, he cares about me. How's that for a sillo … stillo … what's that jismy thing?"

"You mean syllogism."

"Guess I learned something from Philosophy 101."

"How did your father feel toward Cailan? Or Shannon? Or any of your friends?"

"Doesn't care, as long as I don't get into trouble. Trouble meaning something he can't fix. Arrests he can fix. Short of murder, there's little

I can do to get kicked out of this place. Ole Daddy Fixit will see to that."

"Is that what you were trying to do? Get yourself thrown out?"

Gary smiled briefly. "See, I've only talked to you twice before, and you already know me better than he does. Better than my so-called friends who think I'm an ATM machine. Hell, you may be the one person who doesn't want anything from me."

"Except the truth."

Gary's laugh was tinged with bitterness. "The truth? Okay, the truth is I lied. Not about murdering anybody. About my alibi. I wasn't with Reed at the club when Cailan or Shannon was killed. Well, not at the time they were killed."

"What do you mean?"

Gary swung his feet up on the couch. "We were together at Reed's place later the night Cailan was killed, after midnight. In bed."

"You and Reed slept together?"

"Just the one time."

"So you're gay, and Cailan and Shannon were a cover?"

"If I were truly gay, I'd be a nicer person. How many gay mass murderers do you see walking around? Okay, Jeffrey Dahmer."

"There've been other gay serial killers. Spree and serial killers run the gamut—female, young, old, educated, uneducated. One reason I'm not a fan of profiles."

"Well, I'm not gay. It's all the rage to swing both ways. S'called being 'fluid.'"

Drayco made a note to ask Andrew Gilbow that, when he ran into him again, if for no other reason than to see the expression on his face. "You might regret telling me all this in the morning when you're sober."

Gary rubbed his temples. "I regret that last beer right now. You don't have any aspirin on you, I 'spose?"

"The coffee will kick in soon. You told Putnam, Esquire, Shannon didn't kill Cailan. You sounded quite confident."

"She was back on her meds. After we broke up, she decided to take them again. I don't remember seeing her happier or more together.

She wouldn't have killed herself. And she didn't have any booga-booga cult friends who would've helped her do it. As for killing Cailan— would a girl who faints at the sight of blood be able to stab somebody?"

"You saw her faint, or she told you this?"

"I gave myself a deep gash on my hand after I broke a glass. Right here where I'm sitting." Gary held up his hand to show Drayco a fresh scar. "Shannon took one look and was flat out on the floor."

That explained the stain on the carpet under Gary's couch. "Yet she cut herself, routinely."

"She wasn't very good at it. Said she'd make one cut and faint. Did one a week."

"If not together, where were you and Reed when Cailan and Shannon were killed?"

"I was here working on my music. No one would have seen me. Reed said he was at the lab working late. No one saw him, either."

"Both times?"

Gary nodded. "That's why we cooked up our alibi. Mutual dee-fense."

Drayco guzzled down his coffee. "You realize this means you don't have an alibi for the murder of either girl? Maybe you should have stuck to your guns."

"Don't care." He twisted the coffee cup around in his hands. "Don't care what the police think, don't care what my friends think, don't care what my father thinks."

"That's a lot of not caring."

Gary patted his computer equipment. "I care about that. Music won't let me down."

Maybe music wouldn't let you down. Everything surrounding it might, and music could become another casualty. Maybe Gary would get lucky, and it would be different for him.

Drayco said, "So if Reed doesn't have an alibi, he would have had time to follow Cailan, kill her, dump the body, and still meet you at midnight. And if he doesn't have an alibi for Shannon's murder ..."

Gary stood up, slurped the last of his coffee and headed to the kitchen. Drayco took the time to look around while he was gone. Gary's computer setup was impressive, easily capable of generating those music codes.

But you didn't need to be a skilled composer to use the types of software Drayco had researched at home. Type in notes representing the clue-words and have the software add some harmonization. Send the finished copy to a standard laser printer and voila.

Gary returned with a cup for himself and another for Drayco, who was surprised, but accepted it. Gary took a sip of his and looked at the cup, puzzled. "Doesn't taste the same. Guess my beer buzz is wearing off. Enough to tell you you're way off target if you think Reed's a killer. Brow-beaten by his wife, maybe. If every husband like that turned into killers, there'd be a lot more corpses."

"Cailan and Shannon were both in his dissertation project."

"Yeah, but with them both dead, puts his project in jeopardy, doesn't it? It'd be insane. Always did think it a weird idea for a dissertation."

"Where did he come up with it?"

"Don't know. Don't talk school much when we hang out. He's the closest thing to a normal friend I've got. We drink and chill. Cheap anesthesia."

Drayco said, "You didn't date any of the other students in that project, did you?"

Gary laughed and struck a male-model pose, grabbing his crotch. "A sex machine I'm not. If they had it as a major, I'd sign up. Gigolo 101."

Drayco tried not to think of Darcie.

Gary's face grew pensive. "It is kinda odd that project was the only thing Cailan and Shannon shared in common. Outside of music. Think there's a connection? If not Reed, then, what the hell?"

Gary's cellphone on a table went off, with a *Rocky* movie theme ringtone. It filled Drayco's brain with blue circles chained together like links in the Kenilworth fence, and that made him think of Tara Sargosian. Sarg was rightfully proud of the way she handled herself after finding Shannon's body. What would Gary have done under the same circumstances? Called Putnam, Esquire?

The young man returned from a bedroom where he'd excused himself to take the call, and collapsed down onto the sofa. "That was Reed. Making sure I got home okay. Told him what I told you. Wasn't happy."

"If Reed's innocent, he won't have to worry."

Innocent or not, Drayco agreed with Gary the only other thing Cailan and Shannon had in common was Reed's project. Which made it a dead certainty Drayco would pay a visit to Reed in the morning.

And how long would it take for the proverbial feces to hit the fan when word got back to Onweller Drayco was still working the case? When—not if—that happened, his window of investigative freedom would slam shut if Onweller made good on his threats. Drayco needed something to happen and soon.

§ § §

Tara knew it was a mistake when she went into the bar and saw a cloud of cigarette smoke hovering near the ceiling, threatening to rain down into her lungs. She hated cigarette smoke and the way it clung to her hair and clothes. Like anti-perfume.

Since Dad had relaxed his recent smothering, she was willing to give John another chance. Despite what happened on their last date. But where was John? Standing her up? Great, just great. Maybe she should just turn around and go home.

Jessica grabbed her arm, yelling above the clash of loud music and chattering voices. "John'll be glad you made it. He was here, left, said he'd be right back. Told me to tell you to hang tight. Here," she handed Tara a beer. "I bought this one, but you can have it and I'll get another. This is organic amber on tap. You'll love it."

Tara regarded the glass dubiously as Jessica disappeared into the crowd. The bouncer was chatting up a pretty blond girl when Tara arrived, allowing her to slip in without being carded. She shouldn't drink, technically. But twenty and four months was *almost* twenty-one. Still, what if there was a raid? Oh well, when in Rome …

She looked around in vain for a table. When her phone chimed, she put her beer down on a railing and checked the text. Not John, just Cyndi asking about some class notes.

Gary and Cailan used to go to Tuchman's, but Vertigo was closer to campus and easy for Tara to walk to. It was also packed every night. How did all those students manage to get any studying in? She grabbed the beer, gave up on finding an empty table, and headed to a spot under an air vent where she hoped the smoke would be less thick.

Jessica joined her, a frosty glass with amber liquid in hand. "Maybe this will help me sleep better. I can't shake the nightmares about seeing … about that whole Kenilworth thing. You been having nightmares, too?"

Tara didn't want to shout like everyone else, so she moved closer to Jessica. "Not really. I mean it was horrible, sure, but she was already dead."

Jessica rolled her eyes. "I should have known a cop's daughter would take it all in stride."

"He's not a cop, he's FBI. And I do feel sorry for Shannon."

"I guess like I should pray for her soul or light some candles or something. You're Catholic, right? Isn't suicide like, the worst? And murder on top of that."

Tara had long since stopped talking about her religion or any other religion, for that matter. She wasn't sure what she believed—maybe a cross between her mother's deep faith and her father's skepticism. Or none of the above.

And try to tell someone she was raised in an Armenian Apostolic Church and she could see their eyes glaze over. Or they'd try to convert her to their flavor of God. As her Dad used to say, "Vanilla, strawberry, chocolate—it's all ice cream."

She kept turning to the entrance, looking for John, but he was still AWOL. Maybe she'd been stood up, after all. Maybe she didn't mind.

John had caught her attention in World History II, lean and lanky with curly black hair and a smile that had a hint of bad-boy charm. As was often the case, the bright shiny package was empty inside when you opened it up. Unlike her Dad's former partner.

After Jessica had stopped screaming when they found Shannon, she'd pulled herself together enough to notice when Dad and Mr. Drayco showed up. The next day, she'd asked Tara for Scott Drayco's number. As if.

Tara didn't have a crush, truly. Despite what her dad thought. She was protective, that's all. That relaxed air wrapped around Falkor was like a black hole, drawing in everything around him. He'd had a lot of pain in his life. She could tell.

Someone handed Jessica a carton of chili-cheese fries, which she shared with Tara. Jessica had to yell at Tara to be heard though she was standing a foot away. "A friend of mine who sat next to Shannon in art history said Shannon didn't seem upset after her breakup with Gary. Why would she kill herself, do you think?"

Tara shrugged. Then regretted it. The motion seemed to have awoken her insides to the realization the cigarette smoke, beer and chili-cheese fries weren't sitting all that good. Waves of nausea burbled up, and she felt hot and flushed and a little unsteady.

Handing Jessica her beer and excusing herself, she headed toward the bathroom. She spied an emergency door leading to the alley behind the bar that was propped open. Fresh air sounded a lot better than the smell of urine and sickly sweet air fresheners.

She ducked out the door and walked several steps along the dark alley, holding her stomach and bending over in case she had to puke. But the cooler, fresher air was helping. Until a cloth bag was pulled over her head.

Someone grabbed her wrists tightly and half-dragged her down the alley, and she heard an idling car engine they were getting closer to. In her mind, Falkor's voice was telling her what to do in an emergency. Stay calm, take deep breaths, be aware.

She went as limp as a rag doll, her knees sagging to the ground, which made her assailant stop and ever-so-slightly loosen his grip. Tara used a technique Falkor had shown her to twist her wrists free, and then she screamed.

That did it. She heard the steps of the man—for she could tell it was a man from the heavy shoes—as he ran in the direction of the waiting car. As it raced off, she pulled the cloth bag from her head.

She worried no one in the noisy bar would hear her cries, but a couple of guys heading to the john rushed outside to help her up. She was angry she hadn't got a good look at the man or the car. At least she'd focused on the car's engine so she might be able to identify it later.

As much as she hoped it was a random attack, she couldn't shake the chills up and down her spine. Was she followed here, to the bar? Followed, with someone waiting for the right moment to kidnap her? Feeling like she was five years old, she pulled the cellphone out of the zipper bag anchored to her waist and called her father.

PART THREE

All must submit to their appointed doom,
Fate and misfortune will too quickly come.
Let me no more with powerful charms be press'd
I am forbid by fate to tell the rest.

—From the song "Seek Not to Know," poem by John Dryden
music by Henry Purcell

37

Reed Upperman had his head propped in one hand when Drayco walked into the lab. If he was hung over from last night's barhopping, he didn't show it, unlike Gary. His face registered a slide show of emotions—embarrassment, guilt, curiosity, fear. He raised his head a few inches. "Beer's truth serum to Gary. He shouldn't have told you."

"The police don't take lying very well. Makes you look guilty."

"By the time they're through grilling me, won't have to worry whether my dissertation is back on or not. Bye-bye teaching career."

Reed limped over to the wall and lifted his arm as if to rip the synesthesia project chart off. Drayco said, "If you need another subject, I've got a few evenings open."

Reed's hand paused in mid-air, and he slowly swung around. "I could use a sound-color-texture synesthete. It's a less common type." Reed limped back to a chair and eased himself into it. "Sounds as if you don't think I'm going to be arrested soon."

"I can't promise that."

"Dr. Gilbow told me the murder cases were closed. And the FBI thinks Shannon was behind it all."

Drayco wanted to say yes, more than at any other time in the case, after Sarg had filled him in with details on Tara's attack. When Sarg called him from Quantico this morning, he'd passed along the news Onweller was shrugging the attack off as a random incident. Judging from his former partner's tone of voice, his arteries must be squeezing hard to keep his blood from boiling out.

Drayco replied to Reed, "I'm tying up some loose ends."

Reed pulled a form out of a drawer and handed it to Drayco. "You'll need to fill this out first."

Drayco pulled up a chair and grabbed a pen. He filled in the bio and contact details, signed the legal mumbo-jumbo and handed the form back. "Have you discussed your bisexuality with your wife?"

Reed grabbed a lychee from the bowl on his desk and popped it in his mouth. Juice ran down his chin, smelling like a cross between roses and grapes. "Our marriage has been foundering for years. The standard got-married-too-young scenario. Then came the kids, so we've stuck it out. And I'm not sure if I'm bi or gay. Either way, if my wife gets wind of it, she'll initiate a divorce and try to keep me from seeing the kids."

"I know a good attorney. He owes me a favor or two." Drayco pointed to a printout next to Reed's computer. "Is that the info I called you about earlier?"

Reed picked it up and offered it to him. "After you wanted to know of other recent synesthesia projects, I checked ProQuest and found a couple of studies, one two years ago, the other three."

Drayco scanned the printout. "Cambridge College in Boston, and Temple University in Philly." He pointed to names under each. "Are these the participants?"

Reed nodded. "I called the two guys behind the studies. They were grad students at that time, of course. They're profs now."

"And they gave you the names of the students involved in their projects, just like that?"

"I'd never do it, even for a colleague. And not only because of HIPAA regs. But one of the study authors has tenure, and the other didn't care. I did tell them it was for the FBI, so maybe that did the trick. Not sure what that says about psychology or psychologists in general."

Drayco pointed to Reed's computer. "You have Web connectivity on that?"

"Naturally. Why?"

"Mind if I borrow it?"

Reed moved over to another chair and let Drayco park himself in front of the keyboard. Parkhurst money notwithstanding, the seat Reed vacated was as comfortable as a concrete bench. Drayco called up a couple of databases he had access to. After finding a hit, he printed the relevant pages and next logged in to NewsLibrary and printed out a few more pages.

Reed rescued the papers from the printer in the back of the room and brought them to Drayco. He waited for a few moments as Drayco scanned the documents, then asked, "So … what did you find?"

"I double-checked the students' names against Boston and Philadelphia police and newspaper reports dating to the time of the studies."

"Something good? Or I guess I should say, bad?"

"I would call murder bad, yes. One student from each of the two synesthesia projects was murdered in what was called a 'ritualistic' fashion involving a knife similar to the one used on Cailan and Shannon. Do you have alibis for those two dates?" Drayco let him read the accounts.

Reed grimaced. "The first one, three years ago, I was in the hospital with my wife as she gave birth to our second child." He hesitated. "The second date, I'd have to look up."

"I'm not sure that will be necessary."

"You don't think I'm guilty?"

Drayco smiled at him briefly. "I never did."

Reed scratched his head. "And I'm the one who wants to be a police psychologist. So, how'd you rule me out? Maybe I can learn something, for future reference."

"You fit the standard profile. Meaning you are too perfect. Then there's your Legg-Calve-Perthes disease, leaving you with a limp. And your glasses—fairly thick, somewhere around minus 30D?"

"Close. Try minus 40D."

"Glasses that thick are prescribed for severe myopics. Myopics have to avoid rough physical activity that could cause retinal detachment. Plus, night vision is a problem. How would you have carried Cailan and Shannon into Kenilworth?"

"An accomplice?"

Drayco didn't want to give out details about Tara's ordeal and hearing heavy footsteps in the alley. Not limping steps, like Reed's. And Reed's probable accomplice, Gary, stood around five feet ten and might weigh one-sixty dripping wet. "All right, I'll give you the accomplice part."

Behind those thick glasses, Reed's eyes widened. "They'll think that, won't they? Oh, God."

Drayco tapped his finger on his newly filled out form lying on the lab tabletop. "Put me in the computer. I think I'll be free next week."

Reed glanced at the form, then up at Drayco, and for the first time this morning, his face registered hope.

38

"You must be psychic," weren't the words Drayco expected from Andrew Gilbow when he cornered the man in his office. The psychologist added, "I was picking up the phone to call you."

"Then this is your lucky day."

"Walk with me," was more of a "heel" command, as Gilbow headed toward the door and didn't look back to see if Drayco followed.

They passed a small group of students who smiled and greeted Gilbow, although he headed off their questions. He guided Drayco out of the psych building, along a gray flagstone path, and into the gated open-air courtyard of an Italianate building. The sign on the gate read AUTHORIZED PERSONNEL, and the entry into the building from the courtyard was by keycard. No student hang-out this, but an administration fortress.

Gilbow gestured toward one of the tables for Drayco to sit and pulled out a piece of paper from his pocket that he handed over. "I received this yesterday."

It was familiar and different at the same time. Somewhat similar to the music codes Cailan and Shannon received, but written as a one-page song with words underneath the staves. The text read, "Thou shall see the glory / death is swallowed up in victory."

Drayco used a handkerchief to flip the note over and check the back. It was blank. "Was this mailed or slipped under the door?"

Gilbow pulled the folded-up envelope out of his pocket and pushed it across the table. The envelope was the same type as the girls received. White, nine-by-twelve, a district postmark, no return address.

Drayco read the address. "This came to your home, not office."

Gilbow said. "And no, I haven't received any more. That's the first and I hope the last. I'm inclined to think it's a prank."

"The 'pranksters' must know of the other notes, because it's too coincidental."

"It's probably nothing. I was more stressed the day I opened the official letter telling me whether I'd gotten tenure or not."

Drayco knew Gilbow was given an accelerated tenure track and the "official" part was a mere formality. But he let Gilbow have his brief moment of insincere humility. "Have you noticed anything else unusual? That makes this seem more than a prank?"

Gilbow hesitated, then uttered a little laugh. "As you witnessed, I'm often accosted by students to chat, argue a grade, discuss a paper. But the other day I had the strangest feeling I was followed. More your line of work. Unless it was you doing the tailing."

"If I'm doing the tailing and you notice, I'm not doing it right. Did you mention this to Jerry Onweller?"

Gilbow shook his head. "Besides, everything's wrapped up on that case, isn't it? Which would make this," he poked a finger at the letter on the table, "most definitely a prank. It does beg the question of why you came to see me."

Drayco took a deep breath and got a lungful of cedar-mulch air. No manure compost at Parkhurst. "Onweller is wrong. Shannon Krugh is not a murderer, nor did she commit suicide. New evidence has come to light suggesting their deaths might not be the first two."

"Onweller said nothing about that."

"As I mentioned, it's new information. I'm disobeying Onweller's orders by even discussing this with you."

Gilbow rested his elbows on the small table, putting him a foot away from Drayco's face which he scanned over the rim of his glasses. "When I first met you at that trial, I saw a rare spark. You conveyed integrity through your body language, and that was the moment I was certain we would lose the case."

Gilbow surprised Drayco again, as he said, "Jerry Onweller can be pigheaded. I tried to tell him Shannon Krugh couldn't be responsible, but he wouldn't listen. If he's pushed you off the case, he's a bigger fool than I imagined."

The psychology professor continued to study Drayco as he would a lab rat. "You have your flaws. There's too much boy scout in you, living in a legal black-and-white world. In order to succeed in life, you have to see the world as it is—not shades of gray, but silver. Silver that leads to gold. Frankly, I think you're afraid."

"Afraid? Of what?"

"Of crossing that line in the sand. Being pushed to do something you fear will pull you away from your moral code."

Drayco drummed his fingers on the table, realized he was doing it, and stopped. "Moral codes are emotional fingerprints. Unique to each of the billions of people on this planet. Unlike fingerprints, they change, morph into something different, over seconds, days, years. It wasn't fear that led me to leave the Bureau."

"Wasn't it? Not personal fear, no. You're the white-knight kind. More a fear you won't be able to do the right thing at a crucial moment."

From behind Drayco, a nearly colorless voice like crinkled tinfoil said, "Just the man I was looking for. I heard they scheduled you on the *Today Show* later this month, Andrew. Couldn't be more thrilled. You will, of course, put in the usual plugs for Parkhurst." The voice laughed. Drayco turned to gauge the new arrival, who pulled out a tiny paper pillow filled with tobacco from a can marked peppermint chewing tobacco and popped it into his mouth.

"Is this one of your students, Andrew? A grad student?"

"This is Dr. Scott Drayco, George, the FBI consultant Jerry Onweller hired." Gilbow nodded at Drayco, "And this is George Thackeray, President of Parkhurst College."

"Well, Dr. Drayco, it's good to finally meet you. I'm so pleased with the way Jerry handled this whole mess. I'm sure you agree."

"No, I don't agree. He was wrong and so are you."

Gilbow's shocked expression was nothing compared to the look on Thackeray's face as he replied, "I have absolutely no idea what you mean."

"Trying to sweep the murders of two girls under the rug in hopes of avoiding a scandal and appeasing wealthy donors and parents, for one. It was wrong not to have warned all the other students, particularly those involved with Reed Upperman's dissertation project. Shannon Krugh paid the price for it."

Thackeray gripped the tobacco tin in his hand. "Jerry Onweller told me your services were terminated. Which means you're not here in an official capacity and therefore trespassing on my campus. I'm within my rights to call security and have you thrown off."

Gilbow spoke in slow, soothing tones. "Come now, George, you've got a very busy schedule today. Isn't that meeting with the trustees coming up in an hour or so? Let me handle this. You go concentrate on your presentation."

Thackeray glared at Drayco and thrust the Snus can into his pants pocket. "All right, Andrew. I trust your discretion. But if he gives you any trouble …"

"Of course." Gilbow smiled at Thackeray. "And I promise to mention Parkhurst twice on the *Today Show*. More if they'll let me get away with it."

Thackeray swiped his keycard and stomped into the building.

The professor tilted his head. "If you wanted to use Thackeray as bait to agitate the waters around Onweller, you succeeded. So what now?"

"I think a trip to the Eastern Shore is in order."

"You're dropping this case for real?"

"Shannon Krugh grew up on the shore, and her parents have a place in Maxateague. I want to talk with them."

"Is that wise? Mental illness is often inherited. Miss Krugh's parents might not be reliable."

"Or they can shed more light on her condition. I'm willing to take the chance."

Gilbow squinted at a crow squawking at them from a railing. "You said more deaths might be connected to Cailan and Miss Krugh. Did those take place on the coast?"

"Boston and Philadelphia. I'd like to work that angle, but I'm more interested in preventing further deaths in the here and now."

"I haven't worked a serial killer case since Donald Wayne Grear a decade ago. You mentioned Reed's project as a focal point?"

"In three out of four murders, the murderer and victim know each other. And these murders contain hallmarks of ritualistic killing for a purpose."

"A Satanism cult? That would indicate a younger white male, one with low self-esteem who feels alienated and powerless and wants magical power over his destiny."

"Satanist cults these days are more likely to choose religious victims than ones with synesthesia."

"Unless they believe the synesthesia is a gateway for Satan, I suppose. You must be thinking Miss Krugh or her parents were involved in something along those lines. That would be a most interesting interview. I'd like to go with you, Drayco. I offer you my services and I'll throw them in gratis since Cailan was my goddaughter. When are you driving over?"

"Driving? That takes five hours in good traffic. Flying is much faster."

Gilbow turned a shade paler. "Flying?"

"I'll rent a plane and fly over to Salisbury or Accomack. An hour and fifteen each way, depending upon winds. I can be there and back in half a day."

"Well, uh, yes, I see that would be faster. A small plane, I take it?"

"A Cessna 172. One of the FBI pilots got me hooked on flying years ago. Don't tell me the vaunted psychologist has aviophobia?"

Gilbow cleared his throat. "I'm sure it will be fine. If my schedule allows it. There is the *Today Show* to prepare for."

"Naturally." Drayco picked up the letter and envelope. "Can I keep these?"

"Certainly."

"And you'll let me know if you receive any others or spot someone tailing you?"

"And if Jerry Onweller gives you too much trouble, I'll return the favor and speak with him on your behalf."

Drayco wasn't keen on the idea of Gilbow or anyone else running interference for him with Onweller. He waved the hand holding the letter and said, "Keep me in the loop with these." He left the courtyard through the gate and obliged Thackeray by throwing himself off campus.

39

The smoldering shell of the building was a mosaic of blackened brick, charred wood and twisted metal, like a sculpture created by an artist on meth. Drayco dodged the fire trucks and ATF vehicles and waved to ATF agent Carlos Desenza, as a familiar twang called from behind.

Sarg said, "You know somebody in every squad and alphabet soup department, don't you? Makes a guy feel cheated on."

"I never tip back Sam Adams with anyone else, I swear. As toasty as this smoldering heap is right now, a cold Sammy is sounding pretty good."

"It'll be eons before I get away."

"How many warehouse fires does this make?"

"Four. Senator Bankton would hit the roof if he still had one. And naturally, he expects us to drop everything else to take care of his little boo-boo."

The smell was almost enough to wish Drayco had a filter mask. Oil, burned plastic, smoky charbroiled wood, chemical foam. An aromatic stew of poisons. On the bright side, no one had died in the fires so far. No humans, nor stray dogs or cats. "Any motives?"

"We thought it was like New York, homeless men burning down warehouses to get the copper to sell. But why only the senator's properties? A homeless man with a political ax to grind?"

"How many more warehouses does the senator own?"

"A dozen. Guess he bought in when the property values were low, hoping he'd cash in when developers swooped in. Hell, I'd bet a year's salary he had inside knowledge. Or crafted legislation making it easier to develop in those areas."

"Oh, what cynicism—and about a Super Politician, too. Defender of untruths, injustice and the American power-play. You sure this one was arson?"

"The investigators found more gasoline accelerant."

Drayco kicked a broken piece of glass with his shoe. "On a much more important note, how's Tara?"

"Refuses to leave her studies. I did extract a promise not to go anywhere without a buddy, preferably a linebacker. FYI, when Tara told me she started feeling bad after drinking a beer, I insisted on a blood check. They found traces of Rohypnol in her system."

Drayco wasn't surprised, but it worried him, all the same. "Like Cailan and Shannon."

"Roofies are also used as date-rape drugs, so there may not be a Cailan-Shannon link. Don't like any of the possibilities."

"You give her the 'keep an eye on her drink at all times' lecture?"

"Twice, for good measure. And to keep that cellphone handy."

Behind the barrier tape, orange cones marked sites of interest found by arson investigators sorting through the debris. A few tarps covered possible clues. Drayco said, "Sorry to call you so early. Thought you might sneak a look in the database before Onweller arrived."

"Thank God Onweller's morning routine includes stopping by Panera for cinnamon-nut bear claws. I got in and out without him seeing me."

Sarg pulled out his notebook. "The info from Reed was a bombshell. The ViCAP run on the cases in Beantown and Philly showed the local PDs didn't report anything about synesthesia or musical codes. Didn't make the connection, but why would they? The kids weren't music students. And they didn't have their own Drayco music guru."

Sarg flipped over a page. "Oh, and the M.E.'s office found something interesting from Shannon's body."

"I'm all ears."

"News flash—not suicide."

"They're positive?"

"If the killer hoped leaving the knife would make us think suicide, he goofed. He didn't realize killing Shannon on top of a tarp and later removing said tarp would leave signs."

"Blood smear patterns?"

"Yep. And Shannon's fingerprints oh-so-carefully placed on the matches had traces of blood. Kinda hard to light a match to heat a knife—"

"If you're already dead. Guess it's a moral victory of sorts."

Sarg thrust his notebook in his pocket. "So you talked to Gilbow again? You get a vaccination against him or something?"

"After he received one of those notes, he wants to go with me to the Eastern Shore. Thinks it will be 'enlightening.' More likely, he needs material for another book."

"The shore?" Sarg said, with a sideways glance at Drayco. "You might bump into Deputy Nelia Tyler."

Drayco didn't want to roam around in Sheriff Sailor's backyard without checking in, so he had a legitimate reason for seeing Tyler. Besides, she was a good person to have in your corner when the chips were down. "Possibly," he said. "I doubt Gilbow will come. Not a happy flyer."

"The Big Man himself scared of a teensy widdle putt-putt plane?"

Drayco smiled. "Don't diss the putt-putt. Cessnas are reliable. And you get a real pilot instead of a computer."

A flash of something behind Sarg caught Drayco's eye, something fluttering low to the ground, and he headed for it. With one knee bent on the ground, he called out, "Got any evidence bags?"

Sarg disappeared while Drayco examined threads wrapped around a tiny sapling poking through a crack in the concrete. Sarg bounded back with a small baggie and a pair of tweezers he handed to Drayco, who extracted the red material and placed it in the bag.

"What is it?" Sarg peered over Drayco's shoulder.

"Red threads. Looks like cotton."

"Red cotton, you say?"

Drayco didn't have to look at Sarg to know they were thinking the same thing—about the red threads the Medical Examiner found in

Cailan's mouth. An abandoned warehouse would make a good place to carry out a murder before the body was moved to Kenilworth Gardens. Red threads were common, so it was likely a coincidence. Drayco hated coincidences.

Sarg took the bag as Drayco handed it over and said, "Forget dead-eye Drayco. Eagle eye is more like it."

"It might not be important."

"See, you'd definitely be wasted in a corporate security job."

"Wasted or not, I have three days to decide. If I don't give them my answer by then, they'll get someone else."

One of the arson investigators called out to Sarg, and he motioned he'd be right over. First, he asked Drayco, "How long you gonna be shore-seeing?"

"A few hours. That should leave plenty time to chat with Shannon's parents."

That was the main reason for going, but there was more to it than that. The challenge of flying the plane was brain Drano, helping to clear his mind, almost as good as playing Bach counterpoint. The chance to see Nelia—and Darcie, of course—was a bonus.

40

Wednesday, 29 October

Drayco gauged the altitude of the patchy clouds overhead. The TAF was dead on target. Visibility six miles, scattered clouds at four-thousand AGL. He'd filed an IFR flight plan to make it easier to get in and out of the thirty-nautical mile security zone established around Washington after 2001. Better to be a known entity in the system than to get an F-16 fighter jet escort to the ground.

After he'd dutifully called Andrew Gilbow to tell him the takeoff time and Gilbow hemmed and hawed, Drayco was certain he'd be flying solo. Hooray for small favors—the air in a small plane could get stuffy on its own. So when he saw two figures headed in his direction on the tarmac, he was surprised, and a little disappointed, to hear Gilbow's voice.

"You decided to come." He took in Gilbow's ridiculous leather jacket and World War II-style aviator scarf.

"Thank my wife. She's the daredevil in our household, but I figured what's fit for the goose is fit for the gander."

The other figure approaching the plane was Adele herself. She smiled brightly at Drayco and ran her hand along the wing of the plane, brushing Drayco's fingers. "I was going to invite myself and tag along. It's not every day you get to go flying with such a debonair pilot. Alas, I have other commitments."

She peered into the cockpit. "How does a man your height fit inside such a tiny thing?"

"With a crowbar." Drayco indicated the towbar lying on the ground. "That's the co-pilot's job."

Gilbow was distracted, and for a moment, Drayco thought the man had taken him seriously. But he gave a humorless laugh. "Just don't ask me to fly the thing."

As Drayco continued his preflight inspection, Adele followed him around, asking the occasional question and taking the occasional opportunity to get closer to him. Gilbow's reaction was a slight smile that made Drayco remember Gary Zabowski's insight—Adele Gilbow's flirting was a way to keep her husband interested.

Drayco gave Gilbow his own headset, and after a brief delay waiting for their IFR release, they were off and climbing up to five-thousand feet. Gilbow's hands stayed laced into a white-knuckled ball in his lap as he babbled nonstop, not looking out the window. Drayco tried pointing out a few features along the route, hoping to give him something to focus on other than his phobia.

Drayco asked, "What is it about flying that scares you?"

"Oh, I don't know, spiraling down, spending the last moments of your life in terror, knowing you're going to end up in a burning, twisted heap of metal."

Drayco smiled. "I won't let that happen."

Gilbow didn't smile. "You can't promise that, can you?"

"If it's within my power to prevent it, I will."

"There are too many things outside one's power for that to be a comfort."

Gilbow remained silent while Drayco replied to an ATC call over the radio, and he stayed silent for several minutes after. Drayco was beginning to enjoy the flight when Gilbow started babbling again. "Brain scans show different parts of the brain are activated by different phobias. And adolescence is critical to the development of abnormal behaviors and fears."

"Like the link between boys who are cruel to animals and grow up to be serial killers?"

"Certainly. I assume you've checked into Gary Zabowski's background? It would be interesting to know if any pets died of mysterious circumstances in his neighborhood."

"I'll keep that in mind." Drayco doubted there'd be any such cases. It was the type of mass-market pablum he'd expect from someone who charged five hundred an hour as an expert witness. Plus a three-grand retainer and expenses.

Drayco descended to three-thousand feet, and they ducked into a few clouds, making things bumpy. He'd slipped a barf bag into the middle console, just in case. "How long had you known Cailan? I assume Troy Jaffray made you her godfather after he was made her legal guardian."

"She was eight, a very impressionable age. And to lose both parents suddenly was quite a blow. Troy needed all the moral support he could get, and I was happy to help. That was before I married Adele."

"And you saw no signs of any cult influences or secretive behavior?"

"None at all. Typical college student stress. Grades. Romantic relationship problems."

"You're referring to Shannon Krugh. You said you had her in one of your classes."

"Not memorable, academically. The signs of her bipolar were fascinating, from a clinical standpoint. I'm thinking of writing a book on bipolar disorder. My publisher is putting on the pressure for another bestseller. The last one sold half a million copies."

Drayco considered putting the plane into a sudden stall to see how a best-selling psychology guru would handle it. He pointed to a postage-stamp clearing on the narrow strip of land in the distance. "That's Accomack, where we're headed."

Gilbow looked out the window. From his clenched jaw, he must have realized for the first time they were flying over water, Drayco's favorite view of the Chesapeake Bay. Gilbow said in clipped tones, "How much longer until we're over land?"

"Not long. Fifteen minutes or so."

A sudden wave of wake turbulence hit the small plane, making Gilbow flail around for something to hold onto. The first thing he grabbed was the right-seat yoke, pulling it back sharply. The stall horn screamed an alert, and Drayco felt the sensation of the plane dropping out from under him.

He had the Cessna under control in seconds, a maneuver he'd trained for countless times. The heated lecture he felt like giving Gilbow evaporated when he saw Gilbow's hands stuffed under his legs and his body shaking even more than the plane in the stall.

Gilbow said into the headset, "You'd better keep your promise. I don't want to die in some fiery inferno burned alive like a piece of toast."

He kept his eyes shut tightly after that, leaving Drayco alone with air traffic control to talk to the rest of the way. No other planes were in the pattern, and Drayco made as smooth a landing in Accomack as he could.

He taxied to the small terminal and had the plane buttoned down in short order. As soon as they'd touched down, Gilbow was chatty again, acting as though they'd never been in a plane. A Benadryl on the return trip for the professor might be a good idea. Make it two.

The two men were greeted by none other than Deputy Nelia Tyler. Despite his earlier heads-up phone call, he wasn't sure she'd show. "So you really can fly," she teased Drayco.

Gilbow said to Drayco, "Beautiful women see you off, and beautiful women greet you. The pilot's life, eh?"

Beautiful married women, Drayco wanted to point out. Still, he was happy to see her and placed a hand on her shoulder as he introduced her, until he thought better of that and put his hands in his pockets.

Nelia walked them to her patrol car while Gilbow looked around at the environs and commented, "It's flat as a hotcake around here. And quiet."

Nelia chuckled. "Flat, I'll grant you. The area used to be quiet, but we're in danger of losing the sleepy charm due to the Wallops Island development. And D.C. weekenders."

"Change can be good," Gilbow said.

Dies Irae   235

"*Plus ça change, plus c'est la même chose.*"

Gilbow blinked several times. "Your accent doesn't sound French, Deputy."

Drayco explained, "Her mother is French. And a violinist."

"Intriguing. Someday you'll have to tell me how a lovely lady with such a background wound up in law enforcement."

Drayco had warned Nelia on the phone about Gilbow and how he used information from people he encountered as fodder for his books. Without their permission, in many cases. With details changed just enough to avoid getting sued.

Nelia cagily replied, "It's a boring story. And now, I believe you wanted to meet Shannon Krugh's parents? It's a ten-minute drive over to Maxateague."

"Such quaint names over here. Chincoteague, Machipongo, Kiptopeake, Nassawadox. Doesn't sound like there'd be any crime around here for you, Deputy Tyler."

"You'd be surprised. I met Drayco while investigating two murder cases here. Greed, jealousy, prejudice—any place with at least one person has all of the above."

"Such a dark view of human nature, Deputy. You'd make a fine psychologist."

"Or attorney." Nelia was smiling, but Drayco saw the tension in her shoulders. It was the new norm for her, judging by the last two times he'd seen her.

Drayco changed the subject. "I hate to rush things, but I promised to have the plane back by four. Depending upon any storm development ahead of the approaching front."

Gilbow stopped dead beside the car. "Storms?"

Drayco gritted his teeth. Yep, two Benadryl. "You can usually find a path around them."

Gilbow glared at Drayco, glared at the sky and slammed the car door after he climbed in. Nelia gave Drayco a sympathetic look and said, "Follow me, then?"

"To the ends of the earth. Which, on a narrow peninsula between the Chesapeake and Atlantic, isn't all that far."

Nelia glanced at Gilbow inside the car and muttered to Drayco, "Let's hope he's not afraid of water, too. The Krughs live on a marsh."

"Did you tell them we were coming?"

"I did. They refused, at first. This is still very raw for them."

Raw barely described an emotional gash like the one that had slit open the souls of Shannon's parents. Closure was only a dressing, yet it was the best he could give them. Too late now, but he worried Gilbow would be alcohol thrown into that wound, making things worse. Mirroring his thoughts, a turkey vulture on the driveway blocked their exit and stubbornly refused to move. Nelia turned on her siren, and the vulture let them pass.

41

Nelia was right about the marsh, which reminded him of Kenilworth Gardens. Fingers of ocean pushed into the coastlines of the Eastern Shore, creating soft mud banks for minks and muskrats and hosting tall grasses for wintering nests of mallards and blue-winged teal. A natural tidal give-and-take, unlike the man-made Tidal Basin of the Potomac. There, gates controlled the water while a nineteen-foot bronzed Thomas Jefferson kept a brooding, watchful eye.

D.C. was all about control. Out here, no one controlled much of anything, let alone the winds and the waves—one of the reasons Drayco enjoyed his trips to the shore. Another reason was currently standing in the doorway of the cottage before them in a deputy's uniform, introducing Drayco and Gilbow to the Krughs.

Shannon inherited brown eyes and a slightly crooked smile from Beatrice Krugh. But she didn't bear a strong resemblance to her mother or her father. Neither of the senior Krughs was particularly welcoming, but they were polite.

"Shannon was an only child," Mrs. Krugh said, not looking at the photo of her daughter on the table beside the frayed gray sofa. She didn't have to look, the expression on her face clutching a thousand remembered snapshots tucked in a mental file.

Paul Krugh added, "She was a good girl. Or tried to be. It was that demon inside her."

Drayco said, "You mean her bipolar disease?"

Krugh nodded. "That's the fancy name they give it. T'was a demon to her. She tried to overcome it. To obey us."

"Honor your father and your mother, that your days may be long in the land the Lord your God gives you," Gilbow said. "The second most important commandment, or so my own father said. I discussed that with Jaffray once."

"Jaffray?" Krugh gaped at him. "Ain't that the name of the other girl they said my daughter killed?"

Drayco leaned forward in his chair, intentionally blocking Gilbow from a direct sightline with the Krughs. "Her name was Cailan Jaffray. She was the niece of a religion professor at Parkhurst, Troy Jaffray. For the record, I don't believe your daughter killed Cailan or herself."

Krugh whispered, "Troy Jaffray," and jumped up. "I'll go get us some iced tea."

Not the reaction he'd expected. Drayco glanced toward the kitchen where Krugh had disappeared, wondering if he'd come back. Drayco asked his wife, "Did you know Mr. Jaffray? He grew up near here."

Mrs. Krugh smiled slowly. "Knew him? I dated Troy. Thought we'd get engaged, but then he met his future wife." Her voice trailed off. "Paul and I got married not long after. I was pregnant with Shannon."

She quickly added, "I was happy for Troy to get away from here. His parents were junkies, you see. He was raised by a maternal aunt when his mother was put into an institution. And his daddy just couldn't stay out of jail."

Gilbow stroked his chin, "That first-hand fear of not having an anchor made Troy turn to religion as a guiding force." He peered around Drayco to look at Shannon's mother. "That's what he teaches at Parkhurst."

"Sounds like he turned his life around. Always wondered what happened to him. And you say it was his niece, the other girl, who was killed?"

"Cailan and Shannon knew each other." Drayco replied, pausing as Paul Krugh did indeed return, with a tray of glasses filled with sweet iced tea he handed out. "They were rivals for the same boy."

"No boy is worth that," she said, her lips in a thin tight line.

"Mrs. Krugh, were you aware of religious cults Shannon hooked up with? She dabbled in voodoo."

It was Paul Krugh who answered Drayco's question. "That's the demon I was telling you about. Voodoo, witchcraft, bipolar, whatever you wanta call it."

Mrs. Krugh shook her head. "She was a good child. The voice of an angel. We were beyond the moon when she got that scholarship. Couldn't have afforded college for her, otherways. But I don't think she was into any cults or nothing like that."

Gilbow took a loud slurp of his tea and smacked his lips. "Studies on college students and religion show it's a substitute attachment figure. Alternate religions, alternate truths."

"So you think my daughter was involved in some cult, Mr. Gilbow?"

Gilbow shrugged. "It's possible. Her bipolar demon," Gilbow nodded toward Paul Krugh, "Combined with her search for meaning might have led her to such."

Mrs. Krugh scooted forward so her heels were flat on the floor made of the Delmarva's common yellow pine. "Whatever it was, it killed her, all the same. I don't suppose …"

She looked at Drayco. "I don't suppose they'll be releasing her personal things soon? It'd make me feel she's come home to stay."

Drayco thought of the nude photos and the strip club matches, but didn't mention them. In fact, he was scheming a way to have them "accidentally" disappear before Shannon's effects were returned. He said, "Hopefully, within a few weeks," and Mrs. Krugh smiled her thanks.

Drayco placed his own now-empty tea glass on the tray. "Mrs. Krugh, I appreciate how difficult this is, but I just have one more question. Did Shannon mention to you that she had synesthesia? It's where someone experiences numbers, words or sounds as colors or textures, kind of a fruit bowl of senses you eat from all at once."

Mrs. Krugh's jaw dropped open. "Sin-ess … well, whatever you called it, near as I recollect, she never mentioned it. Why do you ask?"

"One of Dr. Gilbow's students is working on a project involving people with synesthesia, and Shannon was part of it. It appears she wasn't a synesthete, only pretended to be."

"Now whatever would possess her to do that?"

"Why indeed," Gilbow scowled. "It could have ruined everything. For my student, Reed Upperman. His dissertation is in jeopardy because of it."

"I'm so sorry to hear that. I have no idea why she'd make up such a thing. Never heard tell of it before, myself."

"Well," Drayco said with a slight smile. "You've both been very kind," he stood up, hoping Gilbow got the hint. Nelia, standing silently in a corner by the door, leaped into action to thank the Krughs and offer her condolences.

Gilbow managed a curt wave to the Krughs, and once outside, didn't waste any time with his comments. "So Troy and Beatrice Krugh were in a relationship. Did you notice she said she was pregnant when she got married? If it wasn't Paul Krugh's, could mean Troy Jaffray was Shannon's biological father."

Drayco reluctantly agreed. "That doesn't mean he knew, even if true. Or has anything to do with the deaths. Unless you think your good friend Troy Jaffray believed it and killed both his niece and his daughter?"

"If he thought he'd find redemption or curry favor with God through sacrifice, perhaps. You said we were dealing with a ritualistic serial killer. One common motivation is revenge."

"Why revenge?"

"For his childhood. For his absent, drug-abusing parents. He transposes the girls as alter egos for himself. Then kills them to hurt 'his' parents."

"And the synesthesia angle?"

Gilbow stroked his chin. "I'm not sure on that point. Perhaps he sees it as deviant behavior. Or one of his parents had synesthesia. Did you or your partner, Agent Sargosian, ask him?"

Drayco had to admit they hadn't. But it was the same convoluted excuse a child comes up with for stealing from the cookie jar. Gilbow might be a renowned TV psychologist, but this explanation didn't gel with what Drayco had seen of Troy Jaffray.

That thought, and Gilbow's unrelenting arrogance, made Drayco a little murderous himself at that moment. He had Nelia drop Gilbow off alone at the Seafood Hut. Drayco knew the owners, both of them Iraq war veterans. It would serve Gilbow right if they cut him down to a size no larger than their fried oysters. Humility on the half-shell.

§ § §

Leaving Gilbow behind wasn't the only reason Drayco's outlook was improving. A trip to the Prince of Wales County Sheriff's Office reminded him of the other occasions he'd spent time with Deputy Tyler and Sheriff Sailor—a man he'd come to respect as much as Sarg.

His disappointment at finding Sailor unavailable, due to his court case, was tempered by seeing his office looked the same. Including the piranha-toothed fish mounted on the wall.

Drayco waited next to Nelia's cubicle while she checked a couple of databases on her computer. She'd taken off her service jacket temporarily to adjust the radio pouch on her duty belt. "Keeps slipping whenever I sit," she explained.

While she focused on the computer screen, Drayco had time to examine her arms exposed by her short-sleeve shirt. Arms that had greenish-purple marks from fading bruises in the faint shape of a hand. It made him think of the bruise on Alice the hooker.

"There's not much about any Jaffray in here, other than the family lived in Wachapreague. No arrests, no complaints." She switched to a different database and tapped the keyboard. "Birth record for Troy Jaffray and one brother. Death records for his father and aunt."

Tara had said she felt sorry for Jaffray when she realized he'd lost his wife, brother, sister-in-law, and niece. Apparently, he'd lost his father, too, and an aunt—the one who'd raised him? Jaffray as Job grew apter all the time. Had this Job cracked, unlike his biblical counterpart?

Nelia looked up, with an apologetic smile. "Not much else without spending more time. And since this isn't an official case on your part or mine ..."

He rubbed his eyebrows. "I understand. Glad it gave me a chance to see your stomping grounds again." Then he looked around, feeling a little wistful. "Guess I should rescue Gilbow and try to beat the storms."

They had no sooner returned to the car when Drayco's cellphone rang.

It was Sarg. "The shit hit the turbofan, junior. Gilbow must have told Onweller about your trip. He wasn't spitting kittens, they were saber-toothed tigers. I am to tell you in no uncertain terms if you continue to persist with your investigations, he'll follow through on his threat to have you arrested. So consider yourself duly warned."

"Duly noted," Drayco replied. "Sorry to put you in the middle. Got any good news?"

"On the murder front, no. On the arson front, no. And don't get me started about having to deal with Senator Bankton. The man doesn't want us questioning his wife, though she's listed as half-owner of those warehouses. If Onweller would pull his face outta his ass, he'd let you help, since you have an 'in' with Mrs. B."

"Humor me, Sarg. The date of that very first warehouse fire was July twenty-third, right? And then the second followed on August seventeenth, the third on October sixth, and the fourth on October fifteenth."

Drayco heard Sarg flipping some papers. "As usual, your memory is correct. Why the interest in those dates?"

"Senator Bankton gave money to the conducting institute on July nineteenth, Cailan was murdered August thirteenth and Shannon on October eleventh."

"Okay, I'll give you the last two might be connected to the murders, if that's where they took place. Why would our arsonist wait a few days between the murders and arsons? And what of that third warehouse fire? Please don't tell me smarmy senator is our killer. Would make my life hell."

"Don't buy a pitchfork yet. And I'll be in touch."

"I'm not supposed to talk to you anymore. Direct orders."

"Just keep me posted."

"You bet," Sarg said cheerfully.

After Drayco hung up, he filled Nelia in on Onweller's threat, to which she replied, "I didn't hear any of that. Officially. La la la la."

When Drayco didn't return her smile, she added, "What's wrong?"

"How did you get those bruises on your arm?"

"Oh, you know, stuff happens."

"One of them has finger marks. Did Tim do that?"

She gripped the steering wheel, staring straight ahead. "It's the MS. Makes him frustrated, angry. He has to vent now and then."

"By attacking you?"

"It's nothing, Drayco. I understand how he feels. I'd want to hit something, too, if I had to deal with what he's going through."

"You wouldn't use someone else for a punching bag. Ever. So when did this happen?"

"After that phone call he made to you."

When Drayco continued staring at her without saying anything, her words came out in a rush. "He had a bad day and was in a mood to accuse anybody and everybody. And he can't control his hands that well anymore …"

"He accused you of infidelity."

She started the engine of the patrol car. "Of being in love with another man, of having an affair because Tim is half the man he used to be. Crazy talk, that's all."

Drayco felt like grabbing the controls and driving up to Salisbury to give Timothy Tyler matching bruises, if not worse. "You don't have to put up with that just because he's got MS. Much as I hate to bring up Gilbow, he's written a book or two on battered women maybe you should read."

Nelia threw the car into reverse and backed out of the lot. "In richer and poorer, in sickness and health. I made a vow, and that vow is as important to me as the oath I took when I became a deputy. And I don't need any lectures from a man who can't commit to anything longer than a couple of years."

The tension in the car was as thick as the marsh mud surrounding the Krugh's house, making Drayco incredibly grateful when his cellphone rang again. The feeling didn't last long. "What? Where are you? Stay put. We'll be right there."

Nelia had to raise her voice as she peeled the car out heading toward the highway. "Sarg?"

"Gilbow. He says he's been shot."

As they sped in the direction of the restaurant where they'd left Gilbow, Drayco couldn't shake feelings of guilt. For discounting the professor's accounts of the threatening note and being followed. For leaving him alone on the shore. The man had offered his services to help and flown with Drayco, despite his fears, which took guts.

Gilbow hadn't sounded too injured on the phone, but they wouldn't know until they got there. Was this attack random, linked to Cailan and Shannon, or some other force at work? Disgruntled student? Jealous colleague? Secret affair?

He glanced at Nelia, whose demeanor seamlessly switched into fully focused cop mode, barking details to the radio dispatcher. With her strength and bulldoggedness, she would have made a damn fine attorney.

The rest of the ride was like a continuous, empty sentence, punctuated only by the barbed, magenta popsicle sticks of the siren.

42

It was dark when Drayco returned to his townhome cave, but sleep was the farthest thing from his mind. He recounted the details of Gilbow's attack, but they made less sense the more he replayed them in his mind. Gilbow went outside the restaurant, someone in a passing car took a shot at him. Seemingly unprovoked.

The professor refused to go to the hospital since he hated doctors as much as flying. Fortunately, the bullet just nicked him, and the cut across his arm was easily covered by a trauma bandage from Nelia's kit. After popping a couple of prescription pain meds he carried with him, he was groggy the entire flight back from the shore.

If Gilbow's threatening note was behind the attack, the shooter knew Gilbow was headed to the coast. He made sure he was there in advance and followed Gilbow, waiting for a chance. That was a lot of risks and variables that had to go the shooter's way. But then, wasn't that a carbon copy of Tara's attack scenario?

After spending the last two hours making phone calls, Drayco now sat staring at the information he'd jotted down. The sudden rattling from the front door's mail slot shook him out of his reverie, and he got up to grab the mail lying on the floor. One envelope in particular caught his eye. White, nine-by-twelve.

He carted it to the sofa, and took his usual precautions as he slit it open and pulled out a sheet of computer-generated music code. Just by looking, he knew it wasn't a Schumann code, probably another Messiaen. He set to work. An hour and three Manhattan Specials later, he picked up the phone to call Sarg.

"How's gimpy Gilbow?" was the first thing Sarg said.

"Hopefully sleeping it off. Does Onweller know yet?"

"I decided to let him find out on his own. Gilbow couldn't give any details?"

"Didn't see the driver. A silver sedan, didn't get the plates. Very helpful."

"Since I assume the fair Deputy Tyler is on the case, and I doubt you're calling about my recipe for Ceviche Verde, what's up?"

"Is Tara safe and sound?"

"Last time I checked. She's staying with us tonight and went up to her room to watch TV after supper. Like old times." Drayco caught the wistful tinge in Sarg's voice.

Drayco relaxed after the news about Tara. "I got another fan letter in the mail."

Wistful turned to worried as Sarg asked, "What'd it say?"

Drayco read his translation aloud, "'TRE CORDE HAUPTSTIMME.'"

"And that means absolutely nothing to me."

"*Tre corde* is an Italian musical term meaning three strings. *Hauptstimme* means main voice, or chief part. It's used in twelve-tone music."

"So … three strings for the main voice? Has our note-sender turned nuttier than before?"

"It might mean a third murder. As far as the 'main voice', it may be why Gilbow was attacked. I was worried it might refer to Tara."

"I don't see how Tara would be the main voice. That sounds more like you, pal."

"Not since Onweller kicked me off the case. If anything, it would refer to him."

"Are you asking me to warn him? He's already pissed at you. And within his rights to have you arrested for obstruction. Might not go far, but you'd still wind up in jail for a day or two. Until Benny Baskin bails you out."

Drayco sighed. "Pass it along. I'll deal with the rest."

"If you ask me, and you didn't, it's a bad idea. Maybe you should call Baskin, Esquire, and give him a heads-up."

"Benny will be thrilled. But I'll wait until I absolutely have to bother him."

"If you hadn't called just now, I would have called you. Heard from the lab today. The red fibers you found at the most recent warehouse fire matched those in Cailan's mouth. Seems the two cases I'm working are linked. Don't know if that's a good thing or bad thing."

"I think it means vengeance is best served hot."

Sarg's voice sounded resigned. "Okay, I'll warn Onweller. Not sure he deserves it. And cheer up—I've heard this year's model of orange prison jumpsuit is adorable."

Drayco looked from the music code to the details he'd jotted down from his earlier phone conversations. The poet William Congreve was wrong. Music didn't have charms to soothe the savage breast, it was a savage beast, an animal, a devourer of souls, sucking them in and never letting go. Perhaps it wasn't surprising so many composers were mentally ill. Throw religious superstition into the mix and you might just get murder.

43

Thursday, 30 October

Gary Zabowski was right on time. He had two coffees in hand, giving one to Drayco. "Couldn't remember if you take it black. Last time we shared a coffee, I was shit-faced. Oh, there's cream and sugar over there," Gary pointed to a table.

As he typically did, Drayco snagged an isolated booth in the small eatery hidden in the basement of the psych lab. Parkhurst ran on old money *and* fresh caffeine. Drayco reached for the salt shaker, as Gary watched agape. "Salt?"

Drayco took a sip, and smiled at the younger man over the brim of the cup. Gary grabbed the shaker and poured some in his own coffee and without hesitation took a big sip. He rolled it around on his tongue. "Not bad. Seems like I've tasted this before."

"I'll get right to the point, Gary. Tara told me Cailan was afraid of her uncle, Troy Jaffray. Did you witness any reason for it?"

Gary took another sip of coffee, took off the lid, stirred the salt around and added more. "He was overprotective. Dictator-for-a-cause. But he cared, you know? She was lucky to have him."

"Being afraid of displeasing someone isn't the same as being afraid for their safety. Was she afraid he'd hurt her?"

"She was jumpy right before we broke up. Thought it was those mystery notes she got. Or maybe Shannon. Shannon was a tornado in a skirt."

"Did Cailan talk to her godfather, Andrew Gilbow, about her fears?"

"Gilbow? Yeah, I think she talked with him. Hoped he'd tame old man Jaffray, tell him to give her some space."

Drayco pulled a copy of the latest music code out of his pocket and showed it to Gary. "Could the same software that created those other codes make this one?"

Gary examined it. "I'd bet on it. The composer programs out there have similarities. You can tell the diff if you use 'em." He studied the paper a little more, bobbing his head and shoulders as he played it in his head. "This is some seriously fucked-up shit." He thrust it back.

"One other thing. After you and Cailan broke up, were you aware of men she dated other than Liam Futino? A relationship she tried to keep secret? Elvis Loomis, for example."

"Elvis?" Gary ran a hand through his hair, making it even spikier than usual. "Elvis had the hots for her, sure. But when she talked about him, it was always how creeped out he made her feel. Shannon and Elvis I could see, but Cailan? Dunno. As to anybody else, hard to keep a secret that huge on a campus like this."

"So she didn't mention a man giving her grief, acting strangely? It could be anybody—fellow students, professors, boyfriends, clergymen, postmen."

"Other than me? She did say she wanted to see a campus counselor. One of those staff shrinks. But I don't think she ever did."

"It was while you were dating she wanted to talk to a counselor? Not after you broke up?"

"Yeah. Guess I didn't treat her like I should have. No good way to ditch someone, you know?"

Images of a few of Drayco's former girlfriends flashed through his mind. He pushed them aside and reached out to shake Gary's hand. "I appreciate you meeting me here. You've been helpful."

"Kinda nice to have someone want to see me. Since Shannon's murder went down, most of my friends are AWOL. I text, I call, they have excuses. Haven't heard a peep out of my father's lawyer, let alone dear old dad. Must be nice to have a friend like that partner-dude of yours."

"What about Reed? I'm headed upstairs to see him next."

"Reed's cool. Think he's getting a divorce. Not on account of me and him. I mean that was a one-time bi-curious thing. Maybe like that Maslow pyramid of needs thing, you know, self-actualization, peak experiences, yada yada."

"Why Gary, you've been listening to Gilbow the Great's lectures."

"Gotta make at least a 'D.' He does try awfully hard to be loved. And an ego the size of Azeroth."

Drayco smiled. "Isn't World of Warcraft passé these days?"

"Played that thing for hours when I was a kid. The Gilbows of this world wouldn't last a day against Ragnaros."

"Ragnaros?"

"The Elemental Lord of Fire."

Drayco shook his head. "Guess I need to brush up on my gaming."

Gary grinned. "It's basically all the same. Swords, dragons, fire, quests, heroes. To tell you the truth, if I'm going to be in front of a computer, I'd rather create music. Speaking of which …"

He hesitated and took a big swig of coffee. "I wrote this piano piece I think is pretty good. I was wondering, I mean—"

"I could give it a look, yes." Drayco took out a business card. "E-mail, fax, or snail mail, take your pick."

Gary took the card. "Thanks." Then his expression turned serious. "You think Elvis is mixed up with the murders?"

"I never rule out anyone until a case is over."

"Including me?"

"Including you. But you're not the roulette wheel number where I'd likely bet my money."

"That's good, I guess. Got someone else in mind?"

Drayco's smile faded. He did, but his chances of proving it were about the same odds as an inside straight-up bet. He just wished he knew who the *hauptstimme* was, to get to her before her number turned up on that roulette wheel.

Gary pulled out some gum and popped it in his mouth. "I'd offer you some, but it's nicotine gum."

"Trying to quit?"

"This makes the tenth time. Not good odds there, either."

Drayco slipped a couple of dollars under the salt shaker as a tip for whoever had to clean the tables. Then he handed a ten-spot to Gary, who looked puzzled. "Think of it as a down-payment bet on successfully quitting."

Gary took the bill and stared at it as if it were his very first A-plus. As Drayco left, Gary said quietly, "I hope your odds pay off." He didn't say whether he meant catching the murderer or him kicking his habit.

§ § §

Gary's "Elemental Lord of Fire" comment followed Drayco all the way up to Reed's lab. It was an apt analogy, given that the knives used in Cailan's and Shannon's murders were heated before plunged into their victims' chests. Drayco called ahead to make sure Reed would be there, so the doctoral student wasn't surprised to see him—though his glum expression spoke volumes.

"Sorry to interrupt your work, Reed. Assuming the project is still on?"

Reed nodded. "But I'm finding it hard to muster any enthusiasm."

"That should be good news, shouldn't it?"

"Good news for the PhD, sure ..." Reed looked at his hands gripping the edges of the desk and relaxed them. "Don't want to go back to my job. I hate teaching. And it looks like I'm going to be moving out of my house there soon."

Drayco stood in front of the chart of synesthesia subjects. "I talked to Gary a few minutes ago. He said something about a divorce."

"Divorce, alimony, child support, no job. That's my future."

"I'm sorry to hear that."

"Don't be. I'll still get to see the kids, the only thing I care about. And my wife would never approve me switching gears to work as a forensic psychologist. She was more into that academic thing than I was."

"You're really giving forensic psychology a shot?"

Reed perked up. "Gilbow thinks it's a good idea. He set me up with an apprenticeship. With a few extra classes, I can apply for board certification."

"You'll definitely find it challenging."

"Teaching spoiled-brat college kids certainly hasn't been."

Drayco had to smile at that. "Reed, who came up with the idea for your dissertation on synesthesia originally? Gilbow said you did."

Reed adjusted his glasses. "He did? That's not how I remember it, but he does have a lot on his plate. Consulting, TV appearances, books, teaching."

"How do you remember it?"

"It was his idea. I was on board right away because it sounded intriguing. Now that I'm switching horses, wish I'd decided on something else. But Gilbow's a force to be reckoned with."

"He comes by it naturally."

Reed looked puzzled. "What do you mean?"

Drayco thought back to one of the phone calls he'd made yesterday after returning from the Eastern Shore. "I'd say he got his ego from his maternal grandfather, a famous and famously temperamental conductor."

44

Hauptstimme, hauptstimme, tre corde. Time running out for someone. After calling Melanie Bankton and learning her husband wasn't at home, Drayco took several shortcuts and ignored speed limits in hopes of making it before the good senator returned home. He didn't think his presence would go over well.

Drayco didn't have to wait long at the bottom of the snaking driveway in front of the gate before a guard came and let him in. A mini-turret at the front of the house sported a yawning mouth of an entry, ready to swallow up any visitors.

A servant of some sort—maid, perhaps?—ushered him into a room so big, it made the Steinway grand in a distant corner seem like a toy. This palace wasn't bought and paid for by a government salary or lobbyist dollars. Bankton had invested his TV-evangelist money well.

Mrs. Bankton soon joined Drayco, dressed in a crisp white two-piece outfit looking like a woman who could be from nowhere or anywhere. She stood out against the vibrant purple and shamrock-green furnishings, a ghost flitting among the living.

He couldn't take his eyes off the Hamburg Steinway. "Is that the type of piano you used on your husband's TV shows?"

"Believe it or not, yes. Pounding out every possible arrangement of 'To God Be the Glory' known to man. At one time, thought I'd be more like you. World tours, Beethoven, Prokofiev, Chopin. But I do have all this," she swept a hand around the room. "A lot easier than the concert life, isn't it?"

He couldn't disagree with her there. "It can be grueling."

"I'd trade it all in a heartbeat. The money, the house. Just to play again and tour for one week."

She wasn't wearing any gloves this time and folded her hands under her arms. "I remember when I first heard one of your recordings on WETA radio. I had to go out and buy it right away. There are so many fine pianists, but you had something special."

"Then I guess all those years weren't wasted."

"Wasted?" She plopped down on a settee. "That would be my youth, I'm afraid. Like most young people, I didn't appreciate youth is the greatest blessing we're given. Such limitless possibilities."

"It's your teenage years I'm interested in. You went to Patuxent Academy High School, the same school Andrew Gilbow attended. At Gilbow's party, you told me you'd known him for some time."

She curled her legs up beside her, catlike, and leaned her arms on the arm of the settee. "Yes, we met there as freshmen."

"You ended up more than classmates, didn't you?"

"We dated. Opposites attract, I suppose. He was the son of a police officer. I was the daughter of an alcoholic and as wild as a fox in heat. I corrupted Andy good and proper, but in my defense, it didn't take a lot of convincing."

"What do you mean by 'corrupted'?"

"Shoplifting at first. Then breaking into people's homes. We didn't steal much. It was more for the thrill. I feel terribly guilty now. He was in love with me, the head-over-heels type. More so than I with him."

She bit her lip. "He wanted to 'fess up. Guess he was so smitten with me, though, he went along with it. Had an odd way about him of being timid and controlling at the same time."

She straightened up and folded her hands in her lap. "I'm surprised I'm telling you this. I feel we have a connection. Or maybe it's those eyes of yours that make me want to confess my sins. My husband knows I wasn't a saint, but he has no idea how wicked I was."

"How did you and Gilbow break up?"

"He got caught during one of our break-ins. I didn't, but I wouldn't give him a false alibi. His cop-father disowned him afterward. Andy told me I'd ruined his life."

"Why? You were both young teens at the time."

"He wanted to be a conductor like his grandfather. And a composer. He had a scholarship lined up to Juilliard and everything. That all ended the day I played around with one of his father's guns and got off several shots next to Andy's ear. I had some minor problems with tinnitus after that, but he was deafened in that one ear."

She smiled at Drayco and shook her head. "After he was arrested for the break-in and got out of juvie, he lost his scholarship and ended up at a community college. Considering the people he hooked up with there, I'm surprised he turned out so well. I've seen him on TV. Read some of his books."

"What kind of people did he hook up with?"

"Fringe religious types. You know, hoods and moonlight circles."

"Celtic Druids?"

"Not the peacenik modern version, more Stonehenge."

"Mrs. Bankton, do you have synesthesia, by any chance?"

She cocked her head at him. "That sounds terribly sexy, so I hope I do. But you'll have to tell what it is first."

"Do you experience words, numbers, or sounds as colors, shapes, textures?"

"Oh that." She laughed. "I didn't know it had a name. Andy was jealous he didn't hear music that way. He used to concentrate so hard, trying to develop it. But after he went partly deaf ..."

She chewed on her lip. "It doesn't matter now, does it? Ancient history."

"It mattered to him." Drayco didn't want to tell her she'd been the inspiration for possibly four murders.

"Really?" She straightened up. "I wouldn't have guessed, he seems so successful. In all honesty, ever since my husband got elected and we moved to D.C., I'd been afraid I'd run into Andy. And then he invites me to his party, out of the blue. I was shocked, to say the least."

Keep your friends close and your enemies closer. Drayco spied the sheet music lying on the piano and walked over to take a closer look. He didn't see this piece often. Hardly ever, in fact. "Are you a fan of Messiaen? I notice his 'Canteyodjaya' here."

"Funny you should ask that. Andy was the one who turned me on to Messiaen's music. I don't get to play much anymore."

"The busy life of a senator's wife."

"It's not that." She held out her hands. Curious, he obliged. Once he saw her hands close-up, he understood the reason for the lacy gloves at the party.

"Rheumatoid?"

"You should see the bottles of pills lined up on my dresser. With all the krill oil, fish oil, cod liver oil, borage oil and soy oil, I'm thinking of opening up my own service station."

Drayco nodded sympathetically, then asked, "Why did your husband donate funds to the Kennedy Center conducting institute?"

"My idea. Forest liked it because he gets a tax break, plus it adds a philanthropic line to his bio. I suppose I was trying to make up for Andy, in some small way."

And not long afterward, the first of Bankton's warehouses burned to the ground. Drayco checked his watch, remembering he wanted to be gone before the senator returned.

She walked him to the door. "If you're in touch with Andy, tell him to give me a call. Forest and I can have Andy and his wife over for dinner sometime."

Drayco stopped buttoning up his leather blazer. "I'll see what I can do." Which he meant, in more ways than one.

§ § §

Drayco wasn't sure where to go next. He found himself driving in the direction of the Jefferson Memorial and pulled into the small parking lot. "Delay is preferable to error," was one of Thomas Jefferson's most popular sayings. Not this time.

He called up Sarg's profile on his phone and dialed. When Sarg answered, Drayco said, "It's Gilbow."

Sarg's voice had an odd muffled quality, but Drayco understood him. "What? What did he do now?"

"Gilbow's our man." Drayco filled him in on his conversation with Mrs. Bankton.

"So, the warehouse fires …"

"Another way to get back at Gilbow's teenage lover-nemesis via proxy. And as we've surmised, empty warehouses make great sites for ritualistic killing. Then you simply burn down the evidence."

Sarg whistled. "Speaking of fires, this is going to put Onweller on the hot seat. Maybe he'll call off the hounds."

"Hounds?"

"After Onweller found out about your trip yesterday, the little prick went ahead and took out a warrant. 'Obstruction' and all. So, you at your place?"

"Playing tourist."

"Might want to hold off heading home. Until I've told Onweller what you told me. There may not be anyone knocking at your door yet …"

Drayco took a sweep of the surrounding area. No one seemed to be paying him any special attention. "I'll try to stay under the radar. But we need proof. Hard to get a search warrant on such flimsy evidence, worse seeing who the target is. Ordinarily, I'd say proceed carefully, build up a solid case."

"But there's that new note you got."

"Exactly."

Neither man spoke for a few moments, Drayco guessing Sarg was going through the same procedural checkpoints he was. Drayco said, "Remember the Wasserman case?"

"You saying we need another act-first-and-apologize-later thing?"

"Can you arrange a twenty-four surveil of Gilbow, either Bureau agents or MPD? If not, I have a few friends in the private biz."

"I'll see what I can do. Least this will make it easier to check into the other murders in Boston and Philly since we know whose travel schedule to sync up."

"And send me a list of Bankton's warehouses to my phone, will you?"

"Drayco …"

"I'll be discreet. It will give me something to do other than skulking around in cop-free hangouts."

"Okay, if you're careful. Ow, goddamnit."

"What's wrong?"

"Nothing. Just keep in touch."

Drayco hung up and sat in his car watching the tourists climb up the stairs to the top of the Memorial, snapping pictures, reading the inscriptions. Mothers pushed prams, fathers chased children chasing ducks. The winds caused a swirl of leaves to fall from the trees, many tinged with orange or blood-red tips.

Such a normal, happy scene. No young men with gang tattoos, no addicts shooting up. But how many of these "normal" mid-belly people were embezzling from work or would go home tonight and strangle their wives?

He pulled out his copy of the TRE CORDE note. They might have another two months before the next murder, but this note had changed the pattern. And that meant everything may have changed, and they might not have much time at all.

45

She hadn't seen it coming. Despite the repeated warnings from her father, despite taking extra precautions, she'd let her guard down. Tara struggled to free her hands, but the rope around them was too tight. Not enough to cut off her circulation, but there was no way she was wriggling out of that.

"Stay calm, take deep breaths, be aware," Falkor's words came back to her. Unlike last time in the alley, her mind filled with a fog, and her arms and legs were growing numb.

What was in that needle? Why had he done this?

Tara paused to take one of those deep breaths. She was in the back of an SUV under a cargo cover, and now, as she listened, she recognized that engine sound. It was like the one she'd heard in the alley.

And it had started out to be such a lovely day. An "A" on her chem exam. John asking her out again. Maybe that's what did it. The first time she'd gone out with him, they'd found Shannon's body. The second time, she'd almost been kidnapped. And now, she agrees to try another date, and this happens.

She strained to hear above the engine and caught snatches of voices from up front. What were they saying? Where was she? Tara coughed behind her gag.

She moved a few inches and felt something poking her in the shoulder, something long and slender. A tire iron. It took her three tries, but she got one end of the iron to slip under her gag and yank it down over her chin.

Streams of twilight through cracks around the cargo cover helped as she managed to hook a finger under her belt that the phone pouch was attached to. Thank you, guardian angel, for making her wear an oversized sweatshirt that hid the pouch.

Inch by inch, she scooted the pouch closer to her hands. She fumbled with the zipper on the little bag for what seemed like an eternity. Finally, she pulled it back just enough she could jab a couple of her fingers inside and force the zipper open. The phone immediately fell out and slipped to the floor of the SUV.

Now what was she supposed to do? Feeling more lightheaded by the minute, she fumbled around for the phone and managed to raise her hips to push the phone so that it landed near her chest.

She maneuvered the phone near one of her fingers she could still wiggle and pressed the button to wake it up. The she scooted her body down to get the phone closer to her face.

The phone's bright screen lit up. Her small moment of triumph was short-lived as she remembered she hadn't heeded her father's words and added a screenlock. No easy emergency call button at the bottom.

Feeling more and more as if she was sinking into a dark pool, she knew she would never be able to press the phone button and then dial 9-1-1 with her nose. She slid the home screen over to her Favorites list and nosed the link to automatically dial her father.

It rang and rang and continued to ring. No answer. "Daddy, pick up!" she wanted to yell, but it went to his voicemail instead. By now, she wasn't sure she was coherent, but she whispered a short message.

Then she nosed another link on her Favorites screen and waited. This time, a voice came on immediately, and Tara found herself sobbing so much, she couldn't speak. She forced herself to calm down, to try and say what was happening. But it was hard, so hard, and everything seemed to be fading away.

§ § §

Drayco knew he'd promised Sarg to keep a low profile, but his curiosity got the better of him. He drove down the street in front of his townhome, looking for law enforcement of any stripe. He didn't see any MPD, but he also wasn't expecting to see the one law officer standing in front of his place.

He opened the passenger door to his car and gave a low, short whistle call. Nelia Tyler, not in her deputy uniform, turned around and hesitated briefly before she slid in beside him, and he took off. "How about a nice tour around the Mall?" he said, pointing the car downtown.

"What's going on, Drayco?"

"I should ask you the same thing. Why are you in town?"

"Had a day off and decided to visit."

"Visit me?"

"Not at first. I wanted to check out a couple of the law schools in town. Talk to a few people about getting my degree through night classes or weekends."

"And your husband gave his blessing?" Drayco added sarcastically, "Just like that?"

"I'll tell him when I'm enrolled."

She fiddled with the edges of her sleeve. "I also wanted to say I'm sorry. I was bitchy with you the other day, at the Sheriff's Office. You didn't deserve that."

He gave her a quick smile, then found a parking place on Fourth Street, a few steps from the Air and Space Museum. That would never happen in summer. He was grateful because he preferred hiding in plain sight.

Nelia turned toward him when he turned the engine off. "Now can you tell me what we're really doing here?"

"Parking. While I figure out my next move."

"What happened?"

"Onweller has a warrant out for me. Which means you're aiding and abetting a fugitive."

"I'm off duty. And I'll plead ignorance if asked. What did you do?"

"The trip with Gilbow. When Sarg relays to Onweller what I found out this morning, I have a feeling that warrant will be forgotten."

"A break in the case?"

"Did you know mistletoe was a part of ancient Druidic rituals? The first time I was in Dr. Andrew Gilbow's office, I wondered why a man with his ego would have a mistletoe print hanging on his wall, taking the place of another award. Mistletoe was called the Druid's herb, with alleged miraculous powers."

"Gilbow and Druids? You're telling me he's behind the murders of the two college girls and it's some sacrificial thing?"

"At least two murders. Maybe more."

Nelia had a way of studying him that was unnerving, her gaze a soul-penetrating missile. "You're not happy about this?"

Drayco drummed his fingers on the steering wheel. "Gilbow can be a narcissistic blowhard. But his books have helped a lot of people. He's mentored thousands of students, many going on to distinguished careers. And there's the cancer center he and Adele are funding."

Nelia placed her hand lightly on his arm. "He's fooled many people."

He was suddenly uncomfortable, whether from the thought that he himself was one of those people or from Nelia's touch, he wasn't sure. "I can just imagine the psychologists who'll be called to testify in his behalf."

"So what now?"

"Now? I suppose that I—"

The ringing of his cellphone startled him. For a moment, he toyed with not answering it, but yanked it out of his pocket and pressed "Answer." Before he could utter one word, a weak, sobbing voice that was so faint, he almost couldn't hear it, said, "Falkor? I couldn't get Daddy and I …" The rest was garbled.

Drayco tried to calm Tara through his voice. "Tara, sweetheart, where are you? We can come and get you."

"I don't know … car … so sleepy."

He guessed Tara had dropped the phone when all he heard was the sound of an engine and something else he couldn't identify. Then they were disconnected.

46

Drayco tried calling Sarg but was sent to voicemail. He left a terse message about Tara, cursed the day when pagers became passé and hoped Sarg had put a roving bug on Tara's phone. He dialed another number he'd only programmed in recently.

"Onweller," the voice answered.

"This is extremely important so don't interrupt. I need you to get a message to Sarg stat. And I need you to put out an ATL on a kidnapping."

"Drayco? You have a lot of nerve calling me after that stunt you pulled with Andrew Gilbow." So Sarg hadn't talked to Onweller yet. Where was he?

"Shut up, Onweller, and listen. I have reason to believe Tara Sargosian has been abducted, quite possibly by our killer, who happens to be Andrew Gilbow. I don't have time to get into a pissing match with you. So do the right thing. I'll see what I can do on this end." Drayco hung up.

Nelia said, "What next?"

Drayco used his phone to see the list of Bankton warehouses Sarg sent along and started scrolling. Three had burned down, leaving the other twelve Sarg mentioned. Drayco briefly considered the one where Happy and Elvis lived, but discounted it. That left eleven.

Nelia peered over his arm at the list on the screen. You think he's going to take her to one of the warehouses?"

"Assuming he doesn't suspect we're onto him."

"Didn't the senator put extra security on all his properties after the first fires?"

"He got ATF to check them out. Too miserly to pay for round-the-clock security."

"Okay. Washington isn't that big of a city. Even if Sarg or Onweller aren't able to call out the troops, you and I should be able to check those addresses."

"Unless we run out of time." Drayco glanced at the clock in the car.

"Sarg will get the word before then and leap into action. So all you and I need to do is start down the list, right? We could go to your place and get my car. Split up and cover twice the territory."

"No time. And I don't want you without any backup."

"If his only weapon is that knife he uses, I can take him. Unless he has a partner or coven, or whatever a group of Druids is called. Cailan's uncle is a religion professor. Maybe he's involved as a partner?"

Drayco clenched his jaw. "I hope not. I don't think so. Not Jaffray."

"Well then. I guess we start at the top of the list and work down?"

Drayco paused. He played Tara's call in his mind and tried to remember every sound he'd heard. In addition to the car engine noise, he'd heard something else. He concentrated. A sound that was familiar, that was … an unusual square pattern of amethyst and silver that felt like needles.

He knew that sound—it was a white-top helicopter, one of the Sikorsky Sea Kings used by the military. If he could hear it that well over the phone, it had to be flying low after taking off or landing.

Drayco quickly scanned the list of warehouse addresses, looking for the one closest to a base. None outside the District, ruling out Andrews and Quantico. Whitetops also regularly flew into Bolling in Anacostia. One of the warehouse addresses was half a mile from Bolling.

Drayco started the car. "I think we can narrow that list in a hurry." By his calculations, barring some VIP motorcade or accident backup—neither of which was rare in these parts—they could make it to the warehouse in fifteen.

He handed the phone to Nelia. "If Sarg calls, give him that address," Drayco pointed to their destination.

For the second time that day, he ignored every speed limit. Even without motorcades or accidents, it took them twenty minutes. And still no call from Sarg.

Like most of the warehouses on Bankton's list, it wasn't in a Disneyfied area of D.C. Another empty two-story building stood sentinel nearby, with every window broken and hardly a square inch of brick up to six feet untouched by larger-than-life graffiti.

Drayco pulled the car into the shadow of that building where they could watch the warehouse without being spotted. To the side of the warehouse, he spied a white SUV with government tags and a Park Service logo on the side.

"Bingo," Drayco said, softly.

He reached under the dash on the driver's side and pulled the cover off a secret compartment. With one click of a latch, he released the hidden gun.

Nelia unbuckled her seat belt to join him, but Drayco nixed that idea. "I'll go in first. You keep trying to get Sarg on the phone. If that doesn't work, call the D.C. police. I've got that number programmed in, too."

Nelia looked unhappy but reluctantly agreed.

The warehouse was impressive, as crumbling abandoned warehouses go. Close to a football field in length, faded blotches of lettering indicated this warehouse used to be a print shop.

He slipped around a corner which took him out of view of Nelia. Noting a door with a lock slightly open, he slipped a finger between the door and frame to test for creaking. It was darker inside than out. The crack of light he'd let in when he entered might be obvious inside. He had no choice.

After a moment to allow his eyes to adjust, he focused on sounds. He didn't hear Tara, but he did hear scraping noises and footsteps from someone moving around. It was painfully slow going as he picked his way through the front hallway toward an opening that looked like it led into the belly of the beast. He had to control his desire to charge in there and snatch Tara to take her to safety.

He'd been looking down every few seconds to make sure he wasn't going to trip over something and give his presence away. It was during one of those quick glances he realized he'd passed a small alcove.

Too late, he realized someone was in that alcove. He spun around, but the figure anticipated Drayco and was now behind him. He felt a sudden sting at the back of his neck.

Reaching around, he grabbed the wrist of his unseen attacker and used his body to push the person against a wall. Adele Gilbow, dressed in a Park Service uniform, looked up at him, smiling. "If you wanted to go dancing, handsome, all you had to do was ask."

"Where is she?"

"Where is who, darling?"

"Tara Sargosian." But as he said those words, Adele's head began to elongate and float up toward the ceiling. He no longer felt his arms and legs. And every molecule of air he breathed in was like a rubber band snapping in his lungs. This was like one of his sleep paralysis episodes, maybe a little worse.

He heard a voice he thought was his own saying, "What was that?"

"Are you referring to this?" Adele held up a mini-rocket, no, a needle. "It's a little Special-K. We used up the last roofie on the Sargosian girl. But ketamine works faster anyway."

A deeper voice floated in from somewhere. "What's going on, Adele?"

"Our *hauptstimme* has arrived. I know we hadn't planned it this way. But why look a gift sacrifice in the mouth?" She lightly stroked Drayco's lips. "And such a nice mouth, too."

He vaguely saw Adele slipping out the door and returning. He heard her say, as if from a long distance, "I don't see anyone else. He came alone."

Drayco knew he'd passed out for a few moments when he found himself on his back on the floor, staring up at the exposed duct work and pipes snaking across the ceiling. It took every ounce of strength he could muster to move, but he'd had a lot of practice at breaking through sleep paralysis.

He flopped his head over to the right where Tara was on the floor near one wall, tied up, and hopefully just unconscious. He couldn't tell from here if she was breathing.

He flopped his head to the left and squinted his eyes to clear the blurriness. This warehouse wasn't empty, filled with the rotting wooden shipping crates and trash from homeless squatters.

He caught odd smells, too, one so strong and so acrid, it was almost sweet. Drayco also saw a blurry image of a figure that looked liked Andrew Gilbow crouched over a fire in the center of the warehouse. He seemed to be holding something long and serrated—a knife?—and wearing a long, white-and-gold robe.

Adele knelt beside Drayco and started unbuttoning his shirt. "I'm afraid that's going to have to come off, darling. Getting the knife in precisely the right place is very important."

She stopped to look him in the eye, answering the question he couldn't ask until he got his mouth working. "It's a shame Tara has to die, but Andrew is very adamant about tidiness. She saw us after we dumped Shannon's body. And when we botched that other kidnapping attempt."

Adele bent over farther and kissed him on the lips. "Did you like the notes? Sending them to you was my idea. The others sent to those girls were Andrew's thing. Part of his whole cleansing ritual to appease whichever God he believes in."

Adele whispered in his ear. "I don't believe in any of that hokum-pokum. I just hate being bored. And Andrew is starting to bore me."

She kissed him again. "You, on the other hand, are a much more interesting game. Even Andrew realized that. When you came along, he knew you were the main course. The girls were the appetizers."

Drayco didn't know how many minutes had passed. The ketamine could be wearing off in a few minutes, depending upon how much was in that dose. He spied a shape on the floor near Tara he'd missed a moment ago. It looked like his gun. He'd forgotten he had it.

If he could just muscle through the paralysis … He tried wiggling the fingers on one hand. After a few tries, he was pleased to find he could do it. Inspired by that success, he tried wiggling his toes inside his shoes.

Adele propped him up, leaning him against her to remove his jacket. Now that he was upright, his vision was clearer. Clear enough he saw the outlines of a face peeking in through a hallway entry straight ahead. Nelia.

Drayco found he could move his toes and also feel the floor under his palms. He blinked slowly and rhythmically three times at Nelia, then moved his eyes in the direction where Tara was lying.

Nelia nodded in response and held up her hand with three fingers, folding them one by one, counting silently to three. On "three," she charged into the room and picked up one of the wooden pallets she hurled at Adele, as Drayco ducked to one side.

Adele almost didn't get out of the way, her eyes wide in shock. She scrambled to her feet and yelled a warning to her husband.

Drayco willed his legs to move, made it to a kneeling position, then hoisted himself up to stand. His less-blurry eyes were seeing better now. Just in time to watch a startled Gilbow lose his footing and fall, his shoe knocking over a can into the fire pit.

With a sudden insight, Drayco knew what his befuddled brain was trying to tell him about that familiar strong odor. Gasoline. The same accelerant found in the other warehouse fires Gilbow used to burn them to the ground.

And now gasoline was pouring out of the can Gilbow had knocked over, straight into the fire and turning it into a growing inferno, feeding hungrily off the large banquet of wood around it.

Adele fled toward an exit from the building which is when Drayco found his mouth was working. "Go after her," he called to Nelia. "I'll get Tara."

Nelia initiated pursuit, and an adrenaline burst pushed Drayco toward Tara. He picked her up and carried her out the same door Adele and Nelia vanished through. He could tell now Tara was breathing. And a quick check of her pulse told him she had a strong heartbeat.

He didn't have anything to cut her bonds, but they didn't appear so tight they'd cause damage. No signs of Nelia or Adele, but he did hear sirens in the background and gauged they'd be here in a little over a minute. Then he remembered Gilbow, as dark smoke poured out of the warehouse door.

With one last look at Tara to make sure she was safe, he took a deep breath and headed into the warehouse, fighting off nausea. No time to analyze whether it was ketamine-leftovers or the nightmarish memory of another burning building that almost claimed a different girl's life just months ago. He'd hoped he would never have to duck into a blazing inferno again.

He heard a scream that made him understand what "bloodcurdling" really meant, as it set off an explosion of black-and-burlap daggers in his brain. It must be Gilbow. But when Drayco stepped into the main room, Gilbow wasn't making any noise at all. He was standing upright, his arms outstretched and waving around—right in the middle of the spreading fire pit as the flames turned his long white robe into a very effective wick. The man was on fire from head to toe.

As if in slow motion, every detail in the room stood out in razor-sharp relief. Drayco looked around for a hose, a bucket of water, a fire extinguisher, a rug, anything he could use to help the burning man. Other than a few small puddles from rainwater seeping through cracked windows and boards, there was nothing. Not that it would matter at this point. It was simply too late.

Gilbow somehow fixed his eyes on Drayco's, and in that lifetime of a moment, Drayco saw what the man was asking. He remembered the promise he'd made to Gilbow in a plane flying across a whole body of water—*if it's within my power to prevent it, I will.* At the same time, in the back of his mind, he heard Troy Jaffray quoting the Buddha, "Mercy and killing can never go together."

Drayco ran toward the spot where he'd spied his gun earlier and grabbed it. With a calm and steady hand, he raised the gun, aimed for the T-box zone on Gilbow's forehead, and shot him straight between the eyes.

He released the breath he'd been holding. Now that he was inhaling smoke, his eyes began to water, and he started to cough. He ran as fast as he could toward the door, almost colliding with Nelia, who'd poked her head inside to check on him.

When they were both clear of the building, he saw several things at once. Tara was free, and the EMTs and Sarg were checking on her. Adele was in handcuffs and being loaded into a police car. Firefighters mustered their gear to tackle the inferno.

And Nelia was staring at him. She'd seen the shot, and the confusion and disappointment on her face were clear. Without a word, she turned away.

47

Drayco sat in a part of the hospital that was empty due to remodeling. He didn't want to be alone with his thoughts, but alone he was. After the EMTs had given him some oxygen on-site, he'd refused any additional treatment, allowing Nelia to drive the two of them to the hospital. That was a long, silent drive. But at least Nelia was unhurt.

This corner of the building had rainbow window coverings that stood out against the brown-and-beige institutional design, doing their best to apologize for the impersonal drabness. He didn't glance up as steps echoed on the painted concrete floor until they stopped and headed in his direction. Drayco turned to the man standing next to him.

"Yo, FBI dude. Fancy meeting you here." A shiny new cast graced the arm of Elvis Loomis.

Drayco pointed to the cast. "How did you do that?"

"Was packing up a few things. Fell over a box. Landed right on the old funny bone."

"Packing? You're moving to new digs?"

Elvis scratched his cast and grimaced. "They told me it might itch. Didn't think it would happen so soon."

"A long pencil or back-scratcher will help."

"The voice of experience. I'll try that. Don't know 'bout the new digs. Depends."

Drayco was too tired to play guessing games. "Depends?"

"On whether the state of Californ-eye-ay throws me out."

Elvis' news was another shock to add to Drayco's day. "What about Happy?"

"Happy's one of the reasons I'm splitting. That play of hers at Signature? It's heading to Broadway. Not much left for me here, nope nope."

"Your son, then?"

"You remembered that? Yep, that's my other reason. Don't know what kind of father I'll make, but can't do worse than my old man. I'm pretty good with a baseball. Was pitcher on my high school team. At least I can teach him how to throw."

"It's a start."

"And a good place to start over. I hope." Elvis bounced on his feet. "Gotta hurry back. Happy'll throw out my things if I don't. Good seeing you, G-man."

Drayco waved a hand at Elvis as the man hurried away. He closed his eyes, enjoying the silence again, and tried to suppress the image of Gilbow on fire. Had he imagined the brief flash of gratitude in those eyes before he ended the man's living hell? Those images would sneak into his dreams tonight. And the next night.

He settled down into the beigeness, with the silence and the lack of colors. His trance was broken once more when Sarg dropped into the chair beside him. "Thought I'd come down and see how you're doing. Elaine's with Tara. She's awake now, and they're not going to keep her overnight. She's already demanding I make her one of my spinach-feta pizzas."

Drayco smiled at that. "With the smoked bacon?"

"She always wants one on her birthdays, too." Sarg looked around the room. "Deputy Tyler?"

"She took a taxi to my place to pick up her car. Her husband called. He's having one of his spells. Just as well—she'll be much safer back home." Safer from crime if not her husband. *Who are you kidding? You're the one who's safer with her far away.*

Sarg folded his arms behind his head. "I like her. Tough, quick-thinking, sense of humor, easy on the eyes."

"She's tough, all right." One of the toughest women he'd ever known. And one of the most appealing women he'd ever known.

Which made it harder to have her look of disappointment playing over and over in his head.

Sarg said, "So … Gilbow."

Drayco nodded.

"A case of displacement revenge. Targeting others instead of Mrs. Bankton."

"With psychosis fanning the flames." Drayco instantly regretted his choice of words.

"Kinda odd he chose to dump the bodies on federal parkland. Was he trying to get caught or something?"

"Regarding Kenilworth, I made some calls yesterday. One was to a Park Service botanist. The gardens were invaded by mistletoe a year or two ago."

"And the getting caught part?"

"Mrs. Bankton said that during their teenage crime spree, Gilbow wanted to confess but was too timid. This may have been his adult version of confession."

"I follow why he targeted synesthetes, a connection to the 'evil' Mrs. Bankton and all that. But his goddaughter? Why her?"

"Parents kill their own kids for far less. He did say he wasn't all that close to her."

Sarg rubbed his hands together. "I'm dying to hear how Adele arranged that staged shooting on the shore. Got the honor of grilling her after the MPD has their turn."

"Psychopaths are thrill-seekers. She latched onto Gilbow because he fed into that. Until the next opportunity comes along." Adele had certainly been quick to save her own skin and leave her husband behind.

"Hope she finds prison thrilling."

Drayco didn't feel like talking. At the same time, he didn't want Sarg to leave. And there was something he needed to say. "I made a mistake in that warehouse tonight. Let my guard down. Passed an alcove without checking it out and got jabbed by Adele."

Sarg didn't respond, but he gave Drayco a quick glance. Drayco continued, "You were worried about my welfare at the warehouse the day Officer Decker was killed. And tonight I was worried about Tara. Same thing."

"But you didn't get an innocent man killed."

"Not an innocent one, perhaps." Drayco could tell, just by the way Sarg cleared his throat, he knew and understood.

"You know, junior. I peeked in the warehouse right before you shot Gilbow in self-defense. That's what I'll tell Onweller. Unless I tell him I shot Gilbow instead."

"With my gun?"

"Found it on the floor."

Drayco tilted his head back, resting it on the wall. "You don't have to take the fall for me as payback. There may be an inquiry, but whatever happens, happens."

Sarg cleared his throat. "Onweller called off the arrest warrant. In fact, he almost sent *me* to this hospital with a heart attack when he said he'd be willing to hire you back. Could be one of those face-saving moves of his. If I were you, I'd tell him where to stick his offer."

Drayco looked directly at Sarg for the first time since he'd sat down. "He said that?"

"Honest and for true. So what are you going to do, take that security job?"

"Oh, I don't know, consulting's not so bad. The hours are long at times, the pay sucks at times, you get shot occasionally, or become an offering to … well, whatever deity Gilbow was going to offer me to. What's not to love about a job like that?"

"If I didn't have two kids in college and a second mortgage, I might join you. I can see it now, up on the office door—Sargosian and Drayco, LLC."

Drayco smiled, then noticed Sarg didn't appear to be joking. "You'd leave the Bureau?"

"In a heartbeat. It's not just Onweller. The organization's changed too much. I barely recognize it as the same place."

"Good bennies."

"I've been saving. A few investments. Barring a major health crisis like Troy Jaffray and his pancreatic cancer …"

Drayco hadn't thought of Jaffray in all of this. The man would have to be told. And how would he take yet another hard knock to his shattered life?

He said, "Gilbow may have been right when he suggested Jaffray was Shannon's biological father. At this point, I don't see what can be gained from Jaffray knowing."

"He's got a lot of religious faiths he can choose from for comfort."

Drayco opened his mouth to retort, but Sarg cut him off. "I'm joking. Maybe I'll shock the wife and go to church with her this week. Great place to learn more about human nature, right?"

Sarg's phone rang with the unmistakable sounds of a polka instead of the default ringtone. Drayco raised his eyebrows, and Sarg shrugged. "Guess you can teach a geezer new tricks." He listened for a moment, said "Okay" and hung up.

Drayco pointed to the phone. "Why couldn't Tara or I get in touch with you?"

Sarg grimaced. "That damned crown. It broke in two when I chomped down on an apple. Hurt like hell. Shooting pains down into my neck, bleeding gums, the whole nine yards. So I got an emergency appointment with the dentist for a root canal."

"Feel better now?"

"Didn't have a chance to finish the procedure. I'd left my cellphone in the lobby, and then the receptionist brought it in and said it was nonstop ringing."

Drayco leaned back in his seat, but Sarg said, "Don't get too comfortable. That call was from Elaine. Tara wants to talk to you."

Sarg led Drayco through the ER patient area and pulled back a corner of a curtain partition to a bed where Tara was half-sitting up, her mother at her side. Elaine smiled at them and excused herself to let the two men maneuver into the cramped space.

Tara had turned on the television hanging in one corner via the remote control she clutched in her palm. Drayco was surprised to see the channel tuned to a police drama. When she looked up at Drayco, it was as if he'd stepped back in time and she was thirteen years old, not twenty.

"Your Dad tells me you get to go home soon."

Her voice was weaker than usual, but he didn't have to strain to hear her. "The sooner, the better. I have an exam tomorrow. Don't think the professor will believe it when I tell him I was drugged, kidnapped and rescued from being barbecued."

"If your father and I each write you a note …"

She smiled. "I think you've already done enough. Swooped in and rescued me just like the real Falkor."

"With the assistance of a warrior princess."

"You mean Deputy Tyler? I'd love to meet her sometime. When I'm conscious."

"Maybe we can arrange something." Drayco didn't want to promise anything, not knowing when, or even if, he'd be seeing Nelia Tyler. Unless she was serious about her law school plans. The idea made Drayco feel a tiny ray of hope he could patch things up with her. To at least maintain their friendship.

Tara said, "Forensics."

Drayco stared at her, confused. What kind of anagram was that?

And then she giggled. "Grad school. Screw the pharmaceuticals. I've decided on forensics."

She switched off the TV and sat quietly for a moment. Then she said, "I can't believe it was Professor Gilbow. What an evil asshat."

Sarg grinned, "Out of the mouths of babes …"

48

Friday, 31 October

The newly widowed Adele Gilbow, having access to her husband's not inconsiderable wealth, was able to afford a primo attorney. Sarg arranged an interrogation session that she'd agreed to—provided Drayco came along.

As the two men sat there with her attorney hovering in the background, all she did was to repeat what she'd told the MPD detectives. She'd only served as a driver and assistant to her husband, the real force behind the murders and kidnapping. She'd gone along with Gilbow's plans because she was afraid for her own life. Adele was quite the accomplished actress. It was clear why she'd been interested in being on the theater board.

Right before Sarg and Drayco left, she motioned for Drayco to sit in the chair next to her instead of across the table. Then, before her attorney could intervene, she quietly whispered in his ear so only he could hear, "Sweet creature, said the spider to the fly. You're witty and you're wise, how handsome are your gauzy wings, how brilliant are your eyes!"

Then she added, "I may not be able to kill a fly, but I enjoy messing with them," and gave him a smile that was part sphinx and part siren. Her parting words, as she stared only at Drayco, were, "You'll hear from me again."

Sarg prompted Drayco afterward, "What was that all about?"

He was half-inclined to write it off as psychopath humor, although he was oddly uncomfortable at her comment. He shrugged and pointed at the date on his watch. "Halloween?"

Drayco and Sarg later stopped by Troy Jaffray's office to see how he was doing. He was buried in boxes and busy packing again. Only this time it was his belongings, not Cailan's.

Sarg put his hands on his hips. "You weren't fired, were you? Because if you were, we can talk with President Thackeray."

Jaffray shook his head. "Not fired. I resigned. Greg Smith teaches sociology, but he's agreed to take over my classes until the end of the term."

Jaffray perched on the edge of his desk. He looked at the now-bare walls and the shelves seeing the light of day for the first time in years, judging from the thick dust at the edges. "I could have stuck it out. Maybe taught until I keeled over in a class. Not that I haven't died already. Finding out my niece was killed by her very own godparents. People I called friends and welcomed into my home."

Drayco asked, "What are you going to do instead?"

"Travel the world. Or as much as I can before I'm planted down in it. Revisit some of the great religious sites like Abydos, Externsteine, the Abbey of Fontfroide, Angkor Wat. I'm thinking of taking Cailan's soon-to-be-cremated remains with me and sprinkling them everywhere I stop. And maybe I'll find some semblance of faith or peace before I'm gone to whatever lies beyond this plane of existence."

"You're handling this better than I would."

Jaffray had seemed distracted, alternating looking down at his feet and off into the distance. But at Drayco's comment, a hint of a smile bloomed on his face. "The Dhammapada says losing what you love brings suffering. But harboring the pain of your loss only brings more pain."

"Something I wish Andrew Gilbow learned."

"Not sure it makes any difference to sociopaths."

"Sociopath? Perhaps. When a musical muse abandons you, it leaves a powerful void. Beethoven contemplated suicide due to his deafness."

"Other men put in that position find ways to help others." Jaffray gave Drayco an intense stare, then turned around to rescue two books from his desk, handing a copy to both Drayco and Sarg.

"Andrew wrote tons of books, and I'd always meant to get around to one myself. I finally did, and it just got published. A small print run, but I want you each to have a copy. It's a history of religion in America. You'll be happy to note, Agent Sargosian, there's a mention of the Armenian Apostolic tradition."

They thanked him, and Sarg added, "You need help with these boxes? Looks like it might take you a while."

"Thanks for the offer, but I have several students coming over in …" he looked at his watch, "About ten minutes. They're going to help me finish up and take everything home. I'd like to be done by five because I have an appointment at a jazz club."

Drayco asked, "The Basement in Georgetown?"

"Liam Futino's group is playing tonight."

Right before the two men left, Jaffray said, "Though I take little comfort in the outcome, I want to thank you both for arranging earthly justice for Cailan."

Back outside, the late-morning sun cast medium shadows from trees speckled with autumnal colors. The leaves had changed a lot in the past two weeks. A sudden gust of wind knocked several leaves and twigs onto Sarg's car, but there didn't appear to be any dings or scratches. None that couldn't be repaired.

Sarg picked leaves off his windshield and unlocked the car door, then paused before climbing in. "If you want a change from peanut butter and marshmallow fluff sandwiches, I've still got those truffles crying out for risotto. I know Elaine and Tara would be happy to have you join us for dinner."

Drayco grinned. "Every time you say truffled anything, I think of chocolate."

"Are you telling me you've never had a real truffle? That's it then, I won't take no for an answer."

"Okay, but they'd better taste as good as the chocolate kind."

Sarg shook his head in mock disgust and drove off.

§ § §

Drayco stopped by one of the few stores in the entire D.C. area that sold Manhattan Specials before going home. Grabbing the lone cold espresso soda left in the refrigerator, he settled down in the den with some days-old Thai drunken noodles that hadn't turned green yet. He'd just lifted a fork to his mouth when his cellphone rang.

Must be Darcie. When she'd heard about his "near-death experience," she'd said she was coming up for a visit. But he was surprised to hear Reed Upperman's voice on the other end. "I guess a lot of people would still be in shock about Dr. Gilbow. Selfishly, my first thought was how this affected my dissertation. When I have time to think about the psychological underpinnings of that, I will. But not yet."

This boded well for Reed's future as a forensic psychologist. "Are you going to be able to finish?"

"I've been in a meeting most of the morning with another professor on my committee. She's agreed to take over as my primary advisor. She thinks I can make do with the data I have if I add another subject."

Drayco smiled to himself, knowing what was coming.

"I know this is a lot to ask, considering how busy you must be. And it only pays a token pittance, but you said you had a few days free. That is, if you're still interested."

Drayco thought about his now-empty calendar. "How much time do you need?"

"If we condense a semester's worth of tests, two weeks."

"I think I can help out a future law enforcement colleague."

"Great! That takes a load off my mind. I do have one other question—did you tie Gilbow to those other two murders in the synesthesia projects?"

Drayco explained how that was one area in which Adele was helpful, if cagey. When asked about the murders, she denied any knowledge. Although she was quick to verify her husband was a guest lecturer in both Boston and Philadelphia at times coinciding with the killings. Drayco was quite happy at this point to have other agents and detectives dot those particular *i's*.

Reed's tone grew more somber. "I know I'm not to blame here. I mean, it was Dr. Gilbow's idea I use synesthesia for my project. I still feel, well …"

Drayco didn't have to envision the other man's troubled expression to know what he was going through. "The Gilbows used you as a pawn on a chessboard filled with land mines."

Reed breathed out a long sigh. "Guess they used you, too. And a lot of other people."

A knock on the door made Drayco wrap up his conversation with Reed. Maybe Darcie? A part of him was secretly hoping it was Nelia. Instead, it was a courier with an envelope Drayco had to sign for.

Drayco slit open the envelope and pulled out a check and card. The check was from Troy Jaffray with a note on the "for" line at the bottom that said "Helping me find peace." Drayco's eyes widened as he saw the amount. It would cover his living and office expenses for a year.

He looked at the card which had a plain white background with a drawing of a blue lotus flower in the center. He flipped over the other side where Jaffray had written, "The narrow mind rejects; wisdom accepts."

Drayco put the check down on the table next to his answering machine. The machine's display indicated two new messages came in while he was at Jaffray's office. One was from Nelia saying she wanted to talk to him when she visited D.C. next week. The other was Brock, wondering if his son had made a decision on the security job.

Drayco's hand hovered over the phone handset, but he didn't pick it up. And he took his cellphone out of his pocket and turned it off.

He stood in the entry for a moment before heading to his piano. He placed the card with the blue lotus flower on the music rack in front of him and then launched into a transcription of "Hymn to the Moon" by Dvořák. In his mind, he heard the violet triangles of Cailan's voice singing a duet with him as he played.

Made in the USA
Middletown, DE
03 April 2022

63552098R00172